A SEASON IN CHEZGH'UN

DARREL J. McLEOD

A SEASON IN CHEZGH'UN

— *A Novel* —

Douglas & McIntyre

1 2 3 4 5 — 27 26 25 24 23

Douglas and McIntyre (2013) Ltd.
P.O. Box 219, Madeira Park, BC, V0N 2H0
www.douglas-mcintyre.com

Edited by Barbara Berson
Text design by Carleton Wilson
Printed and bound in Canada
Printed on 100% recycled paper

Canada Council for the Arts
Conseil des Arts du Canada

Supported by the Province of British Columbia

Douglas & McIntyre acknowledges the support of the Canada Council for the Arts, the Government of Canada, and the Province of British Columbia through the BC Arts Council.

Library and Archives Canada Cataloguing in Publication

Title: A season in Chezgh'un : a novel / Darrel J. McLeod.
Names: McLeod, Darrel J., author.
Identifiers: Canadiana (print) 20230443451 | Canadiana (ebook) 2023044346X | ISBN 9781771623629
(softcover) | ISBN 9781771623636 (EPUB)
Classification: LCC PS8625.L45475 S43 2023 | DDC C813/.6—dc23

If anyone asks you
how the perfect satisfaction
of all our sexual wanting
will look, lift your face
and say,
Like this.

—Rumi

I

Sigwan — Spring

i

He had dreamed about it yet again: his great-grandfather's trapping cabin where he spent his earliest years. Oddly shaped and built with huge glass windows, and cedar instead of pine—almost no right angles—trapezoids on all sides. A cathedral ceiling. The roar of clashing currents at the confluence of two unequal rivers, shimmering rapids, standing waves and eddies. In the centre of a meadow, a colourful canvas tipi. Crimson-tipped Indian paintbrush all around. Scattered in the clearing that surrounded the cabin, animal hides stretched across frames made of bamboo canes—with their unmistakable knobby, round knuckles. One hide was vast with long shaggy fur—an appendage, like an elephant trunk, hanging down. The second had a ferocious head with yellow, dagger-like canines protruding from its mouth, golden fur with brown markings, a stubby tail. The third hide was that of a gigantic bison—plush fur. A man and woman, both elderly, stood by a roaring fire, its base contained by large stones. Sparks spitting and flying into the air. A spiralling haze of smoke—the precious and ingrained odour of wood burning. James stood across the fire opposite the couple, who spoke Cree, smiling and giggling, and he responded in kind. At times, the three of them spoke and laughed in near unison.

As always, when he woke up, James wondered what guidance the dream was offering. Was it meant to assuage the aching hollowness in his chest that had at times overwhelmed him since his mother died? Was he seeing his great-grandparents, Kîkwâhtikowiw and Sâkowêw—the ones she had always spoken of with such reverence? They did live to a ripe old age. The look in their eyes—a disarming gentleness of spirit he hadn't seen for as long as he could remember. The hides of prehistoric animals—what was that all about? And the land ... the pastoral rolling hills covered with Jack pines, spruce, trembling aspen and weeping birch; it was clearly the boreal forest where he was born, to the east of two mountain ranges: the Coast Mountains and the Rockies—perhaps depicted in an ancient era. The river valley. There was always a river or stream in his dreams, as there had been in his childhood surroundings.

The aroma of coffee disrupted his thoughts. Franyo was up. James flipped the eiderdown aside, slipped on his blue housecoat with white stripes, which matched Franyo's with brown stripes, and sauntered downstairs. He spilled coffee into a mug and joined Franyo on the balcony, gave him a quick peck on the lips and sat. He let his mind dwell on his homeland—settling back into the fantasy of buying back a parcel of the territory that comprised his mother's and grandparents' homeland—*his* homeland—which his mother had described with reverence and nostalgia; recalling her childhood living on the land, in simple seasonal dwellings, communing with the birds and small animals, harvesting food and sacred herbs. She had loved to recount stories her father and grandfather told her of their lives as braves, hunting in a vast territory that spanned the plains and went right up to the foothills of the Rocky Mountains ...

James's family hadn't been granted land by the government, neither as Indian reserve nor as private property, as so many others had been. His *mosomak*—grandfathers and great uncles—had been hunting and gathering in the forest the spring the Indian agents and land commissioners showed up. They didn't get counted and didn't get to make their "X" on a document that was meant to provide a definition of what rights they, their children and grandchildren would have into the future. It wasn't just the land they'd lost; it was their entire way of life and family dynamics. In truth, that was the ache he felt in his chest: a palpable yearning to visit unspoiled homeland, likely prompted by his last few visits with his mother, when she'd flown to Vancouver to see him. She had lamented having lost their traditional way of life. After each visit, he'd fantasize about buying the land back. He never told her about it—not wanting to get her hopes up, understanding it would take years if he could do it at all. He felt elation when he thought about this, the precious and full memories of being on the land with his mother, aunts, uncles and cousins—picking gooseberries, strawberries, raspberries, collecting wild mint or taking road trips to just observe the beauty of the rolling hills, creeks and rivers, and to feel the thrill of animal sightings.

This elation drained to emptiness. James knew that getting their land back was impossible. Yet each time he had this dream, he wanted to call his Auntie Clara and Uncle Charles to tell them he was going to do it—he was going to buy back their land one day. But at that moment, he had no money and it would all sound foolish. Nevertheless, he could start to investigate—bare land must be cheap, and it was likely still undeveloped where his community had lived. Well, undeveloped except for pumpjacks, compressor stations and aboveground pipelines. At the onset of oil exploration, the government had forced his family to move and then blew up the concrete bridge they had built only a few years earlier.

He looked over at Franyo, contentedly smoking and scanning the morning newspaper. He didn't need constant conversation, and James liked that about him. Comfortable silence was a sign of acceptance and peace among Cree people, and James remembered basking in it as a child, looking up at the pensive adult faces during long lulls in their confabs—all conducted in their language. But right now, he wished that he could talk to Franyo about his dream, the vision of the old ones—James's ancestors—recurring now, and of his fantasy to reclaim ancestral land. He knew it was important, yet he couldn't discuss it. Franyo might think he was crazy—a savage—and James had worked so hard to get away from all the negative trappings and stereotypes—the poverty, the tragedy, intensity and stigma of being Nehiyaw. This is what his people called themselves: Nehiyaw. It was a neutral term meaning *people of the land*, but he'd only ever heard the word used in a pejorative, condemning way, when someone's behaviour or appearance was repulsive: *mah sôskwâc—kiyapic nehiyaw*… or as kids, they would say *nnnch*—ever *Indian*.

It was Saturday morning, so they followed their routine, which James loved. The two of them jumped into Franyo's van and drove to Granville Island, where they spent the early morning in James's favourite coffee shop, the Blue Parrot, which took up two levels of a repurposed glass-encased pier. Franyo rushed upstairs to nab their usual spot, which had a view of the high-rise towers along English Bay and sat down in one of the colonial-style wooden chairs. In the distance, the cherry-red magnolia and strawberry-parfait camellia blossoms were stunning, still in full bloom. James loved the contrast of the pastel-coloured flowers nested above and betwixt jade-green leaves.

Closer in, sailboats, tugboats and canoes competed for prominence as they navigated past each other. James recalled how just a few years earlier, freshly relocated from the Prairies, he'd been intrigued as he watched the vessels glide through the bottleneck of the recently demolished Kitsilano Trestle, to escape into the increasingly wider bay that led to the vast Strait of Georgia. The two lovers lounged contentedly, knowing they'd beat the crowd. James basked in the waves of different aromas in the air: now freshly ground coffee beans, now fresh bread and cinnamon buns, now the heady scent of stargazer lilies from the flower shops below; buskers tuned their violins. The two men sipped their cappuccinos and tore apart warm croissants; James savoured the golden pieces first, then dipped the ragged doughier pieces into a runny raspberry jam before stuffing them into his mouth and washing them down with foamy coffee. The fluffy texture of the buttery croissant reminded him of his kokum's fry bread—how he'd loved to rip it apart and dip the pieces into her wild raspberry preserves after plastering them with butter.

Once their hands were free, the two men divided up the Saturday *Vancouver Sun*: the Entertainment and Career sections for James, the front page and Homes and Entertainment sections for Franyo. As he relinquished the front page section, James glimpsed the headline, HIJACKED BC FERRY PURSUED BY COAST GUARD INTO INTERNATIONAL WATERS—the incident that had dominated both the local and national news for days now; everyone abuzz about the outrageous attempt to redirect a ferryboat to an unknown destination and the holding of a dozen crew members hostage until mysterious demands were met. Beneath that, another headline caught James's eye: RANCHER BANS NATIVES FROM ENTERING LANDS TO HARVEST BERRIES. James felt a flash of anger but pushed it back—he'd have to focus on that article later, back home when he was alone and could shout and swear. He passed that section to Franyo.

"You woke me up last night, James. You were talking in your sleep again, but this time I think you were talking Cree—I didn't understand a word. It was kind of muffled but definitely not English."

"Well, Cree is my first tongue, and, in my dreams, it seems I speak it fluently. Maybe I was talking about you," James answered and chuckled. "Did I say *moniyaw* or *nechimoos*, white man and sweetheart?"

The two men laughed. In that moment, they seemed so close, so connected that James wished he could tell Franyo about his dream. Maybe one day—not just now. Friends were coming for bouillabaisse that evening. James was cooking, and Franyo was to be his sous chef. They would find everything they needed in the various kiosks and shops of the market: shrimp, halibut, mussels and clams, shallots, saffron, fennel, an orange, and four ripe Roma tomatoes. Baguettes. When they returned home, they would thoroughly clean Franyo's apartment. James would practise a few songs on the piano, the way he liked to on weekends, hours at a time.

He'd felt so fortunate when Franyo had asked him to move in. He could only have fantasized living in a place like this—with a cedar-trimmed deck, skylights and a loft in a trendy part of Vancouver. And Franyo had made room for his worn and bulky piano and let him hang pictures of family on the walls to make him feel more at home. He knew it would always be *Franyo's* place; he was a guest—a very special long-term guest who paid rent each month, and that was a good arrangement.

Once the condo was sparkling and inviting, Franyo would set up the fireplace so that they would only have to strike a match moments before their guests arrived. If there was time after all the prep, they would go for a walk along Kits Beach. James used to wish they could hold hands while strolling, but even though people in Vancouver—Kitsilano—were open-minded, Franyo would've been embarrassed.

James was slurping his second cappuccino and flipping through the Career section when a large ad caught his eye. SCHOOL DISTRICT SEEKS PRINCIPALS FOR TWO REMOTE SCHOOLS ON INDIAN RESERVES. Above the ad was a map of Stuart Lake. He set his cup on its saucer and opened the paper wide—raised it so it covered his face, and read:

> School District 89 is taking over management of two schools on Indian reserves from the federal government in September 1989 to make them fully accredited public schools. The schools are located in two separate communities governed as one: Bilnk'ah, on the northeast side of Stuart Lake with a population of 700 and Chezgh'un on the southwest, with a population of 250. Enjoy unparalleled outdoor experiences in a pristine part of British Columbia: fishing, hunting, canoeing, kayaking and skiing.
>
> Qualified candidates will have cross-cultural experience and a master's degree in education.

James was breathless. For the last couple of years, he'd been monitoring the job market—had sent out his resumé to on-reserve schools across Canada, but to date had had no responses. He'd kept this from everyone—his colleagues at school, and even Franyo. He didn't want to stir Franyo up unnecessarily, and he'd just gotten tenure with one of Canada's most prestigious school districts. Either of these principal positions would take him home *and* be a serious promotion—would double his salary. Well, the location wasn't exactly *his* homeland, but a place very similar, he imagined—*Indian* land. He took a few quiet deep breaths to contain his excitement, then he lowered the paper, folded it twice and tucked it under his arm. He glanced over at Franyo with a tentative smile, tried to keep his excitement at a simmer. Franyo already knew him so well, he would no doubt recognize the wild and unsettled aspect that had come over him.

Franyo's azure eyes captured James's—cedar-bark brown. Perhaps it was true that opposites attract. Franyo's fair complexion made James look even more swarthy, and the ever-so-slight crow's feet at the corners of his eyes made James's face look even more youthful.

James let his gaze rest on Franyo's handsome eastern European face and was, once again, thunderstruck that they were lovers—*lovers*, despite a fifteen-year age gap.

Franyo broke the silence. "You checking out the Career section again?"

"Yeah. I just like to see what's out there. I know I have a great job, and how ironic, all because I speak French. Imagine, a Nehiyaw teaching rich kids to speak French—here, in Vancouver!"

"You were so excited to get that job—remember? And the kids love you—look at the haul of gifts you've had each Christmas and year-end."

"Well, this week, a couple of dads showed up at my classroom door to complain about the advanced math program. One dad said the program was too easy—everyone was getting A's, but the other dad said he thought it was too hard—his kid was bringing home exercises and problems he hadn't seen till twelfth grade."

"Annoying for sure, J, but rare, right? Most of the parents love you. Anyway—any jobs?"

"Oh well, you know—a few for teachers, and two for school principals, but I don't meet the requirements."

James took a deep breath—neatly re-folded and set down the paper. He swished his remaining coffee to capture the bit of foam near the top of the cup and then slowly savoured it. He wasn't ready to have this conversation with Franyo yet—not here and not now, when they're nicely relaxed and feeling so connected with each other. He looked up and tilted his head to the side. "You? Anything interesting in the news, Fran?"

"Some land conflict with Native people in the BC Interior. An American millionaire bought a huge ranch and is now limiting access. The Natives claim it's their territory—want to keep on with their traditional practices there—hunting, fishing and picking berries, harvesting medicinal plants. I guess you know better than some reporter what all they'd wanna do there. The rancher got an injunction, but the Natives say they won't back down. Good for them!"

James placed his delicate but strong hand on Franyo's thick wrist and looked him in the eye with a determined look, as if to say, *let's not discuss that now, please*. He didn't want anything to spoil his Saturday morning with the man he cherished, in his favourite place.

Franyo took the cue. "Ready to get on with shopping then? Can't believe you're really gonna make bouillabaisse for all those people," he said.

"We'll only be six. Theo and Bérénice from work, and Enrique and Julius. And it's fish soup, like I ate growing up—just fancied up a bit, French style. *Sera délicieux—wekasin*."

Another chuckle. Franyo was getting used to hearing this playful banter in French and Cree from James—sometimes he even threw in some Spanish.

Dinner was a success, although Theo and Julius were so engrossed in conversation that they seemed to not even taste the bouillabaisse that he and Franyo were so pleased with—its delicate saffron flavour and colour, its silky texture. Mechanically, they all sucked, slurped, chomped and chewed juicy prawns, blue mussels and buttery slices of toasted baguette, wiping their hands and lips with the cloth napkins James had folded so artfully and placed atop each placemat.

Julius, who was studying to be a French teacher like James and Bérénice, was lecturing Theo—in fact, the whole room—about Latin music and dance. Theo, the tall and balding vice-principal from the school where James and Bérénice taught, offered at length the bits he knew about historical Latin vocal sensations, Agustín Lara, Celia Cruz and Lola Beltrán. Everyone else wished they would both shut up and focus on the food—join in with the moans of pleasure and chorus of compliments: Bérénice: "*C'est délicieux.*" Enrique, Julius's Guatemalan partner: "*Muy rico.*" Franyo: "It's great, J."

"It's *fish soup* ... just like we ate at home. Well, sort of," James said and laughed. Everyone joined in the laughter briefly, but then James's characteristic silence settled over the room. Not all of his friends understood this about him—how he could go silent and through his body language and demeanour bring a hush over the whole room. Some took it as brooding behaviour, but James's close friends had become accustomed to it. They realized that he liked sitting in their presence, in silence.

Right after dinner, Julius put on a cassette tape of music he had recorded—salsa, cumbia and merengue. Almost every time they'd gotten together, he'd coached them in the various types of Latin dancing. Tonight, his plan was to teach cumbia.

"Like salsa, it's an odd seven count, but the movements are more pronounced. You have to kind of swing your hips side to side—so many Anglo men are stiff that way, but you can't get into the rhythm otherwise," Julius directed. The dynamic seemed a bit strained, but everyone got up to try the moves even though there wasn't much room.

Catching his breath after two dances, Theo announced, "I brought some music too. Youssou N'Dour, from Senegal. He's a musician and a griot—a traditional historian and storyteller. Let's put it on. By the way, if you guys like the music, maybe you'll come with Bérénice and me to hear him in a couple of weeks, at the Commodore. The music is phenomenal. African dancing, drumming and chanting—regalia—all mind boggling."

James was immediately annoyed. There goes Theo pushing his tribal stuff again. Any time he had a few moments alone with James he would say something about James's roots—the fact he was Cree, at times lecturing James about getting back to his culture. Maybe Theo saw how ill at ease James was at times—trying to find his place in his new reality—a young professional living in a big city on the West Coast, among white folks: always trying new hairstyles, new fashions (buying any shirt that had a motif that was even remotely tribal), constantly seeking acceptance, striving to impress.

Theo was trying to be kind, but why couldn't he just let it go? James *knew* he was different... And now this—tribal music. What was he to do? Why were Julius and Theo hijacking his party? He glanced over at Franyo, but Franyo's expression provided no guidance. James realized that after putting Julius's music on so readily, he now had to play Theo's music too. Good thing there was more wine—and a special dessert still to come.

"Ah, I studied the griot tradition in a course about the literature of French-speaking Africa," James chirped, trying to sound interested as he reluctantly got up and took the cassette from Theo. "They're historians, storytellers and sometimes shamans. They were colonized by the French."

He slipped the tape into the elaborate sound system Franyo had bought to impress him and turned up the volume. Instantly the room filled with the tritone harmonies of syncopated guitar rhythms and high-energy, yet subtle, tama drums. In spite of himself, James was drawn into the music—he wanted to stand and move to the beat but was too embarrassed to let himself go with it, even after drinking a few glasses of wine.

While his body didn't move, his mind—slightly numbed now by the alcohol—began to wander, and he didn't try to stop it. He let Theo and Julius carry on their conversation, or more accurately, their reciprocal lecture—comparing Latin and African music—how it all came from the same roots, and so on, and so on.

Bérénice, Theo's latest romantic interest, brushed a loose blond curl out of her eye, adjusted her wire-rimmed glasses, and gingerly placed a hand on James's thigh, bringing him back into the moment. She seemed to sense that something was going on with him—that he was momentarily in another world. James looked at her and smiled. He longed to tell her about the job prospect up north.

"Franyo, you've been pretty quiet all night. Maybe tell us a bit of *your* story," Theo said. "I'd love to hear about your escape from Yugoslavia—at what age, sixteen?"

Franyo smiled. "Thanks Theo, I would like to, but it's getting late, and it'll take a while..."

Julius stood up. Enrique followed suit. "That was such a nice dinner, and great conversation, and lovely music, Theo. Thanks for sharing."

"Bérénice and I will have to have you over soon, just to hear that story," Theo said, nodding and smiling. "It was a great night everyone. Oh, by the way, I left a book for you on the desk there, James. I look forward to discussing it with you at some point."

After everyone had left, James went over to the desk and took Theo's book out of its paper bag. He felt a pang of resentment—what was Theo trying to teach him now? Then he saw the receipt and bookmark. The book was new, and it wasn't cheap—Theo had spent good money on this gift; he must've felt the content was important. He glimpsed the title, *The Dispossessed: Life and Death in Native Canada*, by Geoffrey York. A few words leapt off the back cover: gas sniffing, suicide, residential schools, stolen children, missing Native women, growing militancy. He flipped it open, glanced at the table of contents. He tilted his head to one side as he realized he had so much to learn about Native life in Canada. He would call Theo in the morning to thank him.

Franyo got busy cleaning the kitchen, and James went to the bathroom to wash up. The evening was a success—he'd pulled it off—a dinner party with his white friends—well, mostly white. He was still in disbelief that he was accepted by these successful professionals here in Vancouver. He had experienced acceptance to some extent at the hospital where he had worked in Calgary, but this could never happen in Edmonton or Northern Alberta—of that he was certain; there was just too much racism against his people. He washed his face and looked at himself in the mirror—at the puffed-up, wavy hairstyle Enrique's flamboyantly gay hairdresser had given him the week before—its crow-black colour contrasting sharply with the mustard yellow of the fisherman sweater Franyo had bought him for his birthday last year... Slowly the glow from the success of the evening vaporized.

He sat alone at the kitchen counter, slightly inebriated, staring at the one remaining serving of English trifle.

ii

The next morning, Franyo announced he was going to clean and wax his van at the car wash on Main Street. James felt a sense of relief—finally, some time alone, at home.

He picked up the front-page section of Saturday's newspaper. Predictably, as he read the article about the conflict between a large tribe of southern BC and a rancher who had recently acquired a huge tract of land, his anger flared. How could an American rancher tell the First Nation, whose territory encompassed his recently acquired estate, that their traditional practices of elk hunting, fishing and berry picking could no longer occur there? Some of the best medicinal sage came from that region. Hadn't there been enough of this bull-shit already? This had happened to his family when he was a kid; they were threatened by farmers whose lands they had to cross to get to their traditional berry-picking sites. His uncles had even been shot at a few times while hunting on public lands that adjoined with farmers' fields.

"Bastards," James muttered.

He threw the windows open wide and fumbled in the bulky, brown leather briefcase that was a gift from Franyo—the only one he'd received upon graduating from university, even though he'd been the first in his family to earn a degree.

He withdrew a floppy disk from its paper sleeve and popped it into the disk drive. He opened the file containing the last cover letter he had sent out, then added a few lines to demonstrate that he was up on the latest teaching theory and methodology: *hands-on science; a problem-solving approach to mathematics; a local ecological, land-based approach to social studies with monthly field trips; the Kodaly method for reading music and ear training; daily phys. ed.; and a multi-faceted approach to reading and writing.*

The "experience" section still looked thin, but maybe they would give him a chance anyway. He printed the two documents, then neatly folded them and slid them into a legal-sized white envelope. As he tucked the envelope into his briefcase, he got a sudden shiver at the realization that he deeply wanted this principal's job. It would be a chance to put all his educational theories and ideology into practice, to create a wonderful and holistic learning environment for students—Indigenous students instead of students from privileged backgrounds. And, unlike what he'd experienced in his five years teaching for the Vancouver School Board, he would foster a progressive instructional environment where teachers' talents and caring could shine through, a setting where teachers felt validated and supported. Most importantly, if he got the job and moved north, it would take him back to the land.

iii

James was at the piano in his classroom, working on an arrangement of "A Song of Joy," which he'd translated into French for his class to sing at the school's spring concert, when the secretary called him over the intercom to take a call in the office.

"James, this is Louise Bernard, the associate superintendent of schools for the Nechako District."

"Ah, hello Mrs. Bernard."

"Please, call me Louise. I know I may have jumped the gun, but I went ahead and called a couple of your references, and based on their wonderful praise, I'm calling to offer you an interview for the principal positions we posted," she said and chuckled musically.

James's hand was trembling. An interview—how many other candidates were there? What were the chances? Would they consider him for the larger school or smaller one? It didn't matter—he had an interview for a principal's job!

At home, James kicked off his booties and called out, "Franyo, I have an interview! I applied for one of those principal's job up north and they're going to interview me. They called me at work."

As usual, at that time of day, Franyo was sitting in his smoking room listening to music on the radio while sipping coffee and enjoying the view of Vancouver's North Shore, relishing his time off between jobs. The lighting was magical in the afternoon, and there were often birds flying around—bald eagles, northern flickers. Glaucous-winged gulls and the ubiquitous Anna's hummingbirds.

In James's imagination, Franyo would be mildly supportive—figuring, like him, that it would be near impossible for him to land the job. Or maybe he would roll his eyes and quip: *Great, J, you have a paid trip to the outback.* But the expression that flashed across Franyo's face was not at all what James had expected. In a tone of sheer annoyance,

Franyo said, "What on earth are you thinking, James—applying for a job on an Indian reserve way up north? What's this place called... *chez who?* And now you've got an interview. It's at least a sixteen-hour drive from here, for God's sake. Do you know how rough it can be there?"

James had been beside himself with excitement, but the butterflies he'd felt in his stomach quickly turned into a Gordian knot. This was serious stuff. He took a deep breath and responded.

"It's a Dakelh word, pronounced with a light 't' at the beginning, a prolonged 'z' sound in the middle and an aspirated 'n' at the end: *t'*chay-zz-gooh-*n*, not sure what it means. And don't forget where I grew up—all the stories I told you."

"Sure—you were a kid then, James. Go look in the mirror. With your fancy haircut and smooth complexion, men up there'll think you're a fag, and they'll tell you so—to your face, maybe even beat you up if they think you're giving them the eye, J."

"Not everyone is like that. We see what we choose to see, Fran... There will be kind and intelligent people there too. It's probably a lot like the place where I grew up."

Franyo's only answer was a blank stare. James continued.

"You think it's easy for me here, my man? In public, some of the well-to-do parents say they're thrilled that their children have a Native teacher. But just last week a few moms got together to tell the principal that my class was spending too much time outdoors—studying nature..."

"You told me so many times about how you brought your seventh graders around this year from making your life hell to respecting you."

"I just don't feel like I belong here. Since Mom is gone, I've lost my connection to... to *everything* that held meaning and was so precious to me—Mother and my grandparents. The land..." James caught the building intensity in his voice. He jerked his head back and went silent. Then a flash of déjà vu—he knew exactly what he would've said next if he hadn't caught himself—*I'm not fully alive here—a gilded bird with clipped wings*, and that would've hurt Franyo so much. This kind of premonition rarely happened to him, but when it did, it was foreboding—some kind of warning from the universe. It felt like his recurring dream about his childhood home—at once comforting and foreign.

"This isn't the way to do it, J. Hurting people. Abandoning the people who care about you most. Think about it. Just look around you. James... *James*..." Franyo said, willing James to meet his eye.

"We should go down to the water, for a walk," James raised his gaze to meet Franyo's.

"You go..." Franyo turned away.

As he sauntered down Cypress Street, James glanced side to side at the new upscale condos and renovated houses of Kitsilano, an area that had once been a vibrant, pot-smoking hippy neighbourhood, with a few old-fashioned convenience stores run by Chinese Canadian families. In the last decade, the hippies had become affluent yuppies who upgraded their digs, and most of the corner stores had become trendy boutiques or restaurants. Since the gentrification of the neighbourhood, and despite now being an educated professional, James felt poor and out of place here. And everyone, or almost everyone, was white—there were no other Native people to be found in the area. He was so tired of being different, everywhere he went, and of having to try to understand those differences and defend who he was as a person—he'd even had to explain to a Vancouver dentist why the shape of his molars was different, for God's sake. He was tired of people asking where he was *from*, and then upon hearing his answer say, "*No*, I mean, where's your *family from*?" It was no wonder he couldn't talk to Franyo about all this—he couldn't even articulate it to himself, couldn't grasp what was going on in his mind and heart. Hadn't he reached his goal in life, wasn't everything going incredibly well for him? Why wasn't he content?

At Kits Beach James breathed in the lusty ocean air and fell into a casual stroll. He passed the oversized saltwater pool where he had experienced bliss swimming on warm summer days, Alaska-blue skies with snow-capped mountains on the horizon. He recalled swimming in the rain there once. He'd loved the tiny refreshing splashes of raindrops on his face as he propelled his body forward in the front crawl, seagulls screaming all around.

He continued down the trail that led toward the shoreline of Jericho Beach. He loved to jog here, the rugged trail just above the beach. Sometimes he would hasten the pace, pretending he was in a cross-country race or being chased by a bear. When he was younger and freer, before the advent of HIV/AIDS, he had met fetching young men here and invited them back to his Yew Street apartment. After they had begun to hang out more seriously—in a de facto relationship—he'd felt relief when Franyo had suggested they keep their relationship open. He suffered less guilt for continuing this type of contact, and it was likely the same for Franyo. Don't ask and don't tell—this was their approach.

Walking back the way he had come, he ducked into the public washroom by the pool. The cool air always had that effect on him, and he thought this was funny—peeing and a shiver got rid of the chills. To his surprise, at the row of antique porcelain urinals, there stood a man he recognized from his university days—a French prof he'd never studied with but had seen around a lot. The man nodded hello, maybe he recognized James too. Within seconds it became clear the man hadn't gone in there just to relieve himself—or if he had, his intent shifted when he saw James. James felt a flush of anguish and guilt—my God, it was everywhere—even when he wasn't looking for it.

As he left the washroom a few minutes later, James glanced around and was relieved no one was nearby. He was flustered almost to the point of shaking—why could he not have just ignored the man and walked away the moment things began to get sexual? Why did he have to engage?

Back home, James washed his face. Catching a glimpse of his eyes in the bathroom mirror, he froze: What was that look—what was the emotion? Sorrow? Dread? Anticipation? It was a look he hadn't seen before, and it worried him. It was as though he didn't recognize himself.

Franyo sat in a blue haze where James had left him. His energy permeated the place. He had obviously been stewing the whole time James was gone.

James watched Franyo take a long drag off his cigarette. He spotted a photo sitting on the antique table—Franyo with James's mother. She had doted on him—ever since James introduced the two of them, saying Franyo was a new friend. Franyo raved about the sumptuous feasts she prepared every time they went together to visit her in Edmonton.

"You know how I feel about you, J," Franyo said, not looking at him. "Since we've been living together these past two years, my life revolves around you, and it's good."

Franyo's eyes were bloodshot. James could tell that he too was holding back tears—had never seen him like that, not even after the death of *his* mother in Slovenia. Franyo stood and went to look out the window—turned his back to James and spoke.

"I don't know why I don't tell you I love you." He shrugged his shoulders, raised one hand into the air and continued. "Maybe I'm scared you'll think you're in control and take advantage of the situation. Christ, my ex-wife, Elena, took me for a ride—screwed me up royally and even deprived me of my children. I loved her, and she almost destroyed me. I can never replicate that scenario—not with anyone, for anything, but I will never abandon you, J." Franyo turned to face him. "I promised your mother, on her deathbed, that I would take care of you—and I will—as long as you let me."

James gazed into Franyo's eyes and smiled, as if to say, *I know—I know, my man—you love me and I'm so sorry I'm doing this to you—to us!* He felt a surge of emotion coming on, and he didn't want to cry in front of Franyo, so he rushed up to the rooftop deck where he loved to sit and reflect. Why was he so desperate to change his life—now—when things were going so well for him? All he knew for sure was that he felt out of sync with the boy who'd heard Cree—*Nehiyaw*—spoken by all of his family all day long, each and every day—the boy who'd grown up in the bush with no electricity or running water, so close to nature, picking berries, eating freshly caught fish and wild meat: deer, moose, rabbit, beaver.

iv

James stepped out of his rental car on the bleak main street—if you could call it that—of Vanderhoof. In reality it was just a brief interlude on Highway 16, which continued to Burns Lake, Terrace and then Prince Rupert. A sense of déjà vu gave him a shiver…

James looked around. He was struck by the vastness of the blue sky, horizon to horizon, with the occasional puffy cumulus cloud floating along. He walked down the paved street still covered by the sand, salt and debris left behind when the huge snowbanks on either side had melted. There wasn't a soul in sight on the inexplicably wide street, just a few disproportionate three-quarter-ton pickup trucks angle-parked outside of the Vanderhoof Hotel, and the other non-descript single or two-storey buildings with unimaginative storefronts. Simple signs differentiated the hardware store from the government liquor store, from the bank, the post office and the pool hall. Surely, the one saving grace was the beauty of the surrounding countryside, in particular the river.

The Nechako River. He said it out loud, "The Nechako." Mother talked about this river, calling it "The Chalk-o." The story she'd told him so many times reverberated in his head—her emphatic alto voice: *You were conceived on the riverbank. Your father took us there—got a job in the lumber mill, when he wanted to get away from his mother after she scorned him for marrying me, a Nehiyaw woman. She was as Indian as me but wanted to be white. We lived just outside of Prince George, in a tiny shantytown of newly arrived Crees and Natives from surrounding reserves.*

And now here he was, drawn back to this infelicitous and asynchronous part of the world. Who would possibly consider a move up here to be a step forward in their life, progress? Most would consider it regression—a return to a desolate rural area in the North, far away from any major centre or modern cultural hub. Yet he felt a compulsion he couldn't explain toward the job at Chezgh'un—just 150 kilometres north. Hopefully the vibe would be more positive there, on historic Indian lands, than it was in Vanderhoof.

Oh, but the river, even with the diversion of half of its flow, was still mighty and vibrant—a key element in the huge ecosystem of the Fraser River, or the Sto:lo. A few Native communities had been displaced by the shifting of its course and the concomitant, deliberate flooding that had caused the extirpation of Nechako River sturgeon, Nechako and Endako chinook salmon, as well as many sockeye populations.

He knew that the formidable Nechako flowed into the Sto:lo, which in turn emptied itself into the ocean near Vancouver, forming a vast estuary, and that there was a subspecies of sockeye salmon that navigated its way downriver and all the way back up, in four-year cycles. They entered the open ocean and travelled in a wide loop to Japan and then back to Canada. These incredible fish stopped eating as soon as they hit fresh water—swam over a thousand kilometres on energy stored in their bodies until they located the exact creek or stream where they were hatched—sheer determination in response to some little-understood magnetic draw, arriving ragged and ruined, to be predated mercilessly by riots of seagulls, crows and eagles who perched on their heads and pecked at them as they spawned in shallow water, before dying. Anadromous, they were called—fish that could traverse two worlds, first leaving fresh water to migrate incredible distances through ocean brine, only to return four years later to their spawning grounds—shallow streams in Northern BC—to spawn and die.

James's head spun just thinking about it. If they could migrate and transform themselves like that, with such purpose, why couldn't he? He walked back to the Vanderhoof Inn and decided to pop into the beer parlour—to check out the local scene and to have a beer to help him relax.

As he stepped into the barroom, he saw her—perched on a tall stool chatting with the bartender, surveying her domain—a waning woman who awaited the arrival of one or more libidinous or depressed men. Her pink, low-cut cotton blouse had lost its stretch. Hastily applied makeup made the wrinkles of her face appear deeper—fuchsia eyeshadow. James felt her eyes following him as he strode to the far end of the musky, near-empty beer parlour—her will for him to look her way was palpable. Once seated, James stole careful glances at a cluster of five men huddled around a bistro-style table across the room. Enshrouded in a cloud of blue smoke, their baseball caps—emblazoned with the logos of local businesses—suppressed masses of scraggly hair of varying lengths and hues. And beneath this, a mosaic of khaki, red-and-black lumberman's jackets, blue jeans, well-worn beige workboots. Unshaven, dishevelled—just as Franyo had described. Voices in James's head, including Franyo's, were shouting that he should get out of there—but he overruled them. "From a Jack to a King" reverberated on the jukebox, a cover version by Ricky Van something, which was now topping the country charts.

The woman's gaze burned James's shoulder, but he kept his head down, trying to sort out what he would say when she eventually came over and recited her best pickup lines. Uh oh, it was going to happen sooner rather than later, and in that rectangular, hall-like space, there was no escape. She sashayed across the stressed fir floor.

"You know howta two-step?" she called out as she grabbed him by the wrist and tried to pull him up.

James leaned back in his chair as far as he could. His feet, firmly planted on the floor, forced his chair back slightly. The rush of discomfort wasn't because the woman was entirely unpleasant—she wasn't—her lips were full, her eyes were bright and her voice was sultry. If it hadn't been for the thus-far-unspoken, but mutually understood expectation of the handing over of cash, he might've felt flattered. Blatant sexual advances by women always left him feeling inadequate and threatened. This woman's behaviour was stirring up a psychological maelstrom in him—emotions and insecurities he'd long since forgotten. *No,* he didn't know how to *two-step,* but he wasn't about to say that out loud—announce his shortcoming to the world. After all, he was from Alberta, where the two-step was an initiation for the macho country-dwellers' mating ritual.

When James resisted her tug on his wrist, her other hand settled softly on his shoulder—concave pink crescents at the base of her fingernails—between the cuticles and chipped pink nail polish. When he still didn't budge, she sank into the nearest chair and pulled it in close. Instinctively, James's breathing shallowed to limit his intake of the second-hand smoke that clung to her clothes and blended with the cheap perfume she had applied much earlier that day, or perhaps the day before. James knew he couldn't tell her why he was in town—she would likely scoff at him and laugh. *You, a school principal… as if…*

"Ah, thanks, maybe another time." James said flatly. The woman clicked her tongue, then got up and moved toward the table of men across the room. James ran his fingers through his hair and breathed a sigh of relief.

Less than twenty-four hours earlier, he had been nine hundred kilometres south, in a chic restaurant in Kitsilano, sipping a fine Valpolicella, listening to a jazz band with a versatile and emphatic vocalist and trumpeter, and chatting with Franyo. Now—here—in this seedy bar. He should just escape into the fresh spring air, stroll along the Nechako River, even though, after sunset, it would be cold outside. Instead, he had just one pint before heading upstairs to his room.

He sat on the springy bed and looked around. So, this is what rooms in the cheaper hotels looked like: worn and soiled brown carpet, cigarette burns interspersed with stains of spilled hot coffee and cold beer, body fluids. Even a dingy room in such a place would've been unaffordable for his family—they had always stayed with relatives when travelling anywhere.

A worn and tattered bedspread was neatly stretched over the sagging bed and lifeless pillows. Two glass ashtrays sat symmetrically on the chipped veneer of a double-wide dresser. A large floral print in a plain glass frame—yellow and wrinkled at its edges. The omnipresent odour of stale cigarette smoke.

He got out his book, *Une saison dans la vie d'Emmanuel* by Marie-Claire Blais. Surely it would distract him and help him to fall asleep. Reading a good book always did.

One of the main characters, Jean-Le Maigre, a teenaged boy who loves to read and writes poems, is tubercular and has lice, and endures threats by his overbearing and macho father to beat him to a pulp and to burn every page of poetry he ever writes. The novel recounts a story of poverty and oppression in rural Quebec, and it comes as close as any mainstream piece of literature has to capturing the reality that James, his siblings and cousins grew up in.

The story brings James solace. His own family wasn't quite as poor as the rural Québécois family portrayed in the book, and while James himself had been sexually abused and beaten by his brother-in-law, he hadn't been sexually exploited by a priest, or by his own brother or older cousins. Still, what a relief to see some aspects of his reality set out in a book. He wasn't alone in having his sexual innocence and development disrupted and usurped: the inflamed sensuality of fervent yet tentative kisses placed on a cheek or closed lips—a delicate act burned into one's memory forever, anxious reciprocal touching and exploration of a girl or boy about the same age—testing stimulus and response—exploring boundaries. All of it recklessly short circuited cauterized in a matter of minutes by one adult who was unable to control his own lust.

v

The next day was clear and sunny. James pulled the curtains open and said, "*Waseskwan*," the Cree word for a clear day. He smiled, but the bright light made the fog in his head more debilitating. Coffee. He would need lots of it to make it through the day. Louise Bernard, his prospective new boss, had reviewed the schedule with him over the phone: a tour of Fort St. Pierre and a visit to the new high school where they would observe the class of Native students that was the assistant superintendent's pet project—she thought they'd do best in a learning centre of their own. Late in the afternoon, they would drive back to Vanderhoof to allow James some downtime before dinner, to prepare for the evening job interview.

He'd heard there were several other candidates, and he wondered what tours had been arranged for them. Whatever those were, he was glad Louise had chosen Catherine Bird, a local elder, to accompany them for *his* tour.

Louise and Catherine stood side by side on the steps of the school board offices. Louise was taller than Catherine. Neither wore makeup. Louise's smooth, milky complexion contrasted with Catherine's olive complexion and deep wrinkles. Catherine's naturally grey hair was pulled back into a ponytail, held together with a colourful beaded barrette; Louise's was cut into a neat pageboy, grey with platinum highlights. Louise offered her hand to James and introduced him to Catherine.

"*Hadih*," Catherine said as she took his hand.

"Well, we may as well head right out," Louise said as she directed them to her white Jeep Cherokee. "We have a long day ahead of us."

Once they had settled into the vehicle, Louise pointed out the two-way radio between the front seats. "This is to listen for approaching logging trucks. Sometimes they come careering around a curve with a huge load of timber crudely strapped onto them." As Louise turned the ignition and James clicked his seat belt into place, Catherine twisted her body sideways to glare at him in the back seat.

"So, you're Cree, eh?" she demanded, her piercing voice cracking. "Well, one of my daughters married a Cree. Goot-lookin' guy, but he broke her heart. Crees have a reputation up here ya know... Came ta steal our womans ... and our horses—for centuries. The traditional enemihs of Dakelh people," she said, scrunching her wrinkled face into a deep scowl.

Louise glanced at James, obviously trying to come up with something to say, to save the moment, but James spoke first. "Well, I'll try not to break any hearts while I'm here, Catherine—and I won't steal any cars... *Ha ha ha*."

"I jus' lie. Goot to meet you, t'James. Jus' wanted have some fun wit' you 'n scare Louise a bit."

"You're a brat, Catherine. You had me goin' for a minute."

The Fort St. Pierre High School was a modern and stylish building, not huge—two storeys high. "Three hundred and fifty students this year, up ten percent from last year," Louise said and sniffed the air. As they moved around the building, James perceived the shifting odours: initially, the smell of chalk dust wafting through stale air, then the whiff of fresh bread from the home ec room, new plastic and a metallic cough-syrup aroma from the computer lab, a blend of sweaty PE gear and the body odour of deodorant-wary adolescent boys outside of the gym. The squeak of runners on varnished hardwood floors drew James's attention to the gym. A group of tall white boys, clad in shiny green shorts and white tank tops, or bare chested, were completely absorbed in a fast-paced game of basketball. He scanned to see if there were any Native kids in the group but saw none. Where were they? Surely there were some great Native athletes in Fort St. Pierre; with three reserves nearby, one contiguous with the town—there had to be.

How would the on-reserve schools compare to this school? he wondered. Would there be a gym, a home ec room, a soccer field?

Would there be a large adventure playground like the one they'd seen at the local elementary school they'd driven past?

As they reached the classroom at the end of the main floor, Louise became animated. "Okay, James and Catherine, here's what I wanted you to see. Our special centre for Native students. Rich Masch, the vice-principal, has a master's degree in Native education, and he set up this alternative program for our Carrier students. We were sure they would all like to be together, in the same room. Have a look. Isn't it great?"

Rich was leaning over the desk of one student—seemingly helping with a worksheet. He was tall, wearing a pale blue dress shirt and beige pants—thick salt and pepper hair and a matching thick, but well-trimmed beard. Premature greying, James concluded, when Rich looked up and James saw his boyish face. Rich glanced at James, nodded and came over, extending his hand. As they shook hands, James felt the vice-principal's inquisitive look settle on him. James wanted to step into the room to see how Rich operated, but Rich's regard—his raised eyebrows, his stance, stopped James in his tracks.

Feeling defiant—like he had a right to observe these students—James stood his ground for a minute, admiring the teens' thick, shiny black hair and complexions—darker than his. The students *all* appeared to be filling in blanks on math and English grammar worksheets. How could anyone think this represented a true learning situation? Rote learning was so passé—everyone knew that. James was familiar with the erroneous assumption that Native students liked to be together in one room, away from other students, and also with the incorrect notion that these same students needed to work at their own pace, independently, in order to succeed. But he also knew that the learning materials for any alternative program needed to be carefully designed and that the presence of a solid mentor/teacher was imperative for doing mini-lessons, answering questions personally and generally providing motivation and encouragement.

"It's a nice facility—uh, the school," James replied. "Really well equipped."

"We're getting a new computer lab installed, too, so the kids can do their exercises using standardized instructional programs, educational databases—and spell check." Rich said with pride. "A new pathfinder program that's been piloted in the US."

James remained silent.

As the three got back into Louise's jeep, they were all quiet. Then Catherine spoke. "I know some of those young ones—two greatnephews in there and their friends. They're smart kids. Not sure why they're not in reg'lar classes—to get a reg'lar high school diploma. Real important nowadays, the grad 'quivalent diploma is only goot fer takin' trades and not fer university."

"Catherine, let's talk," Louise responded, with what sounded almost like relief. "I'd like to hear more of your views on this. Some in the district consider this approach innovative—like the special ed folks. I'd love to talk to you and James more about this."

James breathed more easily—he looked forward to discussing this with Louise. Seeing that segregated classroom frustrated him—filled him with a sadness he dared not explore or allow to burst his bubble of optimism. The stark reality of there being two solitudes here in the North reminded him so much of his childhood back in Northern Alberta—the racial separation that happened at recess and lunchtime as if it were the most natural thing in the world: the Native kids went to one part of the playground and the white kids to the other.

Just how backward was this school district that he was seeking to join as an educational leader? He had imagined Louise as progressive, innovative and creative. Why hadn't her energy and approach filtered through the entire system? Maybe it was too soon. Change takes time. Hiring him was a step in the right direction—and he, in turn, would hire more Native educators. And, he would operate at arm's-length from the district at *his* school, be it in Chezgh'un or

Blink'ah, and hopefully he would have enough autonomy to run it the way he wanted to. Louise seemed open to his innovative ideas for a customized academic curriculum imbued with local knowledge and culture—the Dakelh language.

On the way out of town, Louise pointed out a historic site that housed monuments to honour important figures in local history: a revered chief who had negotiated a lasting trading arrangement between the local tribes and fur traders, a politician who had worked in the town in his youth and gone on to become the first governor of British Columbia, and a priest who had spent decades in the area as a missionary. Catherine suggested they drive by a shrine that was the grave site of a young Dakelh woman who was venerated by Indigenous people as a potential saint—miracles had been attributed to her, and Native people from all over the North made annual pilgrimages to pray to her. James felt discouraged—colonialism and Catholicism, both oppressive forces, were well entrenched in the area. How would he counter them in his role as school principal?

vi

An evening interview. Somewhat unorthodox, but once James saw who was on the panel, he understood why. Everyone was busy during the day with meetings, classes and appointments. In the foyer outside of the sterile boardroom where the interviews were to be held, Louise introduced James to the selection committee: her boss, Mike O'Leary, a short, balding, middle-aged jock, who stood next to Chief Felix Joe. The chief also looked athletic but was taller and trimmer, with a smooth complexion. He had strong Native features but looked surprisingly fair standing next to Art and Sally Thaddeus, a middle-aged couple who were darker even than James—almost as brown as James's Fijian friend Davith. Art and Sally both worked as teaching assistants at the school. Colin Baird, the band's white director of education; Tara Friesen, the Native education consultant for the school district; and a cluster of nodding and smiling school trustees. Art's handshake was especially warm and genuine—a broad smile accompanied a sturdy grasp. Kindness in his eyes. The chief showed Art and Sally to their seats and gave them each a pen and a notepad to write down any questions they might have during the interview, explaining that if there was time, he would read them out on their behalf.

The two-hour interview was gruelling. James was fatigued by the mental effort required to not only answer the questions well, but to strike the right pose—to not look effeminate alongside the other men who were redolent with male energy, to speak proper English yet not sound overly elegant in his word choice and turn of phrase. This type of thing, others' perception of him in this regard—his masculinity and English enunciation—hadn't occurred to him since he'd left his home in Northern Alberta. In Vancouver, he'd just sort of blended in. It would take a while for him to comprehend the situation here, but he was glad he'd decided to wear his nicest designer sweater and pressed slacks instead of a white shirt and tie—his black leather Paraboots, a style he'd picked up from Theo. Dressed like this, he fit in just fine, and when Art teased him about his fancy clothes just before the interview started, he said, "I dressed up for you, my friend," and this put everyone at ease.

After the interview, Art, Sally and the chief waited for James in the hallway—all beaming. Art towered over the three of them by at least a foot. He offered his oversized, cinnamon-skinned hand once again for a hearty handshake. The black crescents at the end of his fingernails contrasted with those of James's and the chief's, which were scrubbed and white.

"Impressive, didn't you think so?" said the chief, apparently directing his question at Sally and Art. Before they had a chance to answer, he laughed and put his arm around James's shoulder and continued, "Especially for a Cree. S'posed ta be our enemih, right you guys?"

"Yes, Catherine warned me." James said with a nervous chuckle.

James stood there feeling awkward, like a child being given praise and affection by an adult. Maybe it was the chief's manner with Art and Sally, and now him—the leader's air of superiority and condescension when he spoke to them, his subjects, and now to James, a possible de facto employee.

"*Hadih,* we'll keep an eye on you t'James," Art boomed in his resounding deep voice and then let out a belly laugh. Sally smiled and giggled. "We'll see you soon, t'James," she said, as she held her hand out, tentatively, and looked downward. James smiled with amusement and joy. Up north, at least among the Dakelh, that would be his name: t'James—a light *t* sound in front of it. He guessed the sound made by *j* in English didn't exist in their language.

Chief Felix looked James directly in the eye and said, "*Hadih,* James. I should tell you, the school in Bilnk'ah is state of the art, but in Chezgh'un, I have a commitment from the federal government to build a new facility. You'll be a big part of it all, should you become principal there. We'll be breaking ground this summer. It'll be modern with all the amenities."

James's mind kicked into high gear. What was the state of the existing building in Chezgh'un like then? Was it adequate? He didn't want to seem forward asking these questions now, since he might not be offered the job. And, he didn't want to look a potential gift moose in the mouth. Only if he were offered the job in Chezgh'un would he find out.

That night, in the plush bed of a cozy lakeshore cabin at the motel just minutes away from downtown Fort St. Pierre, James awoke in a sweat. He was dreaming about an experience his mother had gone through in her last months. He was there with her, in the treatment room of a cancer centre. Blue circles on her belly and back—a technician positioning her on a stretcher and pointing white, cone-like mechanisms at the circles of ink. The technician was readying to project radiation through the centre of them, seeking a direct hit to the large tumor on her pancreas. A nebulous odour—vaporized chlorine? His mind flashed to his mother's corpse poised comfortably in a metallic casket that sat squarely on a coffee table at his aunt's house in Slave Lake, where they grew up, near Sawridge Reserve.

He was sure there would be more dreams to follow—he realized after dreams like this that he was still mourning the loss of his mother—albeit mostly unconsciously. So much in his new surroundings made him nostalgic for her.

At the crack of dawn, the honking of a throng of Canada geese startled him awake. The geese must have just returned north—he hadn't noticed them on the lake. Oh my God—what was causing the new aching hollowness in his chest? It felt familiar, like the sorrow he'd felt when his mother left him at age ten, or when he moved from Calgary to Vancouver—a world away from his family and territory. Yet this was different—a deeper and more urgent torment. He sat up and cradled his head in his hands as he realized that this time, the grief was of his own making.

He yearned to be with Franyo. Ah, this was the biggest part of this present angst... he was contemplating leaving Franyo, the person who had shown more devotion toward him than anyone else who wasn't family. He would be leaving Franyo and the world they'd jointly built and shared for the last eight years—a world where James didn't belong, but where he had nevertheless been accepted and validated, esteemed by his fellow teachers, his students and their parents—all affluent, and mostly white. This could never have happened where he was from—Slave Lake—or the nearest city, Edmonton.

II

Kekac Nîpin — Early Summer

i

The following Monday morning, James was back in his classroom in Vancouver when the secretary's voice came over the intercom of his room. "Mr. Ward, please come to the office. There's a call for you."

It was Mike, the superintendent of the northern school district. "Well James, last night the board passed a motion, unanimously, to make you an offer for the principalship of the Chezgh'un school. Congratulations are in order for sure, but I should tell you, accommodations at the moment are dicey. There are two large mobile homes where the teachers can bunk up, but we may have to put you up in an RV or vacation trailer to start out—we'll get you settled in a new teacherage before winter. Think it over. An offer package has been couriered to you, and you have two weeks to respond. I'm sure we'll be in touch soon."

"Well, thanks so much, Mike. That's wonderful news, and yes, I will consider it carefully—no question!"

James hung up the phone and flopped into the chair beside him—his mind in manic mode. To live where, and in what? Sure, they'd promised a new teacherage for him and the other new staff, but workers hadn't yet broken ground, and things like that took a while to build.

But what an opportunity it was, to set up a new school and try all the great methodologies he'd been reading about—ways to establish a positive learning environment and wonderful teaching conditions with limited bureaucratic interference in teachers' creativity and enthusiasm. He would take this principalship!

How would he tell Franyo? After all, Franyo had been buying gifts and spoiling him for the last couple of weeks—a bouquet of flowers every Friday afternoon, cakes from James's favourite bakery, A Piece of Cake, every Saturday. And the passion, the lovemaking was as frequent and as hot as it had been when they were new lovers. In all of these things, Franyo was telling him: *I love you, James, with all my heart. Please don't go.*

James went directly home right after the three o'clock bell. He was a bundle of nerves, vacillating between giddiness and angst, but he'd have to keep his emotions under control, or at least feign that. He'd invite Franyo out for dinner—his treat—and after dessert, he would tell him.

Things didn't go as planned. Franyo—a cornered cat.

"I don't want to go for dinner. If you wanna treat me, let's order pizza. We have a bottle of wine in the cupboard."

"Let me get us a glass of wine."

"I might make some coffee."

"That'll keep you awake tonight."

"I likely won't get any sleep anyway. Okay, pour me some wine then."

"I have something important to tell you, and I wanted to do it in a good way."

"You got a job offer—that odd principal's job up north, in the bush."

"Why odd?"

"Anyway, the sensible thing would be to use that to parlay your way into a promotion here in Vancouver. You said there were vice-principal jobs open."

"I need to go," James blurted and then tried to swallow his words. It had come out the wrong way.

"Why's that so hard then? … You can just *go*—nobody's holding you back." Franyo choked on the last part of that sentence.

That statement had its desired effect. James's throat was dry and his stomach tight. His life with Franyo, here in Kitsilano, was the only security he'd had in life and Franyo knew it. The possibility of losing this little bit of stability threw James into a panic. He wanted to flee—to seek refuge in the arms of a stranger—as he so often did to soothe his stress. He had to keep himself together—assuage Franyo's anguish and manage his own fears too. He was going through with this, *coûte que coûte*.

"Franyo, you know it's not you. I wish you could come with me. I love being with you here, but since Mother died, I feel so disconnected from my family—my sisters and brothers and all my relations back home."

"I miss my family too, James. It's time to get real about yours… Why can't you just go see them? Visiting will bring you closer to them."

"Remember your last visit to your family—you said it wasn't the same. You didn't know who to stay with—there wasn't the same family bond… Well, that's what it's like for me, too. Like yours, my family is in disarray now, and will be for a while."

"Thanks. That makes me feel better. You know what, fuck it! Let's go out for dinner after all. But please, don't put on that African music when we get back. All that tribal stuff is starting to drive me crazy."

"I have some time to respond," James said, unnerved and on the verge of tears. "Maybe I'll apply for a leave of absence for a year, from the VSB."

A week later, James found a memo in his mailbox at school.

> Mr. Ward, congratulations on your job offer as principal of Chezgh'un School. Given the nature of this new position, should you choose to accept it, it would not be prudent for

us to grant your request for a leave of absence. We at the VSB wish you every success.

James flushed. Things were intensifying. The safety net had been pulled out from under him—if he were to leave his job, the change would be permanent. But this career advancement would move him a quantum leap forward—into another orbit. Shaking now, he got his letter of offer out of his briefcase, picked up the phone and dialled.

ii

Louise Bernard made arrangements with the Vancouver School Board for James to spend a week in the northern school district. So, the first Monday in June, Franyo drove James to the airport, as James had done for him when he travelled to pulp-mill towns around BC to work his magic as a master craftsman, cladding tanks and pipes—insulating them to preserve heat or cold. A quick hug followed by a forced smile.

When James found his row number toward the middle of the airplane, he was surprised to see that the man in the seat next to his was Rich Masch, the high school vice-principal from Fort St. Pierre, the one who had a master's degree in Native education. Rich's hand flew out in front of him and he smiled broadly.

"James, good to see you. BC's youngest school principal. Congratulations. You must be flying high… *ha ha ha*. No pun intended."

"Thanks, Rich. I *am* really excited."

"Well, please feel free to stop by the high school anytime for a chat. I'd love to hear how things go out there. Maybe we can collaborate on some extra-curricular stuff, cultural programming, once you get your bearings…"

"Oh, that's an interesting idea. Thanks so much."

"Louise says you're pretty sharp when it comes to curriculum design. She expects you'll do amazing things for the folks out there."

During the hour-long flight to Prince George, James was flattered that Rich spoke to him as a peer and wondered if they might become friends and allies. Every time Rich spoke, James peered up into his blue-grey eyes and listened attentively. It was wonderful that, like him, Rich had decided to devote his career to Native education. Maybe the vice-principal had gotten the wrong impression about him when they first met.

Once the pilot announced they were at cruising altitude, Rich raised his eyebrows, leaned in closer to James and spoke quietly, as if he was afraid the other passengers might overhear.

"You know, James, I'm not sure how to tell you this, so I'll just be direct. I don't know if Louise has told you. You'll face some real challenges in Chezgh'un, but there's one in particular you should know about: there's so much inbreeding in that place that it's affected their cognitive abilities."

"Inbreeding... Incredible. Ah... How?" James asked, astonished.

"It's shocking," Rich replied. "A friend of mine, a social worker who apprehended a couple of kids out there, was surprised to see they all carry the same last name, Peters. Just bizarre."

"Bizarre is right. I mean the idea of inbreeding."

"That's the word in the district. I mean not just Chezgh'un—other Native communities, too. So many people with the same last name."

"Yes, I know about the last name thing—in Chezgh'un and where I'm from too. Did you learn about that in your Native studies courses? I mean, why that is the case in some communities?"

"I can only guess..."

The woman sitting beside Rich who had been stone quiet jumped in. "Well, everyone knows about that...yes, inbreeding has affected their intellectual abilities for sure. Explains a lot."

James was flabbergasted. The plane dipped suddenly—he spilled his coffee, felt its warm wetness on his thigh. He tried to dry it with a napkin and reached to unbuckle his seatbelt, to go to the washroom, but the flight attendant announced that all passengers must remain seated and fasten their seatbelts.

"Damn," James said. "What a mess. Listen, the reality is that the priests renamed people—got rid of their 'Indian' names—for convenience. They gave people from small villages the same last name so that when they were taken to residential schools, the priests and nuns would know where they came from."

Rich and his seatmate maintained their gazes straight ahead and didn't respond.

Once it was clear they weren't going to engage, James carried on, "And Rich, remember, other things happen with inbreeding before intellect is affected—like congenital deformities. Asymmetrical faces, clubfoot. Have you read about the royal families of Europe? The effects of inbreeding among them—the Hapsburg jaw and hemophilia? It's well documented. The folks I've met from Chezgh'un all have fine features. They look very healthy. Inbreeding in Native communities is a myth."

The pilot announced they were about to land and spoke about how nice the weather was in Prince George. James breathed a sigh of relief. He continued, unsure if he was being heard or ignored.

"As I imagine things, when the people of Chezgh'un were sent off to residential school, the first generation that is, the priests gave them all the last name of 'Peters,' which displaced their individual Dakelh names, and it carried over. And I've researched their culture—historically, they would marry cousins, but third cousins, which isn't a problem, genetically speaking."

Rich squirmed in his seat, his face red, his eyes bloodshot. Looking straight ahead, he breathed in deeply and spoke. "Do you like to hunt, James? Moose and grouse hunting are huge around Fort St. Pierre. Hundreds of hunters from the south come up every year. Convoys of motorized campers, equipped to the nines—power generators, satellite dishes, crates of booze. You know, it's funny. I was surprised when you told me you're Native. You're so stylish and well groomed. I assumed you were Filipino, or maybe Polynesian. And you're so articulate—impressive."

As they were about to go their separate ways at the Prince George Airport, Rich extended his hand to James and said, "Well, listen. If there's anything I can do to help—let me know."

James took Rich's hand and looked into his milky, freckled face and his grey eyes, trying to gauge his sincerity. He wasn't a harmful person, just ill informed, like many others. James pulled his copy of *The Dispossessed* out of his briefcase and gave it to Rich. "This is a great book that deals with many of the issues facing Native people in Canada right now. I've learned so much from it—I know you'll find it interesting."

James was cruising along the highway in his rented Ford Bronco, *rumbo a* Fort St. Pierre, completely absorbed by his surroundings, the rolling fields, which presently were taking on a greenish hue. In another week or two, the same scene would be completely verdant. He wondered what the area must have looked like before the so-called settlers arrived. Had this area, like the Canadian Prairies, been thick with trees and shrubs, black with herds of bison, or perhaps elk and moose? Or were caribou more common here? There definitely would've been lots of beaver, working their magic, keeping the habitat lush. They were everywhere and were so numerous before the fur trade, which had targeted their pelts more than that of any other animal. In his side mirror, he caught a glimpse of a few crows taking flight.

Suddenly, blue and red flashing lights in the rear-view mirror caught his eye. "Damn," he said as he touched the brake then pulled over to the shoulder. The constable opened the door of his cruiser and stepped out—ticket book in hand. Great, how much would this cost?

The officer—tall, blond, with a developing paunch—asked to see James's licence and insurance papers. James looked at his nametag: GOSSELIN. That name sounded familiar—a French name. The officer scolded James for speeding, even though he had been just ten kilometres over the limit. It hadn't occurred to him that he might become a target for the RCMP up north, stopped frequently, for something or other, like his younger brother, Trevor, had been in Northern Alberta, carded almost every time he went anywhere. James looked around some more as the Mountie wrote the ticket. He noticed an eagle's nest balanced precariously atop a telephone pole on the passenger's side ahead in the distance—that was a new sight. Down south the aeries were usually concealed in the canopies of stands of cedar or Douglas firs—sequoias. The officer coughed to get his attention and handed him a raft of papers. James regarded the policeman's face as he took the ticket and said, "Thank you—I guess."

"You picked up any hitchhikers lately, bud?"

"Ah no, I'm not from around here."

"What's that got to do with anything? Some perp—or should I say perv?—is travelling these parts picking up women hitchhikers—mostly Natives. A few of 'em have gone missing. Just in the last month, there's been two Native women and one white girl who vanished—no trace of 'em."

"I hadn't heard about that. But thanks for the warning—very concerning."

He made a mental note to ask Louise and Catherine about this—the missing women. What was going on?

When he finally arrived in "the Fort," as the locals called it, James pulled into the parking lot of the Kings Inn and dashed into the restaurant, anticipating the spicy and pungent flavours of a Chinese combo dinner. Chopsticks and chili oil. He would get it to-go so he wouldn't have to make small talk with any of the locals, the waiter or the proprietor. Having to explain who he was and what he was doing there—there would be plenty of time for that in the months to come.

The aroma of stir-fried garlic, onions and black bean sauce made his mouth water. He sat in the booth closest to the door to wait for his order. The simple decor of the place reminded him so much of the Chinese restaurant in the town closest to where he'd grown up, and also of the ones he'd visited in many small towns in Alberta and BC since he'd left his village. The food was always to his liking.

He checked into the motel—a simple row of log cabins along the lakeshore—hurriedly, hoping to get the cabin right at the water's edge so he would hear the delicate lapping of the lake's tiny breakers.

He was eager to wander down to the shoreline, find a nice spot to eat and then explore. Later, in the moonlight, when nobody else was around, he would go into shallow water to pray to the spirits of the place and give thanks, the way his mother had taught him. He would spend a week in that cabin—travelling back and forth to Chezgh'un the first couple of days, and the other days to and from the school board offices in Vanderhoof.

How could he get Franyo to visit him there—even for a week in the summer? Franyo would hate the bugs but love the people and the place. The people of Chezgh'un would appreciate Franyo—he had such a disarming smile and a seductive way about him. And he had a soft spot for Native people—he'd even had a Haida girlfriend at one point.

James wasn't sure where this affinity came from, but Franyo had shown him a collection of comics he'd kept since he was a child, about a fictitious Apache chief named Winnetou. Franyo had also seen many movies about this chief. James was intrigued. He'd never heard of the bestselling German author Karl May, who had become famous for his work based on this imaginary Mescalero chief. The concept of the "noble savage" put forth by the French philosophers he'd studied leapt to mind. James nodded and smiled.

But as he read Franyo's comics, he realized that May had depicted both good "savages" and bad. The former were those who were fairer with more subtle facial features, closer to a Caucasian countenance, and more apt to accept a *white* way of life, a *white* way of doing things. Whereas the latter, who had darker skin, were depicted as sinister and undesirable in their appearance, manner and lifestyle. Old Shatterhand, the European protagonist in the body of work, at some point becomes blood brothers with Chief Winnetou and gradually inculcates him with a *white* way of thinking, including *white* values—Christianity—while at the same time, preserving desirable aspects of Chief Winnetou's noble savagery. James guessed that Franyo considered James as belonging to the first group. He was relieved and perplexed at the same time—was Franyo following Old Shatterhand's example in his relationship with Winnetou? Had he taken James on as a project, hoping to refine him a bit, smooth the rough edges to make James an exotic blend of emphatic wildness and New World *savoir faire*?

A mosquito landed on his forearm. He swatted it, leaving a bright red blotch on his hairy skin. His blood, someone else's or a blend? Had he just inadvertently become someone's blood brother?

iii

Early the next morning, James was off to have breakfast with Catherine Bird and Tara Friesen, the Native education consultant for the school district, before heading up to Chezgh'un together. When he stopped for gas at the Chevron station, an aging white guy loitering at the coffee counter asked James what he was doing there. After James's upbeat response, the man said, "Well, you know, us locals won't drive out that way anymore. Too afraid to get shot. The Indians are so violent, and for no good reason. You should've seen my friend's pickup truck after he ventured out that way last summer looking for pine mushrooms. He had parked at the edge of the forest for just an hour, and when he got back to his vehicle, it was riddled with bullets. Ten dents and five holes, right through. Some of 'em near the gas tank."

"There's hardened criminals on that reserve," the clerk added, waving her hand in the air, motioning toward the lake as she continued. "One Indian was convicted of attempted murder and I know there are others out there who have killed—gotten away with it 'cause the cops are scared to go out there—and the Indians all look the same anyways, even share the same last name. Don' know what the fuck that's all about."

Was this blunt racism, or was there a kernel of truth in what the locals said?

When James arrived at the diner, he recounted the dire warnings from the Chevron. Tara became noticeably restless as James spoke.

"A lot of kids have fetal alcohol syndrome on that reserve. Lots of gas sniffing too, as well, to this day. And I'm sure the kids are performing way below their grade levels. But they've likely never been assessed. By the way, how did *you* come to be so well-spoken, James? Your diction and pronunciation are so smooth... elegant even."

James felt himself wince. "Well, Tara, my Scottish-Canadian brother-in-law taught me to speak like this—corrected my grammar and pronunciation every time I opened my mouth for years, even at the dinner table. That, and I've had seventeen years of education—none of it in my birth language."

"Well, perhaps you should call your brother-in-law to thank him. It serves you well."

Catherine shifted uncomfortably in her chair and spoke. "They're goot people t'James. They're misunderstood, and they're scorned by so many because they've kept to themselves, their skin is darker than any other community aroun' here—behin' their back, people say they're *black*, 'n they've kept up the traditional ways." Catherine paused, then raised her open palm in the air and continued, "But you know t'James, more than one noble fam'ly in our region has their roots in that community."

James believed Catherine. He wanted to believe her. After all, he came from a Cree community that had been rife with violence similar to that he'd been warned about here in the North. His mother had told many stories of people chasing each other with axes, or worse, with hunting rifles. He took the warnings of the well-meaning locals, including Tara, to heart, but they only made a slight ripple in the swells of his elation. He was getting his own school—and returning to a Native community much like the one he'd grown up in, he imagined. He wasn't going to let these stories discourage him.

The drive from Fort St. Pierre to Chezgh'un was a blur. James loved studying the copses of mountain alder, trembling aspen and black spruce that rushed by as Louise drove along. He felt a rush of adrenalin at the thought of making this trip on his own. Oh, the freedom and independence of travelling alone through the daunting wilderness—with just a vehicle to both transport and shield him from the omnipresent dangers he was all too aware of from having grown up in the bush of Northern Alberta. Back home, black bears were the largest and most feared animal, although incidents with them were rare. But this was grizzly country—the one animal species that will actively hunt humans as prey. An uncle of James who was a hunting guide loved to recount a story of a grizzly crushing a man's skull in his gigantic jaws, ripping out and eating just the belly, leaving the rest as carrion to be devoured by crows, vultures, hawks, eagles, wolves and rodents—the maggots of blowflies.

The incessant fine dust made James's eyes water. It lined his nose and left grit on his teeth. And the constant shimmying of the vehicle on the rough gravel road made him lightheaded, but, still, none of this could dampen his enthusiasm. He was in his element. Twenty kilometres or so northwest of Fort St. Pierre, Louise veered to the right, onto another gravel road, this one even narrower. With confident dexterity, she manoeuvred around a gravel truck, a grader, logging truck after logging truck. James heard the occasional trucker announce his rig number, direction and "twenty" on the radio phone.

After miles of dips, grooves and interminable stretches of brain-rattling vibration, at last the gravel gave way to a bumpy dirt road and they drove across a makeshift bridge of wooden beams and planks, swerving to miss a couple of giant mud puddles. James knew they had finally arrived in Chezgh'un.

Wooden shacks lined both sides of the street. Weatherworn plywood sheets served as siding, some of which had long ago been painted blue or white, but most had now taken on the silvery-brown hue of aged or untreated wood.

In a meadow past the row of the houses on the creek side, a single large cow, chocolate brown with splashes of white, grazed lazily. The animal looked up as Louise's white vehicle approached, but when it was clear there was no danger, it continued munching grass and young yarrow. What on earth was that cow doing there? It seemed so out of place in this wilderness setting. Then James remembered something he'd read about the residential school in the region: the church and state had colluded to coerce the Dakelh and other people who were students there to become farmers. Perhaps this was a remnant of that era, maybe someone had actually tried to give cattle ranching or raising dairy cows a try.

A stubby wind-worn steeple of a Catholic church lay straight ahead. The paint, which two decades earlier would've created a glossy sheen of ecclesiastical blue, was now peeling.

Louise pulled up to an old two-storey building with worn cream-coloured wooden siding, surrounded by quack grass and gravel. Bare patches of weathered wood stood out here and there—grey asphalt roofing shingles, a number of which were missing, a few others askew. The wooden railing of the entryway stairs and landing had recently been replaced with pine planks that hadn't yet been painted. The large banks of windows that ran almost the entire length of the side that was visible declared it the schoolhouse.

The three leapt out of the jeep, yawned and stretched.

At the sight of the school, James felt shock and sadness. There were no school grounds as such, just a grassy meadow directly behind the schoolhouse, with an off-kilter stand-up merry-go-round and the remains of a teeter-totter: a partial plank protruding at a sixty-degree angle from a rusty fulcrum and frame off to one side of it. Didn't every school in the country have playing fields and decently equipped playgrounds?

My God, what was he getting himself into?

"We'll have to get rid of that broken equipment," Louise said. "It's depressing."

"I wonder if we could build a skating rink," James said, then went silent, worried it was obvious he was trying to conceal the feeling of defeat that was rolling over him in waves. "We'll have to plan a solid outdoor rec program," he continued after a pause of a few seconds, as he, Catherine and Louise walked over to the building.

"Let's have just a quick look inside," Louise offered. "Too disruptive to have so many strangers, especially administrative types, show up in the classrooms. You can come back tomorrow, James, on your own. The whole building will look better, inside and out, with a bit of paint and a few touch-ups here and there, which can all be done over the summer."

James nodded. He stepped onto a patch of quack grass near the school to examine the corroded and barely legible plaque that was screwed into its exterior wall. It read:

CHEZGH'UN SCHOOL, DEPARTMENT OF INDIAN AFFAIRS

The year of construction and the corresponding federal minister's name were illegible. For how many years had the federal government run this school, instead of the local band or school district? Just a couple of feet to the right stood a white flagpole with a ragged, wind-torn, red and white maple leaf flag—snapping haughtily in the spring wind. Nearby, a faded and corroded satellite dish hovered over a badly vandalized telephone booth. The phone booth looked so out of place, and it was hard to imagine anyone ever using it—how strange it must have felt to stand outside of the schoolhouse in this tiny village talking by phone to someone who seemed light-years away—not only physically but psychologically and culturally as well.

Inside, the large bulletin boards in the hallway were bare, except for an official-looking notice pinned to one of them—the page yellowed and curled up at its corners. Louise and Catherine stood farther up the hall, at the entrance to the combined office and staff room. James sensed their discomfort in touring the facility, but he had to get the straight goods. Facing issues and challenges head on was always better—especially the inevitable. A handsome, young-looking elder poked his head through the office door and introduced himself as Patrick, the school custodian.

"*Hadih,* Princip'l, I'll show you 'roun' the buildin'."

Patrick led him downstairs to the basement first. Once there, Patrick hesitated and pointed to a miniature wooden bridge he'd built over an open drainage channel. A thin stream of water trickled through it into a six-inch pipe that had been installed to pass through the very bottom of the west wall.

"We need this for spring runoff… otherwise basement floods—gets real mouldy fast." There were stacks of desks and a pair of rusty filing cabinets—rows of unmatched cross-country skis lined one wall.

Patrick pulled James aside and handed him a raft of papers.

"Thought you should see these, princip'l—the mos' recen' inspection reports."

James glanced at the papers then tucked them under his arm—he would read them later.

"Thank you, my friend. I'm sure you do the best you can with the place," James said and smiled.

Patrick led James back upstairs and down the corridor. He stopped in the doorway of a room that held a rundown-looking photocopier, a beat-up teacher's desk and a round table with six chairs around it.

"This is yer office, princip'l—and the staff room. And right beside it, here, is the school kitchen—we don' use it much, but maybe you will—till you get yer house. *Ha ha ha,*" Patrick said as he patted James on the back.

James stepped into the kitchen and looked out a large picture window toward the lake and the treed hillside that descended toward it.

"Well, it's got a stunning view, that's for sure. I'm sure the school will make good use of it—and me too," James answered with a smile.

"We kin never get goot teachers or princip'l here. The goot ones er too 'fraid ta come or they come 'n jus' stay fer few months or a year."

By the time he packed up his things from the office to leave, James—whose emotions had swamped him in waves of feelings he didn't understand… sorrow, grief, frustration, desperation—was now seething. The Chezgh'un school had neither gym nor playground, let alone an all-weather sports field. James couldn't help but recall the large high school they had toured in Fort St. Pierre, eighty kilometres away, and the large adventure playground at the town's elementary school—how state of the art it was. James felt betrayed.

The federal government was far richer than any Indian band, school district or province—yet this school building was likely one of the worst in the country. It rivalled some of the rundown schools he had seen in Mexico. The irony was too much. Simply because they fell under a federal government jurisdiction, the children of Chezgh'un attended school in an antiquated and grossly inadequate building while just eighty kilometres away, children attended classes in what was likely one of the most modern schools in the Western world. All because it was under provincial authority, which drew provincial funding formulas along with the requirement to meet provincial standards—provincial building codes and regulations about student safety. Now he truly understood why the local Dakelh community leaders had decided to take the administration and control of these two schools away from the federal government—in an attempt to level the playing field somewhat. In any case, he thought, how could any government official, provincial or federal, have let things get so horrendous? He felt his anger growing.

Why hadn't Louise warned him? Only the chief had given a slight hint of the state of the school facility in Chezgh'un. He was sure it was because she really wanted him to take the job, and oddly, somehow, this gave him some reprieve from his frustration.

James had never been good at masking his feelings, but he couldn't let his rage shine through. He had to be on his own for a bit. He tripped down the grey wooden steps of the schoolhouse and wandered down the main road, unsure of where he would end up. One second, he felt gut-wrenching sadness, and the next, optimism and bliss percolated within him. He stopped at the picket fence around the cemetery just outside of the village. Good—here no one could see him. This was perfect. James would speak to the ancestors of Chezgh'un—ask for their guidance and support.

He gazed at the wall of spruce trees around him. He looked up at the mountains in the distance, and then turned to focus on the vast calm water of the lake. Then, with his hands interlocked in prayer in front of himself, he beseeched the ancestors silently, with telepathic messages, occasionally mouthing a sentence or two. He lost all track of time.

A cool breeze brought the new principal out of his trance, and it occurred to him that Louise would be looking for him—worry and concern written all over her face. Community members, on the other hand, if they knew what he was doing, would understand. This tough situation wouldn't defeat him—there was no way. He was determined to make the best of things, and to work with the community to make things work—and work well. They would deliver exceptional, customized learning for the children of Chezgh'un and help them prepare to address and turn around all the historic injustices their community had survived.

When he got back to the school, Louise, Catherine, Tara and, separately from everyone else, two officials from the Department of Indian Affairs—who had shown up of their own volition—stood on the school's staircase with looks of consternation.

"James," Louise said as reached out to put her hand on his forearm, "I was just telling our friends here from Indian Affairs, they'll have to lay off the existing teachers. They're not up to snuff."

James's only response, a blank stare.

Louise and Tara couldn't get out of there fast enough, James was sure. But for now, he just wanted to walk past them and wade into the water to honour the lake and its surroundings, to acknowledge and give thanks to the spirits of the place. He would do that at the far end of the lake, back in Fort St. Pierre.

The next day, James headed out to the logging road that led to Chezgh'un, his mind in manic mode with thoughts of all that he wanted to accomplish. He'd rework the provincial curriculum, incorporate the Dakelh culture and worldview, make it more relevant to the students. He would roll out the eco-adventure program he'd tried so hard to implement at the school in the city—teaching scientific experiences by spending time in nature, in all seasons.

In no time at all, he'd crossed the wooden bridge over the stream that he thought must circle the community. How odd: Chezgh'un was really on an island; the stream around it, a moat.

The front door of the school was locked, which surprised James. Art Thaddeus, the teaching assistant, appeared, seemingly out of nowhere, and opened it for him. Standing there on the landing, he looked even taller than before, towering over James.

"Guess you'll have yer own keys soon, eh princip'l?"

"Do you guys lock the door during the daytime?"

"It's ta keep stragglers from walkin' in at any old time—we give 'em fifteen minutes. If they're not here by then, they don't get in till the afternoon session. But you'll have yer own keys."

"Be nicer if you let me in every day, my friend. Then we can have coffee together and chat."

"*Hadih,* but I need a smoke wit' mine. No smoking inside the building. School rule."

James stepped into the wide hallway alongside the two classrooms on the main floor and was impressed by the gleaming off-white lino tiles. Patrick had clearly worked hard last night to make the place look nice. James took a few steps over to the first classroom and opened the door to a scene that would have been any principal, teacher or parent's worst nightmare.

Primary-grade kids were scattered everywhere—chattering, laughing and bickering. Some were crouched on the floor, engrossed in some game. A boom box produced the constant static of a radio station that had gone off the air, or that wasn't properly tuned in the first place. An older-looking white woman with unkempt, long grey hair was perched behind the teacher's desk, darning a sock that was stretched over a light bulb. Stacks of ripped and ragged textbooks sat in a pile off to one side. A few kids looked up from their colouring or worksheets. One boy took his Walkman headphones off, anticipating James would say something. Once the kids grasped that James was going to stay awhile and guessed that he might be somebody important, they went quiet.

The teacher glanced up at him, then returned to her darning. James walked over to her and put out his hand as he spoke.

"Hello. I'm James, the new principal. Start in September. Nice to meet you."

The only response, a curt nod.

He decided to join a group of kids colouring on the floor near the bank of windows that overlooked forest. As he sat on the edge of a loosely formed circle, he felt a rush of joy, something he was sure must be bliss. Children with hearty, coal-black hair, pretty much growing wild—tattered clothing that had probably been handed down a few times or had been sent by some charity in Prince George or Vancouver. Fresh faces and shiny brown eyes. The fragrance of woodsmoke and Dial soap, and that unique smell young kids everywhere seem to carry of fresh breath and innocent sweat.

As a child, school had been his solace, a safe refuge from trauma and tragedy that had resulted from his mother becoming an alcoholic when he was in first grade—likely as a result of his extended family's forced relocation from their settlement in the woods to the closest village where the established residents were almost exclusively white. James wanted to recreate this safe haven for other children. There had to be a library, or at least a collection of books in the interim. Books had been his *échappatoire* and his salvation.

For a few moments he sat quietly, observing. A couple of children were gripping their crayons tightly, concentrating on colouring within the lines—one with his tongue sticking out—while others, who had decided the whole page was fair game, enthusiastically glided their crayons back and forth and up and down or in spirals. Another observer might have thought he was being ignored, but James knew better. He knew there would be no eye contact, since in both Dakelh culture and his, eye contact with a stranger, an adult, would've been disrespectful. And, predictably, they were shy. Busy work, he thought—*so* not his teaching style. Sure, colouring and printing were important for fine motor skills, but from the stack of loose sheets of hand-coloured pages and arithmetic worksheets strewn haphazardly around the room, he guessed the kids spent many hours colouring and in rote learning mode.

A little girl in a flowery blue dress with white lace trim and white socks inched closer to him and said in a meek voice, "*Hadih,* you da new prinicp'l?"

James caught her stealing a sideways glance at him, so he smiled and said, "Yes. Yes, I am."

A little boy looked up from his work, then looked back down at his worksheet and said, "*Hadih,* they say yer Indian, like us. S'true?"

Before he could answer, another little girl looked up and said, "Kin you coun' ta ten in Indian?"

"Yes, I can—but my language is differen' than yers," James caught himself adjusting his pronunciation to sound less formal. That was something he'd have to weigh carefully—yes, he should model proper English pronunciation and grammar, but for now acceptance was more important. He knew this was a test, and it was important to answer fully and promptly, so he rattled off the numbers one to ten in Cree, "*Peyuk, niso, nisto, newo, niyanan, negotwasik, tepakohp, ayinanew, kekac mitahtat, mihtat.*"

"*Hadih,* efer differen'. Nothin' like Dakelh," said the first little girl. Us, we say: *lhuk'ai, nankoh, taki, dunghi, skwunlai, lhk'utagi, lhtak'alt'i, lhk'utdunghi,'ilho hooloh, lanezi...*

James was dazzled by the girl's pronunciation of the numbers as she counted, convinced she must be a fluent speaker. The difference between the two languages was striking—Farsi to Swedish. The sing-song Nehiyaw pronunciation seemed basic and simple compared to Dakelh. Unlike Cree, Dakelh had clicking consonants, aspirated vowels and glottal stops. Maybe it would be trickier to learn than he'd hoped. James was surprised that neighbouring tribes could have such distinct languages. But the Canadian Rockies kept them apart—kept them from melding their languages, cultures and DNA.

"*Hadih*, will you be teachin' us?" asked the little boy who'd spoken earlier.

The boy reminded James of his own brother, Trevor—Teddy Bear. He was cute, caring and energized as a child, but after spending years in and out of foster homes, his life was plagued by drug use. James choked up as he answered, "Music. Yes." He coughed, cleared his throat, then continued. "I'll teach ya music, but y'll have a homeroom teacher for nearly everything else."

He stood up abruptly, nodded in the direction of the teacher, and stepped into the hallway, across the hall and into the staff washroom. There, he took some deep breaths and said a prayer to his ancestors to give him strength. Strength, clarity and wisdom.

The neighbouring classroom was much quieter and more organized. Lanky middle-grade kids, many with longish hair, sat at desks doing worksheets. Math exercises, he guessed. The antithesis of his math classes back in Vancouver, with the problem of the day, weekly problem, code-cracking contest and activity centres with math manipulatives. He'd have to order all the same books, equipment and supplies he had in Vancouver and scan the catalogues for more culturally appropriate material. These kids deserved the best.

The downstairs space, a combined classroom and woodworking shop, was intended for high school–aged kids, but it sat empty. James took this as a personal challenge. In his prep for the job interview, he'd read that in many First Nations communities students dropped out from the age of thirteen, when they should've been in the eighth grade. He would investigate the situation in Chezgh'un and strategize. Maybe he could visit a few elders to see what they thought was happening with the adolescent dropouts.

Another day, James would return to the school to go through the piles of ratty books to see what could be salvaged. For now, he decided to look through the boxes and filing cabinets he'd seen in the basement. As he rifled through the files and loose documents he found there, his consternation mounted. He flipped through a few student registers, which were legal documents in provincial schools. Student attendance had been carefully documented in September and October, but then trailed off. Upstairs in the office, he located a filing cabinet with a top drawer labelled STUDENT RECORDS. He pulled it open only to find that it was empty.

iv

James had planned to spend more time in the community, but he'd seen enough to know he had his work cut out for him—recruiting teachers, rethinking the curriculum and studying the school's budget. How many teachers could he hire? What quantity of books, equipment and supplies could he order? Apparently, Chief Felix and Mike O'Leary, the superintendent, had negotiated a one-time school-start-up amount—would it be enough? The next day, James drove directly to the school district's offices in Vanderhoof.

The excitement he'd felt upon waking had dissipated, and he didn't try to resolve the angst that had taken its place—the gnawing in the pit of his stomach that he hadn't felt since his university years when he had had to piece together a living, with no idea what the future might hold. His only comfort was the presence of the ancestors, the powerful support and caring of a few of the people he'd met so far—Catherine, Art and Sally—and the sweet faces of the children. And there were the elders he had yet to meet. Catherine had told him the community was rich in that regard—several pairs of healthy elders who all spoke their language—a long life expectancy.

James dropped his briefcase in his temporary office and stepped into Louise's office. He breathed a sigh of relief when he saw Louise's beaming face staring up at him but was taken aback by what he saw around her. The entire surface of her large desk was covered with file folders and papers—the flow continued onto the floor, onto an easy chair and along the bookshelf under her huge picture window.

Above Louise's desk hung a sign that read:

IF A CLUTTERED DESK IS A SIGN OF A CLUTTERED MIND,
THEN WHAT IS AN EMPTY DESK A SIGN OF?

James pointed at the sign and chuckled. "Ha, that's great. Now I don't feel so ashamed of my own occasional clutter. On another note, you were right, Louise. We have to get rid of all the teachers. For certain, the older unkempt woman who looks so burned out."

Louise handed him a stack of résumés from teachers who had attended a teachers' job fair in Vancouver.

"All good candidates, James, but they all want jobs in or around Vancouver. Nobody wants to move north, let alone to an Indian reserve."

James called up the few people Louise hadn't yet contacted and got the same answer—they wanted Vancouver-based jobs, like the position he was leaving. A few of them even mentioned they thought he was crazy, in the present labour market, to leave a permanent teaching job with the Vancouver School Board. Feeling queasy, he went for a walk over to the river. He sat on the ground on a grassy spot for a few minutes, but still felt off when he stood to go back to the district office. He'd given up incredible job security—a stable life and future.

On the way back to the office he had a brainwave. Why not call up head of the Native Indian Teacher Training Program at UBC? Surely some Native grads would consider coming to work up north. It was a good move. Within days, he had set up phone interviews with a number of teachers who were enthusiastic about moving north to work with him, a young Native principal.

When James got back to the motel on the lake, he was astonished to see, perched primly on a log on the beach, the classroom teacher he'd seen in Chezgh'un—younger looking in a coordinated outfit, blue jeans with a matching jacket and a pink top, silvery hair resting on her shoulders, nicely brushed now. *Be extra nice, James, remember—angels unawares…* She waved at him, then motioned for him to join her. What on earth could she want and what was she doing here? Surely, she's not going to make a pitch to keep her job. That would be awkward. There was no possible way that could happen.

As James got closer, he noticed that her fingernails had been clipped and filed. Likely aware that James was taking note of the changes in her appearance, she smiled tentatively, then launched in. "Ah, Sally and Art came to bingo—so I hitched a ride. I wanted a chance to talk to you, alone."

Her voice astonished James, it was sweet and melodic, youthful sounding—in stark contrast with her weathered face. "I'm Laura. Listen, we teachers know the gig's over—that you're going to dismiss us—but that's not why I'm here.

"I wasn't always like this. I just wanted you to know. I was contracted by Indian Affairs about six years ago to do a special needs assessment at Chezgh'un. I fell in love with the place—the place and the kids. At first, I had a lot of energy—thought I could make a difference in just a year or two. And now, all this time later, I'm burned out. Of course, it doesn't help that my family's fallen apart in that time. Also, too, I haven't been able to fit in there. I'd be surprised if any white person could—in Chezgh'un, I mean. People are kind, but..."

"Ah, well, thank you for coming to see me. I'm honoured," James said, trying to sound sincere. In reality, he was wondering what this woman wanted. He was hoping she wouldn't plead for him to keep her on staff. Clearly Louise's decision to get rid of her meant she'd have to leave the community.

As if she'd read his mind, Laura said, "Listen, years of social isolation can do things to a person. I only left the village a couple of times a year. I'm bushed. But I care about the kids. I want to tell you about them. There's things you should know."

James listened intently as Laura described the literacy problem at the school. He had already noticed that the English spoken in Chezgh'un was dialectic—like loosely translated French.

"At the residential school the kids attended, at Lejac, about four hundred kilometres away, most of the nuns and priests were francophones who spoke English as a second language. Yet it was their job to teach English to their charges, not French. Sent by the Catholic Church."

She told him that only a few kids in the intermediate class actually were performing at grade level. She said that she, and Art and Sally, had tried to put together cultural programming in the school, Dakelh language classes, traditional drumming and dance, hide tanning and so on, but their bosses from Indian Affairs, all junior bureaucrats, shut it down, telling them to focus instead on the three r's. She also mentioned fetal alcohol syndrome and told him that a few kids were gas sniffers. James wondered if this was true, or just sour grapes—that Laura was putting the kids and community down because they hadn't accepted her and she was being forced to leave—so he studied her carefully to gauge her sincerity.

"Well, thank you for the information, Laura. It's all very helpful."

"I'll head to the road now. My ride should be along any minute. Oh, by the way," Laura's countenance brightened slightly as she said this, "there's a positive piece. Keep an eye out for Shannon. She's about thirteen. Lorna and Henry's daughter. She's so smart. She can go places. Oh, and there's Bid'ah, Clayton and Dennis. All smart."

She turned to leave, then hesitated, turned to face James and said, "Oh... and there's Anouk. I wish I had time to tell you about Anouk—a very talented carver. But he was devastated by his mother's death a few years ago. Still a mystery. Never met his dad. The man might have demons he's passed on to Anouk. You know... the sins of the father..."

James was relieved when Laura left. The mention of demons gave him a chill and he didn't want to hear more of her thoughts about Anouk—or anything at all, for that matter. As he sat watching the woman walk away, he couldn't help but wonder how many other Lauras there were in other Native communities—burned out, ineffective teachers just hanging on to life by a thread, suffering from religious delusion or some other mental illness, yet holding the huge responsibility of educating Native kids who so badly needed competent and caring instruction and mentorship.

v

Louise invited James and Catherine for dinner at her home. James was dazzled by the huge post-and-beam house that was built on a bluff overlooking the lake with a natural footpath down to the shore. Wood and glass everywhere—including the walls of a huge loft upstairs with a railed area overlooking the great room, kitchen and family room. The 180-degree view of the lake from the doorway mesmerized him.

"The door is always open, James. We never lock the place. Anytime you feel like stopping by to play the piano—please feel free."

James glanced over to where she was pointing and was awestruck by the antique upright grand piano in the family room.

"We'd hoped our daughters would play, but they weren't into it. Janna took up the drums instead." She chuckled and shrugged her shoulders. "What could I say?"

"That's generous, Louise. Thank you." James answered earnestly, although he knew he could never take her up on her offer. In addition to his shyness, his pride wouldn't allow him to accept what felt like charity—the benevolence of someone in a position of privilege and wealth bestowed upon a lesser being. And then there was the optics of it all, if he were to be seen as being too cozy with the local gentrified white folks, what would the Native people he was working with think of him?

The three sat at the elegant pine table in the outdoor seating area. An impressive grill and outdoor stove were built into the exterior wall. The brass hood above the grill funneled into the same chimney as the expansive river stone fireplace in the great room. The chimney was equally as elegant from the outside. Oh, Franyo would've loved that barbeque.

Louise went in to get drinks for the three of them. Catherine and James sat in a comfortable silence, breathing in the fresh air, both tacitly thankful that the bugs weren't out in earnest yet. Late June would be a different story.

Catherine broke the silence.

"Y'know, t'James—the lan' this house was built on belonged ta my grandfather, tens of hectares along this side of the lake, includin' all the foreshore. It was pre-empted by Louise's great-grandfather 'n other settler fam'lies in the late 1800s."

"Well, why doesn't your family go after it? Get it back?"

"There would be war. Louise's fam'ly and mine haven't spoken ta each other for long time—two generations at leas'. Louise 'n I are the firs' ones ta talk. Her great-grandfather got the land for free from gor'ment. That was the law then—they jus' had ta claim it as theirs. The idea was that 'ventually gor'ment would survey and charge a fee, but that n'er happened. And this is just one family site we lost. Other Dakelh families owned other large trac's of land under our traditional system, also along the shoreline of this lake, and other nearby places. But white fam'lies are established here now. We gotta keep the peace, so we're goin' through a long process called specific claims ta get back some of the lan' and get compensation for the rest."

Louise stepped through the double glass doors onto the brick pathway to the table.

"Isn't it a lovely evening, you two?" she said. "Did Catherine tell you? We have common roots here—in this fabulous place."

"Ah yes, she was just telling me."

James felt himself squirm in his chair. He was baffled by the injustice that Catherine had just explained—this was worse than the situation his family found themselves in with the loss of their land and territory. At least his family didn't have to watch the new fee simple landowners develop and enjoy property that was rightfully theirs, day in and day out, as neighbours. He didn't want to harbour bad feelings toward Louise and her family—but now, as Louise poured their tea and smiled at them sympathetically, it felt like she was gloating. James struggled to stifle pangs of resentment. He decided to follow Catherine's patient and gracious approach—this wasn't his battle.

vi

The near-daily phone conversations between Louise and James were usually had to discuss predictable administrative issues: the hiring of new teachers, the role the powerful provincial teachers' union would have in his small school, school atmosphere and discipline. Usually they sang from the same song sheet, but today, with the proposal he was going to float, James anticipated some dissonance. He took a deep breath and launched into his pitch.

"Louise, you know my team and I will face incredible challenges in Chezgh'un. Low literacy levels due to poor instruction more than anything, I suspect. But from what the teachers tell me, there may be some fetal alcohol syndrome present—and almost everyone speaks a strange dialect of English. It's like they've taken some French expressions and translated them directly into English. My team will need a common base of knowledge and agreement on a skillful approach to help the kids master their own language, but also learn to read and write well, in English. I would like to take the teachers to a week-long summer program on the "whole language" program. The McCrackens, the inventors of this approach, are giving workshops. Do we have a pro-D budget?"

"Yes, I'm familiar with the McCrackens' work. They're excellent. Where are they presenting this summer?"

"Monterey, California."

Silence at the other end of the phone line. James knew what Louise was thinking—*are you out of your mind? You've just been hired for a job in a remote community in Northern BC, and you want to take yourself and four teachers to Monterey, California, the haunt of the rich?* Louise was more diplomatic than James would have been, had he been in her position.

"California? Gosh, even if the board did approve this, do you know what the optics would be—in the district? For you—with the board, with other principals? Oh James, this is too much. We've already offered you respite weekends in Prince George. All expenses paid, one weekend out of every month, to be away from the community for a couple of days, to catch your breath, so to speak."

For James, everything was up in the air now. He had rejected life as he knew it—almost every aspect of it, the permanent teaching contract he had worked so hard to attain, a stable and caring relationship with Franyo and a supportive and growing circle of friends. All of this, stacked on top of the loss of his mother two years earlier when he was twenty-eight, disrupted his world completely. What did he have to lose?

The second Saturday in July, exhilarated, driving his shiny new cherry red compact Suzuki Sidekick, James picked up Catherine Bird from her niece's apartment on the east side of Vancouver. Then, in nearby Burnaby, they met Debbie Greaves, the recently graduated primary teacher who hailed from a small, all-white, logging community on Vancouver Island. Loretta, the intermediate teacher—a young and upbeat Tsilhqot'in woman from Williams Lake who was spending the summer out on the land, moving around on horseback to document the important historical and cultural sites of her people—and Harry Wallace, a white high school teacher originally from Vanderhoof, eager to begin his first teaching job, would fly down to meet them in Monterey. The Sidekick was quickly filled with high-energy banter and laughter.

Debbie didn't know how to drive a standard, so she sat in the back seat while Catherine and James took turns at the wheel. While James was driving, Catherine told him stories of her life and talked about Dakelh culture.

"We're Dene speakers, t'James. Our tribe goes from the far north of the NWT all the way down ta Arizona. I was at a conf'rence wit' Navajo people a couple of years ago, and y'know, I could understand their elders when they spoke Dene—it was really somethin'. Dene territory stretches all the way down there—we're the same people. Ain't that somethin'?"

James listened silently as Catherine told him stories about her childhood in the bush, and about hunting moose, cleaning, quartering and butchering it all on her own after her husband had died. Without any measure of self-pity or pride, she talked about raising eleven kids as a single parent. She filled James in about the small "p" politics of the Dakelh tribes in the larger territory.

"The Chezgh'un people have always been at the bottom," she said. "It's all on account of they're humble and gentle peoplez. But they're smart and talented, too. They really suffered in the residential schools—and they all attended, four of five generations. Almost killed their language, culture and even fam'ly ties—mothers don' know how ta nurture like they used ta. Some things are instinctual, eh, like the basics, feedin' and hygiene. But the usual affection and carin' are now weaker in many fam'lies than before. And them priests and nuns really had their way wit' all of us in residential schools—molested many of the boys, lots don' talk about it, some of the girls even got pregnant, nuns too. Some babies died at birth—the nuns just buried their corpses in the schoolyard—no ceremony and no markers, no coroner's 'vestigation. And in the community, you'll see abuse—more than you'd expect. That cycle all got started in the residential schools wit' them priests and nuns. Vict'ms become abusers. Y'know."

Catherine drove like she was driving a large rig—she started out in second gear, double-clutching like a seasoned veteran. Then, it was James's turn to talk. He told her about his childhood. He recounted stories his mother had shared about events in their family. Catherine nodded now and then and occasionally clicked her tongue to show she was listening and present.

Capricious snow flurries began as they ascended Mount Shasta and a hush came over the three of them—the hill was steep and there would be no snowplows out in the middle of summer. James leaned back in his seat, relieved that Catherine wanted to continue driving.

She was clearly skilled and confident in winter conditions, but he and Debbie were taken aback when, near the summit, Catherine slowed and pulled into a lookout area that hadn't been cleared. Oh my God, would they get stuck, or maybe slide backwards, right onto the highway? Catherine noticed the sudden tension in the air and spoke up.

"James, this mountain is the main reason I came along on this trip. Dakelh people have a legend about the power of this place. It might have come to us from the Klamaths, the Indian peoples who are from here, about the healin' powers of this mountain. They had their Indian status taken away and jus' got it back."

"Wow, Catherine. I believe Cree people have legends about the Rocky Mountains near Banff, but not Mount Shasta."

"This is one of the most important energy centres in the world, t'James. Back in the day, only medicine people could go above the treeline. Too much power for ordinary folks to go there—powerful spirits, both goot and evil."

James got a shiver.

"I feel something different here, Catherine," Debbie added from the back seat. "I sensed it halfway up the mountain, but I wondered if it was just me. Almost like heart palpitations—strange energy I don't quite understand."

"We are gonna need the power of this place, all three of us—them other teachers too—ta get through the first six months in Chezgh'un. Don' wanna scare you guys, but some people believe that the Chezgh'un people have been put under a curse, and anyone who goes to live among them will be affected, too. Maybe go mad, get sick, be attacked by evil spirits, maybe even die."

"Oh, Catherine," said James. "You're just like my mom and aunties—scared of bad medicine and evil spirits. I believe if we keep positive, maintain our own individual spiritual practices, we will always be safe."

"That's not wrong, t'James. It's goot to do your own cer'monies—definitely, but we can't be naive when it comes to evil spirits. They are present and real in everyday life. You will feel their presence up north. Be warned."

"I will have my sweetgrass, sage and tree fungus with me. I'm not worried."

"*Hadih*, t'James. I'm goin' off alone for a few minutes. I will include you, Debbie and the other teachers in my requests."

Catherine collected a cloth bag from the back of the vehicle and walked off by herself, disappearing into a nearby stand of trees. James and Debbie remarked on the large eagle feather sticking out of one side of her bag before the two of them wandered off in separate directions. James hadn't brought any medicines or feathers—afraid to take them across the US border. But at the very least, he could pray to his ancestors and to the spirits of Mount Shasta.

After Catherine had been gone for at least a half-hour, Debbie wondered aloud if they should go after her.

"No, she grew up in the forest. She'll be back when she's done," James said.

When Catherine returned, she stood taller, and her weathered brown face was radiant. There was a new depth to her chocolate brown eyes; they emanated peace and kindness. Timelessness.

James drove down the mountain in silence in awe of the snowflakes swirling all around. When they had almost completed their descent, Catherine twisted in her seat to face James and Debbie as directly as she could. She regarded them as she spoke.

"The spirits of this place are incredibly powerful. This land now called California is Indian land, every corner of it was occupied before contact—just that some of the tribes were almost wiped out in the so-called Indian Wars, and others had their numbers greatly reduced when a bounty was put on their heads. Survivors were relocated ta places like Oklahoma—to live wit' strangers, made subservient ta other tribes they had nothin' in common wit'. There were many different languages and dialects here, but most are now extinct—gone forever. Do you guys understand what is at stake, for us—the Dakelh people—in particular, tiny communities like Chezgh'un? European contact happened in California in the 1600s—nearly four hundred years ago. And now tribes have vanished—most of their languages *are gone, forever*. Europeans came to Dakelh territory just *two hundred* years ago. *Hadih*, in less than a hundred years, will Dakelh be long gone, the language—the people of Chezgh'un extinct? They're strong people, but we hafta do what we can to help them to survive—keep their place on this planet."

This was their mission, James realized: to help the people of Chezgh'un to survive, to thrive, prosper and regain their dignity and culture—to do the best they could to undo the colonial damage and live an exquisite life in their own territory, undisturbed.

The teachers' time in Monterey was fantastical, particularly given that the setting and culture they would be immersed in—Northern BC, in a matter of weeks—was such a stark contrast to the glitz, glamour, affluence and warm, oceanic climate of California. Several evenings, the new cadre of teachers dined together, always in restaurants overlooking the bay. They quizzed Catherine so as to learn as much as they could about the Chezgh'un community and its dynamics. Each time the met, their enthusiasm seemed to increase. The speakers at the conference were gifted and inspirational educators. James was relieved that he and his new teachers all seemed to get along—positive team building was taking place—every leader's dream.

On their last day at the conference, James was restless and sad not to have had time to explore the territory in and around Monterey—to make a connection with the local tribe there who had just recently found their way back home to reclaim some of their territory. As Catherine had said, this was definitely "Indian" land, but all he knew was that the tribe had been greatly diminished and may even have been annihilated.

James felt proud that he'd been successful in squelching the sexual desires that had arisen during the course of the week—he had to behave, he was a school principal now—a public figure, of sorts. As it was, he'd have to keep the fact he was in a relationship with Franyo under wraps up north and only let the information out to people he trusted. Maybe after the conference was over, he could seek out some relief. After all, everyone was going their separate ways and he would be driving home alone. Maybe then.

James decided to go for a walk to pray to the ancestors of the place. He went to a site on the beach he'd read about in a tour guide book, where a large, dying cypress tree had become a focal point of tremendous effort by local officials to help it survive, unlike so many others in the area. Oh, the irony of it all: the place was very developed, up to and including the beach, and now, solely to maintain property values, the white folks were trying to save the remaining orphaned trees along that one urbanized stretch.

James sat cross-legged at the base of the tree, contemplating the gentle waves on the water, when a passerby caught his eye. At first blush, the man looked somewhat familiar—a distant cousin perhaps. The man must have somehow sensed James willing him to look at him—he turned and then slowly approached.

"Hello," James said once the man was within earshot. "How are you?"

"I'm Melquíades," the man answered, offering a handshake. "Everyone calls me Mel. Pleased to meet you. From around here?" James tried to stifle his amazement at hearing this name. Melquíades was a character from *Cien años de soledad,* the Gabriel García Márquez book he'd been studying—a wanderer who made people comprehend that there was a reality other than their own—that an outside world, a parallel reality, existed.

"Interesting name," James said. "I'm James... not Bond, unfortunately. I'm Cree, Nehiyaw from Canada," he said and laughed.

"That tree. Dying. Over the years they try to preserve those cypress trees growin' here at the beach, but it's too little too late. Guess they never heard of riparian zones."

"What zones?" James said as he tilted his head.

"Well, you can't make a clean sweep of things along rivers, streams, lakes and oceans—disrupt the habitat completely and expect there won't be negative effects. Trees, shrubs and other plants keep the shoreline intact—keep it from eroding. My ancestors knew this intuitively and respected nature—didn't destroy habitat. We didn't have 'riparian' in our language, but we had the concept down."

"My language is Nehiyaw."

"I'm of the Esselen tribe—originally from here. My people were almost wiped out—killed off by the Spanish a long time ago, and survivors were eventually shipped away to be assimilated into other tribes."

James shivered.

Melquíades asked James to join him for a walk to a local sacred site. He stopped at a rocky bluff and showed James pictographs—paintings in the shape of a hand—as if someone had painted a series of hands. He told James that if a person rested their hand in the painted palm, they could divine all that had happened at that site in the past. James knew he would have to return to try it. Would it be even more powerful than praying to the ancestors of the place? James stood. The man put an arm around his shoulder—pulled him in close.

vii

Franyo had dutifully helped James pack up his cramped Suzuki Sidekick with personal belongings, directing him how to place boxes and bags so he could fit them all. But he'd said extraordinarily little all morning, even while they were sipping their coffee. As he stowed the last items into the back seat, Franyo said, "You can store some of your stuff here you know—this is still your home."

"I wonder how far I should drive tonight. What do you think, Fran?" James asked, shifting his guitar to sit more securely. Maybe the community would ask him to serenade them or lead singalongs in the evenings around a campfire.

"I don't know. You wanna wait till tomorrow to leave? Maybe less traffic on a Sunday, J."

"No. I have to go. No putting it off, Franyo." Catherine had told him that most of the community, certainly all the elders, would be in their summer camp at a nearby lake, netting and preserving salmon for the winter, hunting moose, bear and beaver. *A great opportunity to get ta know them, James... see firs' hand how they live off the land,* she had said.

"Remember to lock your car doors. Don't pick up any hitchhikers. And no speeding. You should stop for dinner in 100 Mile House, the Wagon Wheel Café. Remember that delicious meal we had there on our trip home from Smithers? Such a fun trip. Call me from there—for memory's sake, okay?"

"For sure, but when did you become so nostalgic?" James said and chuckled, straining to control the tremolo of his increasingly high-pitched voice. He knew that he'd better get into his Sidekick and get on the road. *Ekosi. Cemak!*

Deep down, he fretted that a tragic fate awaited him. After all, he had the same genes, the same personality traits and constitution of his alcoholic mother, who had ended up living on skid row, and of his older sister, Dora, whose suicide at the age of thirty had devastated him in his university years.

James was no alcoholic, nor was he addicted to drugs as both his older and younger brother had been, nor was he suicidal. His addiction was to sex. So far, he'd been able to keep it under wraps—a deep dark secret that played out in moments of weakness. Attractive men—or those who were simply needy—were his kryptonite.

Through the Fraser Valley, copses of trees framed cultivated fields, which were now lush and thick. In another month or so it would be harvest time. James recalled that this was Sto:lo territory—the local tribes had taken on the name of the river. He had heard about an extraordinary young tribal chief who was really helping the communities in Sto:lo territory to make great advances—would this happen in Chezgh'un with Chief Felix? Was Felix Joe as much of a visionary as the young Sto:lo chief?

An hour or so later, approaching the town of Hope, James saw the majestic, snow-capped blue mountains that he loved—their avocado-green robes reaching right down to the turquoise river. He and Franyo had made this trip many times, and they would always pause here to take in the scenery. He wished Franyo was there with him now.

Peaches, plums and corn would be ready for purchase farther into the Interior, James guessed. He hoped to come across a fruit and vegetable stand along the highway, but seeing none, he decided to visit a market on the Indian reserve on the west side of Kamloops. There, he would buy enough to last him a few weeks, and extra to share with Art, Sally, Catherine and other elders. The detour would lengthen his already long journey, but it was an inconvenience he was willing to tolerate. The arid rolling hills around Kamloops, giant sand dunes really, had always intrigued James. Their sagebrush covering. He didn't know why those hills commanded his attention—but the one time he had stopped on the side of the road to gather sage and explore, he quickly realized that it was not hospitable terrain for people—the hill was steep, bone-dry, uneven. Instinctively, James knew there would be snakes—dangerous rattlers.

North of Cache Creek, James looked up to the hills to locate the old wagon trail which had been cut into the hillside, built specifically for the gold rush. Apparently some members of a local tribe farther north had led some white prospectors, likely Americans, to a place where gold deposits could easily be seen, and this had triggered the gold rush in this area. His fourth-grade students had been incredulous when he told them about it—that a wealthy prospector had imported twenty-four camels to haul gold ore from the Cariboo down to Lillooet, so it could be shipped by train to the coast. The kids had screeched, slapped their desks and said, in French, "Aw, come on, Mr. Ward—another one of your tall tales—you're not catching us this time." To get the kids to believe him, James had had to show them a photo of a camel mounted by a bearded prospector, his rifle hanging down at his side. He laughed out loud at the memory, then felt a pang of loss. He'd had such a lovely rapport with his students, with every class he'd taught. As a principal, he would be one step removed from students, directing a team of teachers, which would be so different.

Off to his right, away from the highway, movement in the valley caught James's eye. He pulled over. Reaching back, he managed to put his hand on his binoculars in one of the cardboard boxes behind him. A herd of horses, loose and running along the highway. A coffee-coloured stallion with a black mane and swishing tail led the bunch, followed by a mare with a reddish-brown coat and a large white patch, like a saddle blanket, over its back—white at the base of its legs. A colt, white coat with black ears and matching long tail, trotted behind the pack eager to catch up.

These were the wild horses of the Tsilhqot'in. He'd read about them, but he couldn't believe he was seeing them close up! Magnificent animals. He'd remembered his one real experience with horses, the trail ride with Franyo in the Rockies near Banff the first summer after they'd met. He'd fallen in love with his horse and also became completely infatuated with Franyo. He got back in his car, suddenly anxious to get to 100 Mile House to call Franyo—let him know the trip was going just fine.

It was easy to find the restaurant he and Franyo both recalled so fondly—just a block from the highway. James remembered the low mountains in the distance covered by a lush spruce forest, and water everywhere—a river, streams, lakes. He skidded into the gravel parking lot, jumped out of his red Sidekick and rushed to the payphones in the lobby.

Franyo answered on the second ring.

"I thought you would call about now," he said in a husky voice with the accent James found incredibly sexy.

"Just got here. What a trip! I saw wild horses. Stopped to watch them for a bit, but I was in a rush to get here—to call you."

A pregnant pause—seconds felt like minutes.

"J… I just wanted to hear you're okay—that you're doing okay. Go and have your supper now. Enjoy it. And remember the nice trip we had together through there. We'll do it again."

The warmth and sincerity of Franyo's words brought tears to James's eyes.

James found a booth near the window of the rustic restaurant. His stomach grumbled but, to his surprise, his appetite was gone. He was fretting over the menu when he overheard a voice from the payphones by the washrooms. It got louder, to the point of yelling: "What do those fucking Indians want now? They're always bitching about something or other. We're going ahead with the logging of that lot, whether they like it or not. At the crack of dawn while they're still asleep."

James felt his anger rise, then calmed himself. He'd definitely left the genteel ambience of Vancouver. Franyo had been so right in his warnings.

On the way to his vehicle, James noticed a flyer on a bulletin board advertising a meeting of the Tsilhqot'in tribes—to discuss the work their leaders were doing on reclaiming rights and title to their lands and territory. He thought about the intermediate teacher, Loretta, her passionate description of how, from contact to the present, her people had fought passionately to protect their lands and resources from exploitation by so-called settlers. He recalled the surreal story she had told him and the others during their time in Monterey about six chiefs who, in the 1860s, had been invited by colonial authorities to attend peace talks in Quesnel, ostensibly to bring to an end the so-called Tsilhqot'in War, which the chiefs had declared to simply protect their homeland. But the chiefs had been tricked. There were no peace talks. Instead they were brought before a judge and jury, and five of the six were sentenced to hang. To James, those six chiefs were heroes—determined to preserve their way of life, their language, and indeed, their very existence. Someday that story would have to be made public.

III

Nîpin — Summer

i

"*Hadih,* t'James. Goot ta see you again." Catherine smiled her broad and encompassing smile. She was as timelessly beautiful as James remembered.

Her house was sparsely furnished, but the living room walls were covered in unframed photos of her eleven kids, some in faded black and white, some in colour. Above all the photos, there was one photo of a young Catherine standing beside a tall, swarthy young man. Catherine saw James looking at the photo, and explained it was her husband, who'd died young in a boating accident. She'd raised their children on her own—never remarried.

James tried to imagine how the house had been in earlier years—all those kids in a basic three-bedroom bungalow—life must've been both frenetic and cozy. Now it was empty, and James was impressed that Catherine didn't show the slightest sign of loneliness or despair at now being alone.

"So goot you came early—get ta know the community. I decided ta go ta Chezgh'un wit' you—make sure you get there in one piece. And we'll go ta the fish camp at Babine Lake. You'll get ta meet Monique, one of the most powerful elders in the area. It's her place—her fishing spot. You gotta get ta know her, earn her trust and gain her support."

"Sounds amazing!" James said, with a sigh of relief that he wouldn't be making the trek alone. "Hope they don't mind me coming. If they let me, I'll stay for a few days, maybe more. I'll take 'em some fruit 'n early corn I brought from down south."

"If you need ta go buy more stuff, you go ahead t'James—come back when you're ready 'n we'll leaf together, alright?" Catherine said and smiled a reassuring smile.

"We have to pass through Chezgh'un anyways, right? I'll just drop my stuff on the way."

When they got to Chezgh'un, James found his RV set up on one side of the gravel parking lot in front of the school, alongside two large mobile homes. James's heart sank—how many months would he spend in this simple metal box on wheels, parked on loose gravel just metres away from the entrance to the school. He studied the sewer hookup with disdain. Things could flow both ways in that type of crude connection—he'd heard about this. And it was so close to the school. No privacy, no reprieve from the work world. As enthusiastic as he felt, he knew this was important. He stepped inside and looked at the wooden panelling all around, the tiny kitchen, and shook his head. He wouldn't be spending much time there—too depressing.

When he emerged, Catherine had a concerned look on her face. "Is this where you're livin'?"

"Only until they can build me a house."

"Really—chee whiz, that could be awhile James. Ya don' wanna spend the winter in a RV!"

"They're supposed to start construction right away, Catherine."

"Yer gonna hafta keep on 'em about that, t'James."

ii

The road from Chezgh'un to Babine Lake was narrow and fraught with potholes and muddy bogs. Zooming ahead of James's Sidekick, Catherine's red truck barrelled over it all. She obviously knew what she was doing, but there were moments when James wondered if she was trying to lose him. Every ten minutes or so, he had to turn on the windshield wipers and spray volumes of fluid to wash off yellow, green, red and black slime—insect innards and appendages which, once dry, were almost impossible to get off.

The trail, a portage route between two lakes, Stuart and Babine, had been crudely cut during the fur trade era through boggy muskeg and was lined by stands of aspen, alder, spruce and willow. In places, he had to avoid menacingly deep grooves where a heavy vehicle had passed through earlier in the spring or last fall. If a front wheel slipped into one of those ruts, the whole vehicle could get drawn in, and you wouldn't get out—at least not easily. Each large pothole, partially fallen tree and significant curve embedded itself in his memory.

All around him, shifting patterns of bright light flickered on the forest floor. James caught himself holding his breath in exhilaration.

As he got out of his Sidekick, the fragrance of woodsmoke at Babine Lake stirred James's nostalgia for his own home in Northern Alberta. He was awestruck by the scene before him: the vast lake with its gentle ripples, the lush forest, nopal-green foothills and rounded mountains in the distance. A flock of ducks swam soundlessly in the distance. A barking dog ran up to study and sniff the two new arrivals. Good, not a ferocious dog like the ones he grew up with, part wolf, part German shepherd. This one looked like some kind of border collie, husky cross. A gruff male voice called out for it to shut up. Rustic cabins of weathered wood on one side of the lakeshore looked as if they'd always been there. A couple of children sat on the large wooden landing of the cabin closest to where James had parked. They looked at him with curiosity, then continued playing.

Catherine followed a well-worn trail across a meadow to a rustic smoke shack, leaving James on his own. How would these people treat him? Would he be accepted as a fellow "Native" person, or would they treat him like an outsider—a white man?

James looked around for Art and soon saw him. He was with a few other men in the distance, close to the lake, hovering over an ample and boisterous fire. James took a deep breath and headed in their direction. As he approached, he could make out banter and cajoling mixed with laughter, with Art's deep, gruff voice dominating. He was telling a story. As James came within earshot, Art saw him and stopped abruptly, leaving just the ever-present local soundscape of wind in the trees, leaves rustling, and chirping and trilling birds. James felt a sudden warmth as blood rushed to his neck, face and ears.

"I jus' lie," Art shouted, and they all burst into uproarious laughter. He paused and took on a serious look as he said, "Uh oh, here comes that new princip'l, you guys better smarten up—no more swearin'."

James stepped in close but didn't quite join the circle.

"What the fuck? How come no swearin'? He ain't no priest," a shorter young guy said, indicating James with his open hand. "He's the princip'l, and the last one, he swore like us, partied with us and even had his way with some o' the wimmin."

Louise had told James about the previous principal—a divorced man in his forties who was a solid teacher, but had no leadership skills. And, she'd said, he got mixed up in community politics in ways he shouldn't have. And he did have a reputation for partying in the village.

The man who had spoken looked like a miniature, younger version of Art, nineteen or twenty. Unlike Art, he wore a baseball cap.

"Well, this one's different. Don't think he's the partying type," Art answered.

"Is he a *hoo'tup*?" the young man snapped.

James took mental note of the word. He'd ask Art what it meant, although, given the context and delivery, he was pretty sure its literal meaning was something like *bloodsucker* and was the Dakelh version of "fag."

Art continued, by way of introduction: "This is my li'l brother, X.J. And this here is Leyo. That's my brother Henry. And this ugly one is Bid'ah, aka Kenny, my oldest son." James felt awkward as he moved around the circle to shake hands, placing his delicate urban hand into the huge, rough clasp of each of the guys, including the youngest, Bid'ah. Each, in turn, looked up briefly, then nodded, smiled and glanced down. Leyo's touch was gentler than the others, and he seemed to hold onto James's hand a few seconds longer than anyone else had. Bid'ah was the exact opposite of ugly. In fact, the Dakelh men were all fine featured, with well-rounded cheekbones, smooth cinnamon complexions and perfectly shaped, strong, ungroomed hands.

Art paused and then pointed to a man sitting on a large stump, back from the circle near a stack of chopped wood and said, "That one over there is Junior. Jus' got outta jail, so don' turn your back to 'im—or bend over!" He guffawed, pleased with his own joke.

James looked at the man and nodded his head. The only answer was an intense stare. James felt instant stupefaction. He would have to watch this guy. He'd seen a similar look when he worked in the psychiatric ward at Vancouver General a couple of years earlier. Unbalanced energy—with a potential for violence. He'd once been jumped from behind by a guy with that vibe—yes, he'd have to be vigilant around this guy, but never let him sense any latent or real fear.

"Princip'l, we were jus' talkin' 'bout gor'ment," said Henry, breaking the stare down between the two men. Henry was a good-looking man, even with the acne scars and a missing tooth. "How they don' respect none of our rights. You musta seen the land 'round here, eh? Clear-cuts everywhere. Didn't talk ta us 'bout it. 'N now they're even tryna keep us from pickin' berries 'n huntin' 'n fishin' in some places, eh? Our most basic rights. *Hadih,* s'true."

James felt his breathing return to normal. With the possible exception of Junior, these guys liked him. But there was another boy Art didn't introduce. He sat off to one side, way back from the circle—a big teenager engrossed in whittling a small piece of wood, obviously lost in his own world. The teen had a strange expression, and when he looked up there was an emptiness in his eyes. James felt the boy's eyes follow him as he stepped around the firepit to claim a vacant stump as a seat. For a second James wondered why the boy wasn't assigned any tasks, but then recalled situations like this in the village he was from and realized that there was a story here and, in time, he would hear it. If the boy didn't come to school in September, he would seek him out and talk to his parents—there was no reason for him not to attend.

"Well, back ta work, ladies. Coffee break's over," Art bellowed. Everyone laughed.

The men returned to their stations to process the dozens of salmon they had pulled from their nets early that morning—sockeye that had completed their migration up the Skeena River. The fish that came up the Sto:lo ended up in the streams that fed into Stuart River and Stuart Lake. Rustic knives—razor sharp. James looked on as Art lifted the female sockeye with swollen bellies out of the pile, one at a time. Skillfully, he sliced open their soft underside to extract a glossy mass of blood-red roe that he deposited into a stainless-steel basin before tossing each fish over to Henry, who, in one smooth motion, sliced open the belly to pull out the guts and organs in one intact cluster. He then passed the gutted fish to Bid'ah, who cut off the head and passed the fish to Leyo, whose job was hacking off the fins. Looking at Leyo's baby face, broad toothy smile and long hair, James realized the boy reminded him of cousins long gone from his life.

X.J. filleted the larger fish by grasping the tail firmly and inserting a pointy knife, deftly, as close to the spine as possible. He slid the knife away from the tail, gently but with determination, neatly separating flesh and bone. He tossed the loose spines into a heap and set the fillets in a neat pile, flesh side up. Every now and then, the boy who had been whittling by himself would wander over and take a batch of salmon spines into his bare hands and carry them over to the fire, where one of the men would place them on racks. The medium-sized and lighter salmon, once gutted and headless, were tossed into a big tub of galvanized steel to be carried over to the smoke shack. Ring-billed gulls circled overhead, screeching and squawking, anticipating a feast. The ravens were more discreet, waiting off to the side, perched in the pines and alders around the camp.

With the last fish processed, Art slid the heads, tails, a few spines and masses of roe into a large cauldron of gurgling hot water that hung over the campfire. Cubed onions, potatoes and celery, salt and pepper. Instantly the roe separated into large, opaque pink beads that floated to the surface then sank. The heady blend of the simmering salmon broth and eggs, alder wood smoke and the delicate aqua smell of the calm lake habitat was intoxicating.

Leyo broke James's reverie by handing him a roasted salmon spine. "A delicacy for us, Princip'l. Give it a try. The closer ta the bone, the sweeter the meat!"

Under Leyo's curious, amiable gaze, James picked the tender, coral-coloured flesh off the spine with his fingers—the flavour, smoky and delicate, savoury yet sweet. He let the expression on his face—wide-open eyes, raised eyebrows and a greasy grin—speak for him. Leyo responded in kind. James basked in the warmth of the exchange with his new friend, but the moment was interrupted by a sudden pang of nostalgia James felt for his own childhood home that no longer existed. This wasn't the effect he had expected in moving to Chezgh'un. He hadn't anticipated this feeling—he'd only anticipated joy, a sense of coming home. He couldn't settle into one emotion for more than a few seconds. Suddenly, he longed for something familiar—Vancouver, Franyo, his Saturday mornings at the Granville Island Market, walks along Kits Beach or English Bay and dinners in nice restaurants—anonymity. He longed to call

Franyo, to hear his voice and tell him about this amazing place at the lake, the beautiful people he was meeting and the delicious fresh salmon he'd sampled.

He excused himself from Leyo and went over to the hefty teen-aged boy who had been sitting alone. "*Hadih,* I'm James, the new principal."

"*Hadih.*" The boy kept looking down. "Heard about you—they say you from the city—but you're Indian too. I'm Anouk. Art, him, he be my uncle. But I live wit' my Granny, Monique."

James chuckled and stretched out his hand, which startled the boy. After a moment, he put his hand in James's—the boy's was cold and limp.

"Nobody likes me, Princip'l. I sniff gas."

"*I* like you, Anouk, and I just met you."

They sat for a few minutes in companionable silence, until Art motioned for James to take a seat on a stump near the fire. Art's brother Henry had made campfire bannock in a cast iron frying pan that he propped up against the rocks of the firepit—enough heat to bake the bread but not burn it. Art brought him a large mug of soup and a chunk of golden bannock. James blew on the soup to cool it, then savoured every spoonful. Eating the soup took him back to his early childhood—Sunday mornings slurping sucker-head soup with his stepfather and baby sister, but this soup, with an oily red sheen, carried more flavour—still subtle but fuller. The sockeye's diet of shrimp gave their flesh a rich taste and explained the colour of the broth. James knew he would sleep well that night.

He returned the mug to Art, wiped his mouth with the back of his hand, smiled, said "*mussi.*" He got up and strolled toward the smoke shack where he'd seen Catherine go earlier. He pulled open the flimsy wooden door to behold ten or so female elders sitting around the periphery of the shack, each wearing a long and loose cotton shift. All of them, except one, wore paisley scarves with a colourful sheen. Off to one side, beneath a round opening in the rooftop was an oval firepit with glowing embers. A stack of alder wood kindling.

James imagined that this was what the Chezgh'un women had done every summer and fall for countless generations—centuries, millennia—subtle differences in the faces and clothing, but the scene never really changed. James closed his eyes for a second and felt a rush. How was it that he was living this experience—visiting these people in this timeless dimension?

Unlike the other elders, Catherine was wearing blue jeans, her greying hair was pulled back into a ponytail. She looked like she belonged. She looked up at James and smiled, then said a few words in Dakelh to the women, followed by the words *princip'l* and *t'James*. With her open hand, she indicated each elder. As she introduced them, each one smiled and nodded. A spark in the low fire snapped. Everyone startled, then chuckled.

The elders sliced the delicate, tangelo sockeye carcasses into connected flaps, two per side before piercing the tail end with long wooden poles. James looked over at a few loaded poles, probably from the previous day, suspended high above the glowing embers. The flesh of the salmon on those poles had become ochre-coloured and the skin a translucent silver and gold. A short, stocky woman, one eye askew, who had been introduced as Margaret, gave him a sample of the oily, half-smoked salmon. Its flavour was as delightful and sensual as the juicy mangos he had enjoyed in Mexico six or seven years earlier, but of course the burst in James's mouth was pungent rather than sweet. James craved more and smiled when Margaret invited him to return the next day to learn how to slice the fish the way they did.

James stretched out his tent on a lovely meadow overlooking the lake, a patch where the spiky quack grass and sprawling yarrow had been stomped down. Just as James fastened the last corner to its peg, X.J. sauntered by with a teenaged girl at his side. X.J. paused and kicked one of the tent pegs.

"*Hadih,* Princip'l, ya shoulda set up close to my cabin, so if a black bear or grizzly come roun' at night, we'd hear ya holler. Always sleep with my rifle by the bed."

James hesitated. He didn't want to move his tent.

"C'mon, bring yer sleepin' bag 'n foamy into my shack. Kin sleep on the floor—der's plentya room," X.J. said, pointing at a nearby cabin. "Might be a mouse or two aroun', or maybe a few rats, but they won' hurtcha."

Just him, X.J. and this girl. This was really intimate. But the cabin was a decent size; maybe one section was divided off.

"Oh, this is Rachel—my latest squeeze," X.J. said, nodding at the girl beside him, whose straight black hair was cut in an uneven bob.

With his sleeping bag and foamy tucked under his arm, James followed X.J. over to the cabin. On the hillside behind the cabin, he noticed what looked like blueberry bushes. He would have to come back in the morning with a bucket before returning to the smoke shack for his lessons in fish cutting. After dropping his sleeping gear just inside the door, James walked over to the largest log house of the camp and settled down on the steps to watch another elder skin and skillfully butcher a bear. The elder reminded James so much of his great-grandmother—her kerchief, her hands, her leathery brown face.

"That's Monique—my mother," X.J. said with a dry chuckle. "Hafta be careful, Princip'l, not to piss 'er off, 'n she make war on you. She be my mother but even I scared of 'er."

So, that's Monique. Catherine had said she was a powerful elder and had issued a similar warning—in almost the same words. "Make war" must've been an awkward translation of some concept in Dakelh. Where James was from, they would've said she's a medicine woman who, in addition to practising good medicine like healing, could also place curses on people. But those who put curses on people were known to practise *bad* medicine. His mother had warned him that, depending on their powers, a curse could bounce back to its malevolent initiator—seven times stronger. James watched as Monique laboured over the bear carcass. Tirelessly tugging and slicing to separate sinew from flesh with swift precision—her strong hands caked with thickening, translucent blood.

The skinned carcass, which lay mouth-up on a sheet of blood-stained plywood, looked like a human cadaver, and instantly James understood why his people from the Prairies, the Nehiyawak, didn't hunt or eat bear. That, and the fact it was a spirit guide for them.

"We ren'er ta fat, Princip', ta make grease," Monique said, without looking up from her work. James was honoured that she would speak to him out of the blue like that, and at first, he was taken aback by her heavy accent, but then he *got* it: of course she has an accent. Dakelh is her first language. "Tast-ez real goot when you dip salmon jerky or dried moose meat in it," she said, and gave him a wide smile. It was dusky out now, but the woman kept working by the light of two kerosene lamps. "This has to get done tonight, so we can put things away, or wolves and bears will come 'round while we're sleeping. And the flies."

Everyone present at the camp, fifteen or so adults and half as many children, gathered around the fire that evening, sitting on tree stumps, logs or rickety lawn chairs—the kind James remembered having at home as a kid. Women served the children first, placing a chunk of Art's campfire bannock or warm fry bread on their plate, then a chunk of fresh salmon that Art and Henry had cooked on racks around the fire, a dollop of potato salad, a few celery and carrot sticks. The kids took their plates back to their respective cabins and sat on the entry-way landings to eat. Sally and Catherine took plates of food to the elders, who, to avoid the smoke, sat on the periphery of the circle. Art took James a plate of food, careful to point out to him a cluster of cooked salmon roe, and two smaller pieces of salmon he'd just taken off a wire rack. "Gave you salmon belly, Princip'l. Real rich," he said with a broad smile.

After dessert of warm fry bread and runny blueberry jam, Art announced they would have a bullshit contest, to pass the time. Everyone pulled their stumps, logs or chairs a bit closer to the fire. James recalled this type of contest from back home—the telling of amazing stories and tall tales until someone in the circle called "bullshit." Then, the person would have to fess up as to whether their tale had been true up to that point or not. People sometimes placed small bets on who would be the winner of a session.

James was bedazzled by the storytelling, and for each one, he hoped no one would call "bullshit" too soon. Leyo's tale was particularly unforgettable, about a hunter who was charged by a bull moose while peeing in the woods—he'd set his gun down. When the moose lowered his head to attack, the guy managed to jump up and grasp the hard, cold antlers in his hands, then used his own body weight to grapple with the animal's huge rack. He managed to twist the head to one side and had almost wrestled the bull moose to the ground when he got flipped high into the air and tossed ten feet—knocked unconscious. He was later found in the bush with his pants down—had barely lived to tell the tale.

Art's story got the most laughter. "I knew somethin' was up when that bear started payin' attenshun ta me from afar in the woods. Never came close enough for me ta worry… 'n I knew it was frien'ly energy—wasn' in attack mode or nothin. Jus' like humans, female bears sniff out their mates in advance, eh—ta pick their favourite. Well, this one female followed me for days, each time I went inta the woods ta cut wood or snare rabbits. Then one night, when Sally was gone ta her Mom's place, I awoke ta someone nuzzling my neck… kinda got me stirred up—ya know how it is, first thing in the mornin' in a warm bed—still half asleep. Then, I thought. What the hell, Sally's not here—who the hell's in my bed? Well, *then* the nibbling started—like *ouch*… 'n I thought—wow, Sally never done that before—ever kinky. Then, it o'erwhelm'd me—that bear smell… *geezus*—ya know usually you smell 'em before you see 'em…"

"Bullshit!" someone shouted over the laughter. Even though Art was shut down sooner than the other storytellers, he was declared the winner.

Once everyone had called it a night, James went back to X.J.'s cabin. He knocked and heard X.J.'s gruff voice say "come in." Across the room, which was smaller than it seemed in the light of day, X.J. and the girl sat on the brown army cot flipping through a magazine by the light of a kerosene lamp. He'd be sleeping just a few feet from the young couple's bed.

James nodded hello. The couple nodded back then continued to peruse the magazine. James stretched out his foamy and sleeping bag along the wall as far from the cot as he could. He lay down and tucked his journal under his pillow. He stole a glance at the couple long enough to see that Rachel seemed to be sulking, her curtain of hair down over her face.

Without warning, X.J. extinguished the kerosene lantern. James was relieved—he wouldn't have to attempt conversation and it saved him the embarrassment of stripping off his clothes in front of them.

In complete darkness James lay on his makeshift bed, thinking. He was slightly unnerved to be bunking with strangers, but nevertheless pleased with how comfortable his padded nest was. He was grateful that he wouldn't have to worry about grizzlies or black bears paying him a visit in the night. James reflected on his day, gave thanks for the beauty of the place and the acceptance of the people—the exquisite soul-nourishing food that was like nothing he had ever tasted before. Then guilt. He hadn't spoken to Franyo that day. The line was busy when he'd called early in the morning, and the payphone at the grocery store was taken when he went to try again, just before he headed out of town.

James was dozing off when he heard a low moaning sound, then a feeble female voice, "No X.J. Not tonight. Pleasss." He could feel the tension in the air.

X.J. grunted and coughed and then there was silence. Moments later, a rhythmic squeak of the old metal cot started slowly and became quite loud and raucous. James heard the girl sobbing but thought he might've been imagining it. He considered grabbing his gear to head back to his tent, then realized he didn't have a flashlight, and maybe things would get even worse for the girl if he left. It was likely not the first time this had happened to her with X.J. and wouldn't be the last. He'd better stay still, he thought, feign sleep, unless it got violent, or the girl cried out for help.

After ten or fifteen minutes, sudden quiet followed by unmistakable sobbing. X.J. grunted and the cot squeaked as X.J. must have rolled off her. He had forced himself on that poor girl, who couldn't have been more than fifteen, after she had pleaded with him not to—and in the presence of another person, a stranger. What the hell? James wondered if anyone in the community knew what was going on between X.J. and the girl. He guessed that someone had likely tried to intervene—to no avail. Maybe the girl wasn't as young as she looked. Or, perhaps, like in many places, this type of sexual exploitation of girls by young men had been normalized.

Decades ago James had witnessed something similar with his older sister—when she was just fourteen. He'd walked in on her and her much older boyfriend when they were making out. His sister wasn't complaining or sobbing, but intuitively James knew what was happening was wrong. Years later he understood what the man had done was statutory rape. His sister got pregnant and had an abortion. Would this happen to X.J.'s so-called girlfriend now? Was she pregnant already? Would she and her family even consider an abortion, if there was indeed a place to get one in the region? Who would cover the costs?

James would have to watch this guy. The man nicknamed Junior scared him, but now James realized he would need to be vigilant around X.J., too.

Eventually, complete darkness and hypnotic silence lulled James to sleep.

iii

Early the next morning, the hooting of owls and the compelling aroma of campfire coffee summoned James over to where the other early risers were perched on stumps or logs, steaming mugs in hand. Folks were quiet—just the occasional comment about the weather and the quantity and size of the fish the men had pulled up in their nets earlier in the morning. Art told James that he, Sally, Monique, Catherine and a few other elders would like to meet with him at Monique's cabin right after breakfast.

When James got there, Monique was settled in the old wooden rocking chair on her porch, gazing over the lake. A queen surveying her domain, James mused, wishing now that he'd taken the time to wash up and change his clothes. Thank goodness he likely smelled of smoke, like everyone else present.

James's mind turned to his own grandmothers. He wished he'd been able to see them display the same regal, proprietary attitude regarding their territory, but the colonization of *his* people had been rapid and brutal. All because of gold, shiny gold—an adornment and western symbol of adoration and commitment—the Klondike Gold Rush brought trauma and devastation to his people. He glimpsed the gold watch on his wrist that Franyo had given him. Suddenly, he felt conspicuous wearing it—him, a poor boy from the bush desperately seeking acceptance here, among these people who lived such a rich life, but were considered poor by Western standards. He took the watch off, placed it carefully in his jeans pocket. He'd put it back on when he returned to Vancouver.

With everyone gathered, Monique spoke, with the weight of a pronouncement. "Listen, Princip'l. We jus' wanna tell you. No use startin' school on the Tuesday after Labour Day weekend. Nobody will be there—we'll all still be *here*—fishin' and huntin'." She paused for a moment, then concluded, "It's our las' chance before winter. Might as well wait till third week o' September—or maybe the very end..."

Everyone sat in silence. Sally stole glances at James while everyone else looked at the ground.

Comfortable with silence, James waited a few seconds to speak. But his mind was racing: at first flooded with panic, which turned to annoyance, then frustration. He'd imagined the elders would support him in his quest to set up great educational programming in the community, in setting up a successful school. Now this, and not from just anyone—from Monique, the key elder, the lead matriarch. He needed some time to strategize. After the warnings he'd had about Monique's power, he knew he didn't dare challenge her.

"It's so good to have this time with you, Monique. Of course, I understand the community has to get stocked up for winter... makes sense."

Monique coughed and straightened her posture a bit. As if sensing the quandary she'd put James in, she at once offered him some relief and signalled that she needed to get on with her day.

"Let's get some coffee tomorrow, Princip'l—well, I drink tea, but you kin get coffee—'n we kin visit a liddle," she said. "Yera goot man. I can tell."

James wandered off alone to find the berry patch he'd spotted the previous day, but before he got very far, he came across X.J. and Rachel—X.J. striding confidently along the path to the firepit, and Rachel following a couple of feet back, her head down. He nodded at X.J. and got a nod back. He was sure there was a hint of a smirk on the young man's face, as if to say—*so whatcha think of me now—am I* the man *or what*?

Rachel's eyes were tiny slits, but what could be seen of them was red.

"Good morning," James called out, anxious to see if the girl would respond.

Rachel kept her head down, but answered, "Mornin'."

"G'mornin'," X.J. said with a broad smile.

"Goin' berry picking," James said. He heard and felt the tremolo in his voice and hoped that X.J. didn't.

"See ya later, then," X.J. said and continued along his way.

James began picking berries along a hillside. Once he had a handful, he sat cross-legged at the top of the hill to study the lake and reflect on what Monique had just told him about initiating the school year. He popped a few berries into his mouth and was pleasantly surprised by the flavour burst—not blueberries, not saskatoons, somewhere in between. The locals called them "blackberries." He'd have to learn the Dakelh word for them.

James relaxed, breathing in the fresh mountain air and savouring the gentle cool breeze against his face. Sitting there like that, in a quasi-meditation state, it didn't take long for clarity to come.

Of course, *of course*—this is a perfect opportunity. If Muhammad won't come to the mountain, take the mountain to Muhammad. If the kids can't come to school, we'll bring the school to them. This is exactly the type of nature education I've dreamed of doing—tried to do in the city, in the schoolyard, in nearby parks and on the beach. Here, we've got the rich forest, the estuary and the lake—a superb instructional setting—and all these master instructors in Dakelh culture! The ultimate teachable moment!

This would take a lot of planning. His thoughts churned—parental consent, curriculum planning, menu planning, tents, first aid, water safety... There's no way Louise would approve.

James sought out Catherine and asked her to join him for coffee. Cautiously, he explained his idea and asked what she thought of it.

"We kin make it work, t'James. I done work like that before, campin' retreats and workshops for large groups... 'n I even cooked in a work camp for a couple o' years. And we can do Dakelh immersion. A culture camp! I love it."

James was giddy. He knew he should discuss it with Louise and Mike, but he needed to run the idea by Monique first. Maybe he could make it a joint request—from him and Monique. He wandered nonchalantly to where Monique and Art were sitting. As he approached, Monique looked up from the bear paw she was skinning.

"Hi Monique. Listen, I been weighing what you said, about starting school late. I can't really do that, legally. I could get fired. Gotta do two hundred days of school each year. But I had a brainstorming session with Catherine, and we thought, well, what if we brought school here? The whole school—all the teachers and kids. Kindergarten right through to the teen program, for the first week. That way, the whole community, including the little ones and teens, can help out. And we'll make it a learning experience—mostly in Dakelh. Catherine will help me plan it all out."

James stopped and studied Monique's face to see if she was getting ready to react positively or if she would tell him he was crazy.

Art responded before Monique did. "Geez, Princip'l that's an idea," he said, "school at the lake."

Sally nodded and smiled. "Be lotsa work ta get ready, Princip'l. But I bet we could do it," she said.

James looked at Monique one more time, his look beseeching her to speak.

"Sounds goot," was all she said.

The ominous warning Catherine conveyed during their trip to California, leapt to mind: *In less than a hundred years, like the California tribes, the Dakelh of Chezgh'un could be long gone, their specific dialect non-existent, and worst of all—the people extinct. We have to do what we can to help them to survive—keep their place on this planet.* Catherine Bird's call to action would be the school's mission statement.

iv

James got the green light from Louise and Mike to proceed with the school-wide fish camp, so he, Catherine, and Art and Sally dove into planning. Once the teachers had arrived in Chezgh'un and settled into their accommodations, James convened a brief staff meeting to go over the camp logistics as well as aspects of teaching roles. He would provide prep time by teaching music for each class. He reminded them of some of the common instructional approaches they'd agreed upon in Monterey during their evening visits. The teachers told him excitedly how they'd set up their classrooms and how eager they were to kick off the school year—the first year of teaching for all of them, except Catherine, who had been a language teacher for several years now. He then asked the team to meet with Art and Sally, as newly appointed teaching assistants and local knowledge holders, to brainstorm a list of the skills workshops they could set up for the students.

The next morning, they reconvened in James's office to go over the results of their efforts.

"My God, this is every teacher's dream," James said when he reviewed what they'd sketched out. "Traditional storytelling, geography of the lake and ecosystems, canoeing, snaring rabbits, setting nets and all the other steps involved with catching and preserving salmon—smoking and canning, boat maintenance, hide tanning, traditional drumming and dancing." He paused, regarded the teachers. Debbie's face had reddened, and Harry sat quiet with a poker face. Undaunted, James smiled, and continued, "Wow. It's all here, you guys: science, social studies, language arts, math ... home ec and phys. ed."

"'N we kin do most of it in Dakelh, Princip'l," Art said with a broad smile.

Debbie's face was crimson red now, and Harry, the new young teacher from Vanderhoof, wore a sour expression.

Debbie took a deep breath then launched in.

"This all sounds great for a camp, as such. But they say the first few days with a new class are so important—to set the tone for the student-teacher rapport, lay down ground rules and establish routines. We won't be able do any of that in a camp setting, and with so many parents present, of course the kids are gonna listen to them more than to us, the teachers," she said.

"That's exactly right," said Harry. "Working with teens is challenging at the best of times. It's so important to establish power dynamics and communications right from the get-go with a new class. This proposal goes against all the methodology I've learned."

James had expected this. As a young, new principal with only five years of teaching experience—who also happened to be First Nations—he knew some of his team would inevitably challenge his authority. He'd hoped that their time and all the discussions they'd had in Monterey—the rapport they'd built would've circumvented some of this. He knew he had to answer credibly and authoritatively. He sat up straight and took on a serious demeanour as he spoke.

"Clearly what we're doing here is unusual, and I understand your concerns. We had to do this—go with the flow, so to speak—or go against it, and spend a week in frustration with empty classrooms. As soon as I grasped that this isn't some frivolous vacation—that to the contrary, it's about survival—gathering food for winter, something historic the community has been doing for countless generations—right here in this same place. As soon as I got that, I knew what we had to do."

James was sure he saw Harry begin to roll his eyes, but the novice teacher caught himself just in time. "Catherine tells me there's no word in their language for *thank you*—they borrowed '*merci*' from the French and now say '*mussi*,'" he said. "What kind of culture is that? In my culture, Cree culture, we say thank you with our eyes. We do have words, too, but the look happens first." James's voice had gotten a little bit louder, and his tone a bit deeper; the two teachers knew he was becoming annoyed.

"I never thought I'd be working on an Indian reserve," Harry said, sounding exasperated. "I have Louise to thank. Thought I was being hired for the Fort or Vanderhoof."

Loretta, the Tsilhqot'in teacher from Williams Lake, smiled calmly and raised her hand to speak. "It's my first year too, and I think the fish camp is great," she said.

"Sure, it's unusual, but unusual challenges require unusual responses. This is the ultimate teachable moment, and a once in a lifetime experience for all of us—teachers and students alike. Thank you for taking the time to voice your concerns—I hope I've addressed them adequately. Now, let's get on with our day, alright?"

The teachers all stood up—Harry stretched, Debbie smiled and Loretta smiled and let out a slight chuckle. They left, chatting and kibitzing, to go to their respective classrooms.

After the staff meeting, James ordered arts and crafts supplies from Vancouver, including wood-carving tools and kite kits, hoping it would all arrive in time. Catherine and Sally helped James with the menu planning—listing food supplies they would need for the five days of the camp to complement the traditional foods they would harvest: flour, barley, wild rice, tomato sauce, beans, fresh veggies, iceberg lettuce, and bacon. Then James went into wannabe chef mode and added things like oregano, thyme, French tarragon, soy sauce, brown mushrooms, Chinese five-spice powder.

That evening, the eve of the school-wide fish camp, after eating a simple dinner he'd prepared in the school kitchen, James wandered down to the lakeshore, alone, reflecting on how things were going with his team so far. He hoped this was the one and only time there would be a real or imaginary racial divide—the two white teachers forming a lobby against him and a Native teacher coming to his defence.

Day one of the fish camp featured kite-making, something James had done at his Vancouver school, though here there would be no power lines to worry about. The weather was perfect and looked like it would stay that way: a clear blue sky from the forested hilltops to the horizon it formed with the lake. The gentle fall breeze kept everyone cool and refreshed. The songbirds were singing in full voice, as if to squeeze in every moment of life they could before autumn set in and they had to fly south. James spotted Art huddled in conversation with Debbie, Harry and Loretta. Art had them laughing. *Good.*

By early afternoon, kites and more kites were flying high in the air, along the wide sandy beach and in the grassy meadow that led up to the hill covered by berry bushes, including the simpler ones the primary class had assembled. Children ran, strode and chattered gleefully, looking up in amazement at the kites they had spent the morning decorating and assembling. They'd used the ovoid patterns typical of Dakelh culture, and painted them red or black against a white background. The banter and joyful noise happy children everywhere make while at play. James felt at home.

"*Hadih,* look at mine!"

"Going so high—gonna blow away!"

"Teacher help me with this string—g'ttin' tangled!"

"Mine fell down—gotta get it back up!"

As he watched colourful kites bobbing up and down, twirling and rotating, tails flying wildly in response to the same cool breeze he felt on his bare arms, James sighed contentedly. That activity was a hit.

Parent volunteers were on hand, and keen to help—many of them had only seen kites on TV, in books or comics, so the novelty was exciting for them too. They spoke Dakelh to the kids as best they could to explain how the parts fit together—who knew how to say the names of the various parts in their language: frame, flying line, bridle? Spine, tail and string, on the other hand, were obvious.

He watched Debbie grasp the hand of a little girl who had struggled to hold onto the kite string and walk along the beach without falling.

Right after lunch, he saw Harry gather a group of teens out in the shallow section of the lake and was showing them how to do canoe-over-canoe rescue. His big accomplishment was convincing some of the macho boys that they needed to wear a life jacket while in a craft or in the water. James breathed a sigh of relief when he saw Harry smiling and laughing as he interacted with the girls. They've won him over already, he thought. How could they not, with those smiles?

As planned, Catherine was leading a bannock and fry-bread workshop with a group of teenaged girls in the cook tent. Each of the girls was kneading an amoeba-like wad of white dough in a large stainless-steel bowl, wearing an improvised apron. James moved in closer, nodded hello to Catherine.

"*Hadih,* t'James, *t'su in' t'oh,*" Catherine said. The girls chuckled at this.

"*T's 'us t'oh*—I'm fine," James answered. At this, the girls' eyebrows went up.

"T'James, these girls are amazin'. Shannon here talks Dakelh and knows how to make real goot bannock all on er own. The other girls are learnin' fast too."

James caught a glimpse of Shannon's gaze. Her eyes were vibrant—bright and eager, full of a joie de vivre he hadn't often seen anywhere. Laura, the exiting teacher was right, she's a special one for sure. Shannon must've felt that she was being observed, she regarded him for just a second before looking at the ground again.

In another part of the cook tent, Loretta was teaching a different group of teens—boys and girls—how to prepare roasted beaver tail. James remembered his mother telling him it was her favourite delicacy growing up, and he couldn't wait to taste it. He watched as the teens removed four black, slightly puffed-up beaver tails from the grill. They'd been cooked on racks over hot coals in the firepit, then sliced down the middle of their bottom side, the first a layer of skin, which now looked like snakeskin, was pulled away, and the same for another layer which was also thin, but pink and fleshier.

"*Tsache*," Sally said, and the students repeated the word. "*Tsa* is beaver, 'n *che* is tail, or the end of something." She handed James a small chunk on a piece of bannock. It looked like fat or gelatin, but it smelled so good. James immediately grasped why his mother had liked it so much; it reminded him of salmon belly or the "pope's nose" of a roast turkey—rich and unctuous like bone marrow with more texture and a delicate aquatic flavour.

Dinner was self-served. Half-smoked sockeye steamed in tinfoil to complete its cooking, served with steamed quartered potatoes or rice, a piece of beaver tail on a chunk of bannock, dried moose meat, deer stew, boiled mixed veggies and a simple tossed salad. There was a jar of lukewarm bear grease to drizzle over everything, and that's what everyone was doing. This was something new; James was sure it was great nutrition, but his belief that bears are sacred animals kept him from enjoying it as the others seemed to.

After dinner, James got out his guitar and led some singing around the campfire. He knew they would like country music, so he played the songs his mother used to sing. He started with "Jambalaya" by Hank Williams—everyone knew the words to that one—then Roger Miller's "King of the Road" and "I Walk the Line" by Johnny Cash. A couple of guys called out for him to play some George Jones songs. He struggled to remember the chords and lyrics to "The Race Is On" and "She Thinks I Still Care." Then he recalled the song his mother used to sing in Cree, "*Kiy wîhkâc, peyagun tapscotch niya*"—her translation of the Hank Williams song "May You Never Be Alone Like Me." That song brought a tear to his eye—he thought about Franyo back in Vancouver. He didn't want to get more emotional, so he switched to happier songs, ones he thought the kids would like, "Puff the Magic Dragon" and "Rockin' Robin."

At one point, James looked around and was astonished to see that most of the adults seated around the fire were still working—at something. Several of the men had voluminous fishing nets gathered around them and were repairing frayed or broken strings with an instrument that looked like a large wooden darning needle. Others were carving small- and medium-sized pieces of wood—some making art, others making wooden pegs they used in the fishing nets. Some women were darning wool socks and others were sewing by hand. James guessed they were taking advantage of the extended daylight of summer to get ready for winter.

As he packed up his guitar and said good night to everyone, James noticed that his face was numb from smiling so much. He stumbled over a knoll of tussocky quack grass toward Henry's cabin to find his relocated tent. Henry had asked Anouk and another boy to move it to a spot right beside the rustic outdoor washstand in front of his door. There, James would be safe from black bears or grizzlies. James noticed a basin and a bucket of clean water, but he was too tired to wash up, so he just brushed his teeth. In the morning he would have a nice French bath to get rid of the smell of sweat and smoke from the day's activities.

The next morning, James was startled awake when he heard Art's voice calling.

"C'mon, Princip'l!" Art shouted. "Said you wanted ta help set net one day. Guess I forgot ta tell you, we do that at 6 a.m. Meet you by the boats."

James scrambled to get dressed. No time to wash up after all. Oh well, his clothes still smelled like smoke, and he'd have plenty of time to wash when they got back. The teenaged boys were warmly dressed and completely focused on the chore at hand: meticulously arranging the nets in the boats so they could quickly and easily be tossed into the water once they arrived at the right spot. One of the boys nodded and smiled as he took James's wrist to help him into the boat, another teen rushed to place a dry cushion on one of the benches in the middle of the boat to ensure James would be comfortable. Another boy brought him a life jacket and showed him how to put it on properly, seated him on the middle bench, starboard side. These boys were taking care of him—treating James like he was a special guest, or an old man, and out of respect they made no eye contact. James was chuckling inside; he loved this feeling of being taken care of, of being watched out for, of being special. This was a completely new dynamic for him.

Art and Leyo, each perched at the bow of their respective motorboats, gave clear directions as to where they would go to set net: one boat at the mouth of a nearby river that flowed into the lake, and another at the mouth of a prominent stream. Sitting tall and alert, chests puffed out slightly, the boys at the helms revved up the motors. James loved how the bow lifted with the rapid acceleration. The bouncing up and down movement, bow to stern, was exhilarating. As the craft flew over the water, a light mist sprayed his face. James was so impressed by how methodical and efficient the older boys wafted the nets, perfectly balanced with floaters and buoys, into the spumy water. Clearly, they'd done this often, probably since they were small boys. At around ten o'clock they would pull up the nets and unload the teeming salmon then set up the usual assembly line to preserve or cook the fish.

On Friday, the final day of the fish camp, Art and Henry drove their respective pickups to the two smokehouses of the camp: the communal one where James had watched the women smoking fish and the large one behind Monique's place. They loaded the back of the truck with racks full of dried smoked salmon, dried moose meat, boxes of bear meat, deer quarters and a few beaver carcasses that had been hung but had yet to be butchered. Buckets of berries. Anouk helped Henry load boxes of sides of smoked salmon and moose meat into James's vehicle. They suggested he should go back to the community first, and they would follow in a few hours.

The mood in the camp was different now. The frenetic energy of uncertainty and worry of the first couple days had dissipated over the course of the week. Any misgivings that community members had about their new cadre of teachers and principal—and vice versa—had resolved through the familiarity that comes with sharing meals, spending uninterrupted blocks of time together communally, day in and day out, sleeping in the same rustic camp each night. They all shared sensory experiences none of them would ever forget, like the day everyone—elders, parents, kids and teachers—all converged on the lake, splashing and laughing, the little ones jumping up and down; or sitting around the huge campfire savouring the first batch of glossy, golden salmon jerky—smiles of delight all around at the burst of delicious smoky mango flavour—the reward of a week of hard work; the appies of beaver tail on bannock, that new delicacy Sally and the teen group had invented; squeals of delight at rare animal sightings: one day, a golden eagle circling overhead, another day, a grizzly in the distance, everyone vying for the binoculars to have a look, and another day, the largest moose anyone had ever seen wandering across the meadow, with its impressive rack.

Debbie had managed to set up some routines for her pupils: a circle for storytelling and reading aloud, once in the morning and once in the afternoon; playtime, first in the sand, then in the water; fish counting when the teen boys pulled in the nets each morning followed by basic anatomy lessons as the men gutted the fish and the kids got to see and touch fish offal: the liver, kidneys, lungs, heart.

Loretta and Art taught a traditional bone game called *lahal.* It got quite raucous with the pounding of hand drums and chanting of songs in Dakelh. It was a simple guessing game: two teams knelt facing each other while members of one team would guess in which hand their counterpart from the other team had placed their bone fragment. Things got quite tense by the time it got down to one team only having to acquire one more bone to win, and by this time all joined in the chanting.

In the early evening, the whole school joined in games of tag, Red Rover and kick the can.

It was hard to believe the week was over so quickly.

Anouk volunteered to accompany James back to the village, and, not really knowing the boy yet, James was reluctant. Teachers and principals had to be squeaky clean nowadays—rightfully so: there were so many cases of sexual exploitation of children, particularly up north. Anouk was a vulnerable teen, so James had to avoid even the perception of possible impropriety or false accusation. But, with Henry's encouragement, he accepted. After all, it was a short—though potentially perilous—trip through remote wilderness and Anouk knew the area well. James felt so validated—an integral part of the community—entrusted with boxes of precious dried salmon and moose meat to be transported back to the community. Now he was entrusted with a vulnerable teen.

James manoeuvred his red Sidekick around puddles, accelerated through bogs and slowed for low-hanging branches. His shuttle between two worlds came to an abrupt stop six kilometres into the journey. He'd underestimated the length and depth of a mud bog. He shifted into four-by-four mode, then tried to edge forward, but no luck. This was grizzly country, and here he was in the middle of the forest, with no gun or other knife, in his vinyl-top vehicle loaded with smoked fish.

"Looks like we're stuck, Princip'l. I might hafta get out and push."

James jumped out of the Sidekick to look around—he didn't want Anouk to have to get into the heart of the bog to push and get back in the vehicle dripping wet with mud—return home like that. How humiliating.

"Princip'l, us, what we do is put branches in front 'n back—helps with traction, 'n if we hafta push, we don' get all covered with mud."

Maybe there were enough branches on the ground to do this. "Let me try a couple other things first, okay Anouk?"

James put the vehicle in first gear and stepped on the gas slightly. The vehicle inched ahead but then got stuck again. He put it in reverse, and it moved back a couple of inches. He repeated this a few more times, but each time, it seemed the vehicle became more entrenched.

Merde, not only were there grizzlies around here but packs of wolves too. They would smell his cargo for certain. And it wasn't only his life in danger—it was Anouk's too.

James was at the peak of his despair when he remembered that for the four-by-four mechanism to engage, he was supposed to put it in reverse and back up about fifteen metres. He put the car in reverse and let the wheels spin backwards for couple of minutes, until he felt the gears latch on. Then he put it in second gear, slowly withdrew the clutch, and the vehicle hummed and moved forward, steadily. What a relief. He wasn't sure which would've been worse, undergoing a bear or wolf attack, or the humiliation of being found there—him and Anouk stranded and helpless—by the men of Chezgh'un.

v

One Sunday morning, after languishing alone in his temporary lodging for a couple of hours, James decided to attempt to visit Monique in her home. He'd heard that was simply not done. She chased away community members who appeared at her door seeking advice or healing—things had apparently gotten out of hand a few years earlier and worn her down. But his few encounters with Monique had made him nostalgic for his great-grandparents, who had lived into their nineties, well into his youth. He longed desperately for that kind of intimate interaction with an elder.

James had already heard so much about Monique from her family members and from Catherine. Others beyond the reserve had heard of her power and influence without ever meeting her, for Monique had never physically left her people's territory around the village of Chezgh'un. According to local knowledge holders, in the weeks leading up to Monique's birth, there were signs that she would be extraordinary: weather patterns were different, a thunderbird landed and perched on Mount Shas everyday around four o'clock in the afternoon and seemed to peer toward the village. Four o'clock was the hour of Monique's birth and the elders in the region were on full alert that day—they sensed something significant was occurring and word spread rapidly. Within hours of her uneventful birth everyone in the community knew Monique would grow up to be a seer, healer and spiritual warrior. From a young age, her dreams would guide the community's hunters to the location where moose, caribou and bears could be found.

Monique's parents instinctively knew that it was critical that she never be captured by the *Nedoh* and taken to one of their schools to be indoctrinated, brainwashed, acculturated and used as cheap labour—wounding her spirit and stifling her soul. Instead, Monique would be raised by Dakelh elders in their language, steeped in the Dakelh culture and cosmology at a camp in the woods, at her family's winter site, which could only be reached by dogsled or boat. She would not be taught to speak or read English. The exposure associated with learning the language and ways of *Nedoh* would've changed her indelibly, distorted her thinking and altered how she perceived the world around her. Through their culture and religious dogma the *Nedoh* asserted that they were the masters of the universe and instilled this in the mind of their children from a very early age, along with their notions of right and wrong, sin and virtue. Anything good or pleasurable was sinful, yet they themselves, the *Nedoh*, did it all anyway, secretively or with some type of perverse rationalization that it was the Lord's will—or they would feign remorse while confessing to having committed a sin and then seek forgiveness and absolution, which were easily granted in exchange for a tithe or offering. In extreme cases, they would claim they were possessed by the Devil and seek exorcism first before confessing to a priest or engaging in supplication for forgiveness directly with their Lord and Saviour, Jesus Christ.

Whereas Monique's people cut trees for essential uses like firewood and material for building homes, *Nedoh* businessmen had already destroyed much of the local forest habitat, clearing trees right to the edges of lakes and rivers, eventually causing mudslides, which interfered with fish spawning and migration. Monique's people used every part of an animal, whereas the *Nedoh* hunted mammals ruthlessly and wasted so much, leaving moose and deer entrails, antlered heads and hides in ditches along the roadside. Bird numbers decreased dramatically, especially swans and grouse. Beavers were brought to the brink of extinction from trapping for their pelts and for a secretion from their castor gland that was used to season food and enhance perfumes. The *Nedoh* also dammed the Nechako River, diverting over half of its flow and causing the water level of local lakes, rivers and their tributaries to drop, disrupting the ecosystem and the natural habitat, creating avulsions up and down the river, which confused migrating elk, moose and Indigenous hunters.

Monique grew up knowing humans were not above living things: muskrat, beaver, moose, weasel, porcupine, eagle, goose, woodpecker, crow, owl, salmon, cedar and spruce were all relations—cousins of sorts. The lakes, streams, rivers, meadows and mountains were the blessed homeland of her people, and they knew that in order for their good fortune and health to continue, they had to treat nature with tremendous respect—in all of their activities and their lifestyle. The plants and animals that provided food and medicine for the Dakelh sacrificed a part of their life, and, for this, individuals and families were forever grateful. They showed gratitude by placing tobacco in certain locations and by saying prayers of thanks after every harvest.

Monique learned to co-exist with all of these creatures and to understand her place—the place of all Dakelh in the natural world—and she would teach this to others, not by lecturing them, but by modelling a rich life in harmony with it all. Bear would offer itself to her in a dream, and she would tell the men where to find it. Then, as always, she would carve it up meticulously, and use every part of the animal, render the fat for extra nutrition and use it for making medicine along with other body parts.

Monique gave birth to all fourteen of her children, including her three miscarried babies, in her lodge in the forest with the help and guidance of a skilled midwife. She in turn raised her offspring in her language, respecting the tenets and customs of Dakelh culture. She taught them to carry their own weight, look out for and support each other and to be stewards and protectors of Mother Earth—to leave their lands and territory improved, better than they had found them, even if just in some small way.

From the time they were toddlers, Monique and her cousin Abel were told that one day they would become husband and wife. Abel was a second or third cousin and this was important—that he be related but not too closely. Relations always treated their women better. Abel had a gentle spirit which would calm—or at least attempt to calm—Monique's fierce nature.

When James knocked gently on Monique's door, Abel answered, ushered him in and motioned for him to sit on a round of spruce just inside.

Abel disappeared into Monique's bedroom to ask if she wanted to have a visitor—the new principal. Sitting there in the rustic shack where Monique and Abel had raised their family, James had a flash of anxiety—had he made a mistake coming to visit unannounced and uninvited? And how would they communicate one on one—have a meaningful conversation? He hadn't yet learned any Dakelh except for basic phrases like *t'su in t'oh,* "how are you," and the response *t's 'us t'oh. Des ah neh* for "be quiet." Within a few minutes, though, Abel ushered him into Monique's room, and James began to tremble—his eyes filled with tears.

The elder was propped up in her bed—a crimson scarf tied around her head and a thin and faded Hudson's Bay blanket pulled up to her neck. Her long, thick hair was pulled back tightly and woven into a braid that flowed onto her left shoulder and continued over the bed toward the floor—James couldn't see the end of it.

"What's matter, Princip'l? Ain't seen ol' womans in her bet' before?" Monique said with a deep melodic laugh. Ah, that's right, she could speak rudimentary English, and was willing to do so in private, but refused to when her children and grandchildren were within earshot. Remaining silent, James tried to look into her eyes, but Monique didn't return his gaze.

Monique reached into a tree stump beside her bed for a rippled tin can, which looked like it may have once held Campbell's soup. She took a sip from it.

"*Hadih,* Monique. Good to see you."

"*Hadih.* Good ya come ta see Monique. I jus' drink bit o' wine. Haf some..." Monique said as she held the can out for James.

James was honoured that she would share her drink with him, but responded, "Oh. No thanks, Monique. Got lots to do today."

"This my territorih, t'James. Everythin' you see 'roun

here—animals, plants, water 'n sky. But it ain't mine like some *Nedoh* say. I'm part of it—jus' part of it, but we gotta say it's ours or they try to take it from us—always wanna take our land!" A deep boisterous laugh.

"I knew you were comin' to us, t'James. Seen you in a vision. But you won' stay—won' work with us feri long—too scared. Scared ta become one of us. Jus' like yer family—you lef' dem too. Too scared they gonna hurt you. Too much hurt t'James—I see hurt all over your face."

James took a deep breath, trying to control the intense emotions that were overtaking him. What did Monique see? He was feeling so good—he was at the top of his game—the youngest school principal in the province—and Nehiyaw at that! Yes, he'd experienced incredible tragedy and loss. Within the last ten years, both his mother and his older sister had died. The two most important people in his life were forever gone, and he'd hoped he'd put his grief behind him. But time and again, he was forced to acknowledge that he was still grappling with the enormity of the loss. In fact, maybe that was part of the reason he made this landscape shift in his life—it was a powerful distraction.

Why did Monique say he wouldn't be there long? What did she see in his future? Did she perhaps have some insight into his clandestine personal life? Would it ruin him? He hoped not—he had a plan. He would stay in Chezgh'un for a few years, maybe even up to ten years if things worked out, accomplish amazing things and build a reputation as an expert in Indigenous education. Maybe he hadn't weighed things adequately from different angles—hadn't analyzed his strengths and weaknesses, nor the opportunities or threats—in this new life, this new context.

"*Nedoh* power o'er you s'real strong t'James. Them white peoples, they control you too much—control yer mind 'n yer heart. If you wanna live among us Dakelh you gotta break free. See ta worl' like Dakelh see it. Feel it deep inside o' you—be one with us and our territorih. But Nedoh brainwashed you so much—all them years bein' taught their ways 'n talkin' their language. Their way of bein'."

What was she talking about? Did she mean the Catholic Church? Or was it his education—twelve years of public school and then five at university? The influence of all his white friends—of Franyo? He knew he couldn't press Monique for details. That's not what one does with elders; she'd said what she had to say—in vague terms—and he would have to ponder and reflect on her words. Over time, he would come to understand what she meant.

Didn't Monique understand why he was here? That he'd come to reconnect with all of that? To commune with nature, to get back his Indigenous soul, get back to his roots. Didn't she know that he'd prayed to her ancestors at the cemetery his first day here? That the ancestors were guiding and helping him now? Monique's words "too scared" echoed in his head—slammed him. *Too scared* to care deeply—that was what she was really saying. Wasn't it? Would he go through life just skimming the surface—never go deep again, with family, with a lover?

After a few minutes of shared contemplative silence, the sign of a deepening bond, James stood to leave. Monique turned to look at him, smiled broadly, then nodded and said, "My door s'always open ta you, Princip'l. Come see me anytime."

James felt the same powerful connection with Monique and Abel as he'd felt with his own grandparents and great aunts and uncles back home, and he was so grateful for this. At once the visit both calmed and worried him, as visits with elders often do. Still, he hoped that Monique would give him guidance that nobody else could. Guidance and universal love. Assurance that he was on the right track.

vi

One night, James awoke suddenly at 4 a.m. The RV, his temporary lodging, was shaking and shifting. *Good God—an earthquake.* He sat up and rubbed his eyes, trying to get his bearings. But wait, this wasn't Vancouver—it was Chezgh'un—in Northern BC, which was not an earthquake zone. So, what the hell?

The earthquake drills they'd done in his school back in Vancouver were useless in his present situation. What was a guy supposed to do in an RV, out in the country—on flat land at that? Hide under the flimsy table? What good would that do? He sat on the edge of the bed in stillness for a moment, hoping it was over, but then the RV lurched to one side—settled back down for a second before it started rocking side to side and every which way. Jesus Christ—this was too weird. "I gotta get outta this thing," he muttered to himself—surely others would come out of their houses, too, to see what was going on.

James pulled on his jeans and a T-shirt, swept his hair back and stepped into his sandals. He grasped the table and spread his arms out so that he could press his hands against the walls of the RV to steady himself. Moving cautiously like this he shuffled toward the door. Oh great, the swaying was getting more erratic. He unlatched the door and let it fall open to a confusing sight. In the haze of dawn there were batches of golden hay scattered haphazardly over the gravel. He leapt out of the RV and slowly stepped to the front of it to peer around its side. He saw the furry black and white rear-end of some big animal. Then it occurred to him—the cow, the aging feral cow that wandered freely around the reserve. Nobody could remember who'd brought her here. Nobody claimed ownership or tended to her. The beast was forcing her way under the RV to get at the hay that Patrick, the school custodian, had stuffed there to insulate it against the looming cold of winter. The cow pulled her head out from under the camper and regarded James for a few seconds before she continued pulling at the hay.

"Okay, what next?" James said and laughed. He enjoyed the moment, by himself in the morning quiet. As he was about to go back into his RV, a movement off to one side caught his eye. He stopped to look and was shocked to see a tallish man dressed in combat fatigues, a red bandana tied over his head, a bullet strap slung over his shoulder and around his waist—a Native Rambo going to do battle… somewhere. James quickly stepped into his trailer.

vii

Three hard thumps on the door of the RV followed by Art's loud voice. "*Hadih*, Princip'l, ya gotta come ta the church. Agnes gonna scold the youth. X.J., my crazy li'l brother, jus' got back from spendin' the weekend in jail in Prince. He be on the loose with a .303, threatenin' to shoot up the town. Gone freakin' insane! Everyone's there. Come across with me. Let's go!"

As if on cue, the loud double crack of a powerful rifle nearby caused James to bolt upright. *My God,* James fretted, *the warnings were real. Had anyone called the police?* James set aside the paperwork he'd been doing, threw on a coat, stepped out of the RV and got into lock-step with Art on the gravel road.

"Don' worry, Princip'l, he ain't gonna shoot us. Just high and bein' stupid." Art said. Nevertheless, he ushered James into the church and closed the door without coming in himself, which left James feeling like an intruder in this community meeting, an interloper.

The tiny church was so much like the church in the village near to where James grew up: an arched A-frame–type ceiling of varnished pine—ubiquitous dark brown knots. Pine-Sol, second-hand smoke, Brylcreem, leather and smoked salmon. Front and centre: a wide platform that sat about fifteen centimetres off the floor was cordoned off by a thickly varnished wooden railing, leaving a ledge for people to kneel on and pray to an enigmatic medium-sized crucifix that was suspended above.

The first two rows of pews were full: all of the teens from Harry Wallace's class with other teens he'd never seen before, a batch of twenty or so young men wearing baseball caps chatted among themselves, ten or so women with young children huddled together. Patrick stood off to one side. Leyo manned the door, as if to welcome people as they arrived. Agnes, an elder, stood up front with her back to the crucifix and altar. Her face looked stern as she addressed the group in Dakelh. She looked so petite and fragile—a scarf with a colourful paisley pattern over her head, one very wrinkled hand raised in a fist. She must've been older than Monique—and what a contrast. Monique had rejected all the forces of colonialism, including the religion and the language, and here was Agnes, a veritable deacon of the church, who despite all efforts to the contrary, managed to maintain her language while practising this foreign religion.

James listened intently as she spoke. This was his first time hearing the language spoken at any length, and he was once again astonished that it bore no resemblance at all to Cree, though they were neighbouring tribes. Well, of course, it's a Dene language, he reminded himself, and Cree is Algonquian. Dene runs north and south on Turtle Island; Algonquian runs east-west.

Leyo must've noticed the look of intense concentration on James's face—he stepped up, put his arm over James's shoulder and began to translate Agnes's message to the group. "She be sayin' we hafta smarten up… get back ta our roots… our traditional cultures and values. Both those and the teachin's of the priests and nuns go against what's goin' on in our community right how. Should be no violence or threat of violence against each other… our way is peace and carin'… carin' for one another like brothers and sisters, relations, which we all are. Guns are for huntin'—not toys or weapons to terrorize peoples."

"*Hadih,*" James whispered. "Thank you."

Suddenly the door behind James flew open, and mid-sentence, Agnes fell silent, her fist still raised high. Everyone turned to see a haggard X.J. stagger in, one of Art's giant hands firmly grasping his right shoulder. In the other hand, Art held a rifle. The silence of the outdoors penetrated the inside of the building for a few seconds, then the buzz of murmuring voices filled the place.

Art directed X.J. to the front pew, where the two of them took a seat stage left to where Agnes stood. Agnes stepped close in to X.J. and began to scold him in Dakelh. The young man kept his gaze on the floor, and his shoulders slunk lower down with each sentence the elder pronounced. James was impressed by how the crowd listened to Agnes and seemed to take her seriously, the young men and teens in particular. It was good that there was a community response to an incident and dynamic that affected the whole community. James felt sad that religion was in the mix but reminded himself that at least four generations of Chezgh'un had now attended residential schools—the indoctrination was thoroughly entrenched and had undermined their traditional beliefs and governance system.

After Agnes finished and stepped back from the crowd, Art stood and said a few words in Dakelh. Leyo leaned in and whispered in James's ear: "He says his mother, Monique, and the other elders are of one voice with Agnes... we hafta get back to the best of our traditional way... live as one big family... care for each other like brothers and sisters." Art's words brought some sort of closure. All the adults stood and responded to him in near unison, then everyone got up to leave.

"*Hadih*... Sit down," Agnes commanded in a gruff voice. Then she said a few more words, in Dakelh.

Everyone did as ordered, including James. Leyo leaned in and said, "She says since we're all here—she's going ta say mass."

Agnes stepped up onto the stage and then moved behind the altar. James was astonished to see her lean over to kiss it, as he'd seen priests do countless times. James recognized every part of the abbreviated but oddly complete rites Agnes acted out—in particular the *mea culpa* part, which he'd always detested. That part of the mass, Agnes said in Latin—*mea culpa, mea culpa mea maxima culpa.*

James wanted to flee. Painful memories flooded his mind—of being a child and thinking, *my fault, my complete fault. How can any of the hell my family is going through be my fault?* And he thought the same for these people—not a damn thing was their own fault, yet Agnes and all who had attended residential schools were programmed to conclude that all that happened to them, all the bad, was their fault and brought on by their state of iniquity. Three or four generations of locals would have knelt at the edge of the stage where Agnes acted out the theatrics she'd learned in residential school, waiting for the correct moment to tilt back their heads and stick out their tongues in anticipation of the priest placing a thin starchy wafer on it.

This thought conjured for James the voice of the aging priest who'd been stationed in his village for decades—Father Proulx, his tired raspy voice muttering, "*Corpus Christi*" each time he placed a wafer on a waiting tongue. James flushed at the memory of the chant—surprised that it still triggered intense emotions. That this colonial religious rite had been enacted and re-enacted here, in this very spot, so far removed from mainstream society, in a place where people had struggled to maintain their traditional lifestyle and ways since contact with white people, only to be indoctrinated to believe they were hopeless sinners—sinners who needed to confess and take communion in the hope of redeeming their souls—angered him.

He looked at the simple wooden stand on the altar. A basic linen runner covered its centre and hung down the sides. Was there, embedded in this altar, a fleck of bone of one of the apostles of Christ? As had ostensibly been the case with the altar in the church back home, indeed with the altar of every Catholic church around the world. James had always found this idea macabre and inane, but this was the explanation the aging priest had given him when James had asked why the priest, or a visiting bishop, kissed the altar each and every time one of them performed mass.

James waited to see if Agnes would do the rite of communion. She didn't, but she had memorized another part of the Latin mass… *Dominus vobiscum,* to which Art and Leyo muttered, "and also with you," before making the sign of the cross.

Then Agnes addressed X.J. directly in Dakelh. James looked at Leyo questioningly.

"She says the community's gonna send him away—ta detox and rehab... right away. And this should send a message to others... says we're s'posta have a dry community here, and that means drug-free, too."

viii

Louise, Mike and their mostly invisible director of operations, Craig, hosted an annual barbeque for the principals in Vanderhoof the afternoon of the first district-wide pro-D day, on the picturesque riverside grounds of the district offices. The social mixer was the perennial harbinger of a long school year and severe winter, this was clear—the calm before the proverbial storm. James felt insecure about how he would fit in with the group of principals who, with one exception, were all much older and, of course, all white. He reminded himself that in various administrators' meetings, he'd seen one or two friendly faces. He'd seek out those faces and try to get to know them a bit. Plus, Louise and Mike would be there—they were always supportive.

The three novice administrators, James and two vice-principals, were assigned to cook and serve the food to the veteran educational leaders. James was assigned to barbeque and serve chicken wings. He looked short and swarthy next to the new vice-principal of the Vanderhoof high school who manned the corn-on-the-cob station. Youthfulness and their newly acquired career status were all the two men had in common. James wore a plain white apron over his clothes, while the fair man wore a khaki one with blue, red and brown vertical stripes over his red golf shirt and designer jeans. Both men smiled widely, as if competing for the role of Prince Charming in a Cinderella play.

The first hungry person to approach James was a woman in her fifties who wore a string of fake pearls atop a sleeveless emerald green shift. Holding an empty paper plate, she grinned as she approached and said, "The aroma from those wings is delightful. Five-spice powder? I should get the recipe. Are they from your restaurant?"

"I don't own a restaurant. I do like to cook, though." James chuckled, pleasantly amused. He knew where the conversation was going.

"Oh, I just assumed some of the food was from the local Chinese restaurant. So, you're not a chef?"

Just then, a dapper gentleman with wavy salt and pepper hair came up behind her and grasped her elbow. It was Gerard, a principal from Vanderhoof.

"Dear, this is James," the man uttered through gritted teeth posing as a smile. "James is the new principal at Chezgh'un."

"Oh, terribly sorry. How embarrassing. I didn't know they hired a Chinese principal in the district. Interesting."

"Dear, he's not Chinese. He's Indian—originally from Alberta, right James?"

"I'm Cree," James said with a smile and nod. Mistaken identity was not new to him. Since grade school, people had assumed he was Chinese, and he took it as a compliment—after all, it placed him a rung up on the social ladder.

"You look different from the Indians around here, James. You're so clean-cut—and kind of preppy, *ha ha ha*. Well, welcome! You'll have your work cut out for you with the Indians up there in Chezgh'un. Right, love?" The woman turned to give her husband a knowing look. Gerard grimaced as he grasped his wife's arm tighter and steered her to the next station.

James felt a flutter in his chest. It must have been all the laughter he had suppressed during the last few minutes. Oh, the look on Gerard's face as he led his wife away.

Overall, everyone was civil and polite, even jovial. But after lunch, when the women and men separated to visit and chat more comfortably, the men's tone shifted. It was as if he could smell the testosterone levels in the group rising. Before anyone even spoke, James began to feel ill at ease. The dynamic was so very much like what he'd experienced as a youth in Calgary and rural Alberta—cowboy country. He noticed each of the men glancing around, sizing up the others, so he did the same—a quick once-over, subtle but noticeable, deliberate. After this initial posturing, a couple of the men stood a bit taller, another leaned back confidently in a lawn chair, crossing his arms. Two others, who were seated, rested their clasped hands in their laps, as if ready for anything. The party was about to get rough.

The young vice-principal James had chatted with cleared his throat to get the attention of his peers. He'd had a few drams of Scotch, and this was reflected in the smirk on his face—a joke was coming, and James guessed it would involve either racism or misogyny—maybe both. If so, how would he respond?

The young man began to describe a cross-dressing prostitute in Prince George.

"Quite convincing, mind you. And in the dim light, after a few drinks, who would care?"

The men all chuckled, including James. A few glanced around to gauge the reaction of the others—a couple of guys shook their heads.

"In her habitual post in the back alley behind the Grand Hotel one night," he continued. "The heavily made-up, wannabe darling told passersby she had a new offering: the penguin special. After an hour with no takers, one super-eager and inebriated loser offered her twenty bucks. The tranny glared at him with disdain, but reluctantly accepted the lowball offer. She stuffed the guy's twenty into her bra, slowly knelt before him and deftly yanked the dude's pants down to his ankles—underwear and all, but instead of latching onto his throbbing dick, she leapt to her feet, let out a raucous laugh, turned and bolted, leaving the guy flailing in the night air as he shuffled after her yelling, 'Hey—what the fuck? Get back here!'" The new vice-principal clamped his feet together and shifted forward, his hand in the air, index finger and thumb erect—a dumbfounded look on his face.

Everyone guffawed. The man *was* funny—his facial expression and re-enactment were hilarious. He could've been a stand-up comedian. But within seconds, James realized he was clenching his teeth. He glanced around to see if Mike or Craig were there, then remembered he'd seen them sitting off to one side of the grounds, at a table with Louise. He wished at least one of them had been there—he would've felt safer. But then he thought this was childish—what was there to be afraid of? These men were all high-level professionals. He took a deep breath and tried to relax his face, as if meditating. In the future, he wouldn't laugh at jokes like that, but he didn't want to seem like a prude either. He couldn't let on this stupid joke offended him—he had more important things to think about. But the sick macho dynamic of the group was deeply troubling.

He'd witnessed similar things, although not quite as risqué, among his male colleagues in Vancouver, but there he was able to casually step away and join the women in their conversation without anyone really noticing or caring. He took another deep breath, tightened his glutes and calves, then scrunched his toes. He smiled and looked around. He needed to be accepted by these men—couldn't be perceived as a prude or a sissy. After a moment's silence one man proclaimed,

"Musta been a 'skin!"

James gasped. *FUCK... don't go there,* he thought.

"Cocksucker!" exclaimed another man who had been knocking back the Scotch since he arrived. Everyone, except James, roared with laughter.

"Or not!" interjected another, causing a new round of laughter.

When Mike O'Leary stepped into the circle, several men abruptly cleared their throats and put on straight faces.

"What's all the hilarity?" he asked. "James, you see what you're getting into here now, with this group of clowns?" He chuckled and continued, "Guess I should've warned you. Seriously though, they're great guys. Incredibly devoted and skilled. You just gotta get to know 'em."

James straightened his posture. He glanced around the group once more and said, "I'm looking forward to it. Pretty hard to shock me. I'm from Northern Alberta—the bush—and I've lived in cowboy country. I'll keep an eye out though, for that transvestite hooker when I'm in Prince." He paused for effect. With all eyes on him now—everyone wondering what he would say next, he concluded, "She might be a relative."

With that, the group went silent. A few of the men coughed, then made excuses to get up and move around.

James stood to leave too; sure his face was aglow. Who cared what these hypocrites thought of him?—they'd all just lost his respect. He couldn't get out of there soon enough, even though his plan was simply to drive to Prince George to spend the weekend alone in a dreary hotel room. A Native cross-dressing prostitute—what the fuck?

Just as he turned to head for his vehicle, James heard Louise call after him. He breathed a sigh of relief at the sound of her voice, and at the sight of her kind countenance he felt himself relax. He reflected back her toothy smile. Louise had a package in her hands. She held it out to him.

"James—before you go, I have something for you. I know you like to cook. My daughter and I sewed an apron for you. Your monogram is embroidered in the middle of it. "Lovely middle name—*Achakos*. What does it mean?"

"Star. Cree for star. Mom had high hopes," James said with a laugh. He continued. "Thanks, Louise! Thanks so much! I'll cook for you sometime and wear this—at your place as guest chef, or out in Chezgh'un. Sorry to hurry off—I'm meeting up with friends tonight in Prince."

When James got to his car, he opened the package and held up the apron. Sure enough, his initials—*J.A.W.*—were embroidered colourfully beneath the image of a feather.

IV

Takwâkin — Fall

i

As he drove Highway 16, *rumbo a* Prince George, a flash of blue and red lights in the rear-view mirror interrupted his train of thought.

"No! No, no! Damn," he yelled. He pulled over and instinctively pulled his papers out of the glove compartment, rolled down his window and sat waiting. After what seemed like an hour, he saw the tall officer emerge from his patrol car and approach—his hand on his pistol. *Shit. Why's he doing that?* He took his key out of the ignition and put his hands up. It was the same blond guy who'd stopped him before, he was sure.

"Ah, a new, but familiar face. In a rush this evening, are we?"

Sure enough, the nametag read GOSSELIN.

"Not really, just caught up in thought, but I was watching my speed closely."

"Where are you headed?"

"Prince George."

"What's your business there?"

"Got some meetings there this weekend," James said, trying not to let his annoyance come through in his voice. Usually, he would object to this type of inappropriate question, but he was new up north and didn't want to get on this guy's bad side. Better to answer with a partial truth. He handed his papers to the officer.

"Your address here says Vancouver. Whatcha doing up here? Vacation? Scoping the place out?"

"That is my permanent address. I just took a job up here. Not sure how long I'll stay. And what do you mean, 'scoping the place out'?"

"Oh yeah? Well, you were over the speed limit, though just slightly. This time just a warning. You must watch the speed limit signs and obey them. Next time, it'll be the maximum amount." The man's tone was neutral, but his demeanour spoke volumes—the deep voice, the scowl, the intrusive questions he wasn't really allowed to ask.

James looked forward to getting settled for the long weekend in his room at the Holiday Inn, right downtown. He'd brought along his guitar, the books he was reading and his case of cassette tapes. Casual clothes. He had mixed feelings: staying in hotels was still new to him and felt luxurious, and he hoped to enjoy good food and drink. But aside from this evening, when he would be meeting the band's director of education, Colin, who'd been on the selection panel at his job interview, and his wife Ruthie for dinner, most of the weekend would be spent alone in his room—he was looking forward to getting to know the couple better—perhaps they would be strong allies. At the very least, he was sure they would have a unique take on community dynamics in Bilnk'ah and Chezgh'un. All of this had flashed through his mind as he accepted Colin's invitation to dinner at the gas station where they'd bumped into each other in the Fort.

At least he would have company for dinner tonight, but what were the chances of meeting someone to hang out with—someone to be intimate with—in Prince George? Franyo would understand, surely; they were both very sexual beings. What was it about driving that aroused him? Perhaps the result of classical conditioning, a Pavlovian type of response? He recalled riding as a ten-year-old with Garth, his dapper brother-in-law, in a bouncy red pickup. The numerous times the hefty and handsome man had invited him to slide across the bench seat and climb onto his lap, ostensibly to steer the truck as they drove from Canmore to Banff to shop for groceries while James's sister was at work. As a boy James hadn't been conscious in the slightest of being exploited sexually—was completely unaware that Garth was aroused. He'd been too entranced by the scenery along the highway to be aware of anything untoward happening: cascading waterfalls, mountain sheep dotting grottos in the hillside, elk along the roadside and the comforting body warmth of the man who was supposedly teaching him to drive—a white guy. This type of grooming went on for a year or so, but at age eleven James realized there was sexual intent behind the man's touch, when he awoke one night lying face down and uncovered in his bed, and beheld Garth standing at his doorway staring at him. To avoid embarrassment and to see what the guy would do next, James feigned sleep. His brother-in-law sat on his bed beside him—began stroking his behind, slipped his large hand under James's underwear. A probing finger...

When James finally arrived at Prince George, he sat for a moment to allow his arousal to wane before stepping deftly into the dimly lit sports bar and pub of the Holiday Inn. The place was almost empty, so he sat at the bar. At least there he could chat with the bartender or the older white guy who had already settled in. James set his Serengeti sunglasses down beside the paper drink coaster on the counter in front of him. The tanned, fit bartender stepped over briskly, stood directly in front of him and looked him in the eye without saying a word. James hated it when service people did this. With this man, he didn't mind so much for some reason; he returned the gaze and noticed a thick five o'clock shadow. Close-cropped hair in spikes.

"Just a lager if you have one on tap. If not, then a pale ale," James said and smiled.

Without responding, the bartender fetched the drink, set it in front of James and walked off. So much for northern hospitality.

With the first sip, James realized he needed to pee badly.

A few minutes later, he was washing his hands in the men's room when suddenly, the door to the larger stall for wheelchair users opened. There stood the tanned, silent bartender—his imposing penis menacingly splayed across his open palm, commanding James's attention—usurping all rational thought. The man gave James a quick once-over and smiled, but still didn't say a word. James began to tremble. He forced a partial smile and took a deep breath.

As if the man had read his thoughts, with a twitch of his head he beckoned James to join him in the stall. James stood immobile for seconds that felt like minutes. He began to panic. How could he even consider doing anything with this guy—here, in a public place? In spite of his mounting panic, James stepped in and pivoted to find himself staring up into the man's thick auburn goatee and moustache. This was all too familiar: the incredible tension, the excitement and terror of possibly getting caught. The act of resisting, knowing full well he would give in. He'd gone through this daily as a teen, this type of torment, with Garth—would someone walk in, catch them in the act?

The man gripped James's right arm, pulled him in close, shut the door of the stall and locked it. James glanced up into the man's intense brown eyes—now wide open. James raised his hand to grasp the back of the man's powerful neck. Taking this as his cue, the bartender leaned forward to brush his puffy lips against James's cheek then planted them squarely over James's, which were quivering. His tongue began probing James's mouth. The man's breath was sweet, but his mouth tasted of coffee.

Frantically, the man gave James a half-turn then reached around and unfastened his belt, yanked his pants down. He leaned in to nuzzle James's neck. James wondered if the man felt him shudder.

James closed his eyes and collapsed into himself, overcome by the intensity of it all—the sudden caving of his knees, waves of ecstasy that left him gasping for breath. How could this be happening? He'd often fantasized hot sex with a gorgeous muscular man like this bartending hunk, but he hadn't in his wildest dreams thought the conjured intimacy could ever become real—especially here—in the heart of redneck country. James grasped the thick metal grab bar—surely nobody had contemplated its present use.

After five or ten frantic minutes, James's mind-numbing bliss culminated in a volcanic eruption and mutual shudder. The man drew James closer, squeezing him until it hurt, remaining firmly inside the whole time. He lowered his head and bit James's neck—hard. James winced, then let himself swoon.

Gently, but with purpose, the stranger clutched James's shoulders and forced a turn till he and James were face to face, well almost. The stranger was at least six inches taller, and his spiked, military-style crewcut made him look even taller.

Sudden dread in the man's face. He raised his left index finger and pressed it against James's lips. A shuffle of feet outside the cubicle. James went into full alert—eyes wide open, ears in acute listening mode. A security guard. The hotel manager? James fixed his eyes on the beige tiled wall behind his partner in crime as his body stiffened. The headline flashed through his head: LOCAL SCHOOL PRINCIPAL ARRESTED FOR PUBLIC INDECENCY—with a bartender at that. Imagine. And what would the actual charge be? Whatever it was, it would be the end of his career, for sure, and possibly the beginning of an irreversible downward spiral, a fate he'd always dreaded, a fate like his mother's. She had spent years on Edmonton's skid row after breaking up with the truck driver she'd left the family for. Was this the future that awaited James? Personal defeat, perhaps followed by suicide, like his younger brother Trevor? James broke into a sweat.

The odour of bleach and other cleaning products gradually displaced the musky fragrance that had filled the air, making James more lucid. The pounding in his temples became unbearable. He took a deep breath—in an hour or so he would join his prospective new friends Colin and Ruthie for dinner in a classy Japanese restaurant—calm, respected, civilized. He would suppress his angst and remorse to resume the role of a calm, confident, astute and "grounded" professional. When he was Catholic, he would have simply confessed any wrongdoing the following Sunday to receive absolution after saying twenty Hail Marys or some such thing. In his late teens, as a born-again Christian, he would've pleaded directly with the Lord for forgiveness and solemnly undertaken to never commit that sin again. Maybe he would have even rebuked Satan, in the name of Jesus, for tempting him. But now he only had his own logic and personal moral compass to rely on: he'd made a choice and he would have to pay the consequences, whatever those might be.

After hearing the cleaner leave, the bartender put his finger to his lips once again, raised his eyebrows and slipped out of the cubicle. James stood frozen, listening for any movement. Hearing none, he quickly made his exit. He stood tall as he moved along the empty hallway to return to the bar—his mouth suddenly parched. Halfway through his now lukewarm pale ale, he spotted a familiar face in the entryway. Chief Felix had just stepped into the dimly lit bar. A young-looking blond woman stepped in behind him and took his arm. A natural beauty—pretty face, no makeup or fancy hairstyle. A floral blouse and colour-coordinated skirt. James wanted to pretend he didn't see the couple, but it was too late—the chief had spotted him and given a perfunctory nod. James stood to meet the chief's gaze. He stepped over to the couple and extended his hand.

"*Hadih,* James. This is my wife, Sarah."

"So, you're James. I heard about you. You like to play music."

"Pleased to meet you."

"We've gotta go," Felix interrupted, "I just wanted to peek at the hockey scores. We might be back later. Honey, I need to use the washroom—you can see if your friends are at the reception desk. Later, James."

Holy fuck, that was close, James thought. The North is a small world. He'd have to be more prudent. Without making eye contact with the spiky-haired bartender he now perceived in a completely different way, he ordered another pint, which he sipped slowly, occasionally glancing at his nonchalant partner in passion, still incredulous. Only his final glance was mirrored, and oh, the intensity… It said so much: *another time another place, we could've been lovers—thank you.*

James slowly made his way to the restaurant. He had heard that just a few years ago Colin was a school psychologist for a large school district in Southern BC and Ruthie was the head nurse of a pediatric surgical unit in an urban hospital. Such an interesting couple and it was amazing that they'd come to work in the North—James assumed it was because for whatever reason, they, like him, had decided to devote their careers to working with First Nations, and was surprised to learn that they now considered Bilnk'ah their home—indefinitely.

The waitress had just placed a tray with a porcelain bottle of warm sake and three petite matching cups in front of them, when Colin spoke up.

"Big community meeting this Sunday afternoon, James—at the school in Bilnk'ah. Felix Joe is giving his first big speech as elected chief. You should stop by," Colin said with a look that made it clear this was more than a suggestion or casual invitation.

James wasn't sure how to take this. Colin wasn't his boss but was clearly in a position of power with the First Nation. He responded, "Ah sure—be great to hear the chief speak. I'll go."

Colin nodded. "Maybe you should know, James, historically the people of Chezgh'un got a rotten land deal, and the injustice continues."

James sat quiet, trying to maintain a neutral facial expression, even though the topic was one that triggered him, given the way his people had been swindled out of their lands, too, by a government that promised to allocate lands to families as private lands, instead of as Indian reserves, but neither ever happened.

Colin's face got increasingly red as he continued, "The initial land allocations for their reserves were so small, and in the early 1900s a royal commission reduced them even further, based on the logic that, since the Dakelh of Chezgh'un moved about seasonally to fish, hunt and gather, they only needed a land base to live upon—they didn't need vast tracts of land to farm or ranch. However no larger territory was ever defined for the practice of these things. As if that isn't enough of an injustice, now the families in Bilnk'ah are secretly in the process of usurping a couple of their most precious small reserve sites. The oppression continues—but now by their own people. But don't expect the chief to be talking about that this weekend unless it's under the euphemistic rubric of land consolidation."

James didn't know how to respond. Was Colin implying the chief was complicit? He had to be so careful. Was this perhaps a test to see if he would become outraged and vow to try to help avoid another historic injustice against his new friends? He knew it would be hard to resist becoming involved in issues like this, but he had to keep his focus on the school—providing the best possible programming he could—to help the community in that way.

James was relieved when their dinner arrived and the conversation lightened up. Colin focused on the food while Ruthie asked James about his childhood in Northern Alberta and his experience studying and working in Vancouver. James hadn't yet told them about Franyo, but if they had asked about his personal life, he would have.

Over a dessert of *anmitsu* and green tea ice cream, Colin and Ruthie debriefed James about Chief Felix—how he was forcefully taken to attend Catholic residential school as a boy and as a young man stayed away, first to attend college and university, then to establish a law practice in Victoria, BC. Even though he was the hereditary chief, he hadn't lived in the community for over a decade. He returned to the community when the position of elected chief became available and even though most people were glad he'd returned home, predictably, the move had garnered cynicism in some quarters. James squirmed in his seat—this was important information, but he dreaded getting dragged into local gossip. Once he realized that they were going to be discreet, with only mild insinuations he could choose to latch onto and explore, or not, he felt himself relax, and he knew this was reflected in his facial expression.

As they parted ways, each of the satiated trio commented on how pleasant the dinner and visit had been—they'd have to repeat the experience soon and often. James had a warm glow—in part from the sake but also from the notion that had just made two much-needed new friends and allies.

Passing a large parking lot on his way back to the hotel, James observed a man standing beside a three-quarter-ton pickup. What was the man doing? James looked closer and noticed a pool had formed at the base of the man's feet. Wow, this *was* the untamed West! A block farther away, he came up to a dilapidated three-storey building with a large sign above it: THE GEORGE HOTEL. Next door, a rundown Chinese restaurant with a flickering, red neon sign: DINE IN TAKE OUT. A plaque above the entrance to the bar of the George read LADIES AND ESCORTS. James had been warned about this place—the "Indian" bar on the main floor and the upstairs rooms you could rent by the hour—cockroaches.

James's curiosity got the best of him. He'd never been in a country bar like this, so he stepped in, thinking he might have another beer. From the doorway, he looked around, then froze. It was true the place was an *Indian* bar, there were Dakelh people there, men and women—and probably some local Cree folks as well. The patrons didn't look happy *or* friendly. He turned on his heels to leave before anyone perceived and reacted to his presence—challenged him to fight or asked him to join them for a drink (which he knew was code for buy us a round, then another and yet another and to say no would be taken as offensive).

Back in his room at the Holiday Inn, James called Franyo, doing his utmost to keep his voice steady. Franyo sounded morose, and James felt that mood taking over his own psyche too. He had barely fallen asleep when he was awoken by loud voices in the street. James bolted upright and flipped on a light. 1:19 a.m. He stumbled to the window and pulled aside the curtain to see a drunken brawl involving dozens of men and, to his astonishment, a couple of women—fists flying, hair being pulled, even some biting. My God, two men were kicking the head of another man who was on the ground and writhing to and fro. More people staggered out of the bar to join in. For at least a half-hour, the procession continued to stream out of the bar until the street was full. The ruckus got louder—riotous.

"Hit me again, you son of a bitch! C'mon, pussyface!"

"Fuck you!"

"*Astum, hoo 'tup!*"

"*K'leg'ah!*"

"*Scanak!*"

James stood there, naked, concealed behind a curtain, wishing he was somewhere else. Surely the RCMP would come along soon, or bouncers from the bar would intervene. But they didn't. After an hour or so the melee dissipated on its own. James fell into a restless sleep—images of violence he'd witnessed as a child kept coming to the fore of his dreams.

The next morning he awoke in a panic, remembering his encounter with the bartender. This was always the case after anonymous sex: incredible guilt and sober second thoughts about his moments of stolen passion. Stolen for a variety of reasons, not the least of which was the incredible risk involved, including one risk in particular from which folks were dropping dead. He'd studied the stats: the estimate to date was a death rate of ten for every hundred thousand from HIV/AIDS. How long did it take for any sign of HIV to appear? And, what if he and the bartender had been caught?

James stepped outside to a grey sky and cool morning air. Any day now snow would swirl and cover the ground. He would experience the first true northern winter since he'd left the sub arctic region of Alberta twenty years ago. Just how horrendous would it be? How long would it last? Would he have moved from the RV into his new teacher-age before real cold hit? There was a hint of promise—at least they'd cleared, levelled, and built a wooden frame so the concrete slab foundation could be poured—the house would be a decent size.

He hoped the community meeting in Bilnk'ah that afternoon would give him optimism and pull him out of his funk. He was grateful for Colin Baird's suggestion that he attend. He would get to witness an important political event and get to know some of the community dynamics at the same time. At the very least, he'd be surrounded by brown faces for a couple of hours, something he'd sorely missed in Vancouver. He hoped the people there would chat with him even though they wouldn't yet know him.

ii

Parked a few metres from the main entrance to the school, James sat in his Sidekick—suppressing feelings of remorse and jealousy at the sight of the modern school building in Bilnk'ah. He found it impossible to avoid comparing it to the rundown and grossly inadequate school facility in Chezgh'un, with no gymnasium, no home ec room, science lab or library. After observing clusters of community members stream into the school, James took a deep breath and decided to join them. The capacious school gym at the Bilnk'ah Community School was packed with people eagerly awaiting the arrival of Chief Felix Joe, the first top-ranking hereditary chief to also be elected the administrative chief by the community. Like Queen Elizabeth becoming the Prime Minister of England—or the situation with the current King of Thailand. James stood at the back of the room to eavesdrop on nearby conversations.

"Yup—finally we got a chief with a vision."

"Yeah, what he done with the schools is great—got rid of the gor'ment—that Department of Indian Affairs—contracted the school district ta take over. Two new principals and all new teachers—they're real good."

"Felix Joe, him, he's from Chezgh'un, but you'd never know it. He speaks Dakelh perfeck, but ain't black and real wild like them others from over there."

He looked around for Colin and Ruthie and was relieved not to see them. They might've expected him to join them and he didn't know how they were perceived in the community—outsiders—especially white folks working in the band office were likely suspect, and he needed to establish a presence and reputation in his own right.

Wafting through the air were the aromas of bread baking, Labrador tea steeping, coffee brewing and the pungent steam of simmering bear ribs and roasting moose noses. The feast was being prepared by the women of the community—and Fred, the one openly gay person in the community. The local gossip was correct, Fred was flamboyant and funny—everyone seemed to love him. People raved about his classic butter tarts with their deliciously gooey, custardy filling. James wanted to approach the gregarious guy and introduce himself, and maybe lay the groundwork for some kind of future camaraderie. He moved in Fred's general direction to observe him—eavesdrop on the conversation he was having with one person after another, all women, in quick succession. He was feeling a bit giddy about talking to Fred, but quickly realized three things that made him step away: he would have to queue up to talk to Fred; there was no natural pretext for him to introduce himself and, if he did, he would be conspicuous for doing so. Still, James couldn't help but notice how accepting the women were of Fred, at least judging by present dynamics. He noticed no men spoke with him.

Chief Felix stepped through the doorway. He shook hands with community members who had been waiting near the entrance, then strode confidently up to the podium. James scanned the place to see if Felix's white wife was there. He didn't see her. The chief was already practising law. James imagined the chief was a prince of sorts, although his princedom was limited to two villages: Chezgh'un and Bilnk'ah, and a couple of fledging satellite settlements. Just over fifteen hundred subjects in all. Apparently, based on what Ruthie and Colin had told James, Felix Joe had been admired, envied even, by his student peers at university, befriended by academics, anthropologists, linguists, and pursued by women—Indigenous and white alike.

How could anyone handle so much popularity and success without becoming vain? Well, the chief would have to try; humility was an important part of Dakelh culture, and the elders would be watching him.

Recently, Felix Joe had relocated to Bilnk'ah, into the house he'd grown up in, along the shore of Stuart Lake, but his elegant wife would continue to live in their house on Vancouver Island, in the tony Uplands neighbourhood of Victoria, where their two children attended a private school.

Felix opened his speech in Dakelh, and everyone seemed to listen intently, his baritone voice mellow and convincing. After a few minutes, he switched to English, which he spoke with only the slightest Dakelh accent, adding an airy "h" at the end of "o" sounds. Soon the crowd began to grow restless. The chief used jargon and went into some detail on technical points. Felix leaned in closer to the microphone. Someone seemed to turn up the volume. Now, his voice echoed in the large, high-walled gymnasium. James was impressed by how organized his discourse was, especially given that the chief had no speaking notes. Still, James found himself distracted by a group of teens gathered off to one side of the large hall, whispering loudly among themselves and pointing in the chief's direction. A goldenrod buckskin jacket with long fringes caught James's eye. As a teen, James had had one like that, but made of moosehide, and he'd loved it. His mother wore it and went out one night and... well, he didn't want to revisit that now.

After completing his speech, Felix Joe took a moment to soak in the rowdy applause and cheers of the crowd. James wondered if they had really heard anything he had said. Felix's stated goals were so ambitious. In his two-year term, he promised to ensure economic prosperity for all; to reclaim Dakelh Rights and strengthen their culture—including winning back land that had been illegally cut from existing reserves; to initiate pragmatic sovereignty, so that the community would begin to run its own affairs and come out from under the Indian Act—including wresting their multi-million-dollar trust account from the control of the federal government; he would address the housing crisis in both Bilnk'ah and Chezgh'un; improve educational outcomes and post-secondary participation; and last but not least, he would address historic injustices of the Indian residential schools run by the church and government. He would set the band up as a corporation. His motto was: "Our Time Has Come." James was exhausted just thinking about the work required to do all these things. He doubted any chief and council could accomplish even half of what Chief Felix had promised in one term, maybe not even in two, but then what did he know about politics, Native politics at that?

Once the meeting dispersed, most people went to get food and drinks, but the youth stayed put. Gradually, they shifted, en masse, toward Felix. He stepped away from the podium and walked toward them, shook their hands energetically. He basked in their energy and enthusiasm, his face glowing, his smile resolute. He moved through the group methodically until he got to the youth wearing the buckskin jacket. James listened while the introductions took place.

"Nice jacket. I have one just like it—different beadwork, of course. Good to meet you."

"I'm Justa, Celina and Simon's boy."

"*Hadih*, Justa. *T'su in' t'oh*? Nice to meet you," the chief responded, holding onto Justa's hand longer than he had the others. The chief lingered and chatted with Justa as the other youths wandered off to get food.

James looked on as the chief remained in conversation with Justa, hand on his shoulder. James knew he too would've paid special attention to the young man—his self-assurance, youthful exuberance and charisma.

James stood with his briefcase hanging over his shoulder, waiting in line to greet the chief—a pretext to eavesdrop on the rest of the conversation.

"So, you must be almost finished with high school, eh? Whatcha gonna do now?"

"I wanna go ta college or university. Maybe become a lawyer like you."

When the young man's face began to redden, the chief removed his hand from his shoulder and stepped back, but kept his gaze fixed on the young man's face.

"Well, don't be a stranger. Come talk to me about your plans sometime."

Justa could only return the chief's gaze in glances, and after a few of these he simply turned his face downward, blushing intensely. The intense desire James detected in the chief's eyes was unmistakable. He'd known that look as a teen, too—actually as a child. Saw it in his brother-in-law—but he didn't want to let his mind go there. A middle-aged white woman, dressed as if for church, stepped in front of James and extended her hand to the chief and launched into conversation.

As Justa walked away, James stole sideways glances at him—certain that the dashing lad must be struggling to contain a flood of exhilaration, and perhaps confusion, from his interaction with such a powerful man, a Dakelh man at that, the most powerful man in the community, maybe even in all of Northern BC, a lawyer who was fluent in both English and his own language—a cultural icon. The chief oozed power and authority, had the respect and validation of his people and had unshakable confidence in who he was: secure in his standing in his own society and an emerging stature in the mainstream. Justa was obviously smitten by him.

Suddenly the chief was standing right in front of James—his hand extended.

"James, good of ya to come today. Should get somethin' ta eat, it's a long drive to Chezgh'un, no?"

As he took the chief's hand, James nodded and said, "Great speech, Chief. I wish you success." He hoped he'd sounded sincere. The chief turned his back and strode away, leaving James flustered. Why was every interaction with the man unfulfilling—*inachevé*? The chief had dismissed him—just like that—both by what he'd said and by his tone.

At once, James's mood shifted, and he realized he felt a sense of estrangement, even of envy. Not for the sexual chemistry he noticed between the Chief and Justa. It was the whole package, what the two men represented in their own unique ways: unmitigated and unabashed virility, complete groundedness in Dakelh culture, fluency in their language, a clear sense of belonging. James had none of this, had lost it all when his family was torn apart, his community uprooted—and with his father gone since before his birth, he had had few male role models. He was an interloper here up north, a voyeur. His obsession with all things sexual was simply an analgesic, to soothe the profound loneliness and grief he concealed so well—his drug of choice, if you will.

James would have to work hard in Chezgh'un to not become an emotional and cultural parasite. His work would become his obsession—his whole raison d'être, just as it had been when he was a new teacher in Vancouver.

When James stepped outside of the gym, the group of youth were right at the door, almost obstructing it. Instead of saying "excuse me" to get by, James decided to introduce himself as the new principal at Chezgh'un. The teens were polite—in turn they each shook James's hand, smiled and nodded, putting James at ease. Justa was the last to shake his hand as he said, "We heard they hired a Native principal for Chezgh'un—they shoulda put you in the school here."

"I'm looking forward to working in Chezgh'un, but I'll be sure to come here to visit, *mussi,*" James said, and got a shiver.

"Might see you now 'n then. I'll go ta Vancouver next week ta start college," Justa said and nodded his goodbye.

"I'm sure our paths will cross one way or another," James said as he extended his hand to Justa, once again.

iii

Inspired by the vibrant young people he'd met in Bilnk'ah, James was determined to improve registration of adolescent students in Chezgh'un. He knew the kindergarten, primary and intermediate grades would have good registration, based on the scant records he'd found for previous school years, but high school participation rates had been low. The secondary school program had to be one of high interest and relevance if it were to succeed, and they would need a critical mass of at least twenty students for such a program to be viable.

"We have to sign up every last teen," James said to Art and Sally one Monday morning as they sipped coffee in the combined office and staff room. He'd been studying the nominal roll from the previous school year and had seen only one or two students listed who were older than fifteen, yet from his brief time in Chezgh'un, he guessed there were at least twenty more teens who were of school age in the community. "There's no reason they shouldn't all be attending school, especially those under eighteen."

"But James, some of those teens have a criminal record," warned Tara Friesen, who'd come out to offer advice and encouragement to James and his team. "One of the young guys was charged with attempted murder. There are even a couple of young women who've had charges. Lots of B and E's."

James liked Tara's proper British accent, but he was always a bit taken aback by it. How did someone of British descent come to be a specialist in Native education, he wondered? He paused a few seconds before responding, "Everyone deserves a second chance." He paused again to study the woman's reaction, then continued. "We'll keep a close eye on the group dynamics and hire an instructor who has good experience with youth and adults, including those who are challenging and challenged. If a problem arises, the community will know how to deal with it."

James worked with Sally and a few community elders, sussing out names from the band membership list and visiting homes to get enough teen students enrolled to justify the full-time equivalent teaching position Harry had been hired into. James thought they simply should've added the names of all the youth under the age of sixteen, but Sally balked at the idea. But sign them up they did: fourteen-year-olds who had dropped out before starting the eighth grade; sixteen-year-olds, who hadn't attended for a couple of years, and eighteen-year-olds whom everyone had given up on—they'd been good kids, but now they smoked pot, slept around and stole from people—at least, those were the rumours.

"Some of 'em aren' here no more, t'James," said Sally. "Some move ta Prince, and a couple of 'em, girls, we don' know where they're at. Been a coupla years now. Their fam'lies had such a hard time with it."

"You mean they just went missing?"

James saw Sally wince. She went silent and looked down. He knew he'd better not ask many more questions on this topic. Surely with time, he would learn more about the situation and understand how the various families in the community were impacted.

"Kind of... Well, cops didn' wanna file a missing person or put out a missin' notice for the longest time. After they did, jus' a few leads, but that's it."

"And have they kept in touch about the files, like with the families or the chief?"

"When we ask, they say they're cold already. Cold cases 'cause they don' got resources ta keep 'vestigatin'."

James felt himself getting agitated. He took a deep breath and said, "I'll ask about this next time I'm in Vanderhoof," even though he knew full well his query wouldn't result in any new investigative efforts—why would it?

Over the next few days, a number of young and middle-aged adults showed up at the school to ask if they could finish high school. They'd heard there were new adult-ed programs in the Fort and in Bilnk'ah—was there any chance of setting one up in Chezgh'un? James loved the idea, viewed it as an extra challenge.

He had already sketched out the curriculum for the teen program: a week of camping out on the land, learning survival skills, followed by a month of workshops: food preparation, drum-making, canoeing, hairstyling and woodworking. Why couldn't they do the same with the adults, except make it generative—involve students in the design of the learning? During that time, students would keep a personal journal, and once they had gotten used to school again, the academic subjects would kick in: math, English, Dakelh language, local geography, science, art and music. And the teens would run or walk at least two kilometres every day, along with everyone else at the school, including James and the teachers. Now all he needed was the superintendent's approval. Harry was up to the challenge of having a full class and teaching a progressive curriculum.

"What in God's name are you up to, Mr. Ward?" Colin bellowed as soon as he saw James. Colin's cheeks were flaming red and his temples pulsated under his flat, taupe toupee. James was out of breath from rushing to the school after Art pounded on the door of his RV and announced, "Princip'l, they're here ta meet with you—from the band office 'n local college." Colin was seated at the table in the office/staff room—looking imperious. Ruthie sat to his left and the local college program consultant, Kathy Weinberg, to his right. Tara Friesen sat in James's office chair, working on his computer, with her back to the group. She didn't acknowledge James's interlocuters, nor turn to face them, but James was certain she was taking it all in.

The two women looked confounded, and Colin's pupils were tiny black dots, causing James to wonder what type of medication he was on. He motioned for James to take the chair directly across the table from him.

"First you take your teachers to California for professional development before they've even begun to work for you. Then, without asking, you set up a new alternative high school program. And now you're talking about venturing into adult education, which is *my* bailiwick—not yours. Who do you think you are? Now that the school district has taken over the school, the community's expectations are over the top. Bilnk'ah and the Fort are abuzz with gossip about how the school year started with a week at the lake—a freakin' *fish camp*. Mr. Ward, these kids need to learn to read and write. Their parents can teach them their language and culture, hunting and fishing and all that. It's not our business. Those bosses of yours, Mike and Louise, can't they manage you?"

Ruthie and Kathy looked dumbfounded now, and James's breath was short, his eyes wide open, his mind racing. He'd thought Colin was an ally.

Ruthie pulled herself upright. Raising one hand in the air, she said, "Colin, what are you hoping to accomplish here? I simply don't get it." Her face flushed as she continued. "James is a friend, and we're here to support him. You know the school district won't."

"I agree." Kathy jumped in. "I'm here to offer the college's full support. We're eager to assist with the workshops you have planned, James. We certainly have the instructors and the community-based experience to deliver for you. We've even found a local Dakelh hairstylist who's keen to teach the teens basic styling."

James gathered himself to respond. "Colin, most school districts have failed Native students because the curriculum hasn't been relevant—there's tons of research out about this. I grew up learning about a foreign lifestyle, an alien way of thinking for my people, and it hurt me. It was only the music program and the kindness of a few teachers that got me through. If we want these kids and adults to stick with the program, develop in a holistic way, and go on to post-secondary, we have to include their language and culture. The funding mechanisms are there for all of it, and it's the only responsible thing to do—set up a full-service, culturally relevant, community school. It won't come at any additional cost to the band; the funding will come from the Department of Indian Affairs, I assure you." James was on fire. "But of course, I need your cooperation. Sorry, I should've spoken to you as things progressed and included you more in the planning, but it all happened so fast."

"Well James, your boss Mike wonders if you need help out here—getting the school up and running, putting systems in place and managing your budget. He's not sure you're up to the role. You're so young and inexperienced. I'll say it again, these kids need to learn to read and write English—and do math—the three good old r's. Their parents can teach them their culture—not you!"

"Strange, the budget issues originate in the school district offices, not with my staffing decisions. I'll get to the bottom of it all though, no worries. The community, the elders are guiding me, and will give me all the support I need. They're a hundred percent behind the curriculum I've designed. They're tired of losing their kids, their youth, to white ways—assimilation. I'm simply doing what they want. I realize, though, that you're an educator as well and you only want what's best for the students and community—and of course the band should get the proverbial bang for its buck from the school district. The next time we meet, I'd be happy to fill you in on the plan my team and I have come up with—to start gently with core academics, but still cover the required curriculum thoroughly over the course of the school year."

With James's placating statement, Colin's scowl vanished, and his complexion began to return to its natural pale-pink hue. James quietly breathed a sigh of relief. He was shocked by this inexplicable hostility from someone he thought was a new friend. When things seem too good to be true, they usually are. James was certain the real issue had nothing to do with educational principles. He'd poke his nose around carefully, to suss out what was *really* going on with Colin.

Ruthie regarded James tenderly as she spoke. "James, listen, we're having friends over this Saturday for dinner—Gary, a close friend of Colin's will be there. Can you come—maybe spend the night?" She threw a look Colin's way. Colin looked at the floor and said, "Sure, it would be great to have you over, James."

Tara rotated her office chair to face the group. Her face was pale, and her scowl deepened as she scratched her thick, unevenly cut hair. She opened her mouth to speak but reconsidered and rotated back to face the computer. James wondered how much of this conversation would get back to Louise and Mike. Maybe coming to work in Chez-gh'un, alone, was a mistake after all.

iv

Anouk was waiting, slouched on the steps of the school. He wanted to talk, so James stepped over and sat beside the boy, who was almost as tall as him, and much bulkier.

"*Hadih,* Princip'l. Got some problems."

"*Hadih,* Anouk. Nice to see you. What's going on?"

"Some o' them girls, they say I bothered 'em. Tryna get me in trouble."

James knew what he meant by *bothering.* His mother had used that word as a code word for sexual harassment.

"*Hadih,* Anouk. You tell me which girls, and I'll ask them what's going on, okay? And maybe you and I can talk about how you can be around them without having problems of any kind, okay?"

"Won't do no good, Teacher. They jus' wan' me gone from here. Say I should go reform school or place for crazy people."

"Well, we have to try to work things like this out, Anouk. As best we can. Gotta try. We're all here to stay."

"Even you, Princip'l? You here ta stay?"

"*Hadih,* Anouk. Yes, of course. I'm here for the long haul."

James made a point of speaking with Anouk a few times a week—on the steps of the school or inviting him out for a walk. He didn't have training in addictions counselling or expertise dealing with children with fetal alcohol syndrome, so he had to come up with his own way of trying to help Anouk. He knew Anouk had heard lectures about the permanent damage gas sniffing does to the brain. He decided to ask Anouk what happened to him when he sniffed gas—to his mind, his body, his vision. James told the boy about a tribe from Mexico, the Huichol, whose artists used a drug called peyote to bring on visions. They trained themselves to memorize what they saw in those visions as an inspiration for their art. He suggested that Anouk try to do the same thing—if he ever sniffed gas again, that he go to see James as soon as he came down from his high to recount to him exactly what the experience was like. If he could get Anouk to replicate what the Huichol did, maybe it would help to provide a way out of the addiction.

One Sunday afternoon Anouk knocked on the door of James's RV. Upon seeing the hulking teen—eyes glossy and bloodshot—James invited the boy in and sat him at the dining table. James fumbled to find his voice recorder and a notebook. Anouk said he'd sniffed gas the day before, and he wanted to tell James all about it. James listened carefully, taking slow deep breaths, determined to not let the tears that kept forming in his eyes take full shape and leak out.

That evening, sitting alone in the RV, he listened to Anouk's voice and read his notes. He tried to recreate Anouk's experience, in writing—as flash fiction or a short story, in first person, from Anouk's perspective, using all the various snippets the zoned-out boy had spouted, in his words, in his manner of speech. Perhaps he would submit the piece to some journal, a psychology or education journal. At the very least, he would incorporate it into his own personal journal, to forever remember Anouk and the experience of working with him. And maybe, just maybe, reading the text to Anouk would help him realize how these "trips" were messing up his mind.

Anouk

Them girls aroun' my age. They know I like 'em, but they run away anytime I get close, or if there's two or more of 'em 'n other kids too, they make fun o' me—call me names—tease me, Anouk is a dummy... big fat dummy... Loves ta sniff gas, blow it outta his ass... dummy, dummy, dummy.

Went down ta the lake alone, jus' sittin' there when that eagle passed o'erhead a few times then swooped down faster than I efer seen a bird fly—dipped inta the water, then flew up with a king salmon in his claws. Wish I coulda seen him rip it apart, enjoyin' every bite, tearin' it up with his mighty beak. The salmon die anyway, turn a deep red, the female after she drops her eggs over pebbles in shallow water, and the male after he squirts his jergens on 'em.

I still have that rag I soaked with gas last night. Kept it hidden, wrapped in plastic. Jus' once more, then maybe I kin quit. Whoa, the dragon's breath rips into my chest, never fails. I fly outta my body like I done before, go straight up, high above the land 'n trees, up and over, above the lake. I see a thousand fish mouths, puckerin', some tiny, some huge. Shark's teeth and tongues of different colours jutting out of 'em.

I flip over, go into a nosedive. Stretch my hands in front of me. I level off a couple o' feet above the lake, fish mouths poppin' open 'n closin' so fast. Snappin' turtles too. Then, the mouths disappear 'n the water's smooth, grey like steel, and inviting, but I don' fly into it, even though I could. I soar over ta the edge of the forest. On the shore, a tall woman with flowing blond hair and a racka moose antlers stickin' out o' her head waves at me, all excited like. The tips of her antlers are shiny black arrowheads. Her eyes bulge outta their sockets, aqua blue pool balls, red dots for pupils. She knows me—her—'n I seen her somewhere too. I wanna fly over ta her, but I can't. Can't even stop or slow down. Whoa, I'm flying toward a huge maple tree. Hadih, its leaves are bats, they're deep violet, hanging by their shiny black claws. They spread their wings and sway in the breeze.

Beneath the maple tree a giant beaver is restin' on its hind legs. Its spongy nose quivers as it sniffs the air. Long black whiskers stick out in every direction. Bulgin' yellow eyes. Its body's covered with sharp spikes. Porcupine quills long as arrows. Four long fangs. Far away, along the creek, the biggest beaver dam ever, and jus' past it, a large pond. Beaver dives, ripples on the water. He come up for air, I like his blue fur. Wide flat tail slaps on the water, the loud claps echo through the forest and deep into my head. Other creatures show up.

There's otter—ever sleek, and fat! It scurries over a fallen log, dips its head into the water and pulls out a frog with two heads, eight eyes. Frog kicks its hind legs against otter ta free itself. Thick yellow blood oozin' into the water. At the end of the forest, two muleys with giant red antlers stop their battle and look over—must be a female nearby. Behind them the tallest and hairiest man I have ever seen. He pushes his way past them. He's chargin' toward me. With each step closer, his hair falls away, leaves jus' dark brown skin.

The hairless, brown-skinned man yells as he charges toward me "ANOUK. Anouk. DAMN. Ya bin sniffin' again. Yer yellin', moanin 'n flailin' your arms like a lunatic." He yanks me to my feet and drags me toward a huge shack with orange smoke billowing out of its roof.

"Hadih, Anouk! You stay here till you come out of yer high. Don't you dare move from here. Ya hear me?"

The next day, James asked Anouk to stay behind after school. After making sure everyone had left, James broke his own rule and asked Anouk to come into his office, alone. He read the story aloud to Anouk and watched him react. Now and then Anouk raised his eyebrows, dropped his jaw, gasped or sighed. When James finished, Anouk's first response was silent tears.

"Can't belief you could write all that, Princip'l—was so hard ta hear it."

James had to blink back tears, too, and this became even harder after Anouk said, "It be so scary, Teacher, each time I sniff gaz. Everything so real! At leas' it gets me outta this place for a lidle while. Kin forget my problems."

V

Kaskatino Pisim — Freeze Up

i

When James arrived at Colin and Ruthie's place, Colin greeted James warmly, then introduced him to Gary, a clean-cut thirty-something educational consultant. After a quick handshake, Gary offered James a sample of what he was drinking—a boilermaker, beer spiked with whisky. James declined. Colin put on a Neil Diamond album, and soon Colin and James were smiling and laughing while singing along to "Sweet Caroline" and "Song Sung Blue." At one point, when Colin left to help Ruthie in the kitchen, Gary leaned over to James, as if to share a secret, and pulled a thick wallet out of his pocket. He flung a wad of brown hundred-dollar bills on the coffee table.

"See this here? Colin gave me a great contract. A few hundred bucks a day. Contract to set up their adult-ed program in partnership with the college instead of the school district. I'm the instructor too. It's a great gig, and it may become permanent. I was supposed to do this in Chezgh'un, too—you beat us to it!"

Although Gary was obviously drunk, James now understood why Colin had been so angry at him for setting up an adult-education program in Chezgh'un. Done in partnership with the local college, it was a money-maker for him and his friend—and James had stolen the opportunity away from them.

In the course of the evening, the four of them quaffed a few bottles of French Bordeaux. Ruthie had pan-seared filet mignon, medium rare, with her famous potatoes—roasted in olive oil and garlic—and put together a crisp green salad. Ruby port with apple strudel and vanilla ice cream.

The moment they stepped into the guest room they were to share for the night, Gary pulled James into his arms, kissed his neck and nuzzled his ear. James was pleasantly surprised—not really turned on—but intrigued by this come-on from a new acquaintance who wasn't unattractive—maybe they would have an ongoing fling. They ended up on the bed together, clothed, with Gary on top, writhing.

James was reluctant to have sex in Colin and Ruthie's house but managed to convince himself that his hosts weren't prudes—they wouldn't care. After all, they'd put the two men in the same room for the night. After a few moments of clothed contact, Gary rolled off James, onto his back. He unzipped his pants—grabbed James's head and pushed it downward to his rigid, circumcised penis. Just as James's lips touched down, Gary rolled onto his side and pulled back. "Fuck, wait. I can't do this, man. I'm not gay. I'm drunk. I'll go sleep on the couch."

The next morning, when James awoke, Gary was gone, along with his half-empty bottle of whisky and the wad of money he'd tossed onto the coffee table.

Over a full breakfast, Ruthie asked James, "Did you sleep okay, my friend? I see you're an early riser, like me. Colin sleeps in whenever he can."

"Just got up 'cause you're here," Colin mumbled.

"Yes, fine. The booze helped," James answered.

"Oh, I thought Gary might've chewed your ear off. He can really be something. He was the apple of Colin's eye. I think Colin lives vicariously through him."

Colin's only response was a blank stare, directed at Ruthie. James was beginning to feel uncomfortable. He was tempted to probe this a bit, but decided not to. This probably had something to do with their marriage, perhaps would even explain about why they moved up north. Things he didn't really want to delve into.

Ruthie looked James in the eye, smiled, then continued, "James, do you have a partner in Vancouver?"

Such a nice way of asking, James mused. This was normal, like in Vancouver.

"Yes, I do. His name is Franyo."

"Oh," she said. "You must miss him so much."

"Yes, you must." Colin added as he turned to James and smiled. "On another note, we're planning to break ground on your teacherage next month, and on the school in early November."

"Ah, that's good to know. I hope it works out. Sure be nice to get settled in. How is *your* work going, Colin? How is it working for Chief Felix?"

"Oh, uh, it's fine. You know, he wants change—and wants it now. He's hired a new accountant, and they're changing the whole financial management system. They're going to tighten up everything—proper signing authorities, updated policies on conflict of interest—*all* that good stuff."

Colin swirled the last of his coffee in its cup, drank it and stood as he announced, "I've got some stuff to do at the office. Good visit, James, thanks for coming."

Colin gave Ruthie a quick nod and left through the kitchen door.

James drank the last of his coffee and prepared to leave too—his bags already at the door—when someone rang the doorbell. Ruthie peeked out the window. "Oh, it's Damien and the new teacher, Ali." For James's benefit, she added, "They're working closely together on the junior-high program. Colin also manages the teacherages," Ruthie said with a surprise smirk. "So, we're getting to know some of the teachers really well—meet Damien, quite needy—while Ali, here, is just the opposite."

She opened the door and ushered the men in. "Damien, Ali, come in and meet James. James is the principal of the school over in Chezgh'un."

Damien's youthful complexion looked very fair and smooth beside Ali's thick black stubble and olive complexion. Ali, taller than both Damien and James by a few inches, burst into a broad smile as his hand darted out toward James. "James—so great to meet you! I've heard so much about you."

James extended his hand, pleasantly surprised by the man's enthusiasm. Who would've spoken to Ali about him and what might they have said?

As though reading James's mind, Ali explained. "Louise Bernard interviewed me by phone last week. She thought I might be a good fit for your school. Couldn't say enough good things about you! But the principal here in Bilnk'ah grabbed me. Thought I could teach advanced math and science—"

Before Ali finished his sentence, Damien took a step toward James and said, "Yes, I saw you introduced at the all-staff. There was a buzz afterward about this radical young principal hired for Chezgh'un. District's pretty proud they hired you. Some of us felt intimidated even."

Damien's words left James speechless and feeling somewhat guilty. He recalled seeing Damien at the all-staff—sizing him up when he thought no one was looking, his strong wide back, thick biceps and boyish smile. He'd even overheard some of the man's witty banter with others around him. For sure, Damien was attractive and articulate, yet something was *off*. James couldn't quite put his finger on it, not then and not now, but he was willing to set the feeling aside for the time being.

"I saw a guitar in your vehicle, James. What kind of music do you play?" Damien asked with a disarming smile, an earnest gaze.

Ruthie interjected, "I have to head out—Colin is expecting me to help him out at the band office this afternoon. The three of you can hang out and chat if you want to. I'll be back in an hour or so."

"Just wanted to say hello, and I gotta get home," Ali said. "Lots of prep to do. But James, let's get together next time you're around, okay? Could make you some Turkish food—Ruthie says you're a bit of a gourmet." Then he raised his hand to indicate the direction and continued, "My house is just across the way there on the edge of town."

"For sure, Ali. That would be great," James said. "But Damien, I'd love to chat with you a bit before I go—if you're not in a hurry." He blushed at his own boldness.

The two spoke for a half-hour or so. James learned that Damien's mother was from Spain and that Damien had lived there as a child—so he and James carried on in Spanish for a few minutes. They exchanged lists of songs that each of them knew. Finally, Damien had a suggestion: "*Oyes, podemos pasar por mi casa un rato.* We can sing a couple of tunes—ya got time?" James quickly piled his bags into his Sidekick and offered Damien a ride to his house.

James was astonished at the teacherage Damien occupied, the size of it: likely three bedrooms, a full basement and large deck—recently refurbished. Once again, he was forced to swallow a flash of resentment after the quick involuntary comparison with his accommodations.

Damien opened with "The Boxer," a Simon and Garfunkel song James knew well—the lyrics about being a poor boy were so apropos, and he knew the harmony—a major third above Damien's slightly deeper tenor voice, much like the blend in the original version. James was dazzled by Damien's nimble fingers on the guitar frets—he himself had played for years but hadn't managed to reach that level of proficiency or refined style, a blend of strummed chords and a picking out of the melody. When they finished, they gawked at each other in disbelief.

Then Damien pulled his chair closer to James's, until the *v* of his hefty thighs engulfed one of James's equally muscular legs. James's face flushed—his instinct was to pull his chair back, but he didn't.

Damien tucked his guitar into his abdomen and leaned forward until his face was about a foot away from James's. He launched into another Simon and Garfunkel song, "America." James got a shiver. If Damien had spoken rather than sung the lines about becoming lovers and eloping, it clearly would have been a come-on. Damien locked his gaze onto James's—a look so intense it was the most powerful seduction the young principal had ever experienced. A mesmerizing warmth came over him—he let it engulf him. He was in bliss—yet sensed danger. There was something about this guy—compelling charm along with good looks, and a devil-may-care attitude—enticing fearlessness—the exact opposite of James's cautious and tentative approach to life. The lyrics replayed, in James's head, *let us be lovers... we'll marry our fortunes...* as he stood and pulled his chair back. He passed the guitar to James. "Your turn."

James fingerpicked the guitar and crooned Gordon Lightfoot's song, "Beautiful." He gazed into Damien's eyes as he began the song, but then had to look away to focus on his playing and singing—and to keep his voice steady.

"Wow, that was fuckin' awesome man. We'll have to do more," said Damien.

James smiled and said, "Well, I'd better get going. Long drive home, and I see it's starting to snow."

"Next weekend—come over. Saturday, we can jam the whole day. *Mi novia*, Sylviana, won't arrive for another month, with her two kids, so we have the place to ourselves. You should stay over."

"That just might work."

James was bursting with both elation and terror as he trod to his Sidekick on the freshly fallen snow, which was now gradually taking over the landscape. He enumerated all the common interests he and Damien shared: speaking Spanish, music—playing guitar and singing, hunting—birds and big game. *Literature*. James had been dazzled by the collection of books in the makeshift shelves in Damien's guest room—books by authors like Jane Austen, D.H. Lawrence, Joseph

Conrad, Dostoevsky, Chekhov, Blake, Voltaire... He couldn't help but reflect on the common interests he and Franyo shared, just three really: good food, listening to music and relaxing at home. And, of course—sex. Hot, passionate and frequent sex.

James didn't know what to make of the comment about Damien's "girlfriend" and her two kids, and didn't want to be too inquisitive with a new acquaintance. He'd learn what he needed to know in good time. For now, the important thing was that it was clear Damien had a strong attraction to him—where it might lead was another question.

On his way out of Bilnk'ah, James spied the house he guessed was Ali's. He decided to stop in for a quick visit, to calm down a bit and also to see if he could glean any information from Ali about how things were going in the school in Bilnk'ah—if they were doing anything particularly innovative that he should consider replicating at Chezgh'un. People from the two communities were definitely comparing notes on how new activities and programming were unfolding in the two schools.

Damien had been cynical in response to James's questions about the Bilnk'ah school, saying it was a mess—the teachers were unhappy with their class assignments, the students equally discontent with their assigned teachers. And James was sure the situation couldn't be that bad so early in the school year—it would be good to hear another teacher's perspective.

Ali was pleased to see James. He offered him a cup of tea and a piece of Turkish delight. The two men chatted about their lives. Ali had studied in the US, had his master's degree in economics and had won a scholarship to do a PhD in post modern educational psychology, yet the BC College of Teachers had still insisted he take a senior level math course to become certified. James talked about his experience teaching French immersion in Vancouver, at which point the two educators switched to French and carried on the conversation that way—each very pleased at this newfound connection.

"The elders of Bilnk'ah are all abuzz about you, James," Ali told him in French. "A Native principal. They wish you'd been hired for their school. Apparently, there was quite a battle in the decision-making about which school you would be assigned to. I have coffee every Saturday morning with a group of elders, mostly men. You should come—meet them one weekend."

Ali had a calming effect on James. He seemed to be able to put everything into perspective. Most of all, though, it was clear from the get-go, Ali had James's back, to whatever extent that might be necessary.

ii

Struggling to hold back the tears, Sally hastily brushed her carbon-black hair, pulled it back into the usual ponytail and stretched a thin red elastic band over it. It was two years ago today that her daughter, Victoria, went missing, and each week of those tortuous years, she'd spent hours in front of the little shrine in the centre of her living room—disconsolate. Her weeping gradually shifted to meditation—hoping for a vision of where Victoria might be found, and in what state.

Initially the shrine had been a photo and a tea light candle, but it had since expanded. Art and Victoria's brothers added to it from time to time, as did Sally: now a wild tiger lily, now an agate from the lakeshore, now a morsel of candy cane. Once a week Sally would remove it all so they could refresh it with new tokens of love. When the new principal had stopped by, she noticed him studying the shrine with curiosity, but she didn't want to say anything to him about it—not yet. People always had so many questions, and with the best of intentions, they tried to explore new angles on the disquieting disappearance—little did they know each question was like another dagger into her heart.

The aroma and gurgling of percolating coffee helped to calm her and focus her thoughts. As she listened for the gurgling to slow, still in front of the mirror, she took stock of the white hair that had begun to appear within the last year. She washed her face and stepped over to the stove, which sat unevenly along the north wall of the unadorned shack that had been home for the twenty-five years she had been married to Art. In a while, she would fry thinly sliced, frozen moose meat and eggs sunny side up and serve them with beans and warm bannock—Art's favourite breakfast. They'd had their challenges in the time they'd been married, but she still loved to cook for Art, and he loved being able to provide her favourite foods in abundance:

moose nose, bear grease and ribs, sockeye, steelhead, different kinds of grouse, wood duck.

Victoria was Sally's only girl and that made her absence even more painful. Her boys were kind and considerate. She'd raised them to be close, close to her and Art, and to each other. Historically, that was the Dakelh way: family bonds were crucial to survival and happiness. Many others in the community didn't raise their kids like that, and didn't show that kind of affection for their siblings, cousins or even for their parents—but Sally understood why. Four generations of Chezgh'un children had been taken away from their parents from an early age—to residential schools—where they stayed for at least ten months of each year. The chain of affection and caring had been disrupted and eroded, along with the language and culture. She knew she was lucky. She'd only gone to Lejac Residential School for one year—ten long months.

When she returned home that June, her grandparents took her to live with them in a remote area that was only accessible by boat or float plane and in the winter months by dogsled or skidoo. Neither police nor Indian agents ever ventured that far—she would be safe there. Sally's grandmother had been strict but caring—had doted on Sally and taught her the traditional ways. Her grandfather was sometimes overly protective, but it was his way of showing his adoration. They only spoke Dakelh.

Clayton and Merle, her two youngest, were in the primary class and they loved their teacher, Debbie. They'd frolic through the front door soon, hungry as wolves, likely singing one of the songs they learned from that new principal. Even though the songs were in English, Sally loved how the carefree melodies they sang brightened the place. Her oldest boy, Bid'ah, aka Kenny, had had his struggles too, but was now working steady and helping to support the family.

Sally romanticized the traditional lifestyle her ancestors had had and wanted to replicate it, to the extent she could, with a few select modern conveniences added in. Like every house on the reserve, their house had a fridge and stove, a radio, VCR and TV hooked up to an aging satellite dish that had been vandalized several times and now only provided a signal about half of the time. But there was no couch, easy chair or dining room set. There were a few log rounds Art had cut to size, with cushions on top of them and more cushions strewn around for the kids to grab and sit in a circle on the floor to eat together, or to lounge while they watched TV or listened to Art or Sally tell stories in the evenings, in Dakelh.

Sally absently ran a finger along the long scar on her cheek, in front of her right ear. That was from her last fight with Art, about ten years ago, before their youngest was born. Well, it wasn't really a fight. Art was drunk and beat her like he used to do, till the time she left him for a week, took their six kids with her to her sister's place in their home village, near Fort St. Pierre. She farmed the kids out to various aunts and uncles. Except Kenny. He wouldn't leave her side in those days. He constantly nagged her to take them home, back to their father. The other kids loved the experience, and it gave her a chance to pull herself together, to decide what to do next, where to go. Art showed up one day in a new truck—showed her his freshly printed AA membership card and promised he would never touch another drop of alcohol. What could she say? That was exactly what she had prayed for.

She sat on the plank Art had suspended over two logs, her cup of steaming coffee in hand, and let her mind wander some more. She treasured this time—fifteen minutes, or a half-hour, every morning all to herself—her only time alone, all day. She conjured the face of the new principal and smiled. He was sweet to everyone, and serious about his work, yet he liked to make people laugh. She remembered how relieved she was when the school district sent a letter to her and Art saying James wanted to work with them, and sure enough, he constantly asked their advice and opinion on the school's operation. She smiled as she recalled the first weeks of classes. She let out a slight laugh as she recalled the first morning of school after the fish camp.

Art had elbowed her in bed, and barked: "*What in the hell, woman? What's that racket? Sounds like we're in an army camp or somethin'.*"

Ta ta ta-da-da ta ta ta-da-da ta ta ta-da-da ta taa-daa resounded in the fall air a few more times.

"*Geezuz, that's re-va-lee,*" Art had said. He had thrown on some clothes, dashed out to the truck, determined to find the sound—see what was going on. If it wasn't one thing, it was another. He found the principal standing on the front steps of the school, cheeks puffed out, blowing into a trumpet. It was 8:45 a.m. and he was alone at the school.

But not everyone in the village liked James. Sally's and Art's enemies had become his enemies, and they would hate him even worse when word got around that not only did he keep the two of them on staff, he gave them proper job descriptions, titles and each a big raise—they would earn the same wages as the TAs for the school district in the Fort or in Vanderhoof. People are asking around how much money he makes—is it six figures, and what about those new teachers—how much do they earn?—they say the community could make better use of that money.

Agnes too was working hard to get rid of him—*he's anti-Catholic, he's a sinner and he ain't given nothin' to the church,* she'd said, when lobbying other elders to join in her efforts. Margaret was Agnes's eyes and ears in the community. But Monique protected the new principal—and her support eclipsed Agnes's undermining.

And there were even rumours that the principal in Bilnk'ah was trying to get James fired—so he could take charge of Portage School, too. Get a big raise. Making up stories to prove James couldn't manage the school in Chezgh'un right.

James wanted to help the people of Chezgh'un, that was clear, but there was so much he didn't know—could never know—about the longstanding spiritual warfare between different factions of the community and between the villagers of Chezgh'un and Bilnk'ah.

Getting the school up and running successfully with new teen and adult classes was one thing, but assuring his own survival was another. She and Art would do what they could to support him—to keep him in the community as long as possible.

iii

Bella

The cloud of dust rolled closer and closer, until it was near enough for the group who stood on the steps of the schoolhouse to make out a low-suspension blue and silver pickup at the heart of it. The truck skidded into the gravel driveway in front of the schoolhouse, creating a new cloud of dust. James was getting used to having the gritty powder stuck to the surface of his teeth, but he still hated it. Who wouldn't? Shallow breaths until it died down. Darn, his eyes had started to water—dust particles under his contact lenses.

A young woman with an olive complexion and shoulder-length, wavy auburn hair stepped out of the driver's side onto the pebbles, regarded the welcoming committee and flashed a broad smile. "Hello there. I'm Bella," she chirped. "The new teacher." Bella's smile shone. She rushed over to shake James's hand.

"You must be James, the principal. Nice to meet you," she said, and laughed some more. Before James could respond, she went on. "It was quite the drive here from Bella Coola, but I made it. I'm really looking forward to setting up the adult-education program. You know, in my community, they set one up through the college, and it's a disaster." She smiled silently, then released a boisterous and intoxicating laugh.

James smiled back and shook her hand again. "Welcome, Bella. You'll be working with good people. It'll be great to get the adult program ramped up. Better late than never."

The new teacher stood opposite James, smiling and nodding emphatically.

James chuckled, in spite of himself. He wanted to set a professional tone with this woman—but she was so disarming. For a moment, his smile reflected Bella's, but it collapsed when he caught a glimpse of three local men standing on the steps of the mobile home—the teacherage, across the way—who were clearly leering at Bella's denim-clad backside. One of the men put his fingers to his mouth, as if to do a wolf whistle, but didn't go through with it. The other two elbowed him and laughed out loud—a sinister look on their faces. Was Bella single? Would she know how to handle guys like these? She would be sharing the largest mobile home with the intermediate teacher, Loretta, and her cousin, Angie, who James had recently hired as the new school secretary. So she would be safe there at least.

Once word got around the community about the arrival of the hip and fetching adult-education instructor—a Nuxalk woman from Bella Coola—the class filled up in no time. Young and middle-aged men and women, and even a few elders, flocked to the school to catch a glimpse of Bella and sign up. For the elders, Bella set up a part-time, afternoon and evening self-study program. She began with an introduction to computers in the new lab James had set up in the basement, so that the adults, including the elders, could work on literacy development and math skills. She even made house calls to elders to follow up on their progress.

One day, after a few weeks of doing these visits, she came into James's office with a mischievous smile. She sat down, leaned close and whispered, "You wouldn't believe what all is going in this village." She whispered even lower. "Some of these elders are foolin' around—with other elders, you know—*having affairs*. In this tiny community." She let loose her loud trademark laugh, which had already become well known in the school. "Those grannies and grandpas are getting more action than we are for God's sake, James."

James squirmed in his chair. What did Bella know about *his* sex life? She was open and direct from the get-go—would she ask him about it? He was often aroused in her presence, and this confused him. Was it the fragrance of her shampoo, her gentle body odour blended with residual cigarette smoke, which reminded him of the smell of his mother and aunties when he was growing up? Or was it her charmed presence, the bubbly personality, hypnotic smile and gaze, the caring touch? Whatever it was, it got to him, and many days he rushed home at recess to masturbate—conjuring images of Franyo or Damien for instant arousal and gratification. As he rushed back to the school he wondered if he and Damien would ever have sex, although it was almost a *fait accompli*. When would he next have relief?

One afternoon Bella stepped into James's office, a look of consternation on her face. "Did you know about Sally and Art's daughter, Victoria? She's been missing for two years already!"

"Yes, I've seen the shrine. Victoria went to Prince one weekend to visit an aunt... and shop... She never came back. Sally doesn't talk about it, but Art told me. It was so hard on him. She was his princess."

"I've been contemplating what we could do to address this—healing from loss of a loved one and from personal trauma—as a class project. I found a series of training workshops, designed and delivered by Native professionals, to equip individuals from communities to pass on new knowledge and therapies to help others to move through their own healing process—establish a community of practice."

"I'm sure I can access funding to do something like this, given we don't have a counsellor or social worker on staff."

The adult students chose Leyo and Marlene, and three other couples, and sent them for training in Williams Lake. After the first session, the four couples came back on fire with insight, telling James and Bella, one after the other, about the various eureka moments they'd each had during the course:

"No wonder our mom didn't show us any 'ffection... She was raised by nuns in a residential school for ten years... And her mom, my granny, was raised by nuns for five years. Never got over their trauma—no caring or affection showed by them toward us kids!"

"My dad used ta cry tellin' us how he and his brothers were taken on different nights, from their beds—ta go ta the dorm supervisor's room, where they were molested. The man didn't think the brothers would tell each other what happened. At the time, they tol' *each other*, but no adults. I didn' have the heart ta tell him the same thing happen ta me, in Lejac."

"Tore my heart out ta realize I never held my liddle girls the way most moms do. Mom never held me as a chil', and now I realize why."

"Our natural and cultural way of raisin' kids was completely broken up in four generations of residential school ..."

"Vict'ms of abuse at the residential schools came home, as older teenagers, with all kinds of psychological problems—the victims themselves became abusers. Couldn't help themselves it seems. Their addiction ta sex and bad type of touchin' was set up in those schools. Like, you know, when a person is abused sexually, daily, well, like with anythin', you get dependent on the high from the physical sensations—even tho' ya never 'cepted it or got used ta it, or wanted it..."

"It's habit forming for sure," James said, staring at the floor, breathing deeply to contain the powerful emotions the adults' comments stirred in him.

Then, James moved around the irregular circle, looked each of the adults in the eye and offered a warm handshake.

iv

One weekend, Bella took a few of her adult students to an addictions workshop in Kamloops—a course on prevention as well as on stemming existing addictions. Bella's brand-new truck could only accommodate two passengers, while James's Sidekick could accommodate four, if three squeezed into the back seat. So, James drove Bella's beautiful new truck to Bilnk'ah, to visit and jam with Damien, have early morning coffee with Ali and a group of Bilnk'ah elders, and later, another nice dinner with Colin and Ruthie.

Saturday morning was beautiful and bright. The country soundscape of chirping, singing and trilling birds and the occasional bass drone of a raven—the synesthesia of all this and the stunning view of the nearby lake and distant mountains and foothills, and the wonder of having intriguing conversation with the gorgeous and smart man next to him—energized James. He struggled to not be too effusive in his glee as they set out for a day of off-roading with him at the wheel and Damien as navigator.

"Nothing too wild now, my man," James said as they turned off the highway onto a logging road.

"Oh, the ground is solid here, plus Bella's truck is powerful—with that motor and its four-by-four function—it'll get us through anything."

"Maybe, but I still don't want to get it all mudded up..."

James got through the first two mud puddles easily, but the third one looked vast—it took up the entire width of the logging road and there was no way to know how deep it might be.

James braked slightly, thinking he might turn around.

"Whatcha doin'? Gun it! Don't slow down going into a bog."

James did... and the water swooshed up both sides of the vehicle—for a couple of metres. Rapid forward momentum was followed by a dull thud as the vehicle came to a stop and the two men lurched forward.

"Put it in reverse—then give 'er."

The engine revved, but the truck only budged an inch or so each time they shifted into second gear then reverse—an inch forward, an inch back.

After ten minutes or so, the two men lowered themselves into the murky, coffee-coloured puddle, which went halfway up their calves.

"Fuck… now we're going to have to try a few tricks to get ourselves outta this mess!"

"I don't want to wreck Bella's truck. And it's filthy!"

"These things are built for this—you're just helping to break it in."

"Great… and how will Bella feel about that?"

"I'm sure she'll be cool. Woulda happened sooner or later up here anyway…"

Thwack… a blob of mud hit James on the chest and splashed up onto his face.

"What the hell?"

"Gotcha… might as well have some fun before we hafta walk back to the main road," Damien said and guffawed.

"You're fucking crazy!" James said as he stooped down and grabbed a handful of mud. Damien must've thought he wouldn't toss it—he just stood there with a smirk—but James did and got Damien squarely in the face.

"You *did* it… didn't think you had the balls. Now you're really in for it!" Damien said as he scooped up more mud—but just as he was about to toss it—another mudball hit the top of his head. When he stood up straight, the mud drooled down his forehead and over his angular nose.

"Okay, wait there… stay still… This is so good—I have to get a photo," James said. He wiped his hands on his jeans, then carefully took his new 35mm camera out of its case and snapped a picture. "This is blackmail material, my man. *Ha ha ha*."

As the two men walked the five kilometres through the woods, swatting blackflies, horseflies and mosquitos from their faces and arms, they talked about their days at university. They'd both studied at UBC. And James learned that Damien had aced calculus and physics. When James had asked him why he didn't pursue a more illustrious career, Damien simply said, "That's not me—being a doctor, engineer or lawyer. That corporate and bourgeois world isn't for me. I wanna move to Costa Rica—open an orphanage."

"What? You wanna be a male Mother Teresa? *Ha ha ha!*"

"You could say that... Ah, there were complications in my personal life, too. Then... I was married to a lawyer, but left her for Sylviana—a huge scandal."

"But this kind of thing happens all the time."

"Ah well," Damien said and coughed, "Sylviana is my first cousin. She was married too—also to a lawyer."

"Geez Damien, even my people know better than to get involved with a first cousin. What were you thinking?"

"It was such a powerful attraction, James—like I'd never felt before. Something like what I feel for you—if you were a woman, I'd fuck you."

James was speechless. Was that some kind of twisted challenge—hope and defeat meted out in equal quantities—one designed to stifle the other?

The next Monday, Bella and James sat in the staff room to debrief on their respective weekend experiences. James sheepishly explained to Bella how he and Damien had gotten her shiny new vehicle stuck in a mud bog. They'd had to hire a skidder from a local forestry company to tow it out, then get the vehicle cleaned and detailed in Prince George Sunday afternoon. Bella took it all in stride, laughed it off and said, "Well, thanks for breaking it in, bud. And thanks for letting me use your Sidekick."

James nodded with relief and smiled.

"Oh James, there was some powerful physical attraction going on among our students and people from other places. And I met a sweet guy, but the counsellors had warned us to not get involved, to avoid romance or sex for the entire weekend, so we could focus on our addictions issues or learning about how to help others—as in my case."

Bella's face took on a longing look. James had to cheer her up.

"There's a song about that you know, about resisting temptation."

"Really—a *song*?" Bella shook her head, puzzled.

"Yes." James broke into Freddy Fender's "Wasted Days and Wasted Nights."

He and Bella burst into boisterous laughter, staring into each other's eyes. "Good one," Bella said loudly as she reached over and touched his hand. James was surprised at the instant tingling sensation he felt, head to toe, at Bella's touch and look. He guessed it was the combination of her smell, her touch and her sultry voice—her look—that had this effect on him. He was tempted to reach over and brush her long silky hair away from her face.

After Bella left his office, James wondered whether he should have gone to that workshop, to deal his own addiction—at least see if they consider it an addiction. Maybe it wasn't addictive behaviour as such, but he didn't seem able to control it, and it certainly put him at risk—lethally so, since the spread of HIV. So far, he'd been able to keep his compulsion under control, and it hadn't limited him in any way, or affected his well-being, at least he didn't think it did.

One evening James went to observe Bella tutoring the elders on computer skills in one of the classrooms downstairs. He was so proud of the computer lab which had brand-new Macintosh machines, thrilled that the elders had asked to learn how to use them. He loved spending time with the elders, in small groups or individually, joking and kibitzing.

Just as he went to enter the basement classroom, a stocky man with messy hair and an unwashed face stepped into the doorway in front of him, blocking his way. It was Junior—who'd been in and out of jail. James recalled the unexplained enmity he'd felt when they first met. Bella seemed to sense the animosity between the two men; she stepped over and, in a calming voice, said, "James, this is Junior—Alfred Junior, Art's nephew."

"Hey, Junior. Think we met at the lake last month. How you doin'?" James said. He was taken aback by the tremor in his own voice, so he quickly forced a smile and extended his hand to the young dishevelled man. In response, Junior gave him a blank stare, then like a seasoned magician, he pulled a cigarette out from behind his ear. He retrieved a silver flip-top lighter from his jacket pocket, tapped the cigarette on a desk, put it to his lips, then dramatically flipped open his lighter and flicked it to produce a dancing blue and yellow flame.

James glanced up at the new smoke detector he'd had installed and wondered if it would go off and trigger the school's fire alarm and sprinkler system. With his eyes open wide now, James stepped in closer to Junior, looked him in the eye and said, "Hey, buddy—great to see you again. Did you know we installed really sensitive smoke detectors, and that the community has set a rule about smoking in the school?"

Junior flew toward James with rage in his eyes. He raised his hands in front of himself, as if he were about to do a chest pass on a basketball court. He thrust his arms forward pushing James hard into the wall behind him.

"I should fuckin' kill you. Stupid fuck of a princip'l. Don't you know who I am? I'm *Chew-nee-yer*—the one and only. 'N I done time for 'tempted murder. Ain't ya heard? Yer real fuckin' brave, or just plain retarded ta talk ta me like that. Guess no one warned ya, huh? I make fuckin' X.J. look like a pussy. 'N guess what? I got connections dude—in high places."

The elders had gone silent, and one stood to intervene when Bella swooped in and stepped between the two men. She put her face close to Junior's and forced the widest smile she could. Then she put her hand on his shoulder and said, "Junior—my pal, I was just going out for a smoke myself. Why don't you try one of mine—c'mon. Let's go outside?" She held out her blue package of Player's. Junior took two and placed them behind his ear.

"Yer fuckin' lucky, mister. She saved yer ass." Junior stumbled out the door behind Bella.

v

"You take the condom out of the package like this. Tear one end open, carefully, and then make sure you're holding it the right way. If all the lights are off, you'll have to figure this out by touch. When you hold it correctly and place the nipple-like top over the head of the penis, it rolls on easily, like this."

As James explained this technique to the wide-eyed teenagers, he placed a condom atop a banana and unfurled it. The teenagers burst into laughter.

"Could never see bananas the same way," one boy called out.

"I sure won't be eatin' 'em no more," a girl replied, laughing.

James had hired Ruthie to collaborate with him in presenting a "family life" session to the teen group, using the methods he'd learned in workshops given by the Vancouver School Board. Ruthie had a bachelor's degree in nursing and was working on her master's in counselling, but more importantly, she was kind and sensitive—motherly. James handed her a box of condoms to pass down each row of students.

The boys clamoured to grab as many as they could and stuffed them into the pockets of their jeans or their desks. Only one girl took any. "They're for my older brother," she groaned, scowling at accusing faces.

Bella stood at the back of the room, taking in every word. Beside her, Mr. Wallace—Harry—the classroom teacher, sat rigid, a quizzical expression on his reddening face. James knew that Harry had gone to Catholic School and it was likely the first time he had sat through a session that was so open and direct about sex and not using euphemisms or the common vulgar terms. Harry looked apoplectic when Ruthie began to explain to the teens how conception happens.

"There is only one way to get pregnant," Ruthie said to open. "The guy's sperm encounters the gal's egg. But sperm are tricky little guys—they can survive in a woman's uterus for up to five days and impregnate her long after the thrill is gone—so guess what, a girl or woman can't go thinking that just because she's not ovulating at the time of sex, that she won't get pregnant."

Ruthie paused for a moment to let the information sink in. The room was so quiet, you could've heard conception happening.

"Also," she continued, "if the gal performs oral sex on her guy, which is properly called 'fellatio'—geez, sounds like an Italian word—even if the guy doesn't fully *come* in her mouth, which we properly call 'ejaculation,' he may still release a few spermatozoids in what is called 'pre-come.' Then if they kiss—and then he decides to reciprocate by orally pleasuring the gal, performing what we call 'cunnilingus'—he may inadvertently plant his seed."

Harry held his head in his hands—ears crimson red; Bella had a wide grin across her face.

After school, James, Ruthie and Bella made their way over a thick bed of brown, yellow, orange and red leaves to the new portable classroom that housed the adult-education program to make a similar presentation to the parents of the teens and to any other community members who were curious. It hadn't occurred to James that there was a need, until Patrick, the custodian and one of the parents, asked him. "*We don' want 'em to know more 'bout the birts 'n the pees, than us,*" he had said with a chuckle a few days ago. "*Them priests 'n sisters didn't teach us nothin' about that stuff—sex 'n produshun in Lejac.*"

Halfway through the adult session one of the women said pensively, "Nobody has ever given us this information before. It's so helpful. We figure it all out for ourselves—and sometimes it cause big problems."

"So, you can't get AIDS from a light kiss with a womans, or a handshake with a gay?" One of the men asked partway into the presentation, looking solemn and fixing James's gaze.

“That is correct. Research is ongoing, in terms of what exactly leads to the spread of HIV, but they know that, like most other STDs, it cannot be transmitted simply. There must be an exchange of bodily fluids. A deep French kiss could possibly be dangerous if one of the participants is infected,” Ruthie said in a calming tone.

“I was amazed ta learn about the different trimesters—of the baby growing in the womb and why it’s so important ta not drink liquor or do drugs when yer preggers.”

After the session, which went way longer than they had anticipated, James strolled back to the school with Ruthie, tired but content. The genuine gratitude of the parents was heartwarming.

James felt the warm glow fading as he sat down in his office to go over budget numbers again. Money was missing out of the salaries line—and the amount was going up incrementally every month. He was heading for a deficit, and this would reflect badly on his competence as a new principal. He had just laid out the accounting worksheets on his desk when the satellite phone rang.

“What the fuck, James?!” It was Mike, the superintendent of schools calling. “You did a condom demo in your sex ed course this afternoon—with a banana? You know there are staunch Catholics in that community, including elders, just as there are Baptists and Pentecostals here in Vanderhoof—some are even school trustees. We discussed this, I told you. The policy is that you can show the condom in its package, but you can’t open it. You’re not in radical Vancouver now. For Chrissakes, James, what next? A live sex demo? This *will* get to the board. You can count on it.”

“Mike, I apologize for the controversy. I did what I’ve been trained to do in this field, and I ran it by several elders, including Monique, a local matriarch. They thought the idea of doing sex education with the teens was great.”

Despite his calm tone, James was in a panic. He had used the information and materials from the Vancouver School Board’s sex ed program. And he'd consulted both Damien and Ali about it, Damien insisting he be direct and blunt in his presentation. His passion about it had made James even more sure of his own position.

Ali had been more circumspect, suggesting that James talk things over with Louise first—about just how explicit he should be. After all, unlike city kids, the students of Chezgh'un likely lived a pretty sheltered life, and some of the elders were pretty religious—still—thoroughly indoctrinated by their experience in the residential schools run by the churches.

He wished he had taken Ali's advice more to heart, despite his own preference for being as direct and open as possible. That had been fine in Vancouver—an approach more aligned with city dwellers who are exposed to sexuality and sexual diversity all around them on a daily basis—and it was the approach set out in the curriculum, but here—being explicit like that in Chezgh'un was to push the community quantum leaps beyond their comfort zone. In the next academic year, he would still do the session, but would be less graphic—leave the damn condom in its package. No banana.

He felt so off balance, he needed to call Franyo. Franyo would understand. He dialled up the satellite phone. Six desolate rings. No answer.

Well, he'd talk to Damien about this issue on the weekend.

James stepped into his office to find Margaret, the elder who had taught him how to slice fish for smoking, slouched over the table in the staff room, sobbing mutedly. What tragedy could have occurred now? Had someone ventured across the frozen lake prematurely with their skidoo to get to Bilnk'ah only to break the surface and sink? Had someone been shot in a hunting accident? Did someone else disclose a scandalous secret they'd been holding in for years?

"Margaret—what happened? What's wrong?"

"They say you're gonna be fired, Princip'l—wanted ta warn you. So silly, jus' because of a stupit French safe. Who ain't seen one o' those before?"

"Oh, Margaret, who told you that?"

Margaret didn't answer, and James's mind went into high gear. Faces flew through his mind—not Patrick, not Monique... definitely not Art or Sally. James tried to make eye contact with Margaret, and it happened for a split second. Her irises were off centre, and she looked permanently sad. James guessed the elder had some serious health issues and had had a lot of trauma in her lifetime. Was she here of her own volition, or had someone put her up to this? What could be her motive?

He put the coffee on to brew and looked out at the reedy shore of the lake through his office window. He rehashed in his mind his conversations with Monique and several other sets of elders about the presentation.

When he had gone to visit, Monique had been sipping wine from her soup can again. She wasn't really drunk, but she wasn't stone cold sober either. *Mellow*, that would be a good word to describe how she was—*chill*.

"Dis is my week ta relax, Princip'l. Worked hard the last two weeks dryin' salmon, skinnin' 'n cuttin' bear meat, and slicin' moose meat to make jerky—we call it *t'sung guey*. Gatherin' berries 'n medicines. Now time ta rest." A boisterous laugh. "So ya came ta visit. They say you wanna talk ta me 'bout sex. *Hadih*, so crazy, Princip'l. Go ahead. T'll be goot!"

Another elderly couple James had never before visited, Maisey and Moise, had been more clear-headed when he had stopped in on them to have the conversation, and their answer was similar. Moise had spoken first: "'Bout time someone talk to our kids about them things—sex 'n produshun. We never learned nothin' from those perverted priests 'n nuns—'cept how ta do it funny ways—or steal it at night. They were gettin' way more action than anyone else. Wasn't so bad when they did it 'mongst themselves—like they did—lots. They didn't know we seen 'em, but we all knew who was screwin' who in that place. After a few sips o' that communion wine, they weren't too good at hidin' things."

After a brief pause, Maisey had taken over. "It was real horrible when they did it with the students—both girls 'n boys. Some girls got big from them priests 'n Christian brothers. Yes, it's time ta teach our kids. I wouldn't know how ta talk to them, 'n they prob'ly wouldn't listen to an ol' lady who had eleven kids."

Then it hit him. *Agnes*. He hadn't talked to Agnes before the sessions. He slapped the side of his head. *Ah!* She's more Catholic than the Bishop of Rome. She must've heard about the session from her grandson Curtis, or her son Patrick. And she must have gotten angry.

James decided to go see her—better late than never.

Agnes was a few years older than Monique, at least eighty-five, James was told, but nobody knew for sure. Without making eye contact, she motioned for James to take a seat on the couch of her small living room. James stole glances at the old woman as she moved about her kitchen. Neither spoke for at least ten minutes, but with tension hanging in the air it seemed much longer. Agnes set a steaming cup in front of James and spoke.

"*Le te muus dje*, t'James. S'goot med'cine."

James recognized the fragrance of Labrador tea. He looked up, smiled and took the cup.

"It was goot, Princip'l. That Lejac School."

James was taken aback by her accent as much as by what she was saying. Somehow it was different than Monique's accent—or anyone else's in the community. She spoke in more complex phrases with a wider vocabulary, but the pronunciation was more guttural.

"I whas whun of de firs' from Chezgh'un ta go ta Lejac Residential school. And it was goot—big, mod'rn, clean. We sleep on real beds and eat offa big wooden tables. I work in de kitchen ta serf de nuns and priests, in der dinin' room. Didn' have ta go classes like udder kids."

"What did the kids get to eat, Agnes?" James interjected.

"Mush. But dey like it. Well, firs' dey did. Got tired o' de watery powdered milk real fast."

"What did you serve the priests and nuns, Agnes?"

"Mostleh tings like ros' beef. Mash potatoes wit' grayfee and boil carrots. Sometimes lettuce 'n stuff. But fer special occasion, dey make meat pie dey call *toort-ee-yair*. Dey woult devour it. Kids woulda love that. Sometimes dey let me ta taste it leftovers. Some Chezgh'un parents bring garbage bags full o' salmon—fresh or smoked—for de kids, 'n dry meat, dey knew dey missed our Indian food. Priest 'n nuns ate it all tho, on accounta it mighta not been safe. Wasn't stored right, dey said. People had no fridges den, jus' kept fresh food in wells or dried food in smokehouses."

James felt himself stiffen with an anger that bordered on rage. He recalled stories his mother had told him about *her* time in residential school—how wicked the nuns had been to her, and to her sisters, cousins and aunts. He remembered the stories he'd read about the Haida and Nuu-chah-nulth people from the West Coast—their tongues pierced with needles for speaking their languages, deprived of food and drink in secretive nutritional experiments. He wanted to mention to Agnes the case of a bishop in a nearby diocese who'd admitted to getting a fifteen-year-old pregnant. The man had supported her and the baby, off the record, for years and eventually was charged with statutory rape, but he got off scot-free when a Catholic Crown counsel botched the case. No, he didn't dare mention that case to Agnes—she was unwavering in her devotion to the Catholic Church—that was clear.

"Agnes, I should've talked to you about the sex education classes before we held them. I did speak to some elders about it. They gave me the go ahead." James was surprised by the slight tremor in his voice.

"De only thin' dem teens need ta learn is dis—jus' don' do it. No sex till yer married in fronta God 'n ready ta haf kids. But my son Patrick, him, he like what you say ta the adults in the evenin'. And my gran'son, Curtis—him too. He like what you say to dem teenagers.

But don' know why you handed out condoms. That ain't goot, Princip'l. The pope, him, he preaches against that you know—any kind o' contraseptic. It's a sin, he says. He was jus' in Africa talking to them people about it—said they shouldn't use condoms. Sure, they got that AIDS disease spreadin' there, but they need ta learn ta control themselves. That's all the kids here need ta know too Princip'l—howta control themselves."

"Lots of people believe that doesn't work, Agnes, and I agree with them. The more you suppress nature, the more it comes out in uncontrolled ways. But in any case, I'll come to visit you every couple of weeks, okay? To let you know what's happening at the school."

"You don't need ta, Princip'l. I know what's goin' on. Wit' the school, and wit' you. They tell me. They tell me everythin'."

There was that word again, the mysterious *they* that perplexed James so much. He was learning he had to guess who *they* might be in any given situation or conversation—and it was useless to try to clarify in the moment.

VI

Kekac Pipon — Early Winter

i

"James, Mona's been crying non-stop for fifteen minutes now." Debbie, the primary teacher who was just months out of university, stood in the doorway of the principal's office/staff room. Beside her stood Mona, a slight child with matted hair. One hand held Debbie's while the other fidgeted with the hem of her worn blue velvet frock.

"I've tried speaking to her one on one. I've tried reading to her. I tried singing a lullaby. I even got out her favourite art project and offered her a cookie. I don't know what else I can do." As if on cue, Mona broke into gut-wrenching sobs.

James stood, motioning for her to lead him back into her classroom. "I've read about a holding technique for children in distress, and I'm willing to try it out—in your classroom, of course."

"Sounds like it's worth a try," Debbie said meekly. "I'll focus on the rest of the class—distract them."

James took Mona's hand and asked her to go with him to the cozy reading centre Debbie had set up at the back of her classroom. Mona had calmed a bit but was still blubbing. Without looking up she grasped James's hand and took one careful step after the other. James sat cross-legged on one of the cushions. He gently rotated Mona's tiny body and pulled her into the hollow of his embrace. The girl relaxed into his hold; her hot cheek pressed against his bare bicep. She calmed even more, and he guessed she would fall asleep like that, but, suddenly, gasping and choking sobs took over. In no time James's arm was moist with tears and he could see Mona was going to have to blow her nose.

What could this disconsolate six-year-old be lamenting? He gazed out the picture window again at the yellow and brown alder leaves flitting about among the swirling snowflakes which had now gotten much larger.

James stood and offered Mona his hand. He led her over to where Debbie was now doing arithmetic games with a cluster of kids, using the manipulatives she was so pleased with: beads and buttons, plastic ladybugs, pinecones. James's gaze met Debbie's. The brief exchange between the two educators made each of them aware how much the other cared about the children of Chezgh'un, and about each other. James was so glad they'd had the week at the fish camp to truly bond with each other and with the kids.

"I'm taking her home, Debbie. There's nothing else we can do."

As they cut a diagonal path across the freshly fallen snow, James sang to Mona—making up his own words to "Hush Little Baby." As they walked, James studied Mona's tiny brown hand in his. Hers was delicate and still held dirt as evidence of yesterday's play and chores—a couple of her tiny fingernails were slightly chipped.

James spotted Mona's mother, Mable, in the distance, across the vast schoolyard. She was approaching them. She must've heard somehow. He paused the song and breathed a sigh of relief—Mable would take over. She had been so helpful with the primary class at the fish camp.

"*T'su in' t'oh*, Mable," James ventured, suddenly feeling odd about holding the little girl's hand, standing there with her in front of her mother. Mable didn't look at James and didn't address him either. Instead, she grabbed Mona's free hand and launched in, "Where you guys goin'? What's wrong with you enawayss, Mona?"

Mona sobbed some more.

"She's been crying all morning. We can't calm her, so I decided to bring her home," James cooed.

"Mona! Smarten up!" Mable shouted and continued walking toward the school. James stood in stunned silence, the crunch of snow under Mable's boots resounded in his ears as she walked away.

"Ah, we've gotta take you home, Mona." James said. "Is your grandmother home?"

More sobs.

Mona's older sister, Terri, met the unlikely pair at the door. Her bottom lip protruded slightly and when she tried to smile her teeth were partially blackened. She took a step back and spit black juice out of the side of her mouth into a tin can, like James had seen his *mosom* and other old men do when chewing snuff.

"*Hadih,* Terri," James said, perplexed to see the ten-year-old at home instead of at school. "Terri, what are you doing home, and why are you chewin' snus?"

"They give it ta me. I like it. Mona too, her, she like it, but t'day they didn' give her none. No Coca-Cola this mornin', neither. They run out of it."

"Can you tell your grandma that Mona's gonna have to stay home the rest of the day. She's really upset. And since I'm here, let me walk you to school—not sure why you're missin' today. We got some of your favourite activities. Can you get your coat and boots?"

With Terri in tow James traced the same route back to the school, anger now clouding his mind. Who was giving these little girls chewing tobacco, and why? And Coca-Cola too? *Jesus.* Well, it had to be some old man—only they chewed snuff. What was their motive? James suspected the worst and became infuriated. He had to try to get to the bottom of this—as soon as possible. He strode back to the school and found Mable who had come to volunteer with Debbie's class—doing a beading project.

"Mable… It seems Mona's been chewing snus... maybe often, and today she didn't get any, so she was in a terrible state."

"Them kids, they sneak it sometimes from the ol' men. They seen 'em chewin' it and they think it mus' be good."

"I hope nobody's giving it to them. That would be so bad."

Mable's face was expressionless as she said, "I'll talk to the ol' men—tell them they gotta lock it up."

"And we'll do something at school—tell the kids how bad it is for them—that it's addictive and can cause mouth cancer."

"Should tell them ol' men 'bout that, too, then!"

"We will. And we'll get some of that special gum to help everyone get over it."

"Goot idea, Princip'l. We kin get some wild spruce gum, too—it'll help."

It was time for Terri's daily literacy session with James. He selected the next oversized book in the series for vocabulary development: tasty fruits and vegetables. He and Terri had been through the A foods: apples, apricots, asparagus, and B as well: beans, bananas, berries. Now they were moving on to C.

Just then, Ms. Zamisky, the literacy specialist, walked in. She smiled and said, "I can take over here if you like, James—free you up to do your principal stuff. My ten o'clock didn't show."

James stood up but lingered a moment to watch as Ms. Zamisky took up her place beside Terri, and pointed to the first picture—a cantaloupe, cut into quarters. Terri became animated and said, "*Hadih*, Miss, what's that big fruit, so orange inside with too much seeds?"

"It's a cantaloupe, Terri, a tasty fruit—not real sweet but it tastes so good. Can you say cantaloupe?"

"*Hadih*, it ain't a real fruit, right? It's 'maginary."

That night, James had a panic attack. What had he done, making such a sudden and drastic change in his life? What kind of long-term life could he have here in Chezgh'un? And his connection with Franyo and his Vancouver friends seemed more tenuous each day. He frantically punched Franyo's number into the keypad of the satellite phone in his office and held the bulky receiver up to his ear.

"Hey J. Having a dinner party—Theo and Bérénice, Enrique and Julius. Can you hear me over all the noise?"

"Oh—that's great, Fran. Say hi to everyone for me and we'll talk tomorrow."

James walked to the lake's edge and sat listening to the gentle waves lapping the shore until he calmed and felt sleepy enough to go back to the RV and go to bed.

ii

"James. How are you?" Chief Felix called out from across the bar at the Blue Parrot. "Better question—what are you doing here? Aren't you s'posed ta be in Chezgh'un?"

"Long weekend—a four-day weekend for us." James said with a smile, coming around the bar to join Felix. "So, I came home to visit."

"James—this is Justa. A cousin from Bilnk'ah. He's down here studyin'. Doin' real good in school." He put his hand on James's shoulder, looked at Justa and said, "James here is the new princip'l in Chezgh'un. He's got a tough job."

James offered Justa his hand. The two smiled in an apparent tacit complicity to not tell the chief they'd already met, albeit briefly.

"Where're you goin' to school, Justa?"

Felix answered for Justa, "He's going to Langara—thinkin' of goin' into law at UBC, like I did. Well, was good to see you, James. We gotta lot to see and do today. We're gettin' our coffees to go. See you back at the ranch—uh wait a minute—I guess I should say the *rez, ha ha*."

The three men nodded goodbye.

As he and Felix walked off, Justa glanced back at James, who stood leaning against the counter. Justa seemed incredibly bright, but James wondered how he was adjusting to life in the city—and to attending a big academic institution like Langara. He recalled his own university days, how so often he felt like an alien who'd just been beamed down to that place from another planet. In those days, everything seemed so foreign. He was breaking new ground for Native youth, but there were no student supports. So he hung out in the mature students' lounge where he found a bit of support from the older students who had befriended him. It's great that Justa had Felix as a mentor, but what supports did he have here in Vancouver?

And was Felix just his mentor? What was going on with those two? Why didn't they join James or invite him to join them? That's what they would've done if they'd met like that up north. He ordered coffee for himself and Franyo, "*Deux* cappuccinos, *s'il te plaît, mon ami.*"

"*Alors, tu connais ces deux gars-là*?" the barista demanded—an inquisitive look on his face.

"*Oui*—yes, I know them from up north, from Fort St. Pierre, where I'm working now."

"*C'est un beau couple. Très cute*! I been tree planting up in those parts. Never saw guys *si beau* up there. Most of the Natives were down and out."

"There are lots who *aren't*," James answered, looking directly into the barista's eyes. The barista passed him the two cups carefully centred on their saucers. James stirred sugar into one side of the foam of each cup, careful not to mess up the tiny brown tree images the barista had made when he poured the white foam over the rich, brown crema. Then James rushed back upstairs to Franyo, to discuss his suspicions about Felix and Justa, which he felt had been validated by the barista's comment.

"My God, Franyo, he assumed they were a gay couple!"

"Well, who knows, J. But a person has to be careful with assumptions like that. They could just be close buddies. Hey listen, I saw an article about that French movie you and Bérénice have been talking about, it's playing downtown tomorrow afternoon. About society going downhill on account of people over-indulging in sex and stuff. Not my thing, but maybe you wanna go see it."

"Oh, *Le Déclin de l'empire américain*... yes I definitely want to go."

James loved going to the movies or renting videos to watch at home—when something new came out in Spanish or French, he was right on it. For the first few years, Franyo would always join James and their friends, but more recently he'd become reticent, saying he didn't like sitting for so long. James knew Franyo meant sitting *so long* without a cigarette, but was embarrassed to say it.

The two of them shared morning coffee and breakfast. Then James visited Kits Beach and English Bay before going shopping on Fourth Avenue for clothing, computer accessories and books on his own—rented a couple of Almodóvar films and picked up some lamb—determined to keep out of trouble.

iii

The next Monday, Chief Felix and Morris, the band manager, invited James to their offices in Bilnk'ah for a meeting. James scolded himself for not asking for an agenda to consider in advance. He recalled Theo's advice: never agree to a meeting if they don't tell you what it's about, and if you must, stall until you're ready. Had they heard about the problematic sex education class, the banana and condom demonstration? Had Agnes or someone else complained? The chief and band manager weren't his bosses, as such, but they could make his life very difficult if they so desired.

James decided to make the most of the trip—stop in the Fort for coffee and a piece of pie, and after the meeting, he would stop in to visit Damien. Together they would strum their guitars and try out their latest harmonies, starting with their current favourites, "Jack & Diane" and "Lovers in a Dangerous Time." Maybe afterward they would go for Chinese food in the Fort and invite Ali to join them, even though Damien hadn't really warmed up to the man. "He's too much of an optimist, and he's a conformist," he'd said. "A total good news bear."

James didn't agree, but Damien seemed so convinced, there was no point discussing this with him.

After the customary formalities, Dakelh-style—a handshake, a few jokes and a slap on the shoulder—Felix opened the meeting. "*Hadih*, James, I know I still owe you a piano."

In response to the puzzled look on the band manager's face, Felix explained. "I promised him one if he got the job—at the interview. He wants to set up a good music program in Chezgh'un. Even if we have to send it by barge, we'll get a piano out there."

"Okay, well I look forward to getting that piano, Chief—really important for music classes. I use my guitar right now, but it's not the same. And the kids love music."

Felix and Morris exchanged glances, and then Morris took over the conversation.

"You know James, we had problems with the last princip'l in Chezgh'un, and we don't want ta see this ever again. You must have heard by now that there is some animosity between the Chezgh'un people and the band administration here in Bilnk'ah. Was bound ta happen. We manage all their affairs, and they don't like how we do it. And now, we have two things coming up that the people in Chezgh'un won't like—won't like them at all: a money decision and a land swap. We invited you here ta warn you ta keep your nose out of community politics.

The chief cut in, as if the two had rehearsed their approach. "*Ha ha*. I know, it sounds pretty dramatic, eh James? But Morris is on to something. There'll be conflict. Ol' Monique will make war on us—with her medicine and maybe a few others will too. We'll be getting a cash settlement for a railroad trespass across Chezgh'un's lands. We're going to invest that money in a local cement plant right by the rez here. You might've seen it when you drove up. Will be a good money-maker, and they'll get their share of the profits, but they won't like it—they want a lump sum payout so they can distribute the money among themselves—not gonna happen. The other transaction is a land transfer. We're going to transfer a couple of modest land parcels from Chezgh'un to Bilnk'ah. They were incorrectly registered to Chezgh'un decades ago—the fish camp at Babine Lake, where they have cabins. That site rightfully belongs to families from Bilnk'ah. The Chezgh'un people will most likely ask for your help in fighting these two things—ask you to go to the tribal council or to the federal government, or even call up a lawyer."

James felt his face flush. He was speechless. He loved that place. And all of the families from Chezgh'un had cabins and fishing sites there. Before they were forced to move to houses in Chezgh'un, that was their preferred place to be. They spent as much of the year there as they could. He wanted to say something in protest, but he knew better.

Just when he'd felt himself settling, sure that his countenance had returned to normal, the chief continued. "Don't get involved, James. Even if they come to you on bended knee—Patrick, Monique or Art. If you implicate yourself, there will be trouble, lots of it, and fast. Those people get flabbergasted and grasp at straws—lobby others to help them."

"I'll take that under advisement, Chief. Thank you."

James remembered the warning he'd received from Colin in the Japanese restaurant. He wanted to learn more about the issue from the chief's perspective, but he knew he'd best not ask any questions just then. There would be lots of time to learn about local political dynamics.

"Oh, and there is an issue with your teachers' salaries."

"I have that one sorted out. There was an accounting error—simple as that."

"Glad you got that one under control, James—but there'll be more money issues. The government just announced a funding freeze and cap on all Indian programs across the country. Doesn't matter how much the actual operating costs go up, like salaries and materials, we can only get a two percent funding increase each year."

"That's incredible, Chief. The funding level is already so far behind regular schools. Special needs students have to move to Prince George and go to a public school to access services—even the least needy cases."

"Things aren't getting better even though the government leaders say they want to improve things—they're actually getting worse. Wolves in sheep's clothing if you ask me. But James, all we're asking of you right now is to keep your nose out of community politics. Am I'm being clear?"

James was sure his colour had now drained. He imagined how deep the scowl on his face was—an ominous, sad mask. Up until then, he'd had no intention of getting mixed up in community politics, but now he would, albeit covertly. He wasn't going to be so easily intimidated.

"Well, Chief, I had no intention of interfering—of playing on your turf. I have enough on my plate just running the school. No worries there. And that really sucks about the funding cap."

"About the salaries, James," Morris said. "Some Chezgh'un members—and ya know, they're my family—I'm from there, eh? So is the chief. Well, some think that your teachers are makin' way too much money. More than anyone in the community. They want their salaries cut, or to get rid of 'em and hire teachers who will work for less, like they used to have."

James took a deep breath. He recalled Margaret's warning. He looked at the chief's face and saw the resemblance to hers. Then he remembered—someone had told him that Margaret was Felix's aunt. So, *he'd* put her up to that dramatic scene. James took a deep breath, then spoke.

"Well, we all know the answer to that one. The teachers have a collective agreement—contracts with the school district. They make the same as teachers in the Fort and Vanderhoof, and it has to be that way. If we want qualified teachers, we must pay them as such, and by law, we must have qualified teachers," James answered calmly.

"Fine and good to tell *us* that, James, but you'll need to convince the community—in particular, the elders."

What was Felix talking about? James visited the Chezgh'un elders regularly and they were onside with what he was doing. Only Agnes had been trickier to convince. A bluff… a smokescreen… a sad way to use the elders.

"No problem. Leave it to me," James said as he stood to leave—it was clear the meeting had ended.

"Oh James, just one more thing… It looks like school construction might be delayed a short while. Just a few months. But no worries—the commitment is firm," Felix said.

James's felt something grab him by the side of the throat, and he felt the blood drain from his face. The new school was a key part of his reason for moving north, and it was badly needed.

"Is there a new timeframe? And what about the teacherages, my house? Sure don't want to spend the winter in a frozen-up RV."

"They're going to start framing the teacherages soon," the chief said as he stood to show James to the door.

James stepped out of the ATCO trailer that served as a band office and took a few deep breaths to calm himself. It seemed too coincidental that the request for this meeting followed so quickly on the heels of his chance encounter with Felix and Justa in Vancouver. Was the chief really telling James to keep out of *his* business—his personal affairs—masking it as a warning about community politics? He couldn't be sure, but something didn't sit right.

As James approached his vehicle, he saw a hostile-looking Dakelh man standing beside it—deep pockmarks on his face, likely from acne, and a long scar across his forehead, probably from a knife. The man looked to be in his late forties or early fifties and about the same height as James. No customary nod, no *hadih* or hello, so James looked down and felt in his pocket for his keys. Without warning, the man raised a fist and yelled at James: "Ya fuckin' pervert! Keep away from my boys. I'm watchin' you. You cocksuckin' priests, you're all the same."

James jerked his head up and struck a confident pose so the man wouldn't think he was afraid of him, even though he was shaking now.

"*Hadih,* what the hell are you talkin' about?" he shouted back as he glanced around to see if there were any witnesses. "I'm no priest! I don't know you, and I don't know your boys. I'm not from here."

The man stepped right in, toe to toe, and put his face squarely in front of James's. "*Hadih,* you know what the fuck I'm talkin' about, *hoo'tup*! Don't you bother my gran'sons 'n nephews no more!"

Vibrating now, James turned away, opened the door to his vehicle and climbed in. He slammed the door and glared at the man as he turned the ignition. What the fuck had he gotten himself into, moving up north?

iv

James was barely halfway into his account of the meeting with the chief before Damien's cheeks burned bright red. "How dare they threaten you like that, James! You're a high-level professional—you can do whatever you want. Don't let yourself become an agent of oppression in petty local politics. Know your rights, and help the Chezgh'un people to understand theirs."

James had second thoughts. Had he made a mistake telling Damien about all of this? He didn't expect such an extreme reaction—it didn't help. Instead of having the calming effect he was hoping for, the conversation pushed James from anger to despair. And he didn't want his new friend spewing off to random people about what he had told him. "You wanna go for Chinese food in town?" James asked. "I need a drink."

"I wanna play guitar with you and sing, my man. Best therapy to heal your frustrations. We could drive down together in my truck, then back here to jam. If we continue late into the evening, you can spend the night and drive home early in the morning. Might be safer that way anyways."

The excitement of the moment dazed James—Damien was asking him to spend the night. He set aside his worries about the odd encounter with the chief and the band manager and settled into being in Damien's company—welcomed the distraction. The two of them would be spending the night together, in his house—alone. What was Damien up to, and what would his girlfriend think of this? Would he tell her?

James loved the drive from Bilnk'ah to the Fort. The mountain that the men said looked like a woman lying supine, breasts and belly turned upward. The seemingly impenetrable wall of greenery that lined the sides of the road. There was a good chance they would see a black bear or a deer along the forest's edge. True wilderness, like the place where James had grown up, but even more pristine.

At the Kings Inn, they bumped into the chief and band manager paying their tab at the counter. The chief gave them a curious look, then approached them to shake hands.

"*Hadih*, James. Long time no see," he said with a chuckle. "So, who's your buddy?"

"This is Damien, a junior-high teacher in Bilnk'ah. Teaches English, music and gym."

"Oh yes, I heard about you. Really good guitar picker, eh? And a black belt in karate."

"Good to meet you, Chief. James, here, is a good guitarist too—and a singer."

The chief studied the two men for a minute, then nodded and turned to leave.

During the ride back to Bilnk'ah, Damien lectured James about Nietzsche's philosophy.

"You have to learn these things, my man, if you're going to advance in this world. You're in a position of power now, so you will face direct challenges from people," Damien warned, with a flash of intensity across his eyes.

"'You solitary one, you go the way of the lover: you love yourself, and on that account you despise yourself, as only the lover can despise.' That's Nietzsche. 'Be extremely subtle even to the point of formlessness. Be extremely mysterious even to the point of soundlessness.' That's from *The Art of War* by Sun Tzu."

Why was Damien quoting Nietzsche to him with all of this intense negative energy? The thrust of the Sun Tzu quote was somewhat more obvious, but he wasn't sure how it applied to him exactly.

"Y'know—you can't be naive, my friend. You're an administrator now—a leader. You're fair game, for so many," Damien said, looking straight ahead with his hands at ten and two on the steering wheel. "And you should know, the school district really screwed me here: don't want to pay my moving expenses and are charging me more rent than the other teachers 'cause I'm officially single and occupying a three-bedroom house. They didn't care that Sylviana and her kids plan to move in with me. That Louise Bernard is a shark."

This assessment of Louise took James's breath away. Louise had been nothing but kind and supportive to everyone, as far as James knew. Yet Damien didn't trust her. James was definitely infatuated with this guy, but he seemed to be a loose cannon—or maybe a rebel looking for a cause was more accurate. The adamant misanthropy Damien seemed to embody left James feeling drained. Why such disdain for those around him?

Back at Damien's house, the two men wasted no time in getting into their music session. As Damien plugged the instruments and microphones into his oversized PA system, James did a few breathing exercises and vocalized quietly to warm up his voice. Playing music with Damien was an important respite for James—from the stress of his new job, from the scrutiny of the community, from his sorrow about being so far away from Franyo—from the related uncertainty of where his life was going from here.

They started with an a cappella version of "Early One Morning." James knew a killer harmony for that song, and Damien loved it, even though it was a folk song—the theme song for the kids' TV show *The Friendly Giant.* Anyone who could hear them would've concluded they were so immature—or crazy—Damien gaily belting out the lilting melody and James boldly singing a flowery counterpoint—in that place, in a house on an Indian reserve in the wild outback.

Next, they did "The Boxer," which, once again, made James's voice warble with emotion as he sang the harmony, especially the opening part about being a poor boy with a seldom-told story.

Then they improvised, both playing the same chord progressions on their guitar, an eight-bar loop with James strumming a set rhythm pattern and Damien plucking out fancy leads. After a half-hour or so of this, Damien sat up straight and said, "Hey James, why don't you do some improv with your vocals, man—making up the melody and the lyrics?"

It was a strange and novel experience, but James got into the groove of it. Within a few minutes, his song turned into an ode to his mother and great-grandfather. After another ten minutes of wailing a phrase his mother had sung, *"Kiy wîhkâc peyagun tapscotch niya,"* James's voice began to tremble. The tremble grew into a waver, then he set his guitar down and began sobbing. Damien stopped and set his instrument down.

"I'm sorry." James sat upright, dried his eyes. "My God. So embarrassing. The phrase means '*may you never be alone like me.*' Mother used sing it when she was drunk and lonely."

Damien came closer, put his arm over James's shoulder and said, "Let it out, my man. Don't ever be embarrassed to show your emotions—least of all where music is involved."

"Okay. Sorry. Let's try again."

"No, let's take a break. Come here." Damien took James by the arm and led him to the couch. He sprawled out and pulled James into the crook of his right arm. James draped his arm across Damien's chest and nestled his head into Damien's muscular shoulder. He coyly unbuttoned Damien's shirt to slide his arm inside, to place it squarely atop Damien's muscular chest. He fell asleep.

v

It wasn't long before the chance to get involved in local affairs, against Felix's warning, presented itself. After supper one evening, when James returned to the school to do some work, Patrick was in his office, seated at the round table, poring over a worn old map. A large wooden box filled with scrolls and other documents sat on the floor beside him.

"We need your help, t'James," he said. "Band office in Bilnk'ah is goin' after our lands—Babine, Whitefish, 'n other fishin' sites."

James began to sift through the pile of documents: old maps, tattered survey reports and water-stained land registration documents. He couldn't believe Patrick kept these important legal documents stored at his house in this old wooden crate—likely hidden under his bed or behind a panel of drywall.

Combined, these documents—historic band council resolutions, sworn affidavits and other loose pages with faded print, likely undecipherable notes from the records kept by an Indian agent—set out the community's ownership over several postage-stamp reserve sites, including the site where they had built their village: a few fishing camps and registered traplines. James was astonished that there was no historic treaty in place for Dakelh people as there was for his people: Treaty 8.

These old and tattered documents were all that the Chezgh'un people had to prove any degree of ownership and historic rights over their lands—and many of them had probably never seen these documents, and never would. Of course, there was oral history—the deep knowledge of elders like Monique and Abel, or Agnes—but so far nobody official had given the oral tradition evidentiary merit. Did the band office in Bilnk'ah have copies of these documents or perhaps more official documents that were safely guarded? And what about the right of the Chezgh'un people to hunt and gather, and their ownership of lands and resources—where was this described? It had to exist somewhere, if the national railway company was paying out compensation for trespass, as the chief had said.

After poring over the documents for a while, it became obvious what the government's intent had been when allocating parcels of a few acres here and there for subsistence farming and seasonal fishing to the people of Chezgh'un: leave the maximum possible land mass available for pre-emption and homesteading by white settlers.

James knew that, short of having tens of thousands of dollars to hire a lawyer, there was nothing that he or anyone could do directly to help his new friends. The Chezgh'un people had relatives in Bilnk'ah, brothers, uncles and aunts. Maybe they would stand up to the chief. But he couldn't approach them, and there were longstanding grudges between family factions—which is likely why those people moved to Bilnk'ah in the first place.

Still, what *he* could do was educate the community—increase their capacity to manage their own affairs. Yes. Education was the answer. This was exactly in line with the approach Bella had decided to take with the adult class: to help them develop a critical understanding of their social reality through reflection and action. It occurred to him he could enlist his new friend, Ali. Ali had already earned the confidence of a number of elders in Bilnk'ah, elders who were closely related to many Chezgh'un families. Those elders likely didn't know that the chief was intent on dispossessing Chezgh'un families of their land base.

vi

Loretta came and stood—near tears—at James's desk. Her class was out of control. A few students had started acting up right after they'd written in their morning journals, and it got worse during math class when Loretta tried to check the math homework from the day before, multiplying and dividing fractions. They were not responding to her requests or direction. The class ignored her. Before entering the classroom, James peeked in to get a read of the students' mood. The kids weren't being insolent; they just weren't relating to the topic at hand, it seemed. He'd seen much worse in one of his seventh-grade classes in Vancouver: paper airplanes flying, spitballs being fired, one student had even mouthed the words *fuck you* in James's face, but cleverly from a particular angle, so that no one else could see. These kids were mellow by comparison. James asked Loretta if the class had artwork they hadn't completed. Yes, Loretta said, they were working with pastels doing drawings of skies, trees and northern lights. James suggested Loretta switch to art until morning recess, and then spend some extra time outdoors with the kids. Ten minutes later, James peeked into the classroom again—everyone was on task, and the mood had shifted. He made a mental note: art was therapy. This was a trick he'd suggest for all the teachers—when academic subjects were weighing the kids down, switch to art. For advanced intermediate math instruction, he would order more manipulatives—objects for teaching fractions—and he'd order games. He'd also suggest Loretta use an application in the computer lab for this topic. James had had lots of training in effective math instruction and had become somewhat of an expert on the topic in Vancouver, so he was happy to share this expertise with Loretta, and she was more than willing to learn it.

Harry stormed into the office/staff room. Anouk had had another outburst. This time he was throwing desks around. The other students were afraid, and he'd sent them outside. But what was he to do? James rushed downstairs with Harry on his heels. They found Anouk in the empty classroom, a pile of wooden desks off to one side.

"Anouk, what's going on?" James asked, trying not to sound perturbed.

"They all be teasin' me again. Makin' fun o' me."

"Anouk, I didn't see that," said Harry, shocked. "I don't think they were. Everyone was busy working on their drums."

"You don' see the looks they throw my way, Teacher. Or hear what they mutter in Dakelh."

"Let's go for a walk, Anouk—a walk and a chat. We'll work this out," James said.

He'd given Anouk what advice he could on self-control. James knew he'd have to get the district counsellor to work on anger management with Anouk and a few of the other boys. The other kids weren't mean or bad, and he was sure a lot of it was perception—maybe paranoia, a possible side effect from sniffing gas. He was sure Anouk had stopped doing this, but there might be lingering effects. Maybe Shannon, Henry's oldest and one of the top achievers in the school, could work with Anouk, helping him with his homework for a half-hour right after school, in a quiet corner of his office where James could keep a watchful eye.

vii

James got used to spelling off each of the teachers for their prep time with music sessions he enjoyed as much as the students did. It gave him a joyous break from his administrative role. He taught them songs like "Wild Mountain Thyme," "The Wind Beneath My Wings" or "Mr. Golden Sun," depending on which class it was. He would teach the lyrics first, getting the kids to clap the rhythm as they pronounced the words, then taught them the melody, by getting them to sing it to "la." Then he would put it all together, pluck and strum for the guitar accompaniment, and, eureka, they had a song. After a couple of months, when music classes started, the kids would call out the title of their favourite song, hoping for it to be the next one up. James was so pleased that they liked the songs he selected. Everyone sang in tune, and he even taught the classes songs sung in rounds to get the students used to hearing themselves singing in two, three or even four-part harmony. Faces brightened when singing "Row, Row, Row Your Boat" and "Kookaburra," but the same faces were filled with joyful amazement at the sound of harmonies after they'd learned to sing "White Coral Bells" as a four-part round. When this happened, Art, Sally and any other adult passing by would stand at the door and listen to their students making this beautiful noise.

The skills-development workshops for teens accomplished what James had hoped. They built up the self-esteem of those who needed it most and instilled a positive attitude toward school life, and they were well attended. The older teenagers didn't complain about the routine of arriving at 8 a.m. to make soup from duck, deer-bone or moose-bone marrow broth and bake bannock under Sally's watchful eye. In fact the soups were getting more elaborate and even tastier. Some days they'd make cinnamon buns instead of bannock.

All the teens learned how to cut hair—some of them had become expert at it and were in demand as budding stylists—resulting in hairstyles that ranged from neat and clean to funky and city-chic. The drum group practised every day from 9 to 10 a.m. while in an adjoining room another group beaded moose-hide moccasins and vests. James loved the sound of the drum in the background while he worked in his office on adjustments to the curriculum, lesson plans for more cultural camps, and teacher evaluations. The smell of the smoky moosehide was ubiquitous.

Art and Harry completed a series of workshops with the teen students—they all had hand drums and knew the moves of traditional Dakelh dances. Art and Harry decided they would invite a teen class from a school on a reserve near Vanderhoof to join them in their drumming, singing and round dancing.

The week of the event, nobody was late for class. And everyone was alert and attentive to whatever their teacher, Harry, or one of the TAs had to say. There was a quantum shift in the students' energy; everyone was in high gear, even the most reticent. All of the skills they had learned came to the fore. Those who were good stylists were asked to cut the hair of the others—the teens paid whatever they could or traded in trinkets, toys or an equivalent favour. Even Anouk got a slick haircut, and everyone commented on how handsome he looked. Those who were good at baking and cooking, four girls and one guy, were busy planning the menu. They would make the best moose stew ever, using garlic, smoked paprika and oregano the way the visiting Native chef from the local college had taught them, and they would serve it with warm fry bread. Beforehand, as an appetizer they would have pieces of canned salmon jerky, and roasted beaver tail spread onto freshly baked bannock (this delicacy they were particularly proud of since word had it that other communities had long since stopped harvesting beaver for food). For dessert, whipped Indian ice cream, cinnamon rolls and pumpkin pie.

On the day of the event, as the teenagers strode into the building, single file through the main door, trying to act nonchalant while sporting their new hairdos, best jeans and shirts, and new runners or leather shoes, all the teachers and parents, aunts and uncles who'd come to observe were awestruck. The kids knew they were *hot* and had attitude like teenagers anywhere who know the power of their youth.

"Hey, what happen ta yer baseball caps, you guys?" Art teased.

"And you girls ditched your jean jackets. Oh my God, you're all gorgeous!" Bella raved.

"Geez, we should do this more offen, eh Princip'l?" Art said. "Didn' know we had such good-lookin' kids, Holy!"

"Well, maybe you guys jus' didn' pay enough attention," Shannon said with a chuckle as she walked by. Her look hadn't changed much, since she was always stylish and nicely dressed.

As the guest teenagers filed into the school, it was obvious they'd gotten all dolled up, too.

"Goot' thing it ain't an evenin' dance, Princip'l. Ya'd have ta go out 'n buy more o' those condoms," Art said with his usual guffaw.

"There'll be a few sparks of romantic interest this afternoon, you can count on that," James said. "It's great. Glad we did teach them about sex and reproduction though."

"They could prob'ly teach us a few things 'bout that, Princip'l—*ha ha ha*. These young ones are more open-minded than we were. Back in the day, we thought 'oral sex' meant talkin' about it," said Art with more boisterous laughing.

"Geez, maybe *we* shoulda spent more time jus' talkin' about it, Arthur—then we wouldn' have so many damn kids," Sally said with a giggle as she elbowed Art in the ribs.

"Hey, not my fault we n'er got central heatin'," Art answered with a smirk.

James was breathless as he watched the teenagers drumming and dancing in a type of round dance, similar to the one Cree people did back home. He was so taken by the beauty of the moment, tears came to his eyes. How in the hell anyone could've seen this cultural activity as evil—all of this was illegal between 1885 and 1951. Why would anyone want to suppress the magnificence of this incredible art form?

viii

The literacy program was going well. The books they ordered that were sequenced from basic to more advanced had come, and to James's and the teachers' delight, they were more culturally appropriate than the books they'd grown up with. There were families of all sorts depicted in the books: different races, including Natives, Chinese, Indian, Blacks, as well as white Europeans—single-parent families, poorer families and wealthier ones, even families with same-sex parents. The teachers all loved working on reading skills with the new resources. And more importantly, the kids loved reading those books. Within months, most kids were on track to catch up to the level of reading they should have had for their age group by the end of the school year.

Some of the kids, like Mona, had genuine learning disabilities, but were progressing well with basic literacy and numeracy. The kids all loved the math games and manipulative objects James had ordered. The daily and weekly problem-solving board was also a big hit. The kids loved the code-cracking type of problems. And the outdoor-ed group for the oldest teens—wilderness survival, first aid, canoeing and kayaking—had gone so well. James couldn't believe the new life he saw in the eyes of the teens the afternoon they returned from an excursion. They sauntered into the school, exhausted but exhilarated—projecting a new attitude, new hope. He wanted some of that for himself. He longed to spend time in the bush, camping.

James bought shotgun shells so a few of the teen boys could go hunting after school, and in exchange, late every evening, they brought him Canada geese and a variety of ducks to clean and dress as food for himself, and for the school's busy kitchen. Just as he'd planned, before recess every morning the whole school went outside to run or fast walk, including the school secretary who'd said she wanted to lose weight. The stragglers would spend their recess getting back to the school. Hot soup and bannock for everyone.

Bella often referred to the work of Paulo Freire, a noted Brazilian educator and philosopher, and asked James if they had a budget to bring an expert to the community to help her map out her curriculum, learning resources and methodologies for the term. She told him the other teachers had raved to her about professional development they'd had in California on the whole language approach and how much it was helping them. Bella said she thought it was only fair that she get to do something similar—but of course, at home, in Chezgh'un.

James agreed, and within days Bella had arranged for a consultant from a prestigious adult-education resource centre in Salmon Arm, BC, to come to the community for a series of workshops on personal empowerment and escaping oppression. The consultant was a Latina woman, Carolina, who had studied with Freire. Bella and the consultant worked with the adult students to identify all the ways in which they felt they were being limited or oppressed, not only by mainstream society, but also in the North and by their own local powers that be. They then designed a strategic plan for community and regional activism with four pillars:

a) consolidating Chezgh'un's hold over its lands and resources;
b) addressing social issues in the community, like addictions, overcrowding of homes, youth suicide, preventable health problems, special needs education, the legacy of abuse arising from residential schools;
c) restoring and strengthening Dakelh language and culture; and
d) restoring traditional stewardship over the environment, including restoration of controlled burning and the use of riparian zones in timber harvesting

James was giddy like a child when the adult students went over their plans with him. He was so thrilled with their work that he invited Bella, Harry, Art and Sally, and the consultant to a dinner at the log cabin restaurant in the Fort, the best one in town apparently. Bella didn't mind when James and the consultant spoke Spanish to each other excitedly about the centre she worked with, as a consultant, and their work all around the country.

The next day, Bella informed James that the adult-education students had decided to immediately launch a research project related to Chezgh'un's ownership and use of lands and resources. To help out, he decided to ask Patrick to let him make copies on the weekend of those documents in Prince George. That was innocent enough—build this into the curriculum: local history, geography, economics and sociology. James stood and carefully rolled up the maps then replaced the red rubber bands that held them in a scroll. He rifled through his desk to find a few unused file folders. He put the other records inside of them and carefully placed the folders into the wooden crate. He breathed a sigh of relief. He had a plan: he would do what he could to make the adults in the community cognizant of their situation, if they weren't already, and leave it to them to decide what to do, if anything.

ix

The snow was piling up all around Chezgh'un, including on the lake, which had gradually frozen, starting with its shores and each day moving farther inward toward its centre. Eventually, the snow formed an expansive puffy eiderdown that covered the solid surface of the lake, the village grounds, meadows and streets. On sunny days it became a glittering white amoeba that engulfed everything. Clumps of it weighed down evergreen boughs unevenly. Gradually the bumpy and uneven surface of the gravel road became smooth and slick with the layers of packed snow, then ice—onto which sand, fine gravel and salt were applied for traction.

James relocated from the RV to the unoccupied medical clinic beside the school; the portable heaters the school district had provided for the RV weren't adequate and many nights he awoke shivering. "Just another month till your house is ready, James," Colin Baird had promised when James had asked. The clinic was intended for an itinerant nurse and had everything he needed—a bed, kitchen, sofa and desk, and thankfully, it was well heated. At least some of the time he would have his own space.

But then, something unexpected started to happen. People with minor medical problems began to seek help from him. During his college days, he'd worked as an orderly, so here at the clinic he started cleaning wounds, applying pressure dressings and stretching tensor bandages over sprained ankles, even though he knew he shouldn't. One person even came with a toothache and all he could recommend was biting down on a clove or chunk of yarrow root, home remedies his mother had taught him.

One evening, he heard a knock at the door.

"Come on in—it's open," he called out without getting up.

"*Hadih*, Princip'l."

James glanced over and saw Jeremy, a rambunctious student from the teen class, standing in the doorway wearing, as usual, his blue baseball cap and grey sweatsuit.

"Step in, J. Close the door, it's cold outside."

Jeremy entered and pulled the door closed behind him. It was hard not to notice the large bulge in his loose-fitting pants. He looked James directly in the eye with an odd smirk on his face.

"I hurt my leg, Princip'l. Maybe you can take a look."

James's mind kicked into high gear. This was a test. He couldn't be sure what all was behind it. Were there other teens waiting outside, ready to peek in a window to see if he would take the bait? Or had some of the men from the community put Jeremy up to this? Perhaps Jeremy was acting on his own—sincerely looking for some relief from an easy target who he imagined would enjoy sharing a few electrified moments. James stood and stepped toward Jeremy. He brushed past the teen to re-open the door.

"On second thought, Jeremy, I could use some fresh air. Let's leave the door open," he said.

Jeremy just stood there with a goofy smile now, watching James.

"*Hadih*, Jeremy. Doesn't look like you're in pain—with that smirk on your face. I can radio Christine, the health rep, to come over. Pretty sure she's home. Maybe you're in shock. Do you want a drink of water?"

"Jus' take a minute, Princip'l. For ya ta have a look." The smile was gone, but the teen's eyes had taken on a new naughtiness. He moved in closer. The bulge in his pants commanded attention, but James forced himself to ignore it.

"How's school goin', Jeremy? Your teacher tells me you're doin' good—you're in class every day and doing your homework. Proud of you."

Jeremy looked at the floor and spoke, "*Hadih*. Well, I jus' wanted ta visit you, Princip'l—hang out wit' you."

James grabbed his coat and pulled it on. "You're a great kid, Jeremy. I like you," James said as he grabbed his parka. "Let's go for a walk."

James and Jeremy walked side by side in step with each other down the main street of the village, with vapour wafting from their faces as they breathed and spoke. It just took a few minutes for Jeremy's cheeks to take on a rosy hue. Before long, he was chattering away about the various animals he had spotted just outside of the village: porcupines, wolverines, martens.

"Harry, him, he's teaching us all that stuff—how ta sort and classify animals—mammals, 'phibians, reptiles 'n so on. So funny. Us Dakelh, we jus' call 'em two-legged, four-legged, those that fly and those that swim."

James listened—amused, nodding now and then and saying, "Oo-oh ye-ah," in the sing-song way Cree men did. "Us Nehiyawak, too. The same."

There had been another situation. One Saturday night, Leyo and another young man from the community asked James for a ride home from Fort St. Pierre. The two men had been drinking and there was constant homoerotic innuendo most of the way back to Chezgh'un. Both men hinted that they yearned for a blow job, and James was pretty sure they meant performed by him—maybe even right then and there—even though it was the middle of winter and they'd have had to leave the vehicle running. James was sorely tempted to pull into a side road to find an isolated spot in the forest to see what happened, but he knew it was a test—a power game. He was the local school principal, for God's sake, and if he'd had sex with anyone local, even completely consensual sex between adults, it would have shifted the balance of power and set the rumour machine in motion. While the men wouldn't outright tell anyone that they had had sex with him, they might find a sneaky way to let the information slip. Maybe there would even be graffiti painted on the school—JAMES SUCKS, or,

FOR A GOOD TIME GO THE PRINCIPAL'S OFFICE. Perhaps someone would even try to blackmail James. He had to be squeaky clean—be celibate as a devoted Buddhist monk—at least in the community and in the Fort.

But James burned with desire. He was in his prime, physically, and so much around him fed the fire: the sights, smells—the raw and vibrant countryside; the phosphorescent northern lights; and the ever-present banter among the teenaged students, teaching assistants and adult-education participants. And then there was something he had learned about in zoology classes in university: pheromones. In the city, people showered—some up to a few times a day. They used deodorant, talcum powder, cologne or perfume, and for their laundry, fragrant fabric softeners. Each of these things masked the aroma of their humanity—blocking the transmission of delicate airborne molecules of androsterone from the sebaceous glands of one person's body to the chemoreceptors of another's—while here, in the country, folks were hygienic but not over-sanitized. All James knew was that after a long chat with some of the women or men he worked with, to his own consternation, he experienced a potent arousal. Flirtatious glances from young women, men cajoling and flirting with each other—but in a coded macho way, fleeting touch, inadvertent or planned, between him and some of the other guys in the community. Whenever Art's son Bid'ah was around, he'd gotten into the habit of kneeing James's butt every time James bent over to tie up his runners or boots. Some days, the combination of these things left James vibrating.

x

On a quiet Sunday, right after breakfast, James decided to go for a walk to the cemetery—to plead for guidance and strength once again from the ancestors of the place. At the first cross street, he was joined by Jeremy, who explained he was going to his uncle's place for coffee. A few steps later, Henry stuck his head out of his door and shouted, "Hey you two *hoo'tups*, where you goin'? Princip'l, better watch out for that Jeremy—he's always up to no good." He reached back into his house for his coat. Pulling it on, he ambled over to James and Jeremy, fell into stride and launched into some banter: "*Hadih*, I saw a big bull moose jus' across the creek yesterday, gonna start stalkin' 'em today—get ta know his habits. Lorna wants another hide to work on. Last week I got a silver fox—ya should come over after 'n see the fur. Maybe you wanna buy it off me, Princip'l."

Jeremy, who hadn't said a word since Henry appeared, sighed and broke rank. "I'm goin' home. My show's comin' on soon."

Henry and James kept walking, in the direction of the cemetery and bridge of wooden planks at the entrance to the village.

"Christ—las' night I dreamt 'bout residential school," said Henry. "About when I was in the marchin' band, playin' a bugle. They gave us uniforms and we got ta go ta Prince George ta march in parades."

"You went to Lejac School, right? For how long?"

"Too damn long—ten years. At least I got ta come home most summers—didn't forget our language. I can still speak Indian. But there were boys from all over the place, and we fought. The kids from up north were nasty to us. But we learned howta farm—the gor'ment figgered that was the answer—teach us how ta farm and give us some patch o' land to work—turn us into *Nedohs*."

"Funny, Henry, you guys say *Nedoh* for white people, us Crees say

Moniyaw, or *Wêmistikôsiw* if they're French—people who go away in canoes."

"Most o' the priests and nuns at Lejac School was Frenchmen. But they made us ta learn English."

"I was raised Catholic, too. My mom went to residential school at a place called Buffalo Bay. But I left the church when I turned fourteen. Didn't make sense to me. I'd go to confess my sins and start out by lying about how long it was since the last confession."

"I did the same! Been years now I ain't been ta confession or taken communion. Agnes, her, she always gets after me ta go."

"Do you believe in that stuff, Henry—Father, Son and Holy Ghost? Transubstantiation?"

"I can't think about it, Princip'l. I get scared whene'er I try. We learned not ta question things—never spos'd ta try ta read the Bible on our own or pray to God directly. Jus' accept what they teach us and pray to Mary or one of the saints."

"But you can free yourself, my friend—pray to God, directly. You don't need a priest or a church. Pray to the universe and to your ancestors. Light a smudge of sage or sweetgrass—maybe you guys use some other medicines."

"I do those things, t'James, but can' let go o' the other. Can't do it. Anytime I let my mind think about different beliefs or pos'bilities, I see the fiery pictures of hell the nuns used ta show us. Scares me shitless. Start havin' nightmares about burnin' up in them flames, wake up screamin'. Jus' can't." Henry went silent for a moment before saying, "*Hadih*, come ta the house, Princip'l. Wanna show you pictures from Lejac School days."

Henry's house was similar to Art's: two rooms with a floor of plain and dirt-impregnated wood, at least where you could see it—the breaks in the sea of foam mats and blankets. Kids everywhere. A miniature cross with a tiny metal or plastic Jesus hung above every doorway—just like at home, James decided. Crosses above every doorway to keep out evil spirits. A well-worn couch with a tattered Hudson's Bay blanket sat under the large picture window that looked out into the street. And there was a crude home-crafted pine table with matching benches running lengthwise along both sides of it.

Shannon, Henry's oldest and the smartest kid in school, was holding a baby in one arm and had a toddler clinging to her free hand. The boy had spread Shannon's fingers, as if he wanted to count them. She looked up at James and smiled vaguely. A few kids James recognized from Debbie's primary class sat in a circle, cross-legged, playing jacks—dropping the red ball and frantically scooping up a precise number of the little metal widgets and grabbing the ball out of the air before it hit the floor and bounced again. James was impressed by how adroitly they moved their tiny brown hands. Henry's wife, Lorna, was in their worn, rustic kitchen, chopping carrots and onions. Appearing washed-out, she looked up at James and forced a smile.

Henry must have seen the look of despair on James's face. He piped up, "We have runnin' water now, Princip'l—an' 'lectric lights. It was a big deal a few years ago when they put 'em in."

Henry got out a tattered Catholic missal and flipped it open to the place where he had tucked a couple of curling photos, glossy black and white with a white border all around. Without looking up, he handed one to James. It was a picture of a shy-looking boy wearing a neat cadet-style uniform, holding a cornet. The boy—Henry at age twelve, James guessed—wore a forced smile and his eyes brimmed with a plea for mercy, empathy, salvation. James knew that the terror, loneliness, sorrow and suffering he saw in Henry's eyes would trouble him for days—even return to him in dreams. He stifled a moan, swallowed his anger. Those bastard priests and nuns tortured these kids, tried so hard to make them white.

"Whoa, incredible pic, Henry. Sometime, maybe you can show me more, but I gotta get going now," James lied. There was no place he needed to be just then. He still had an hour or two before his appointment with Patrick to go over the plans to build a new fire escape for the school. But he was overwhelmed with emotions he could barely contain.

"Talk to you soon, Henry. See you, Lorna. See you, Shannon."

James let out a moan as he pulled the door shut behind him. So many memories of his childhood home and the houses of his aunts and uncles—but these people were even poorer. His family at least had had linoleum on their floors.

Staring at the ground in front of him, James walked slowly toward the cemetery. Once there, he looked around to make sure nobody could see him or was close enough to hear him. He moved around the graveyard—to the other side of the grey picket fence that encased it and turned to face the snowy forest—when the sound came out of him. A powerful chant he had never sung before.

"Ha-iy ha-iy ya... Ha-iy ha-iy ya..."

It was his great-grandfather's chant. He muttered the phrase over and over, swallowing back the sorrow that was threatening to take him over.

xi

December. Christmas rapidly approaching. But this year, for the first time in his life, James was not enthused. In November, the breathtaking surroundings of the snowy meadows and forest enclosing the frozen lake had buoyed his spirits, and, really, he should've been breathless in anticipation of two weeks off with travel to Vancouver for a joy-filled Christmas with Franyo and his Vancouver friends, and then off to Cancún for a sunny getaway. The prospect of fun times did afford James moments of relief, but he'd been staying with Debbie and her partner in their two-bedroom trailer for over two weeks now—this after several months in an RV followed by a month in the nursing station with little to no privacy—and he was distressed. The couple were kind and accommodating, for sure. They even asked him to join them for dinner each day, but he didn't feel comfortable sharing their space—not at all, and despite his fierce determination to succeed, he couldn't persevere—fulfilling a high pressure and very visible role in the community, doing his utmost to support a team of novice teachers, improvising and scrambling to meet student needs, and responding to seemingly endless administrative demands by the district office, all while homeless. He needed a safe refuge to escape to at the end of each day. After spending three months in their own cramped quarters—a two-bedroom trailer with one bathroom, inadequately heated and mouse-infested—Bella, Loretta and her cousin Angie, were equally fed up. However, neither James nor the women complained openly. Most houses in the community, which weren't much larger than their trailers, housed between ten and twenty people, a blend of adults and children.

One day after school, James and Bella met in his office to brainstorm a strategy to force the accelerated completion of their accommodations. They each poured themselves a cup of Labrador tea and sat at the round table, looking sombre.

"Well," James opened the discussion, "as the union shop steward, maybe you can just tell me, as your principal, that living conditions in the accommodations provided by the band and school district are inadequate—and that you and Loretta refuse to continue in those conditions."

"Then you'll take that to the board—tell your bosses that we're taking job action?"

"We shouldn't have to go that far—no formal ultimatums, as such. I'll simply write a letter to the superintendent saying that living conditions are unacceptable, and, as a result, the teachers and secretary are considering involving the union. So, I, as principal, have decided to close the school a week early. I'll inform him that neither I nor the two teachers or secretary will return to the community until our accommodations are ready."

An hour later, Margaret was at James's office door, in tears, saying she heard that he and Bella were leaving the community for good, and she was so sad. Somebody obviously overheard their conversation and started a line of gossip. Minutes later, Art and Sally popped into James's office to say they'd heard the same thing—the school was closing until the accommodation issues were addressed—and they guessed that could take months.

The next day, James sent a note home to the parents to inform them of his decision.

Most school days, Art joined James in his office for coffee—early, before anyone else showed up. They'd catch up on all the latest gossip, speculate about the weather and politics, joke around and laugh. But the second last Thursday before Christmas break, Art showed up, at 7 a.m., at Debbie's trailer instead. He knocked loudly. James was sure that at that hour, any visitor would be there to see him, so he opened the door. In an outstretched hand, the tall cinnamon-skin man held a frozen vacuum-sealed package, and in the other a scrunched-up black garbage bag that looked quite heavy.

"I 'spect you'll be headin' out this weekend. Got somethin' for ya here, Princip'l, for yer Christmas Dinner down south. Deer tenderloin, some of my own salmon jerky and some canned smoked salmon. Gotta have somethin' good ta eat while you're in the city." Art smiled his broad smile and let out his loud laugh. "Don't wantcha ta forget us, ya know. We wan' ya ta come back."

As he took the precious gift from Art, James smiled as tears rushed into his eyes.

xii

James's fire-red Sidekick flies over the layer of white powder that covers a bed of packed snow and ice on the logging road between Chezgh'un and Fort St. Pierre. In the vehicle with James are Art's eighteen-year-old son, Bid'ah, and two villagers who hitched a ride. It's the Friday before the Christmas holiday, and James will drop them off in the Fort to have Chinese food, try their luck at bingo and get supplies for the coming week. They'll hitch a ride home with Art, or someone else they meet at bingo.

At James's request, Bid'ah is driving. Everyone says he's the best, should be a race car driver—and he *is* driving fast: a hundred kilometres an hour, like all the skilled drivers from the community do on the snow-packed winter roads. The men are gleeful—tickled to be heading into Christmas holidays, and to be in each other's company. They're so pleased with the way things are going at the school and in the community. As usual when driving over snow-covered roads, they slide, swerve and bounce. The air is full of noisy banter and laughter.

James feels it first: the vehicle is drawn as if by some powerful magnet toward the ditch. One of the front tires has been pulled into a deep rut. Bid'ah has a firm grip on the steering wheel and tries to steer away from the ditch, but it isn't working. Everyone gasps. Bid'ah clutches frantically and jams the brake. James reflexively stomps on the non-existent brake under his foot. Suddenly the vehicle swings in a circle and continues to fly around again and again, until finally the centripetal force wanes and it lurches over a high embankment of crusted snow. In the second it's airborne, the Sidekick flips over. James watches it all happen in slow motion. The hood touches down, but lands softly onto a bed of snow. Instinctively Bid'ah cuts the engine. James is frantic. Is this how he'll die—*where* he'll die—with strangers he'd just met a few months earlier, in the bush of Northern BC? He imagines the headline: YOUNG SCHOOL PRINCIPAL DIES TRAGICALLY IN CAR CRASH. Each year so many people die like this back home in Alberta—their vehicles flipped into the ditch—instant death when the roof crushed on impact, or when shattered glass penetrated their body—some even get decapitated. At least they'd survived that part. James takes a deep breath to focus as they glide, in case he has to take some sudden action—what that could be he has no idea—he's hanging from his seat for God's sake, held in by the seatbelt. What could he possibly do?

The vehicle is now a four-man luge in an Olympic event—careering forward on a blanket of snow—fresh powder atop a solid base, with Bid'ah, James and the two back seat passengers hanging upside down from their seatbelts for this astonishing and horrifying ride. James prays there'll be no tree stumps or boulders—the area's been clear-cut, so he's not worried about standing trees. The headlights are still set to high beams, so James can see where they're going and for what it's worth, he remains vigilant.

"Fuck! We're gonna die," he yells as he grabs Bid'ah's arm. The contact calms him instantly, then he feels stupid.

When at last the vehicle comes to a stop, James breathes a deep sigh of relief. Bid'ah sputters, "Wow, ever lucky, Princip'l. Soft landing, no trees or boulders in our way."

"Everyone okay?" James shouts. "Everyone okay?"

"Yup, fine here," the men say in near unison.

"Now ta get out a here 'n get this thing right side up," Bid'ah says. "Brace yerself on the roof with one hand, Princip'l, 'n hang onta the handle above yer door, 'n I'll release your seatbelt. Then you can release mine."

Both doors open easily. The men roll themselves awkwardly out of the overturned vehicle. James inspects them visually. "No blood—no broken bones? Anyone hurting anywhere?"

"How about you, Princip'l? You were pretty scared there. Y'okay?"

"No broken glass anywhere and no fire—thank God. Just glad nobody's hurt. *Arghh,* we gotta get moving. I have to get to Prince George by seven o'clock. My flight's at eight."

"No worries, Princip'l," Bid'ah says. "We been through much worse. We'll have this vehicle right side up and on the road before you know it."

Within minutes, a loaded logging truck appears and pulls over. Two men leap out and rush over. James had heard this about the logging-truck drivers in the North—aggressive drivers, but they never fail to stop to help out when they see a vehicle in trouble.

"Everyone okay? Anyone hurt? We got a first aid kit."

The driver flags down another truck which luckily has a winch to pull them out of the ditch. Bid'ah leads the effort to get the Sidekick back on its wheels using the brute force of six men—rocking—then flipping it, first onto the passenger side, then onto its wheels. With the powerful winch, they manage to pull the vehicle onto the road in a matter of minutes. No damage.

James is in shock. Every one of the teachers in Bilnk'ah, except Ali, was in an accident, in the fall or winter, and now it has happened to him. He feels incredibly fortunate yet cursed at the same time. He's just had his first brush with death. He knows he doesn't dare tell Franyo about it—he would never hear the end of it.

xiii

James stood on the corner of Robson and Burrard Streets and watched the shifting masses flow around him. It was one of those rare mid December sunny days in Vancouver. There was a chill in the air, but James couldn't see his breath like he did every time he stepped outside in Chezgh'un. After only a few months of living away, James felt like a complete stranger here. Not one of the hundreds of faces that rushed by him was familiar, and, unlike people of Chezgh'un or Bilnk'ah, not one person here made eye contact or nodded in acknowledgement of James being there. He saw young and chic Asians, tall and handsome Indians with turbans, others with a mahogany skin tone he assumed were from the Middle East, an occasional Black person, and of course white people of all skin tones, sizes, ages and social classes. An older balding man was camped out on the sidewalk right at the corner of Robson and Burrard—shirtless. He held up a cardboard sign which read, BIRTHDAY TODAY. 53 YEARS OLD. NEED BEER. James passed a cluster of Hare Krishnas, their heads shaved, with parallel white lines of their *tilaka* in the middle of their forehead. One squeezed a miniature accordion, and, in unison, they chanted their usual prayer.

He tried to imagine anyone from Chezgh'un being there with him. How would any of one of them have felt, standing on that street corner, alone, in a city of more than a million people, none of whom would say "hello" or even acknowledge their existence. And if something were to happen to such a visitor, who would they turn to for help? In the North you could count on your neighbour or even a passersby you didn't know if you ran into trouble on a country road or in town. They might even buy you a coffee when you were broke.

James popped into a bistro for a light lunch. Suddenly, he felt nostalgic for Chezgh'un—the place and the people. He glanced around and recalled the fall day, a Friday, when he had given Bid'ah a ride to Prince George to visit a relative for the weekend. They had arrived early in the evening, so James invited Bid'ah to join him for supper at the local White Spot—a low-key family restaurant that was reasonably priced and modest. Bid'ah became speechless the moment they entered. He stared around the restaurant in complete disbelief.

"Princip'l, I can't be here," he had said softly.

"Why Bid'ah? It's just a restaurant. And you're here with me. I want to buy you supper."

"But they won' let me stay. Pretty sure I'll get kicked out—not styled up for a fancy place, and I been wearin' these clothes for a week. Didn't comb my hair this mornin', just popped this cap on my head."

James convinced Bid'ah to stay for a burger and fries and a glass of coke. But Bid'ah had squirmed in his chair the whole time, saying little, anxious to leave. How would Bid'ah or any of those teenagers from Chezgh'un, or adults for that matter, cope in Vancouver? And that was his reaction to a simple place like White Spot. James didn't dare tell him or any of the adults in the community about the fancy French restaurants where he loved to dine with friends, in Vancouver. And he hadn't told anyone except the teachers about his upcoming trip to Mexico—thinking it would completely blow their minds. Maybe he would show them pictures when he returned.

The sky, which was bluer than a starling's egg, was fully reflected in the calm Caribbean Sea, making it impossible to define a horizon. The four travellers could hardly wait to get to the beach, spread out their blankets and feel the warm rays of the sun on their pale skin. His travel companions—Franyo, Lena and Janine—were naturally fair, but after months of winter, even James's skin was paler than he liked it to be. James was surprised his lesbian friends had wanted to join him and Franyo but was glad for the company. The bus ride from the Cancún airport to the hotel took forever. Their rooms were basic, with rustic furniture, but the two couples were so mesmerized by the sweeping view of the sky and ocean that they were oblivious to the decor.

"I'm having a piña colada as soon as I get changed and zip down to the pool," Lena announced from her room across the hall.

"We won't be far behind you," Franyo answered, laughing.

"I can unpack our suitcases, Franyo, if you want to go find us a good spot on the beach," James offered.

"My favourite beach blanket," Franyo said as he smiled and grabbed a bright yellow Mexican blanket from his suitcase. "We've had this for years now."

"See you down there, then," James said.

James was alone now, which was what he had wanted, a few minutes to maybe write a quick poem or sketch an entry in his journal—in Spanish or French of course, in case Franyo stumbled onto it.

James had just placed his and Franyo's beachwear into the wooden dresser when he heard a knock at the door.

"*Mantenimiento,*" a male voice droned.

"*Voy,*" James responded and moved toward the door.

He opened, and a man in a white uniform stepped in. He was slightly taller than James, and tawnier. After a quick once-over, James decided that the man was younger than him, and better looking too.

"*Buenas tardes. Voy a checar el ventilador,*" the man said in a baritone voice.

"*Me parece que funciona bien,*" James answered, pointing up at the rotating ceiling fan. The young man turned the speed-control knob on the wall beside the bed, but nothing happened—the blades continued to whir at the same velocity.

"*Vez? Hay que arreglarlo,*" the Mexican said as he nodded and set his tool kit on the floor.

James kicked the door shut, and the young man moved in closer. His smile widened to show a line of beautiful white teeth.

"*Que hay que hacer?*" the man asked with a chuckle.

James didn't understand the question, but he understood the look in the man's eyes. He closed the slight space between them and touched the man's shoulder.

James's heart was still pounding as he stepped out of the hotel onto the veranda by the pool. He couldn't believe the powerful sensations that flooded every inch of his being when he realized the young maintenance man wanted sex. All the pent-up sexual frustration he'd felt being around Damien, Bella and other new friends in the community who, unaware, turned him on incredibly. And the sexual release—in sync with the handsome Mexican—left him trembling. He took a few deep breaths and stood still, admiring the surf and the vast blue sky. He stepped onto the beach and savoured the sensation of the warm sand filtering though his toes. After a few strides, he paused a moment, until he was sure his colour and expression had returned to normal, he hummed a bit to make sure his voice would be calm before he addressed Franyo.

"Where you been?" Franyo called out.

"Oh, the maintenance man showed up to check the fan and air conditioner. Didn't want to leave him in the room on his own. Y'know, with all our things there."

"I just ordered us drinks. Lena and Janine are by the pool. But I wanna hang here for a while."

James gazed at the sugary-white sand around him and at the translucent blue Caribbean. He couldn't believe he was here—that he had escaped the snow, the icy roads and below zero temperatures. He pictured Damien—fingering his guitar and strumming. What were his plans for the holidays—staying in Bilnk'ah to hunt, ice fish and play music? Damien had simply said he had plenty of entertainment there—with his passions—he didn't need to go anywhere. James felt so fortunate to share one of those passions—music. The two men had three out of four weekends together, making music for hours every day, each month since they'd met.

Then his mind turned to Art, Sally, Bid'ah, Catherine and the teachers and kids at the school. Even though he missed them, a week in this paradise wasn't enough. He had wanted to return up north to spend a few days with his new Chezgh'un friends and Damien before classes resumed. He prayed that his house and the other teacherages would be complete when he returned, that his letter had had the desired effect and the board wouldn't call his bluff. The foundation had been laid and the frame was up, the insulation and roof had recently been added, but who knew if it would be completed by the time he got back.

"Hey. Why are you thinking so hard, J?" Franyo cooed. "Come here—sit and relax. We're on vacation now."

As a foursome, the two couples visited the Mayan ruins of Tulum, climbed the El Castillo pyramid, strolled for miles along the beach, exchanged countless smiles with kind brown faces, snorkelled along a coral reef—marvelling at the brilliant colours of the vast array of fish of all sizes and shapes—savoured garlic soup, *chile relleno, aguachile,* sipped piña coladas with fresh pineapple juice and coconut milk and laughed at Lena's craziness—befuddled by her story about how, using obscene hand and mouth gestures, she had asked the male housekeeping staff, who spoke little English, if they were gay.

Occasionally James took time away from the group and wandered along isolated sections of the beach, hoping to encounter some Mayans—Native Mexicans. He knew this was their territory and that they were very populous and must have still lived and worked here. In town, in souvenir shops and craft stores, he'd asked a few strikingly beautiful cinnamon-skinned people if they were Mayan or knew Mayan people. "*Soy indigena de Canada—Nehiyaw, es por eso que pregunto,*" he said as a preface, so they wouldn't be offended by his question.

To a person, the people he asked were taken aback. They would get a puzzled look on their face and say things like, "*Creo que mi abuela si, hablaba el idioma, pero yo no.*" Your grandmother, but not you… James thought each time, incredulous. James kept asking, until one of the men he asked answered differently, "*Si, claro. Soy Maya.*"

The man invited James to go with him on a Mayan tour the next day, promising he'd have him back to his hotel by dinner time. James was apprehensive, but decided to go, thinking the man was sincere and kind but then wondered what pretext he would have to make up for his friends to justify leaving them for a day and spending it on his own? If he had told them he was going to visit a Mayan community, they would've wanted to go with him, and he wanted this experience to be an Indigenous to Indigenous experience—through and through. Without dozens of queries and well-meaning but potentially offensive comments about Mayan culture. Besides, like most people, likely his friends thought all Mayans were dead—extinct like the Beothuks of Canada.

"*No importa,*" James said to himself. He would do it anyway.

As promised, early the next morning the Mayan man was waiting with another man in the hotel driveway, standing beside a beat-up Volkswagen Beetle. In what seemed like no time at all the three men reached an area where the jungle appeared impenetrable, even thicker than the densest brush back in Northern BC. James trembled with anticipation. He became aware of the fluttering in his chest and sighed. He couldn't believe he was on his way to visit a present-day Mayan village and tour some of their territory.

"*Bahauz kaw wa lik,*" said the man who greeted the three of them. James guessed he was a cacique or leader of some kind.

"*Meeksba,*" the guides answered.

Hearing the language, James became even more emotional—sad that it hadn't occurred to him to bring a gift, as was the custom in his culture.

For years afterward James would dream about that day, wondering what was real and what he'd imagined. Had he really stood atop a Mayan pyramid, gazed across a thick jungle with a couple of colourful toucans flying overhead? Had he really heard his hosts warn about the *aluxes,* the protector spirits of the forest? Were *aluxes* like Dzunukwa—the wild woman of the woods of the Indigenous people of the Pacific Coast in Canada and the United States? Had he truly ventured down a lush trail to a deep crevasse where spider monkeys leapt overhead in the canopy? He wondered how he had been brave or foolhardy enough to be led into a deep river where blind catfish lurked and swam to a cave to share in a traditional, millennia-old ritual in the Mayan underworld. He would never forget helping to collect the white resin from chicle trees, the source of the original chewing gum, a medicine for the Mayans—much like the spruce gum Cree people chewed. Not only was it tasty, but it had health benefits too. Every damn textbook or article James had read about the Mayans had made it sound like they were a historic race that had disappeared. He wanted to yell out loud, write a letter to every snooty encyclopedia, saying, *they're here—they're alive, they're real and they're beautiful.*

After his hosts convinced him to spend the night, James had one of the best sleeps of his life, in a hammock, but he awoke in panic. What would he tell Franyo, Lena and Janine? Had they already reported him missing? Were the police out looking for him? This was so irresponsible. He knew he would pay the price with Franyo now—no sex and possibly a lot of sulking for the rest of the week. How could he make his friends understand the magical, once in a lifetime soul-connection he had experienced with these people, much like the communion he had felt with the people of Chezgh'un? As kind and progressive as they were, his friends really had no reference points for appreciating how meaningful this was for James—it wasn't simple exotic tourism, as it would've been for them.

The chief of the Mayan village presented James with a gift, a figurine of the Kinich Ahau, the sun God. As James rode back to the hotel in the back seat of the Volkswagen that morning—quiet and pensive—it occurred to him how he could appease Franyo. He would gift him the figurine—well that's what he'd tell Franyo, but what he would really be doing is storing the God figure at their shared place. It would remain his and, at some point in time, come back into his possession.

Maybe the God would protect and inspire Franyo while James was up north—and help him to get through their eventual breakup. James balked at his own involuntary thought. This was the first time he'd let himself go there. *Their eventual breakup...*

Franyo was already down at breakfast when James got back to the hotel. He just smiled and nodded when James stopped by his table to say he was just going up to change—he'd be right back.

James studied himself in the bathroom mirror. The look in his eyes had changed, yet again; something had shifted, he could see it in his soul and feel it in his heart. Why hadn't Franyo questioned his absence like he would have just six months ago? Did he realize their relationship was falling apart? James wondered if he should initiate a conversation about this while they were here, in a neutral place? But, did he dare when he didn't know where his life was going? Franyo had been the centrepiece of his life for years now—his rudder in uncharted waters. Who would provide that stability in the future? Suddenly, he dreaded going back to Vancouver. He didn't *belong* there. He wasn't sure he belonged up north either. For certain, he didn't belong in Bilnk'ah. There was something very odd going on with Chief Felix—his tense attitude toward James. This made James feel unwelcome, insecure.

On the flight home, James hid his face as he wept while peering out the airplane window at the idyllic Caribbean as it faded into the distance. He didn't want to leave that place, nor did he want this trip with Franyo to come to an end, ever. What awaited him back home? The rain of Vancouver for a couple of days, and then the trip back north—to uncertainty, cold and danger.

James's flight up north was turned back to Vancouver three times in two days. Both times, he took a cab back to Franyo's place where Franyo welcomed him with open arms and a delicious dinner. When he did finally get to Prince George it was forty below and his Sidekick was under a metre of snow somewhere in the hectare of white blanket that covered the long-term parking lot of the airport.

Fortunately for James, he bumped into Justa at the Prince George airport. He'd been booked with a student standby fare for a flight to Vancouver and didn't get on. Justa offered to help him shovel his way out of the massive snowdrift that covered the entire parking lot. In exchange, James offered Justa a ride to his relative's house in downtown Prince George. Justa would try to get a flight again the next day. The cheeriness the two men brought out in each other distracted them nicely from the miserably severe winter conditions.

James invited Justa to join him for lunch, where the two men shared stories about their Christmas experiences—Justa with his family back home on the reserve. Coyly, Justa told him the chief had picked him up at his parents' house in Bilnk'ah one day, and they'd spent a couple of days together in Prince George, watching the Spruce Kings hockey team live, dinners at the Greek place and the Japanese restaurant. James wondered if Justa was trying to signal something about the relationship he had with the chief without giving away too much—unsure how much he could trust James as a confidant. After all the cheerful back-and-forth banter, the men exchanged phone numbers.

xiv

James awoke and glanced at his gold watch. Seven o'clock. JAN 4. He'd considered leaving the watch in Vancouver but couldn't. It held so much meaning—the most incredible gift he'd ever received from anyone. Whenever he missed Franyo, he just had to touch the watch to ground himself. While up north, he would keep it tucked away and only wear it or hold it in private moments. Here, in Damien's house, he liked wearing it, even though Damien had said it made him look wealthy—intimidating. James lounged awhile in the extra bedroom of Damien's teacherage. He loved the odour of the sheets. He was sure it was Damien's musky fragrance he smelled.

Even though Christmas vacation had come and gone, both the school district office and the band office remained closed due to the forty-five below zero weather. Electricity was out and phone lines were down. It was impossible to check the status of the teacherages in Chezgh'un. It was just the two of them in the house. Damien's girlfriend and cousin, Sylviana, who had finally moved in with him, had travelled to Vancouver so her two kids could be with their father over the holidays.

As James lay there, his thoughts intensified—he worked himself into a frenzy, as he often did these days. So much had happened these last few weeks: he'd issued an ultimatum about his teacherage, he felt guilty about how he'd behaved on his Mexican vacation—he'd slept in the same bed with his lover for a week, and not initiated sex once, and he still had no idea if his teacherage was ready (if not, he guessed he would simply drive to the school district office in Vanderhoof and ask to be assigned other work); and now he was allowing himself to be crushingly beguiled—by a man he knew truly little about, which put his relationship with Franyo in even further jeopardy. At times he was convinced that his life was in danger, and he wasn't sure if it was because of the wildness of this source of temptation—Damien—or if it was simply due to the dangers of life up north.

Even if James had wanted to drive back to Chezgh'un, it wasn't safe to do so. The forecast called for lethally dangerous cold. Every year, somewhere in Northern BC, someone froze to death in a vehicle—a breakdown or accident—either with no emergency supplies or an incomplete kit. One could succumb to a frosty death in less than fifteen minutes if not dressed for winter.

James dreaded this fate for himself or anyone, but he also harboured an irrational premonition of coming across such a car on the side of the road, perhaps in the ditch, and looking inside to find a body, frozen stiff. He shivered at the idea, and, suddenly, he needed a warm body beside him—human contact. He thought of Franyo, who loved to cuddle and was always there for him, patiently awaiting his return. But for now, the man closest to him physically, and the one he was presently drawn to, was sleeping in the master bedroom across the hall.

James got up and stumbled across the hallway. The windows of the bedroom were frosted over, blocking the view of the layered white mounds between the house and frozen lake. Ice and packed snow had sealed every crack, crevice and vent, making the indoor air unnaturally humid. James stood in the bedroom doorway, listening to Damien's rhythmic breathing. He spotted a hunting rifle propped in the corner near the head of the bed and was taken aback, but then he recalled Damien had told him that in Bilnk'ah he always slept with a gun at his side. James had found this an extreme measure but guessed Damien had his reasons. He'd mentioned concerns about all the rough rednecks up north.

Had Damien heard him approach? Was he feigning sleep? James shuffled over to the bed, gently lifted the covers and climbed in. He hesitated for a moment, then wrapped his arms around Damien's warm, near-naked body and snuggled in close. Surely, after the intimacy they had shared, playing guitar, singing cheek to cheek and then cuddling on the couch, Damien wouldn't mind him taking this liberty. Their connection was sealed, James was sure. He had sensed it, and he knew Damien did too. James had just gotten cozy when Damien's phone rang. Damien groaned, disentangled himself from James and got up to answer the call.

Damien was sulky when he got off the phone. He and his girlfriend had had a nasty argument. There were issues with her living up north with him—with children to support and no job. How would they survive on the salary of a first-year teacher even with the subsidized housing? What would she do all day there? How would her kids, both very fair, get along with the "Indian" kids?

Damien said he wanted to play scales on his guitar and be alone for a while, so James went into the kitchen to put on a pot of coffee and plan the menu for their dinner. Damien had loved the brie en croûte he made previously, and yet it was so simple: throw some prefab pie crust over a round of cheese and bake for a half-hour at 350 degrees, but Damien didn't want to hear that—for him, this was haute cuisine.

James was increasingly at ease with Damien, although at times he was taken aback by the intellectual challenges his new friend tossed him. Nobody had ever questioned him so mercilessly. Damien would ask things like, *Are you truly happy, or are you simply content? What is happiness, in reality? How do you define yourself?* After a long, drawn-out discussion like this, Damien had once said, "James, your life is truly a tragedy. The only thing that could've made it worse is if you'd been born female—then the tragedy would've been complete."

James was stupefied by these discussions and attempted to defend himself with statements like, *of course I'm happy,* and *doesn't that include being content, why split a hair four ways? I mean of course there are elements missing in my life, but… And, how could you say that? Of course there've been tragic moments, but look at me, my life is far from being tragic—I'm on a great path.*

After these intense sessions, James was eager to get to Ali's house. There, he could relax—enjoy a reprieve from Damien's deep scrutiny and challenging conversation. The two educators and aspiring philosophers would sip bourbon and debrief on community politics and dynamics. Ali discussed the philosophers he had studied and admired most in his graduate studies in the US. He went on about postmodernism and the thinking of a French philosopher, Michel Foucault. And Rumi.

xv

When James finally returned to Chezgh'un after a week at Damien's house, his teacherage had been completed. Patrick had kindly moved his things there and hired someone to set it all up. When James entered the bedroom of his new home, however, he discovered that the window had been jimmied—part of its frame was on the floor. Someone had laid or slept in the bed, but the only things missing of his belongings were a bottle of Eau Sauvage, his pricey French cologne, and the sweatshirt he had worn the day he gutted and skinned a moose by the roadside, at the behest of the men from the village.

Art was infuriated when James told him about the break-in and theft.

"Some goddamn *hoo'tup*, Princip'l. I'll get ta the bottom o' this. Don't worry."

"It's not that serious, Art. No damage and almost nothing missing. They didn't even take the coins from my change jar."

A few hours later, Art trudged over to the school and stepped into the office, where James had settled to work. His imposing figure towered over James. He leaned in close to James's face as he spoke, "Fuckin' X.J., Princip'l. Ashamed ta say it, my own little brother broke inta yer room. No sooner gets back ta town, then does this."

This was one of the few times James had heard Art end a sentence without his characteristic guffaw. His face shadowed with anger and embarrassment, Art turned abruptly and left.

James sat at his desk, perplexed. Why would X.J. break into his home—lie in his bed, and then steal those two items? How would he react the next time he came face to face with X.J.? Although James didn't understand why, the fear he'd felt upon meeting Art's youngest brother hadn't yet dissipated. Each time they came face to face he'd perceived a strange intensity. Yet, James was convinced that X.J. liked him. Then, he recalled the September morning X.J. had shown up at the door of his RV with a plastic container, asking to borrow sugar. James had just finished shaving and washing up, so he answered the door shirtless. He was baffled when he saw X.J. standing there with an empty sugar jar—this was so cliché. As X.J. gawked at James's shirtless torso, his expression shifted from a smile to a look of shock and embarrassment. James had been convinced he saw glimmers of raw desire in that moment—a frustrated longing. He got some sugar for X.J. and let the incident slide.

xvi

James was settled in at his desk with a steaming cup of coffee when Bella, Art, Loretta and Angie walked in. Bella and Art each poured themselves a cup of coffee, smiling and chatting with each other while Angie and Loretta sat down at the table. Catherine walked into the room and flashed her inimitable broad smile—taking time to share it with everyone in the room as she glanced at each one and nodded before settling her gaze on James. "Welcome back, Princip'l—so goot to see ya! *Hadih,* they finished our houses o'er the holidays. So glad!" she exclaimed, then smiled again and continued, "*Hadih,* t'James, did the girls tell you their story yet—Angie and Loretta? We almost had a tragedy here last week."

James looked over at Loretta and Angie and raised his eyebrows, inviting them to tell their story.

The night of January 3, Loretta and Angie had decided to make the trip from Williams Lake to Fort St. Pierre and onward to Chezgh'un. Extreme temperatures didn't phase them. They were country dwellers who had been through worse. Besides, over the holidays, Loretta had bought a brand-new four-by-four Chevrolet Tracker, and they'd thought about spending the night in the Fort, but after having driven five hours, coming north from Williams Lake—what was another hour to get to Chezgh'un? So, under a sky lit by a half moon, the two women set out for Chezgh'un. They wore winter coats, but to avoid being uncomfortable during the long ride in a heated vehicle, they had opted to wear light winter boots instead of the heavy wool-lined ones they typically wore in Chezgh'un and Williams Lake. Just north of Fort St. Pierre, the scenery was idyllic. "The moonlight was so magical," Angie said. "I love that drive."

The sturdy, white-flocked spruce trees that lined the road for the first ten or fifteen minutes of the trip comforted them. Such a familiar sight: snow-covered branches picking up the moonlight—occasional sparkles. A perfect tableau for a Christmas card. Angie, mesmerized by the scenery, said she had begun to recite a Robert Frost poem that she had memorized in fifth grade: *Whose woods these are I think I know...* when suddenly, she smelled oil burning.

Even though the vehicle Loretta was driving was new, and the dealer had filled it with oil, the oil indicator light was on. How could that be? Slowly, they advanced a kilometre farther. When they saw smoke wafting from the front of the vehicle, and the temperature gauge was as high as it could go, they pulled over.

"We had to walk—what else could we do?" Loretta said. "We were past the turnoff, so we knew it was less than five kilometres to Chez-gh'un. We walked fast, to try to keep warm. The howling coyotes. Or was it wolves? Their call and response—even though we heard it so many times growing up—was blood chilling."

When they finally got to the trailer their toes were numb, so they knew they were frostbitten. They soaked their feet in warm water and wrapped themselves in blankets.

James was left speechless by their story. He'd grown up in the North and spent time on the Prairies, but eight years in the moderate climate of Vancouver had spoiled him. He'd forgotten about the very real dangers of the North. After a moment of silence, James said, "I'm so sorry you two had that incredible close call. What a horrendous experience." He went quiet and looked at the floor, knowing that there was really nothing further he could say without sounding trite. He glanced over at Catherine.

"Ya coulda spend ta night at my house in the Fort, you girls. Ya know that," Catherine said in a quavering voice, wiping tears from her eyes.

VII

Pipon — Winter

i

A mayhem of noise—vehicles and voices, frantic and frenetic—wakes James from a deep sleep. *What the hell is going on?* Half asleep, he pulls on a heavy sweater and jeans, then rushes to the door and slips into his bulky winter boots. As he steps out onto the porch, flashes of red from the direction of the school catch his eye. *Fuck—Henry's house!* Furious flames burst out of the eaves and windows—ready to devour anything in their path. It's a scene from another century—a house on fire and men rushing around in the snow on foot with buckets of water. They can't get close enough to the burning house to douse the flames. Bright orange and crimson flames burst through the roof, sending a thick cloud of black smoke billowing into the sky.

To quell the fire would require jets of water blasting from a powerful hydrant or fire truck—Chezgh'un has neither. The talk around the community was that the federal government for years had promised to build a basic fire hall, but plans had been cancelled time and again—insufficient budget, government cutbacks.

This fire is unstoppable without a fire truck.

The blaze flashes higher and higher into the sky, more emboldened with each passing moment, obscenely lighting up the reticent grey sky. Sparks spitting in every direction. James rushes toward the house. It is as if he is invisible—everyone is so focused and intent—their movements robotic, even though they must know their efforts are futile. *My God, where are the kids, Lorna and Henry?* He doesn't see them anywhere. Are they huddled in the surrounding vehicles to keep warm? He hurriedly scans the trucks, but the air is too hazy and the headlights from a couple of the vehicles blind him. Has someone taken Lorna and the kids to Monique's or to Agnes's or to another house nearby?

James looks around for a bucket, even though he knows that throwing water is useless—it's simply building up a bizarre ice sculpture around the base of the house. Anouk appears and brings him a bucket, shows him where the water source is. Each new frozen layer promptly covered by soot, then the next one forms. From out of nowhere, a huge ember vaults toward James. He jerks backwards. *Oh God, please let Henry's kids be safe!* Is Henry in the Fort—partying again? He wracks his brain, trying to remember if he had seen a smoke detector in the house. Smoke detector? Fire extinguisher? These are city things. *Get real.* Where are Henry, Lorna and the kids? Who could he ask? He has to ask someone—*now.*

He spots Sally in the distance. She's a mess. Her face is covered with soot and ash, as is her parka. And she's blubbering, incoherent. James runs to her, puts his arm around her shoulder to comfort her, but she is stiff and cold, reeking of smoke.

"Two kids in the house, Princip'l. Henry, too. He was tryin ta drag 'em out. Didn't make it."

"Nooooo!" James screams and charges toward the burning house, still wailing, "Noooo! Noooo! We have to get them out!"

Art steps into his path. "Can't, Princip'l. You'll die. Smoke 'n heat are too much," he grunts. "We arrived too late. The other kids are at my mom's with Lorna. Helicopter is comin', ambulance too. But too late. All too late."

"Shannon! Is she okay?"

"She's with her mom, but she's really shaken up, Princip'l."

By 8 a.m. James was on the phone to Damien in Bilnk'ah. Damien was getting ready to leave for work.

"Damn, I wish I'd had the insight to do something before—something preventive. I should've seen the risk—even for my own safety, for God's sake."

"You can't think of everything, my man. You aren't their saviour. Remember, these people have survived thousands of years on their own without you there to look after them."

"I know that. But there must be ways I can help—now."

"Sure, James. But you need to get over your Jesus complex."

Damien's words stung, and James decided not to respond. Of course, Damien was right—he couldn't save these people, or anyone, from anything. But there were so many ways he could help—so why shouldn't he? And why should he settle for the status quo—alternate realities are possible. Damn, why did Damien want to put a damper on things?

James pulled on his hefty parka, wrapped his wool scarf around his face and stepped outside for fresh air. The RCMP had come to investigate. This must have been their first trip out here in years. He saw the constable who'd issued him a ticket on his first trip out this way—what was his name? Gosselin? He was now chatting with X.J. and Leyo. He likely knew that X.J. was on probation. Other than the break-in at James's he's been doing great—even chopping wood for the elders. What business did the cop have with Leyo? Just then, the constable glanced over at James. He interrupted what he was saying and approached to offer James a handshake.

"Settling into Chezgh'un okay? Sure appreciate what you're trying to do here. Good luck," he says with an expression that puzzled James. Is he earnest, or being sarcastic? Will he ask more intrusive questions the next time he stops James, or will he be more respectful? James leans in close to the officer, and says, "*Merci. Vous parlez français, j'imagine… L'incendie a été une vraie tragédie! J'en reviens pas.*"

That should do it, thought James. A bit of schmoozing in the cop's own language. Maybe from now on he'll respect me.

James decided to order basic smoke detectors for each house using the school's budget. He'd have some explaining to do, but he didn't care. He asked Bella to mobilize the adult-education class by getting them to do research on the number of fire-related deaths each year on Indian reserves in Canada.

Within a few days, Bella and her class had completed the work and what they learned motivated them to write a paper they planned to send to the band office and federal government. James was so impressed—they even had an executive summary. Bella was really something. He studied the paper carefully. He made a mental note to set up a session for the students to present their report to the band leadership before sending it off, with a covering letter, to the Department of Indian Affairs in Vancouver. Surely the powers that be would now feel compelled to do something to address the situation in Chezgh'un and similar communities across Canada.

SUMMARY OF FINDINGS RELATED TO FIRES ON INDIAN RESERVES IN CANADA:

prepared by the Chezgh'un Adult-Education Program Class

Based on current official national statistics:

a) The fire-related death rate was 1.6 for First Nations people per 100,000 person-years, compared to 0.3 among non-Native people, an increased risk of five times.
b) The fire-related death rate for First Nations people living on reserve was 3.2 per 100,000 person-years. More than ten times the rate of 0.3 among non-Native people.
c) The burn-related death rate was one death per 100,000 person-years for First Nations people, which is five times the rate of 0.2 among non-Native people.

d) The hospitalization rate for fire injuries was 7.5 for First Nations per 100,000 person-years, compared to 1.7 among non-Native people, which is an increased risk of four times.
e) The hospitalization rate for burns was 13.9 for First Nations per 100,000 person-years, compared to 4.3 among non-Native people. This is an increased risk of three times.
f) Building and structural fires were four times more likely to be the cause of death than other types of fires such as ignition of highly flammable materials, forest fires, campfires, intentional self-harm or assault.
g) Native males suffered statistically more fire-related deaths, burns and hospitalizations than Native females.
h) The social determinants leading to higher fire deaths and injury for Native people included poverty, inadequate housing and lack of working smoke alarms.

A key issue we discovered is the chronic underfunding for fire services in First Nations communities resulting in a lack of fire halls and firefighting equipment, as well as a lack of legislation mandating compliance with building and fire codes on reserves.

Lorna and her remaining six kids, all grief-stricken from the loss of their father and two siblings, crowded into Art's house while the elders sorted out where they could stay in the short and medium term. They decided that the oldest would sleep at their grandmother Monique's place most nights. All the other houses in Chezgh'un, mostly two-room shacks like Henry's and Art's, already had between ten and twenty people living in them, combinations and permutations of babies, toddlers, teens, adults, elders.

To make matters worse, the band wouldn't be able to build a new house for Henry's family for at least two years because there were ten other families on the list for new houses in Chezgh'un alone, and twice that number in Bilnk'ah. The band manager had soberly recounted to James this harsh reality the following week when they'd bumped into each other in the Chinese restaurant—James's astonished facial expression was met with an angry retort: "Where the hell you been...? This is the fuckin' norm on Indian reserves, all over the North. Big families—so many peoples bunked up in shacks... firetraps, every goddamn one of 'em. Gor'ment don' give a shit."

ii

James and Bella sat sipping beer at the pizza joint just around the corner from the Crest Motel in Prince George—chatting about social inequity, the dynamics of oppression and popular response. Bella dazzled James with her summary of the Freirean approach to pedagogy: "Antidialogics and dialogics as matrices of opposing theories of cultural action. The former as an instrument of oppression and the latter as an instrument of liberation," Bella said. "The characteristics of antidialogical action are conquest, divide and rule, manipulation and cultural invasion, whereas in dialogical action we see cooperation, unity, organization and cultural synthesis."

"Whoa, slow down, wait a minute—you just swamped me with jargon. Tell me what this all means in plain English."

Bella laughed and said, "I studied this stuff so damn much, I can quote Freire off the cuff like that. It simply means that instead of the usual one-way conversation that political leaders and educators have with their people and learners, respectively, we should encourage active dialogue—an exchange of ideas and thinking to understand the reality one is faced with, and once this is accomplished, collaboratively find solutions that work for all. We need to treat people as if they're whole, empowered, inspired beings—as opposed to empty vessels that need to be filled, or sheep that need direction, guidance and salvation."

"Thank you. That's more like it. It's a brilliant technique, especially with adult students. Good God, they have life experience and a wealth of knowledge and problem-solving capacity to draw on. They wouldn't have survived to adulthood if they didn't."

"The group I'm working with in Chezgh'un is amazing—so much knowledge and life experience. It's the usual pattern we see with on-reserve learning—adults with years of training under their belt. But it's a patchwork of skills development. Nothing to pull it all together as a diploma or degree—industrial first aid, basic carpentry, computer skills, home maintenance, basic electrical skills and so on."

"Well, listen, I've been stumped trying to find a way to be a catalyst for the community to defend its land base and rights, and expand them to meet their needs. I know that for a lasting solution to occur, the community has to do the work. And, besides this, I've been warned by the chief to keep my nose out of local politics."

"I know exactly where you're going with that, James, and I'm onside. We can get the adult-education class on the issue—to investigate the history of how they ended up in the situation they're in, with respect to their land holdings and governance. We'll get right on it."

The two educators were so excited by this meeting of the minds—by the hope of being able to make a difference as catalysts as opposed to taking the issues on themselves—they both bolted out of their chairs and hugged.

The hug turned into an embrace. James felt aroused and he felt that Bella did too. As they moved apart, they looked deeply into each other's eyes. James leaned forward, and his lips touched Bella's. Her lips firmed up slightly to return the kiss—then they caught themselves.

"Wow. That was close."

Bella threw her head back and laughed loudly, then said, "Too close, James. But oh my God, would it be nice."

"It would ... it really would. You're amazing."

"Maybe another time, another place—when we're not working together so closely, with you as my boss—and me as the union rep. Can't have the union in bed with management now, can we?"

"Listen, I'm sure stranger things have happened. But better for us to not go there, right?"

They sat back down and continued the conversation, discussing all the government cutbacks and how they were affecting First Nations. They both expressed consternation and wondered aloud if the new school construction at Chezgh'un would be delayed—or cancelled altogether. Bella's classes were in the new portable, but James couldn't bear the notion of working in the unsafe dilapidated main building another year, and the government had already backtracked on its promise to build a community fire hall without delay. The public outrage stirred up by the deaths in the fire at Chezgh'un had dissipated in no time at all, it seemed.

Bella lightened up the conversation by recalling some of her experiences over the brief time she'd been the adult-ed teacher at Chezgh'un—how amused she'd been hearing from the elders about their sexual escapades. Who was having a fling with whom in the grey-headed crowd of Chezgh'un. "A regular seniors' Peyton Place," she said with a laugh.

Her tone got more sombre as she said, "There's been disclosures, James—partial disclosures of childhood sexual abuse from some of the women in my class, against elders I won't name, and political leaders. I had to end those conversations before they told me too much. After all, I'm not a counsellor, or a cop. I had to be very clear about this with the adult students." She sat silent, pensive.

"Everyone knows, or should know, that the current situation is part of a cycle arising from massive sexual abuse at residential schools over several generations. Victims of abuse by priests or nuns became perpetrators themselves, and it will take a large-scale community-wide intervention to deal with the situation. It likely won't happen in our time there."

"But surely that doesn't mean we can't try to get help for the students who are ready to begin their healing from this, James."

"I agree. A case-by-case basis of doing our best to get help. Then it'll be up to the community as to how they approach their collective healing. I just hope they do."

"What are ya doin' tomorrow, James?"

"I was supposed to meet up with Damien to go for a hike, maybe some bird hunting, then Colin, Ruthie and Ali for supper. See you back in Chezgh'un day after tomorrow?"

"Sounds good," Bella answered. "See you then. Drive safe."

iii

At spring break Damien and James left for Vancouver together in Damien's truck. Damien had precipitously left his teaching job in Bilnk'ah—everyone knew there was a story here—but Damien and his principal had somehow managed to keep the information from leaking out into the gossip mill. James knew that if he really wanted to find out, Louise would likely have told him, but he preferred not to know, in order to preserve the caring and respect he'd developed for the man in such a short timeframe. What good could possibly have come from him knowing more of Damien's shortcomings and flaws? After all, Damien had been good to him—a solid ally.

He'd intended to confront Damien about persistent rumours in the community—about him sleeping around with young married women—which if true, would have put him in a dangerous conflict with the men of Bilnk'ah. And, there were rumours about issues with his criminal record check—someone had finally gotten around to looking at the results for all the staff. This long road trip south would have been the perfect opportunity for a heart to heart, but what was the point now?

With his own reputation to protect, James knew that he would have to pull back on his friendship with Damien—whether or not Damien stayed in the community. It's a small world up north, he reminded himself. Everyone knows everyone else's business. Better to not take any more chances. In addition, his so-called girlfriend, Sylviana, had left with her children and moved to Prince George in another cloud of mystery. Like James, she had befriended Ali, and sought his kindness and assistance with the relocation—much to Damien's consternation.

Just north of Williams Lake, Damien suddenly swerved his truck to the left and slammed on the brakes—but the front right fender hit something anyway.

"Fuck," he yelled. "Fuck, fuck, fuck, fuck, fuck." He pulled over to the shoulder on James's side and stopped—killed the motor.

James straightened up and went into full alert. What now? There was always such calamity and drama with Damien. It happened in a flash. It took a second for James to grasp what was going on. The animal had come out of nowhere. Was it a deer? Must be a female—he would've seen the antlers if there were any. Damn—must've hit the head or elongated neck.

"I hit a fucking moose—just what I needed. Did you see it?" James stayed quiet. He'd learned that at times like this saying even the most consoling of words could set Damien off into an angry tirade—directed at him—for supposedly missing some important point of logic or sensibility. The two men jumped out of the truck. There lay the animal on its side—twitching. Laborious breathing. The powerful smell of wet animal fur and urine caught James by surprise. This cow moose was about to mate, or had just mated—a cow who had selected her mate, rolled into a mud pit the lucky suitor had dug and peed into. Once he'd gotten over the surprise of the odour, James looked at the animal more closely. Its thigh muscles were twitching. He was so tempted to touch it, to stroke its fur—a blend of hickory and sepia, which he knew covered a soft velvety layer of skin. How tragic—maybe this cow moose had just been impregnated.

Ravens had already gathered, squawking loudly. One bird flew at the others menacingly as they hopped haphazardly around the dying moose. Suddenly it pounced onto the moose's disproportionately large head and started pecking the giant moose eyeballs with its curved, obsidian beak. An overwhelming sense of hopelessness came over James. He stood there, immobile, while Damien swung into action.

"It's in agony—I have to shoot it."

He jumped into his truck and grabbed his hunting rifle. He clicked the magazine into place and yelled out, "Stand clear!"

James turned on his heels and moved toward the back of the vehicle. He heard the deafening explosion and knew it was over. Now, he'd accompany Damien to file a police report. The police in turn would phone the game warden who would contact a local First Nation hunter to pick up the carcass for the meat and the hide. Road-kill, James thought. How many times had his family been summoned to get roadkill, because they were so poor? Sometimes the animals were badly mangled and very little meat could be salvaged, the hide a mess, but this was a clean kill—not much would be wasted.

This thought consoled James as he climbed back into the truck, knowing he was in for a sombre ride with Damien. The vehicle rocked as an eighteen-wheeler flew past. Damien jumped onto the bench seat without uttering another word. He didn't have to. His foul mood permeated the air.

Just north of Kamloops, James realized they were nearby to a site where conflict had been building between a resort development and Native land protectors. He asked Damien to make the slight detour to visit the protectors' encampment. The so-called Native "occupiers" had now taken control of one of the roads that led onto the resort site, to a lake that was considered sacred and believed to have healing properties. The lake had circular spots on its surface that had a lustrous sheen, apparently caused by the minerals suspended in the water. Sure enough, an improvised wooden guard station had been set up just outside of the large metal gate of the ranch. A few Native men stood in front of it to control access. Presumably, the encampment the media had described was just ahead, out of view from the main road. James was filled with excitement but tried not to let it come through in his voice. Even though they weren't lovers, Damien had a jealous streak James still struggled to understand.

"Can you stop the truck please, Damien? I'm going to walk over and have a chat with them."

"We gotta get to Vancouver tonight, man. And they're not gonna wanna see me, a white guy. C'mon now."

"I have to do this. You wait in the truck. Won't be long. Please, my man."

James pulled on his parka, even though the weather here was milder than up north. He jumped out of the truck and strolled over to the men. He stopped just in front of them. He could smell their smokiness. They'd likely just come from sitting around the fire. The men didn't say a word—they studied him quizzically.

"Hi, I'm James—I'm Cree from Alberta, but I'm a school principal in a reserve called Chezgh'un, up north. Our adult-ed students have been keeping up-to-date with the situation here, so I wanted to stop by to meet you guys, to tell you that you have our support. They want you to know: they could send some guys down here in a flash if things flare up—if there's any violence or if the military shows up."

The men looked apprehensive at first, but their faces softened once they'd sized up James and gauged his sincerity. The tallest man, decked out in camouflage gear, introduced himself as Thunder Cloud. He shook James's hand and asked him if he wanted to join them for a cup of tea around their fire—try some of their campfire bannock and dried fish. James was impressed with how organized and equipped they were and suddenly wished he'd made the trip on his own, to have more flexibility.

"Don't have time. I'm ridin' with a *moniyaw* teacher friend here. We gotta get to Vancouver tonight. Just wanted to see for myself how things are with you guys. Never know what to believe in the news, eh?"

"We have warriors posted at every entry to the development site. We know who all's coming and going. And bro, the media hasn't reported this yet, but the cops and military have set up a parallel camp about ten kilometres up the road in a provincial park. They have heavy weaponry and a couple of military vehicles—they're ready to do real battle. They've closed the park for now—for everyone. But we plan to take the park over, too. That park is our land—it has traditional burial sites on it. All hell will break loose in a few weeks we think. People are planning to come from all over Canada and the US. Even the Mohawks are coming—and they have weapons. A couple of their guys are former US Marines, eh."

"Well, we'll be watching the news. In Chezgh'un there's a group of adult learners who are watching the situation closely. They'll drive down to back you up if need be."

James held out his hand to the man who shook it briskly before turning his back and walking away. As James strode back to the truck, he debated how much information he should share with Damien about the protest. Damien could be so intense...

iv

Franyo had waited up for James. They had an energetic, tear-filled reunion. James became aroused, but when the intensity began, he instantly felt remorse for fantasizing, yet again, that it was Damien in bed with him rather than Franyo. He conjured Damien's hands, his face and his muscular chest, but the new reality flashed into his mind. Things were over with Damien. They would never be lovers, and he let himself settle into the present moment. It was Franyo he was with—reliable, caring and ever affectionate Franyo. Once the passion had ebbed, Franyo held James so close that thoughts of Damien dissipated as they breathed in each other's exhalation. Face to face like that, they fell asleep.

Early the next morning, James and Franyo made their habitual trip to Granville Island. James wondered aloud if he would bump into Chief Felix again, with Justa. He hadn't spoken to Justa in a while—since that chance encounter in the Prince George airport. He suspected that the chief would be mortified if he knew that James knew about him and Justa. There was still so much homophobia in the North—and Bilnk'ah was no exception.

James would make paella that evening. He and Damien had spoken about the recipe James had developed and refined over the years since he and Franyo had first tasted the earthy dish in a quaint Spanish restaurant on Davie Street while they were still getting to know each other. Damien had bragged that his mother, who was from Spain, made the best paella ever, but James was sure his recipe would be comparable, if not better. He thought about inviting Damien over to help prepare the meal, but Damien would've been awkward around Franyo—and vice versa—if it was just the three of them. He was certain.

As he and Franyo wandered through the public market, stopping now and then to listen to tattooed, bohemian buskers, James kept an eye open for Justa and Felix Joe. He made a few excuses to linger, manipulating the situation to delay their return home, until finally, Franyo said, "James, come on, we've gotta prep for company."

Once he realized what he was doing, James became flustered, wondered what that was going on with him, before realizing he was worried about Justa. After exchanging messages regularly over a couple of weeks, it had now been a while since James had heard from him. He wondered how Justa's studies were going—how his social and love life were going—if he'd seen Chief Felix a lot or a little. Those were the usual things they discussed. He would call Justa when he got back up north.

As soon as they returned home, James began the preparations. For him, cooking was a form of meditation—all encompassing. A few hours of relief from the stress of life, preparing gourmet meals. He didn't do this in Chezgh'un, where simple fare was the norm for everyone.

James marinated the prawns in olive oil, garlic, Dijon mustard, paprika and tarragon. He soaked the mussels and clams in cold water for an hour before scrubbing and cleaning their shells. A half-hour before the guests came, he would place the large casserole dish in a heated oven until the rice was swollen but not quite cooked. Once everyone was seated at the dining table, he would place the seafood medley atop the rice mixture and place the dish under a hot broiler until all the deep blue and cream-coloured shells had popped open and the prawns had turned bright pink. The pungent, briny juices from the seafood would seep into the rice to enhance the land-based flavours. James would accelerate this by turning the seafood into the rice a few times with a large wooden spoon.

The guests arrived in quick succession; Enrique and Julius, Theo and Bérénice, James's Fijian friend Davith and his partner Cynthia... Wait, where was Damien? He should have arrived by now too. Damn. Had he gotten lost, or decided to spend the evening in other company?

James took off his apron and made the rounds with hugs and cheery banter. When he got to Bérénice, she held him still for a moment and gazed into his eyes. James felt himself shudder and he knew Bérénice felt it too. He took a slow, deep breath before anyone else noticed that he was getting emotional. He raised his head and gave Bérénice a quick *bec* on the lips then moved on to Theo.

Everyone had sat down to eat when the intercom rang—Damien.

"I'll let him in," James said to Franyo, as he hastened out of the apartment and downstairs to the foyer. In spite of everything, he felt a rush seeing Damien there. He was one amazingly talented and bright man—with so much to offer. Damien had been such an anchor for him through a huge life transition and uncertain times. He hoped his new friend would get another chance, in another school district with another principal, another doting friend. The two men studied each other's faces for a moment, then embraced and held each other before heading up.

James was proud to introduce Damien to all of his friends. Yes, Damien was truly an anchor in the white world, in his new life in the North.

Once Damien was seated at the table, James returned to the stove for the final prep. As he stirred the rosy-red prawns, deep blue mussels and white butter clams into the saffron-infused rice, he surveyed his group of friends via the pass-through. He still cared about them, of course, but the connection he had with them was shifting—he could feel it. With the exception of Bérénice, who was incredibly empathetic, he felt he was simply going through the motions of closeness with his friends—emulating the bond they had before. When he looked at Damien, he felt an exhilaration he couldn't understand or explain, even here, in the love nest he'd shared with Franyo.

The paella was a hit. Everyone raved about it, and, for once, Theo and Julius enjoyed the food along with everyone else. Enrique addressed Damien in Spanish, and Damien did his best to respond. James caught the smirk on Enrique's face when Damien spoke with a

Castilian accent—a lisp: "*Grathias. Es un plather estar aqui con ustedes.*" Damien then shifted his attention to James and said, "I have to admit, James. This paella is as delicious as my mother's. *Muy rica.*"

After dinner, James and Franyo set up an improvised stage at the edge of the dining room. Everyone moved to the living room to sit on Franyo's comfy sectional couch. Bérénice, wine glass in hand, made herself a front-row seat on the floor with a cushion from the couch, directly in front of James.

James and Damien crooned, in a smooth and consistent flowing harmony, about wanting and needing each other, about tasting each other's wine-coloured lips. They warbled "All I Have to Do Is Dream" by the Everly Brothers, gazing into each other's eyes as they sang. Next, they blasted out "Seven Bridges Road." After each verse, Damien flat-picked a fast-paced solo. When they sang their favourite song—an intense love ballad—James set his instrument down to focus on the intricate harmonies. Some passing notes were discordant, and James loved the contrast—harmony is somehow sweeter when it emerges from dissonance.

James worried about this moment. He knew Franyo would see the intense emotional dynamic between himself and Damien. Franyo could read him like a book. Would he believe that Damien and James were sexually and romantically entwined? Likely, *everyone* would make that assumption.

There was a split second of silence after the duo completed the last line of the song, then boisterous applause. "*C'était éléctrique!*" Bérénice shouted, grasping James's thigh before standing to kiss Damien on the lips.

Theo, Julius and Enrique all raved as well. Cynthia said, "That was magnificent. You should do a show." Franyo sat silent, but when everyone other than he had said something, the group turned to look at him, to discreetly gauge his mood.

"You guys are brilliant! Quite an act," he finally said, as he stood to approach the couple where they sat on their improvised stage. He shook Damien's hand and then pulled James up into an embrace. He held him for a moment, then abruptly let go.

Damien stood and raised his hands in the air as he spoke. "Thank you, everyone. So good to meet you. James has spoken a lot about each of you. Sorry to do this, but I have to leave—my friend Joel is expecting me at his house—another performance," he said and chuckled. He made the rounds to shake everyone's hand. As he approached Franyo, James could see the sadness in Franyo's eyes.

James showed Damien out. As they said goodbye, tears welled up in James's eyes, and he blinked them back. The two men held on to each other longer than they normally would. James savoured Damien's powerful embrace for a moment then tilted his head upward and kissed Damien's right cheek. He muttered, "*Te quiero. Tu sabes. Cuídate mucho mi, Damien,*" and turned quickly to leave.

"James… My man."

James turned to face him. Damien didn't want to leave him either.

"*Oyes, mi,* Damien. I'll see you soon, back up north."

Damien stepped up to James and put a hand on his shoulder.

"My man… I hate to ask you this, but you know I'm out of work now. Could you lend me some money to help tide me over, till I get on my feet again? I don't need much—like maybe five hundred."

"Tomorrow. I'll meet you tomorrow after I go to the bank."

James turned and rushed upstairs, fighting back tears of frustration.

VIII

Miyoskamin — Spring Breakup

i

The piercing ring of Franyo's home phone awoke James at five o'clock. Intuitively, he knew it was for him, but who could be calling him at Franyo's place so early? Another family emergency? Since his mother had died a couple of years earlier and even before that, after she'd quit drinking, he hadn't had any late night or early morning calls. Every time she called at strange hours his mother had been inebriated and distraught about something that had happened ten, twenty or thirty years earlier—maybe even in her childhood, but she just had to discuss some angle of the incident she had in mind with James, urgently.

"Ah, hullo."

"James?"

"Who's this? Why are you calling me at this hour? How did you get this number?"

"*Hadih,* James. It's Caroline, Justa's sister. Sorry ta call you like this. I heard you were in Vancouver, and I need a big favour. Could you go ta see Justa? He's in emergency at Vancouver General. They say he tried ta commit suicide during the night."

"My God. Yes—I'll call them to confirm he's there and I'll go right away—well if they let me."

"I talked ta them, and they say they'll let you in—in place of fam'ly, if you'll go."

James threw on the clothes that were closest to him. He was anxious to get going but baffled. Why were they calling him instead of the chief? Maybe the chief was home in Prince George, as would be expected, with his family. Or maybe his family wasn't so keen on his friendship with Justa.

Tousled hair, pale blue cotton pyjamas. Puffy face, eyes tiny slits. James saw a flash of recognition and maybe relief in Justa's eyes. Obviously sedated, Justa sat on a threadbare white sheet that partially covered a thin rubber mattress placed atop a cement mound in the middle of the tiny square "quiet room." Behind him, a shiny stainless-steel toilet was an unnatural outgrowth from the drab cement wall. James remembered working in these quiet rooms, where new admissions were placed for the first twenty-four hours or until the psychiatrist had seen them for an initial assessment.

"Can I leave the two of you alone for a bit?" asked Justa's casually dressed duty nurse. "We'll leave the door open."

"Fine with me," James responded. "Justa?"

Justa nodded without looking up.

"Just call if either of you need anything," the nurse said as he turned his back and hastened out of the room, pulling the door until it was left slightly ajar.

The two men sat in silence staring at the floor. James knew he just had to be patient. Chances were there would be no eye contact during this visit. Dakelh people were like that and so were Cree people: when emotions were heightened, they avoided eye contact. After what seemed like an eternity, James stepped in close to Justa and spoke.

"Caroline asked me to come. So, what's going on my friend?"

Justa remained silent for a long pause then cleared his throat slightly and said, "Not sure I should tell you."

"Well, you don't have to tell me. I came because I'm concerned, and because your sister asked me to. Not sure how I can help, but I want to, if I can."

"Maybe they let me leave with you—don' wanna be *here,* that's for sure. You wouldn't believe all that's going on in this place."

Out of nowhere a silky soprano voice with a slight vibrato echoed off the stark cement walls silencing the two young men for a moment.

"*There are pigeons on the roof of the little chapel that belong to the Mother of God.*

White and purple and grey and dapple, they preen their feathers and promenade."

James recognized those lines from a song from his high school–choir days. How odd that someone would be singing this obscure song here in the psych ward in Vancouver. He took it as an omen—he was supposed to be here with Justa.

"Justa, I really need to know where your head is at if you wanna get outta here. Most likely, the emerg doc and psychiatrist will have you committed for up to two weeks. So, today or tomorrow they'll move you to another ward, or if they think you're okay, they'll sign you out—discharge you into *somebody's* care."

"Everyone back home knows you live with your lover."

"*Hadih,* Justa, why are you telling me this? Shouldn't this conversation be about *you*? I'm not the one who's needing care right now. But listen, if you don't wanna talk to me, I might as well just go. But before I do, I should ask you, do you want to see Felix? Shall I give him a call?"

"Don' call the chief. Please don't call the chief. I don' wanna see him again. Never. He walked out on me. We're done."

The two young men sat for a moment without speaking, then Justa broke the silence.

"First it was all fun. He'd come ta town, and we'd go ta hockey games, work out at the gym together, run some trails. Overnight trips ta Whistler ta ski. Everyone assumed we were father and son or that he was my uncle. We went along with it, but sometimes I would tease Felix, tell 'im, 'I dunno what you and your father do.' He would get so mad. Then one day, after a hot session, I did it… I tol' him I *loved* him. Fuckin' tol' him I loved him. So stupid. He hasn't called since."

Justa paused. He stared at the floor, then looked up at the ceiling. "You can't tell anyone."

James nodded.

Justa clasped his hands tightly in his lap. "I fell for Felix harder than for any girl, and we had way more sex than I had with any woman so far. I was willin' ta give up everythin' for Felix—my girlfriend, my close ties to my family. They woulda ditched me if they knew 'bout me 'n the chief. Even my grades started to slip."

He told James how it all happened—Felix's gradual but powerful seduction. It had begun innocently enough: meals at fast food places before or after hockey games, shopping trips for clothes and sports equipment. Felix wanted Justa to have the best runners, the trendiest sports clothing—shorts and muscle shirts, designer sunglasses, top-notch golf clubs, baseball equipment, a flashy tennis racquet. Even a professional frisbee. *You're a natural athlete—you can do anything,* Felix had told him.

Justa leaned forward and put his head in his hands. James thought Justa might cry. He himself was on the verge of tears—full of this young man's angst.

"I know a good counsellor, a clinical psychologist if you wanna go see her."

"Like, I'm not even fuckin' gay. I told Felix that. I like pussy. He's the one that pushed it all. Came by more and more—made the sex hotter each time. I tried ta hook him up with my Dutch friend Christine from college, but he didn' want another woman—he wanted me. I was blown away that this incredible man, a hometown hero wanted me—*me!* So powerful and convincin', eh? Anyways, after he didn' return my calls for a week, I got real distressed and took some pills, tranquilizers—a whole bottle."

James could feel wetness on his cheek, a tear that he quickly brushed away. His sister had committed suicide in this way:

chlorpromazine—CPZ. It took her three tries to succeed. There was no way in hell he'd let this happen to Justa. No way. He took Justa's hand, looked him in the eye and said, "*Kisagihin nsims*. Means I love you, little brother."

As he strode down the long stark corridor with its drab greyish walls and tiled floors, he pondered the treatment options for Justa. The psychiatrist would likely put him on a waiting list for a community care team and discharge him within a day or two. He considered talking to Felix, confronting him about his relationship with Justa and asking him to find some way of mitigating Justa's suffering—maybe an apology, maybe a travel junket somewhere or some time back in the community, at the chief's expense. But then he quickly decided that this would be a surefire way of making real enemies with the chief and being shunned from the community—probably fairly quickly, costs be damned. No, he would just call Justa's sister and advise her on the best course of treatment. And he would call Justa more often—a few times a week. And visit him when Justa returned home in the spring. Maybe invite him to Chezgh'un for a weekend.

James flew back to Prince George early Sunday morning. He planned to drive to Bilnk'ah to see Ali and Damien. He'd deliver the Gitanes cigarettes and Wild Turkey bourbon for Ali then drop some gourmet items at Damien's for them to enjoy the following weekend.

Ali was so happy to see James—he invited him in for a cup of tea.

"*Hadih,* James, would you like to stay for dinner? Simple fare, but it'd be nice if you could join me."

"Oh, that's sweet, my friend. But I'm going to pop over to see Damien. We'll play some music."

"For real? He didn't tell you? He really didn't tell you?" Ali said, his right hand flailing in the air.

James responded with a blank stare, a look of bewilderment. "No... what?"

"He's gone. Gone for good. He got back from Vancouver and packed up his truck—left just like that. Plans to drop his stuff off at his mother's place then go back to Vancouver to stay with a friend named Joel while he looks for another job."

James was dumbfounded by two things: Damien absconded like that without telling him, and he was going back to stay with his friend, Joel, who, for some reason, he had insisted on referring to as his rich, gay Jewish friend.

"Damn. Did he leave his contact information with you—or anyone?"

As James drove back to Chezgh'un, his thoughts were frenetic. He felt dizzy and nauseated. How could he have given Damien, a complete stranger, a central role in his new life? How could he have been so mistaken about Damien's character—placed such importance in his friendship—even compromised his relationship with Franyo, as a result. He knew he'd been getting warning signals but had dismissed these thoughts. James had had a lot to process at the time: a fear of the unknown, a response to Damien's daredevil approach to life and lack of respect of the very real dangers of being in the northern wilderness—untamed nature, and his overwhelming and confusing seduction. He'd become so emotionally entangled with the guy—now he'd have to rethink their relationship—completely. One huge source of solace and emotional support in his new life in the North was now gone.

ii

Art burst into James's office with a strange smile and an unhinged look in his eyes. "*Hadih,* Princip'l, they ask me to go to Argentina." His boisterous baritone laugh. James smiled at him but didn't say a word. Instead, he raised his eyebrows and tilted his head to one side. Then he leaned back in his office chair, knowing he would have to wait for Art to stop laughing and explain. Art took a deep breath, made fleeting eye contact, then said, "Goin' ta hunt beaver."

James swivelled his chair slightly so he could look out the window. The creek that ran around the whole community was high, and the giant mud puddle in the school driveway continued to expand. After a few seconds, he swivelled his chair back and said, "*Really*? Hey Art, I know you won the bullshitting contest last week—undefeated champion and all that—but it's just you and me here now. No audience. No prize. Besides, you got lotsa beaver right here buddy, all you can handle!" James snickered at his own double entendre, and Art joined in, squelching James's laughter.

"No shit, Princip'l. Band office radioed last night. They want me ta go ta Argentina ta hunt beaver, and I tol' 'em I would, but only if you kin come along. You speak their tongue—Spanish, right?"

James got near frantic at the thought of travelling south—the winter had been long and cold. He glanced out of the picture window of his office at the brown patches around the mounds of dull grey snow. It would be nice to get away for a while and come back to greening grass and pussy willows and blossoming flowers—but he had to control himself, avoid disappointment. He took a deep breath and let silence hang in the air for a few seconds before launching into his response.

"To hunt beaver, eh? Right, Art. You're not sucking me in, man," James said as he stood and walked to the doorway to see who was in the hallway, eavesdropping, waiting to see if he would fall for the ruse.

No one. James turned to face Art, who was leaning against the door frame, arms akimbo, a smirk on his face. Art sat in James's office chair, so the two men were now almost eye to eye. Dogs began barking and growling outside. The vicious German shepherd–wolf cross tied up in the yard across from the school grounds must've gotten loose.

"Art, did you make a bet with someone, that you could fool me? Are you recording this?"

Art laughed again, then made a straight face and said, "*Hadih*, ever-suspicious Princip'l. No, t'James. It's for real. Sometimes gor'ment do stupid things, eh? Well, in the forties, when the fur was worth somethin', gor'ment captured fifty beavers from aroun' here and shipped them ta Argentina—alive. Ta start a fur industry there. My *'atsiyan* was involved in that. He tol' me about it—said he had warned them it was a hare-brained and risky scheme, said it might be hard for beavers ta get used ta the place, but if they did, watch out. If they were gonna transplant them beavers, they shoulda taken some bears and wolves, too. Beavers breed like rabbits, and they can reshape an ecosystem o'er time. And sure enough. Tee-yair-ah del Foo-eh-go—or somethin' like that, some big park anyways—is being ruined."

James was still suspicious. Discreetly, he studied Art to make sure there wasn't a tape recorder strapped to his belt or tucked into the pocket of his plaid shirt. If this *was* a bullshitting scheme, it was getting elaborate.

"Well, *Arthur*. And just what do they want *you* there for? Are you an expert on beavers?"

"I like ta think so, Princip'l. Dakelh have been eatin' beaver since time h'immemorial."

Art roared with laughter and James joined in although he always felt his laugh was feeble alongside Art's. The laughter died down, then Art continued, "They want me to hunt and trap as many as we can down there, and show the local tribe—they call 'em Mapuche—how ta trap beavers 'ficiently. Teach 'em ta tan the hides into nice furs and cook the meat so it tastes goot. The tail is a delicacy, Princip'l. 'N there's a gland that produces a thick, waxy grease. S'goot medicine for burns and cuts. We keep some in the house all the time."

"Well yes, I know that part, Art. I'm Cree, remember? My mom used to tell me that she loved to eat beaver tail, and she talked about that gland under the tail that produces a thick goo. Cree people used it as medicine, too, and top chefs use it to flavour soups."

"We do the same, Princip'l, but those tribes in Argentina, them Mapuche, don't know nothin' 'bout beaver. They have their own delicacies and medicines I figure."

"When do they want you to go, Art?"

"The week of Easter, Princip'l. Let's go."

James had planned to drive to Vancouver again for Easter vacation, but if this *was* for real, the temptation to travel to South America would be overwhelming. He'd call Franyo right away, and Justa too—to tell them he wouldn't be spending his vacation in Vancouver. Surely, they'd understand and share in his excitement.

That night he investigated travel logistics for getting to Argentina from Chezgh'un. It would be early fall there, the exact opposite of Canada. Patagonia was in the extreme south. Some said it was a lot like British Columbia: mountainous, four seasons, similar habitat, a paradise for beavers—streams and forest, and no natural predators. He and Art would have to drive a few hours to Prince George, fly two hours to Vancouver, five hours to Toronto, then eleven hours to Santiago de Chile, then a final two-hour flight to Buenos Aires. From Buenos Aires they would fly or take an overnight bus to Rio Negro. They'd be fatigued when they got there, but they'd be *on*—James attempting to translate Art's non-stop stream of consciousness banter and then the eager responses of his Mapuche interlocuters.

James helped Art apply for his passport, signing the form as a referee. Chezgh'un was abuzz. Art was going to Argentina—to hunt beaver, and James was going with him. What an adventure! James and the teachers researched Argentina further and decided to use the trip as a "teachable moment" for the whole school. They planned lessons about the geography, history and culture of the country. The teens assembled a gift package of cultural items: smoked jerky of salmon and moose, a moose-hide vest, beaded moccasins and gloves. A video of the high school class singing in Dekelh, drumming and dancing. A recorded message from elders, Agnes and Monique, in Dakelh with a Spanish translation. A painted drum.

As he did his research, James was shocked at the parallels between the colonial history of Argentina and that of Canada. But there, the colonizers of course were Spanish rather than British, and they were after gold, primarily, although they also usurped the lands and set up a type of feudal system, using the local tribe for cheap labour, and demanding a percentage of the tribe's harvest of maize, beans, squash, potatoes and chilies in a crude taxation scheme. Like the British, the Spanish used germ warfare, spreading smallpox throughout Indigenous communities by trading or gifting blankets they knew to be infected, in order to reduce the overwhelming majority population of the local tribes. But the Spanish also used armed massacres, and at one point the Argentine government even put bounties on the heads of individual Mapuche.

In Canada, there was no large-scale warfare as such, and a bounty was also offered, but for bison instead of humans. The bison were intentionally exterminated to starve out the Plains Cree—to force them to enter prescribed treaties and then move onto reserve lands, to be confined there. The collusion of the Catholic Church with the Canadian government helped convince rank and file "Indians" to pressure their leaders into signing the cryptic treaties, which had colossal implications, and into accepting what little was offered to them by way of provisions to prevent mass starvation.

Mapuche men were fierce warriors who staved off Spanish colonization for more than a century. They were a proud and sovereign nation. The Spanish Crown negotiated treaties with them, nation to nation, but those historic treaties were declared invalid by the post-colonial government of Argentina.

The research gave James and the teachers plenty of information, but several questions arose for James and Art to ask of the tribes in Argentina: Did they still speak their languages? Did they lead traditional lifestyles, eat traditional foods and how was their health? What were the predominant social challenges they were facing? Were they endeavouring to get their lands back—re-establish their historic sovereignty? Had they developed a relationship with the new and invasive species from Canada, the beaver?

Art chattered frenetically during the entire two-hour drive from Chezgh'un to Prince George. It would be his first plane ride. In the airport, he studied the other passengers, the passing flight attendants in their official-looking starched uniforms, pilots in their pressed white shirts and black caps, and the security guards. He studied his ticket—the rectangular onion-skin pages looked so tiny in his big hands. Wide-eyed with curiosity, he called out, "YXS, YVR, YYZ, SCL, EZE. What the hell's all that for, Princip'l?

James reached up and put his hand on Art's shoulder to calm him, aware that it all must have been surreal—and this was just the beginning of the adventure. James had warned him about having to remove his baseball cap going through security, and that he would have to remove his belt and boots—maybe even get frisked.

Art laughed and cawed in his smoky voice, "You sayin' they gonna feel me up, Prinicp'l? If I'm lucky, it'll be some hot womans."

"No Art, it'll be a guy."

"Geez, well, I better not get a hard-on. Be hard to miss—and real embarrassin'."

James giggled.

They got through security without incident and Art continued his cheery chatter as he slid his bulky brown belt through its loops and slipped his feet back into his huge leather work boots.

"How many pilots will be flyin' the plane? Do they use autopilot? How high do we go?" Art chattered. Before James could answer, he continued, "Geez, what if we crash, Princip'l—somewhere in remote bush—and survive? Who'll eat who? Or what if we go down in the ocean, get eaten by sharks and our scraps get eaten by seagulls and crabs. At least then our flesh won't be wasted." Another guffaw.

"You'd be tough as hell, Art, and smoky to boot," James said and laughed some more.

"And I s'pose yu'll be fresh, tender and juicy, eh?" Art said as he elbowed James and smirked.

The drama started as soon as they left the Ezeiza International Airport to drive into Buenos Aires. In a dialect of Spanish unfamiliar to James, punctuated by odd guttural sounds, the taxi driver asked where they were from. James introduced himself and Art as Cree and Dakelh men, respectively. "*Indios de Canadá*," he said in summary. The taxi driver snorted and replied, in a lovely lyrical intonation, "*Sha no hay indios en Ar-jun-tina. Los matamos—a todos.*"

James was baffled. How could he translate this for Art, especially given that they were on their way to work with the Mapuche. "Art," he said through gritted teeth, "he says there are no Indians in Argentina anymore. They killed them all."

Art cleared his throat and said, "*They*—who is *they*? That's fuckin' weird, Princip'l. Tell 'em, we're gonna work with the Mapuche—and what about all those tribes we read about in the rest of the country? The Kolla, Diaguita, Guarani—and the others I can't remember the names of?"

James didn't want any conflict right now, especially in his third language—with a racist. He was captivated by the landscape outside, and he and Art were both exhausted. They studied the pampas—a kind of South American version of the Canadian Prairies—with huge umbrella-shaped trees breaking the monotony of the horizonless, flat, brown fields. Art was no doubt hoping to see big game, while James was studying the plant life and birds. They must be having a drought.

Here and there along the road that traversed the pampas, clusters of men, young and old, sat in the shade, beside parked cars, drinking from shiny metallic cups through straws, passing the time—seemingly *a gusto*. Ah, they're drinking yerba mate. James couldn't wait to try it—*la bebida típica de los Guaraní,* he recalled reading. The drink was supposed to be a powerful antioxidant and stimulant—it made him recall the powerful fragrance of the wild peppermint he used to harvest as a child, for his mother and grandparents, for tea.

To break the silence James decided to change the drift of the conversation with the taxi driver. "*De donde es señor? Bueno, su familia?*" he asked.

The fair-headed taxi driver said his family was from Germany and that they had arrived in Argentina with nothing but the clothes on their backs. They had worked hard to get ahead, and now owned houses and properties.

James asked in what year the man's family had immigrated.

"*Como* 1945," the driver answered before pointing at some Indigenous-looking people on the street. "Lazy bastards," he yelled in Spanish. "Why don't they work?"

Ah, okay. James cogitated—1945... So they were possibly Nazis fleeing Germany after the war. But he wasn't willing to pursue the idea just then. He didn't want anything to burst his bubble of bliss and fascination.

They were in the city proper now, but what area, James wasn't sure. He knew that Buenos Aires was enormous, a Latin American version of Toronto or New York, with all kinds of adjoining neighbourhoods and municipalities—*barrios*. Finally, he saw a sign that read CENTRO and knew they must be approaching the hotel, where they could at last shower and have a nap. The streets were lined with people carrying placards and wielding sticks shaped like broomsticks, but thicker and longer. They were banging on makeshift shields, making a thunderous noise. Most of the protestors had chestnut or mahogany skin tone and wore ragged clothes, but even the most rough-looking among them had fine Indigenous features.

"Every Monday afternoon this happens. Sometimes they managed to shut down the whole downtown core," the driver growled in Spanish before pulling over and stopping in front of a tall, narrow cream-coloured building with a large sign that read HOTEL.

"Sha shegamos. Cien pesos por favor."

James's stomach fluttered at the sight of the man at the front desk—swarthy, with a broad smile of strong white teeth, a dimple in his chin, a dark and thick growth of facial stubble.

"Bienvenidos cabasheros. Como le va?"

James was melting. The man's voice was a deep baritone, and his pronunciation so sensual. James cleared his throat, hoping his voice would sound normal, not pitched high as was typical when he got excited. Art was attuned to anything sexual, so for sure if James didn't contain things, Art would pick up on James's attraction to this man.

Before James could respond, the man said, "*Ay. Están cansados. Se nota. Les doy las shaves y sha.*"

James chuckled to himself at the pronunciation. He'd been warned about this: the *y* and *ll* consonants are pronounced as "sh" and sometimes double *r*'s were too. And there were other anomalies, like "*voz*" instead of "*tu*." And everyone called them "*caballeros*" pronouncing it as "*cabasheros*."

The two travellers collapsed onto their beds and slept for two hours. Art awoke first and rousted James.

"Come on, Princip'l. We ain't got much time. Wanna see a little bit before we head out tonight and I'm gonna be hungry as a bear in spring."

They took a cab to the plaza in San Telmo, and the first thing they saw was a man changing from jeans into tight black pants. He pulled his white T-shirt off his trim and hairy chest and then wriggled into a long-sleeved black shirt. His coal-black moustache was perfectly trimmed, and his longish hair slicked back—lots of Brylcreem. "He put bear grease in his hair, t'James," Art laughed. "Plenty of it."

A young woman with a porcelain complexion and pronounced cheeks and jawline appeared out of nowhere in a strapless bustier and matching skirt that was slit on one side almost right up to her waist. Blood-red fabric with a black sheen—black and crimson lace trim along the hemline. Her long raven-coloured hair hung loose over her shoulders. Shiny black pumps with stiletto heels. Art's jaw dropped and his eyes bulged.

"Holy shit! Gotta get a picture of *her*, Princip'l. Never seen a woman decked out like that before. Ever ssssexyyy."

"Just wait till they start moving, Art. It's like vertical sex."

"Geez, Princip'l. Never heard you talk dirty before."

"'Cause I just *think* dirty. Never say it out loud."

The two men laughed. Art slapped James's back. A flock of pigeons, just like the ones back home, flew over the two men and landed near the dancers to pick at crumbs someone had scattered.

A man in a black suit appeared out of nowhere. He sat down behind the dancers and opened a boxy, hard white case to carefully extract a large accordion. Another man showed up with a set of conga drums.

Within minutes the stage was set. A few reedy-sounding long notes sounded from the accordion—a call to duty. The couple came face to face, embraced and stared intensely into each other's eyes. The conga drums started up, and the music became frantic.

The woman threw her head back as she lifted one foot high behind her, almost poking her own curvy buttocks with the spike heel. In response, the man thrust his chest forward and stood erect. Then all hell broke loose. Brazenly the man stepped forward, forcing the woman to step backwards. They jerked their heads in opposite directions energetically—chin to shoulder. Then they shuffled into a side-by-side position and began partial turns. The man raised a cluster of their four clasped hands directly over the woman's head and spun her in a complete turn to the right and then all the way back again. Their feet flew in every direction as they writhed and brushed up against each other. The woman's right leg—or was it her left?—glided out of the slit in her skirt for a second, then back in, and the man spun her again. She leaned back and kicked high into the air. Once she was back upright, the man pulled her in close and peered down at her. The woman jerked her head back to meet his gaze. It looked as if they would kiss, but they didn't.

James was breathless. He didn't want to take his eyes off the dancers, but he stole a glance at Art's face and smiled at Art's look of amazement. He was captivated.

"*Hadih,* she's gotta know what she's doin', t'James," Art declared. "One wrong move and she'll nail his balls with those pointy pumps. Lookit how she kicks up between his legs—and glides her knee up through his thighs. Holy fuck. Wait till I tell Sally! She ain't gonna believe this. We gotta take lotsa pics."

They watched three long dances, the middle one slower, like a waltz. Art's stomach started to grumble.

"Geez, Princip'l, their dances are way sexier than ours! Gave me a hard-on just watchin'! *Ha ha ha.* They must be horny as bucks in ruttin' season after dancin' like that."

"Good thing you and Sally don't dance tango then, Art. You already got lotsa kids! And we're not sleeping in the same room tonight—definitely not the same bed," James said with a laugh.

"How else me 'n Sally s'posed ta keep warm at night, Princip'l? Even after we got lights 'n furnaces, lotsa power failures up there in the bush." Uproarious laughter.

Off to the side of the plaza, they observed a man behind a crude barbeque full of red embers with smoke pluming upward. The aroma made their mouths water. They moved in closer and saw the large reddish sausages the man was grilling and serving on what looked like crusty Portuguese buns. The sign above his head read, *CHORIPAN.*

"We gotta try those sausages, Princip'l. Look delish!"

The rest of the afternoon was spent on a whirlwind tour. A local recommended they catch the weekend market in *la Recoleta*—an upscale neighbourhood with fancy hotels and restaurants. Apparently there was intriguing *artesanía* for sale there along with more delicious Argentinian food, but Art was happy in San Telmo, so there they lingered.

An olive-skinned man pushed a cart over to them and called out "*Figuras. Arte indigena de los Mapuches.*"

"Lookit these, Princip'l! Outta wood. That carver's a Mapuche. Tell him where we're goin'! ... Wow! Look! ... A hummingbird feedin' from a flower, a crested bird in its nest, a hollow frog with humps up and down its back with a stick ta move over it ta make noise. Sally and the kids'll be all over this stuff."

Art and James bought almost all the carvings the man was carrying. The man told them there would be a lot more artwork like his where they were going.

The two travellers went back to their hotel to pack up their bags and store their purchases, then went out for supper. They came across a *Criollo parrilla*. Art froze in front of the plate-glass window to watch a chef in a white coat rotating huge skewers of large chunks of meat. The skewers were secured diagonally over the fire at the right distance for a slow, smoky roast—a beef hindquarter and a side of pork.

"Holy, Princip'l, that's how we use ta cook salmon, steelhead and deer. We used big branches from alder trees as skewers. Added firewood now and then to keep hot coals goin' till the meat was cooked jus' perfekly, jus' like they're doin' here." He paused for a second, swallowed his mouthful of saliva and said, "We gotta try it, t'James. Let's do it."

"Okay, Art, but you know I have to have a glass of Malbec. From Mendoza. Just have to. Supposed to be the best in the world."

"Li'l ol' wine drinker, you," Art chanted, making James think of the Dean Martin show his family used to watch every Sunday night. Art must've watched it too.

"Hola caballeros. En que puedo servirles?"

"Una parillada para dos personas por favor y una copa de Trapiche Malbec."

Ten or fifteen minutes later, a mountain of meat appeared at their table, topped with four sausages: two juicy pork chorizos and two of blood pudding. There were pork chops, pork ribs, chicken legs, a large chunk of filet mignon and barbequed intestines, which the waiter called *chinchulines*. A large container of chimichurri. Art and James were almost drooling, so sure they would relish all of it. They looked at each other with a look of bliss as they each took a bite of the juicy chorizo. The reciprocal look happened again and again as they tasted each cut of meat. Their feet trudged as they made their way back to their hotel and to the *central de autobuses*.

At eight o'clock the next morning, in the port city of Bahía Blanca, Art and James were greeted by a large group of men and a woman who whisked them into a minivan to take them to their *ruka*—a traditional Mapuche lodge. They were served a breakfast of scrambled eggs, *sopaipillas*—which was their version of bannock—and a soup they called *pishco*, which had wheat, peas and fava beans. In the place of coffee, they poured James and Art a fermented drink they called *muday*. One version was alcoholic and the other wasn't. They explained that the drink was traditional, that their people had been making a fermented drink from maize long before the Spanish arrived.

James and Art were puzzled when each of their hosts tipped their glasses to spill a few drops of their drink onto the floor and called out "*por la Pachamama*," before taking a sip. But they quickly surmised that it was a ceremonial ritual, so they did the same, and one of the men leaned over to James to explain that this was one way of honouring Mother Earth and the universe—their beloved Pachamama. Right after the meal, the women ushered James and Art into the courtyard. In the centre they saw smoke billowing out of a small ceramic urn. It smelled like sage but was slightly more pungent. The group had formed a circle and slowly everyone approached the burning smudge. One after the other, with cupped hands, they pulled the fragrant smoke around their heads and torso, then shuffled along. James and Art looked at each other with astonishment. This was so familiar. The herbs were different, but the ritual was the same.

After everyone had partaken, they stood in a circle, hands held out, palms up, slightly crossed. An elder moved slowly around the circle and placed a few pale green leaves in the hands of each person. As he did this, he looked into their eyes and muttered something inaudible. When it was James's turn, he was determined to apprehend what the elder was saying, but it was in Mapuche, not Spanish, so other than the reference to the Pachamama, he had no clue what was being said. The man next to James leaned over and said, "They're coca leaves. We chew them to calm ourselves and bring focus, *y disipa la animosidad entre gente*."

Art and James regarded each other, slightly confused. Would they get high from those leaves? Isn't that what cocaine was made from? Art had sworn off drugs and alcohol—sober for ten years. What should he do? James didn't do drugs either. What was the right thing to do? They had to maintain their integrity but not offend their hosts. With no chance to confer, they tacitly decided to participate in this traditional rite. They followed the example of everyone present and put the leaves into their mouths and chewed.

Within seconds after chewing the leaves, a calm came over James—a clarity he hadn't known before. A few of the young men stuffed more leaves into their mouths and chewed energetically until they had a bulge in the side of their cheek where they tucked the growing wad. Then everyone went back inside, where the tables had been assembled into a circle. The woman who appeared to oversee everything directed James and Art to the head of the table.

Everything was surreal. Their minds were still foggy from the arduous trip—fifteen hours in the air and eight hours by bus. The adventure of it all. James was on the verge of tears from the time they arrived at the *ruka* and saw the intricate symbols and animal figures that had obviously been hand-painted with tremendous care. Their hosts had noticed and said, "*Mira. Se emociona.*"

Once everyone had settled, an elder spoke in an animated tone about a historic prophecy about the condor and the eagle—how one day they would meet up. James translated for Art as best he could: "When the Eagle of the North flies with the Condor of the South, the spirit of the land will re-awaken. Art and James wiped tears from their eyes, and Art told James to tell them that his *'atsiyan* had recounted the same vision, saying this prophecy had been passed down for generations among the Dakelh.

"Princip'l, tell 'em—we don't have much time. Gotta get onta the beaver issue. That's what we're here for. Remind 'em, we're not spiritual leaders or politicians. Just everyday, ordinary *Indians* here to hunt beaver." Art's resounding laugh. He pointed at the two rifles he and James had brought—the two .17 Hornady Magnums that sat over in the corner. James grunted and regarded the guns with annoyance, recalling the hassle it had been getting them all the way to Argentina—locked in foolproof cases, with the ammunition packed separately. He'd had to reiterate time and again the justification for transporting weapons across international borders, as well as show incredulous officials their formal letter of invitation from the government of Argentina.

"Yes, I know Art, but first, let's share the recipes for beaver. Remember, we plan to host a big feast after the hunt and the demo on how to tan the hides."

James got the handouts the adult-education class had put together, which he had meticulously translated into Spanish. The first slide was a recipe for braised beaver. He stood and moved around the circle handing out the copies of the recipe—Art had the English version in front of him. When James sat back down, he caught the brief smirk on Art's face. He elbowed Art in the side and gave him a look to persuade him not to start giggling as he reviewed the ingredients:

1 boneless beaver
8 large potatoes
2 large onions
Salt and pepper

But looking down at the list, he himself started to giggle, recalling how he, Art and the whole class of adult-education students had doubled over with laughter upon reading the first ingredient. Of course, Art, with his twisted sense of humour, had had to comment on it, saying, "Jesus, Princip'l. A boneless beaver? You Crees are too much!"

Art's snicker prompted James to lean in close and whisper, "*Please* don't laugh. The joke won't translate here, and it'll be hell to explain what's so funny!"

But it was too late. Art was already into a fit of giggles, and without knowing what he was laughing about, their hosts joined in. Within minutes, the whole group was laughing so much they had to hold their sides. James was laughing hard now, too, but also trying to focus his thinking. What the hell could he say by way of explanation without offending anyone? Within seconds, the laughter became deep belly laughs all around and some had tears streaming down their cheeks. Alright, no explanation necessary—the laughter had bonded them, the Mapuches, the Dakelh and the Cree.

Once the laughter stopped, there was silence and then an air of seriousness took over. The local leader, who was also the leader of a fledgling national Indigenous organization, stood to speak. James sat up straight and opened his notebook to jot down keywords for reference when he translated for Art. After speaking for a few minutes, the leader nodded for James to translate.

"It's an honour to have two brothers travel so far to be with us," James conveyed. "You *are* our brothers, in spirit and in truth. It's important to acknowledge that. We'll do all we can to make sure you enjoy the few days you have here with us. We want this to be the beginning of a long relationship between our two peoples."

James noted that although Art was moved, he was now getting jittery with impatience. James continued with the translation:

"We appreciate your willingness to share your skills with us for how to hunt, trap and utilize the meat and fur from the beaver. We know the Canadian government must have picked a man who is very skilled in his traditions. We will go out hunting with you a few times over the next few days. We're eager to taste the flesh of this animal which is such an important part of your people's culture. Bony or boneless."

Everyone had laughed, but after a few seconds their leader's gaze brought silence.

"The government wants to use us to extirpate this animal from our territory, and we won't do that. The Pachamama has her ways, and we must respect them. This animal, your beaver, is part of the Pachamama, and the Pachamama will adapt. We will taste the meat, and if we like it, we will begin a relationship with this animal—if it works out. If not, well, we just have to wait for nature to adjust itself as it always does. We know you'll understand."

James sensed Art was getting frustrated, but he was relieved to see that he calmed as the message sank in. Art knew he had to respect these people and their ways. And exterminating the beaver was both impossible and reckless.

A few minutes later, when James and Art were alone outside of the *ruka*, Art put his arm over James's shoulder and spoke in a low tone.

"It won't be enough, t'James. Even if they decide they can use the fur and want ta eat the meat. It ain't enough. Huntin' beaver is damn hard work. And they'd have to eat a whole shitload of it every week ta even make a dent."

Art laughed, but James didn't. Now *he* was frustrated. What a waste of money and time. The damn government brought us all the way here when they didn't even have the local tribe onside with their plans. All the stupid and harmful things the government in Canada had done to Indigenous people began to roll through his mind—banning the potlatch and traditional ceremonies, making it illegal for First Nations to hire lawyers, trying to force Dakelh people into farming, sending them to industrial schools and forbidding them to speak their language, trying to pass the 1969 White Paper, a document that sought to eliminate "Indian status" and abolish Indigenous rights in Canada. A familiar anger surged from James's heart into his throat and head—*stupid fucking government.* But something gave, and he came back into the moment. He was here on this remarkable land with a tribe he had never met before—and they were showing love, to both him and Art, so soon after meeting them. In a minute, they were going to share their dances, drumming, music and have a feast.

Art stopped laughing. His huge brown eyes looked deep into James's as he said, "*Hadih,* Princip'l. We still have love. Big pieces of our culture are still intact, and we have Indigenous brothers and sisters here, too—in the same boat. We'll survive and evolve. Lighten up."

That night, back in their hotel room in Buenos Aires, James was vibrating with excitement. Finally, something important had surfaced and sunk in—James knew where he belonged. He belonged with Native people on Native lands. But, he would also occasionally step over the line and into that other reality—the one where he'd spent most of his life, the parallel reality where, as a rule, life was easier, more genteel and comfortable, more refined. So, this is what it took to make him understand what was significant and valuable in life: rich, meaningful contact with tribes in California, Mexico, other parts of British Columbia, and now Argentina. He was still afraid to live fully in this reality completely because so much of his support and learning had come from the other side, but all of his work now—all of his career—would be with Indigenous people, somewhere in the world. He was determined, and this notion gave him joy with a heavy dose of trepidation. Who would accompany him—and who would understand?

Five days later, James pored over the huge international departures board of Ezeiza Airport to find their flight. Everyone in the departure lounge stared at Art as he walked in—some coyly, others openly gawked. With his complexion a shade or two darker than James's, long, straight black hair, exceptional height and a red baseball cap, Art was a spectacle for sure. To James's surprise, Art simply returned their stare, flashing his broad smile and nodding hello to each person who was brazen enough to hold his gaze.

iii

Things couldn't have worked out better if James had coordinated it with the festival organizers. The entire staff and student body of the Chezgh'un school was on the huge stage of the main tent at the Prince George Children's Festival and was about to perform for a large audience. The event host had asked for volunteer participants starting with a principal, then some teachers, and, lastly, they invited up several rows of students—which by chance included all the kids from Chezgh'un. On their own, not one of those Dakelh kids would've gotten up onto the stage, but in a cluster, they were fine—especially seeing their teachers already there. Justa was now home for the summer break from college, so he had come along to help out.

James and the teachers smiled in anticipation. James was so glad he'd taught the whole school the song "Rockin' Robin," convinced that the kids would sing it loudly and enthusiastically here, but the gregarious festival host had something different in mind. He said that in just a few minutes, he and a couple of his friends would teach hip-hop dancing to those on stage, including the principal and teachers. He divided them into groups of eight, and each group went off with a dancer to learn their moves. James was overjoyed. He'd seen some of the kids breakdancing in the hallway or on the wide school porch.

The brown faces James had become so fond of were vibrant, now—sparkling eyes, lips stretched wide to reveal perfect white teeth—joy had temporarily displaced pervasive despair. Oh, and the funky styles the talented teen hairstylists had given them for this trip to the city were so sweet. The music came on, so loud that James and the teachers found it overwhelming, at first, but they got used to it quickly. The thuds of *ba ba PAH pa-ba pa pa* on the kick drum made the whole stage vibrate. James recognized the song—"Get Up Everybody (Get Up)" by Salt-N-Pepa. Justa had played it for him a few times, months ago. James felt a flash of sadness at that recollection, but his grief was quickly flushed away by the sight of the first group of newly minted dancers. They shuffled out in single file, steps and arm swings coordinated, until they transitioned into a move the host called "the Smurf": continuous subtle hip thrusts while punching the air left and then right, in sync to a four count. My God, the smiles. The next group took the stage and began a move the host called "lock it down": side-to-side hops and foot glides with arms rhythmically flailing in the air. Another group flounced onstage, attempting backflips and cartwheels, and to James's amazement, most of them completed the moves successfully. The other group took to the stage in partial front flips, one after the other, until everyone was on stage. For the finale, the host asked James to stand at centre stage. The host then got everyone to do the Smurf. They began in a single line, and then, as if driven by centripetal force, the dancers spiralled around James, moving in, tighter and tighter. It had been years since James was surrounded by energy like this—beautiful brown bodies, hyper-charged, glistening with perspiration. It all reminded him of the social dances his sisters, brothers and cousins did under the Prairie sky in the cool air of the evening after the sun had gone down. But this here was so much more fun than the bunny-hop, the limbo or the "Oh! Johnny" mixer dance they did back home.

Hamburgers at McDonald's for dinner. James found McDonald's food tasteless, and he hated their corporate practices, but it was the only place that could handle a group this large, and, of course, the kids were all worked up about seeing Ronald McDonald, getting a handout of plastic toys and sampling, for the first time, the heavily marketed burgers, french fries and pop. Soft ice cream for dessert. Even the kids of Chezgh'un who'd never been to Prince George knew about the chain's offerings and gimmicks.

Monday morning, James walked into his office and found Bella sitting in his chair beside his desk, sipping on coffee. She tilted her head to one side and said, "Well thanks a lot for that, James."

"Was fun, eh?"

"Well maybe *you* had fun."

"Whaddaya sayin'? We *all* had fun."

"You weren't on the bus on the way home, pal."

"No, I told you all, I planned to spend the weekend in Prince George with Justa. He's become a great friend."

"The gas, James... Oh my God, the gas."

"The bus ran out of gas?"

"No. The kids had never eaten at McDonald's before, and they're not used to dairy. Cheeseburgers, then ice-cream? They farted all the way home. I thought I was gonna die," Bella said as she laughed maniacally and stood to punch James's shoulder. Between laughs, James forced out, "Geez Bella, sorry. So sorry you had to go through that—but better you than me."

Tuesday morning as James approached the school on foot, he spotted Louise's vehicle parked outside. She would've had to leave Vanderhoof early to get here before school started—what was going on?

James glided into the building and noticed the lights were on in the primary classroom. He went up to the closed door and peered through the window. Louise was talking to Debbie, and Debbie was dabbing at her eyes with a tissue. What in the hell was going on? Was Louise doing a school inspection without telling him? Had Debbie complained about something to do with his performance without telling him? James went into his office, sat at his desk and booted up his computer. He went through the motions of making coffee—making noise so that Louise and Debbie would realize someone else was in the building now.

He had just sat down at his desk when Louise walked into the room. Her eyes were all bloodshot too—what was going on?

"James—I have some difficult news, and I wanted to tell you in person. I've been diagnosed with lung cancer—stage four—it doesn't look good."

James took her hand and looked into her eyes. "Louise, I'm so sorry," he said and then went speechless as tears welled up in his eyes.

"It's okay to cry, James," Louise said. And he did. She took him into her arms.

"It's okay, James. It's okay. Sorry to do this to you so early in the morning and all—but word is out in the district, and I had to tell you now. Let's have some coffee. I brought some homemade cookies for your staff."

The sound of hand drums and voices chanting resonated from the basement.

"That's a lovely sound," Louise said.

"Oh, I forgot. Art and Sally started a drum group. They get together each morning before classes—to get the day off to a good start. Isn't it beautiful?"

"Yes. Exquisite."

iv

James had become quite close to Justa—like an older brother or a first cousin. They'd spoken on the phone often and visited each other a number of times when Justa was back up north, doing a co-op work term in Prince George. Justa had opened up to him—told him more than James had wanted to know about his sexual episodes with the chief, about how he'd been sexually abused by a priest while serving as an altar boy. Justa had named other men from Bilnk'ah who'd come on to him, seeking sexual favours—and James had listened, sometimes for hours.

Now, he wished he'd done more—gotten Justa counselling, encouraged him to speak to a trusted elder and suggested he date other people to help him forget about his romance with the chief.

Justa was dead.

James was here in the dank basement of Vancouver General, broken-hearted, staring at a cold, pallid body. Caroline had called him at Franyo's place again, in the wee hours. Would he go to VGH and identify the body? The family would drive down from Bilnk'ah the next day—too expensive for so many to fly, she explained.

Justa's body had washed up near the Burrard Civic Marina—fully clothed. Guesses were that he had jumped from the Burrard Street Bridge. There were no witnesses—at least no one had called in any reports. Vancouver Police had found an envelope on the kitchen table, addressed to no one in particular. No one opened it—best left for the family to read, they resolved.

James tried his best not to let the pervasive mood of mourning overtake him as it had the strangers around him in the morgue who had come to identify or pay respects to their loved ones. Their moans, sputters and wailing made James feel emotionally volatile, too, but wouldn't it be incongruous if he broke down like that for this young man who wasn't family? Besides, he'd already had his share of that kind of gut-wrenching grief. Thank God they hadn't become lovers—if they had, after the suicide, James would've wanted to die too, he was certain.

A morgue attendant began speaking loudly to a Chinese Canadian family, telling them that it really *was* time for them to leave, telling them they had been there for a *full hour* and, no, they couldn't leave behind the yellow chrysanthemums and white roses they'd brought.

"We have no place to store flowers and the hospital morgue is not a private funeral home. That is where you should take your flowers once the body has been transported," he said.

"We want to visit a while longer," a plaintive voice protested.

"I'm sorry, you can't."

James understood. You don't want to leave your loved one alone in such an impersonal institutional setting—a stark warehouse of death, but he also understood the morgue attendant's dilemma. He'd been in a similar position. There was work to be done, and members of the public couldn't be left unsupervised in the morgue.

What was going through Justa's mind in the days leading up to his suicide? James had heard from him just a couple of days earlier, and Justa had sounded so good—like he'd moved on. *Wait a minute. FUCK.* Why hadn't James realized what was going on? *Justa had a plan.* Just like James's sister had—she was so calm, even cheerful in the weeks leading up to her death. After James's sister's death, a doctor had explained that once a person suffering from suicidal ideation has a plan—a surefire way out—they feel relief. Had James been with Justa in person in that last week, maybe he would've twigged to what was going on.

Damn. Had Justa not been able to comprehend how final this all was—that his life would be over at age twenty—all his hopes, dreams and plans abandoned? How could he have known that whatever message he was trying to convey through this drastic act, it wouldn't get through? Not to anyone. Suicide was simply overwhelming, for everyone around—even bystanders who just heard about it. Justa would never have wanted to hurt his loved ones. Maybe he simply needed to put an end to the anguish and horrible betrayal of being kicked to the curb by the chief. Couldn't they at least have remained friends as he and Franyo would—friends for life? James regretted not telling anyone about the affair—it *was* an affair, wasn't it?—but he still felt it wasn't his place. Not his place to out the chief, nor Justa for that matter—to their community, to the world. James didn't know if Justa had discussed this with anyone else, but he was sure others knew. After Justa's unsuccessful first suicide attempt, the chief spent two weeks in Vancouver—at Justa's place. He didn't bother to book himself into a hotel.

Justa had confided in James about those weeks. He thought that if he could improve sex with the chief, he would rekindle their relationship. Did he really think that Felix would ever leave his wife and children? James tried to talk sense into Justa, to no avail. It was when Justa tried to get Felix to try pot or cocaine—he'd heard from his college buddies that pot helped diminish inhibitions and that cocaine-infused sex was astonishing—that the chief finally left, saying he'd been clean his whole life and wasn't about to start doing drugs now.

Tears welled up in James's eyes as he took Justa's cold hand in his. He'd had friends who were "the other woman" involved with accomplished men and had heard about their suffering. He couldn't imagine how disempowering it must've felt to be "the other man" for a strictly closeted man who sought to protect his heterosexually masculine image at all costs, likely to safeguard his political and personal future.

The morgue attendant interrupted James's thoughts. "So, then that's a positive identification. Thank you for your time."

"Thank you," James said. "The family will be coming tomorrow. I should just take a photo for them. For their peace of mind... so they know for sure... ah... "

As he took this final photo of Justa, James studied his lifeless body that had always exuded vitality—healthiness, wholesomeness. Sorrow began to shift into anger. He hated that Justa was there in the morgue at VGH, on a sliding tray in a large stainless-steel refrigerator while the chief was probably comfortable, warm and content in his home with his fair wife and their three kids. Yes, this was a cynical view, but he wouldn't put it past Felix.

As he stepped into the antique elevator to leave, James tried to understand the implications of what had just happened—and his involvement in it all. What did Justa's suicide note say? Would he ever get to read it? Did the chief know about Justa's death yet? Was he implicated in Justa's note? Should he call the chief to tell him? After all, in addition to being Justa's lover, Felix Joe was still the leader of Justa's community, and Justa's family was huge—held political clout. In any case, the community would expect a public statement from the chief.

No, he couldn't call Felix. He wouldn't be able to adequately disguise the resentment in his voice, and even if he could have, the chief would view the call from an outsider as an intrusion—into his role as chief, or his role as Justa's executioner.

James let out a sigh as he stepped into Franyo's apartment. He was always safe and welcome here—even when he least deserved it. He loved that about Franyo. He was quick to wrath, but he was also able to forgive equally fast and move on. And, he never gloated about being right about the North—never uttered the words, "I warned you, James—I told you so..." Maybe graciousness came with age. From the entryway he could see a vibrant bouquet of flowers atop the square glass coffee table in the living room. The fragrance of stargazer lilies, butter, garlic and smoky paprika filled the air. Wonderful, Franyo was making dinner. They would have a lovely meal together.

At Justa's memorial service a week later, James's grief had turned to rage as he listened to the chief's speech. The matter-of-fact way Felix spoke about the alarming suicide rate among Indigenous youth in Canada. How it's four times the national average for non-Indigenous youth. He went on to speak about important research work being done on this topic by a leading psychologist at UBC, as if Justa was a statistic now, as if he himself had nothing to do with it.

James couldn't say anything—nothing at all—but that didn't keep him from going up to the chief after the ceremony was over to offer a handshake and say, with a twist of irony in his voice and fire in his eyes, that he appreciated the chief's words about youth suicide, and that Justa's death was indeed a tragedy, one that could have been prevented.

v

James had forgotten what spring thaw looks like up north. Tiny rivulets appearing everywhere and coalescing to form larger ones, until eventually they found their way to the permanent stream that circled the community, causing the stream to swell dramatically, clearly making the land Chezgh'un was built on an island. Pussy willows and catkins, brighter red willows contrasted with the dull, ubiquitous straw-brown grass that had been weighed down by tons of snow and pushed into dormancy by the cold and darkness. Songbirds whistled, sang and trilled in a joyous but subtle melodic cacophony. And the village was livelier too—everyone getting ready for spring hunting and gathering. Spring rabbit tasted so good after a winter of moose and salmon jerky, beaver and bear meat. Jeremy, Bid'ah and Marlene showed James how they set snares for rabbits or hunted them with a .22 rifle. "Remember, Princip'l, them rabbits move in circles, counter-clockwise fer some reason. Maybe jus' to confuse us," Marlene told James, and chuckled.

The school programming had worked like a charm. Most students, even the teens, were at, or at least a lot closer to grade level in math, writing and reading. Cultural programming had gone so well, kids could be heard speaking Dakelh around the school and all over the community. The teens had truly become cultural artisans, making snowshoes, beaded buckskin moccasins, gloves, vests and jackets—as did those adults who weren't previously skilled at these crafts.

The federal health nurse reported the lowest rates of respiratory diseases in the community since Health Canada had become involved there. The daily exercise program was credited for this change. Miraculously, with the exception of the occasional backslide by Anouk, there was no gas sniffing in the community, and even then, Anouk reported it to Art each time he partook.

Bella's idea of bringing the social activism of the Freirean approach to the adult program was paying off in real and concrete ways. The first big change she, James and Catherine noticed was in the adult students' self-esteem. They now held their heads high and participated enthusiastically in all discussions and activities. They'd taken hold of so many of the issues that the community, region and even province were facing, analyzed and tackled them head on, coming up with made-in-Chezgh'un solutions. After decades of neglect, the road to Chezgh'un had been graded, with gravel being added as necessary to deal with large potholes or washboard sections; the local forestry companies had agreed on the importance of riparian zones and implemented them in their annual harvesting plans, and where they'd previously harvested trees right to the shoreline of a river or lake, they promised an aggressive reforestation plan; and the adult students had started an inventory of the resources in their territory, using mapping and computer-based inventory systems.

There were days James thought it was all too good to be true, but for the most part it wasn't. There were real improvements in the community, developments in which he knew he'd played a small part as a catalyst. He'd believed in the power of education and in the community—and resisted falling into negativity or factions.

Bella scheduled a time for the local college to administer assessments for high school graduation equivalency for students who wanted to go on to a post-secondary education. James and Louise had congratulated her on this—thought it was brilliant. Bella had good reason to believe that all of her students—except maybe one—would succeed, so she and James were gobsmacked one day when they arrived at the school to face a sit-in, in his office, by a group of elders who did not want the testing process to happen.

James dropped everything for the morning, to listen to what the elders had to say.

Agnes began. "Princip'l, we know you mean well. Ya done lotsa goot things wit' us here. But we can' let this GED thing, or whatefer you call it, go ahead."

Margaret spoke next. "We wen' ta residential schools, 'n what for? Ta lose our culture—they try ta kill our language 'n culture. Yes, you done some goot work here… but we don' wan' our young peoples 'similated to white man's ways."

Monique stood up and faced James then looked askance when she spoke. After she uttered a few words, it was clear she was going to speak in Dakelh only, so Sally moved in to translate. "She says the Nedoh, the white man, tried ta change everythin' about us. The way we live, the way we raise our kids—'n they even interfere with our sex life—tellin' us when, where, how and with who we can have sex. Tell us it's efil if we do it jus' for love 'n pleasure. That wasn't our way. We had no shame about our bodies—no shame 'bout our ways of bein' together fer sex. Dey try ta change the way we see the worl', the way we interac' with it."

James squirmed in his chair. He knew what the elders were saying was very important. The cultural programming they'd put together was good, but it was still not enough to counterbalance the impact of the Western, mainstream education process. His seventeen or so years in the school and post-secondary system had assimilated him, and he hated that, but still, he didn't understand the elders' concern with the GED exams. What exactly was it?

Then Monique's husband, Abel, Art's father, stood to speak. This time Art translated for James and Bella.

"Princip'l, he says you done good here. You're a good man. So many here got really close to you. But you hafta understan', you're workin' for the white man here, doin' what the white man want. We wanta see our kids get schoolin', succeed in life. But every time one of 'em goes ta college—they never come back. Sure, they come back to visit now 'n then, but we lose 'em, and we don' wanna lose more of 'em. That's why, Princip'l, we don' wan' these tests."

James was stunned. Of course, they were right. He thought about Felix, who'd only come back to the community recently because someone recruited him for the top leadership role, and even now he didn't reside in Bilnk'ah—just went there for business. He thought about all the Chezgh'un relations who lived in the Fort, Prince George or Vancouver. They would never move back. What a quandary. Justa had gone away and would *never* come back.

"Okay. I have an idea," Bella said. "How about we ask the adults what their plans are after getting their GED. And how about we get each of them to make a commitment to work with the community after they graduate, in whatever field that be. If they get band funding for college or university, they'll agree to work for the same community the same length of time they're sponsored for."

"I have another idea," Art said. "How about get fundin' ta work with the school district and college to come up with a five-year trainin' and employment plan fer the community. We can't keep teachers here for more'n a year or two, so why not train our own peoples to become teachers—even the *princip'l...*" Then he guffawed. "Sorry, Princip'l. We love you, but there goes your house above the lake I promised you."

Catherine spoke up. "We done somethin' like that in my community—in about five years, mosta the professionals, the big wage-earners who now come from the outside, will be our own peoples. It kin be done."

"You can go a'het wit dos tests then, Princip'l 'n Missus Bella. Gosh you're a smart one, Bella," Monique said with a chuckle. "Real sexy too! So prout o' you." She smiled her timeless smile.

The GED testing showed that all of the students met their goals: a few had wanted tenth grade equivalency to go on to get training in a trade, and others wanted complete matriculation. Bella and James wrote a letter to Carolina, the consultant from the Native Adult Education Centre in Salmon Arm to give her the good news, and to invite her to work with them on the program design for the next academic year. They told her they would like to take a generative approach to curriculum development, where the community worked with the educators to design their own programming, the content and methodology of the learning. Could she help them with this?

Soon after, Carolina called to tell James that she was now the interim director of the centre. She congratulated him and Bella on the wonderful success and invited James to travel to Salmon Arm for a meeting of the centre's external advisory committee.

James was thrilled.

vi

It was unfair, and they knew it—those who had masterminded James's visit to the region in the middle of the province, where winters were mild and summers were hot and long. One of the best fruit-growing areas of Canada.

The meeting of the advisory group to the Provincial Native Resource Centre was a pretext. What the board of directors was really up to was an unabashed recruitment of James to work with them, as their new executive director. They wined and dined him—highlighted the progressive work they were doing with Native communities all over British Columbia and even in other parts of Canada. The team travelled to exotic and fabulous places like Bella Coola, Bella Bella and Kispiox. To Victoria, BC, for regular meetings with their funders, the provincial government. The Sunshine Coast and Peace River Valley. The Nass. They were consulting with First Nations and urban friendship centres all over the province—on community development, conflict resolution, negotiating skills, adult basic education and even more technical things like land and resource management. Their work was to assist and inspire communities to advance, and they wanted James to be their new leader.

James loved the drive south and back in his Sidekick, traversing three climate zones each way—from snowbanks and frozen lakes, snowy owls and dark-eyed juncos of the Nechako to sparkling streams, sapphire-blue lakes, mountain bluebirds and western tanagers in the Shuswap. He was still astonished by the job offer, for a senior position in the post-secondary world. He would be a director in a college setting—in what seemed to be paradise. But how could he even consider it? He'd only just begun his work in Chezgh'un and surely planning for the new school would begin soon. How could he miss out on the excitement of that? Well, he'd have to ponder this one long and hard. And despite the weather up north, the prolonged winter and slow spring thaw, he was happy to be returning home. Yes, he did feel at home in Chezgh'un, now, in his comfortable two-bedroom teacherage. He was exhausted, but upbeat.

He'd just unpacked his suitcase and was making a pot of Labrador tea when he heard a knock at the door. He opened and was aghast at what he saw: a familiar face he cared about was now barely recognizable. Puffy purple eyes, nose crooked, permanently altered, missing teeth. The mangled face of his gentle and kind friend, Leyo. Speechless, James motioned for him to come in and take a seat at his dining room table.

He had been beaten by a group of men, presumably locals, and left for dead in the ditch at the final turnoff to Chezgh'un. Leyo didn't offer any explanation—in fact, he went and sat down without a word. When James went over to shake his hand, Leyo stood and the handshake became a hug. "Goot ta see ya, t'James."

"Let me pour you some tea."

"I jus' wanna sit here with you. Don't hafta say or do anythin'."

After a few moments, Leyo broke his silence.

"You could be nex', Princip'l. I jus' hafta warn ya."

Initial rumours were that the attack was the result of an unpaid bet, or money owed, but weeks later, Bella recounted to James the real cause: yes, the altercation was initially about a financial debt, but when his aggressors suggested Leyo hit up the principal for the money, referring to James as his "*hoo 'tup* bum buddy," Leyo became furious, and his adamant defence of James's reputation got him a beating.

vii

It was the first concert the school had ever had, and everyone was involved in some way. Since the school had no gym, the event was held outdoors, with the school steps and landing acting as the stage—a makeshift amphitheatre. There were folding chairs for the elders and teachers, while the students sat on blankets on the recently cut quack grass. Fortunately, the morning dew had already evaporated. Bug spray and suntan lotion for all. The monstrous mosquitos weren't too bad yet, but they were already making their presence known, as were the blackflies. All the birds had returned as well—the ducks had built their nests in the tussocky grass of the creek and could be seen swimming along the circle of the stream that surrounded the village. James loved waking to the dissonant honking of Canada geese very early each morning. The large flock of lily-white trumpeter swans had settled into their usual spot at the north end of the lake and could be seen in the distance from the steps of the school or from the window of the school kitchen. Art had told him that it was too bad they were now protected, because their meat was delicious.

The kindergarten and primary classes stole the show with their traditional dance—decked out in the new regalia their parents and the adult students had sewn for them: little buckskin vests with fringes and fine beadwork. Each class sang a few songs in both Dakelh and in English. The intermediate students sang a few of the folk songs James had taught them, with two-part harmony thrown in the mix here and there. The teen students, caparisoned in their quirky but convincing outfits, recent catalogue acquisitions or savvy clothing swaps, did a variation on the breakdance they'd learned at the Prince George Children's Festival, to huge applause. They followed this with drumming and singing in Dakelh—the songs they had worked on with Art all year.

For the English part of their performance, James accompanied the teens with his guitar as they sang songs they'd learned with him. They finished their part of the concert with Neil Young's "Harvest Moon." Everyone joined in for the chorus that sang of being "still in love with you." A few of the teen students who had been learning guitar on their own played and sang. The adult students who were musical took turns playing the fiddle or guitar or drummed and sang traditional Dakelh songs. To close the concert, Art and the teen group led everyone in a round dance.

James took in deep breaths of the pure spring air and gazed around at the wall of forest, a blend of evergreens, aspen, alder and poplar, and at the lake nearby against a backdrop of the serene Mount Shas, in the distance. He felt rushes of bliss followed by intense sadness. He was going to be leaving this place and these people in just a couple of weeks. And while his new job had a big title, he had no idea what was in store for him. He knew there wouldn't be—*couldn't* be—the same sense of community and togetherness he'd felt here with the people of Chezgh'un. The same reciprocal love.

As various students shuffled past him, coming to and going from the stage, he studied their faces. Darcy and his chubby cheeks that were always slightly rosy; Jeremy, with his endless provocation of the principal—unkempt hair—the only teen who'd resisted getting a funky hairstyle from the budding local stylists; Caroline, with her serious expression that broke into full sunshine when she smiled; little Clayton, with his sweet laugh and kind nature. He was going to miss them all. He was glad he had hundreds of photos of his time here—and he'd gotten duplicates of them all to leave behind for the community.

The last Thursday in June was Fun Day—and the weather cooperated. Vibrant helium balloons and hand-painted kites flew in the air, these ones were larger than the ones they'd made in the fall at the lake—keepers, works of art. A few of the adults had set up the stations for the various activities and events: face painting, three-legged races, a collaborative treasure hunt, outdoor volleyball, pin the tail on the beaver. Everyone paused for a lunch of salmon or moose burgers with fresh homemade wild strawberry sauce and ice cream for dessert. The mood was upbeat and happy. Most of the afternoon was to be spent at Sandy Beach for swimming and water sports. The kids had started water safety and swimming lessons, so they loved being in the water to practise floating—face down, on their backs, or the jellyfish. Of course, the boys had to show off with handstands in the waist-high water.

James revelled in the joyous scene before him. The sight of Anouk floating by on his back brought him out of his daydream. "Hey Anouk!" he shouted. "How cool is that? My good buddy... floating by... stealthy like a seal." The attention prompted Anouk to roll onto his side to show off his mastery of the side stroke and scissor kick.

"Wow, that's amazing Anouk!" Marlene called out and swam toward him. "You picked that up so fast. The group counselling sessions seemed to work. The girls no longer teased Anouk, nor did they appear to feel threatened by him.

Things were starting to wind down when Patrick pulled up in his pickup and jumped out—looking as if he'd seen a ghost. He called for Art—or Sally—to come.

James watched as Art and Sally hurried over to Patrick. After he spoke to them, Sally began to cry. Art put his arm around her, pulled her close. James was alarmed, hurried over. But it wasn't bad news, as he had feared.

Victoria—their precious daughter—who had been missing for more than two years, was home.

viii

James convened a school assembly for his surprise announcement. By the time he'd finished telling them he had accepted a challenging job in the Shuswap region, everyone, including James, was wiping away tears from their eyes. His team had wanted to organize a farewell feast for him, but he asked them not to. He felt he was abandoning them all—his friends and the entire community—so he wasn't deserving of a feast.

But a feast was had. The Saturday before last week of school, James was lured to the school with the promise of parting gifts. A single dancing drummer, Agnes's grandson Curtis, dressed in a beautifully beaded buckskin suit greeted James at the door and led him to a metal chair in the middle of the room. The drum group from Harry's class, a blend of teenaged boys and girls, also dressed in their buckskin regalia, formed a circle around James.

As James studied their exuberant faces, tears formed in his eyes. How could he be leaving these fabulous people who had been so kind to him—accepted him as family? James focused on his breathing, deep and measured, to keep from becoming overwhelmed by emotion. He couldn't cry. He had to get through the event with his dignity intact. This was all his own doing. At present, to shed voluminous tears would be disingenuous.

Curtis stepped over and whispered in James's ear that he was going to perform the eagle dance and that James was to follow suit by imitating each of his moves. As James spread his arms like the wings of an eagle and moved his feet in rhythm with the drums, the teachers, students and parents clapped boisterously. He swooped low, then rose up again—moved in a semi-circle—quickly, then slowly—then swooped low again. The crowd howled with delight.

Next, they put James on a team of men who would play *lahal,* the bone game, against a group of women. All eyes were on him as he drummed, chanted and danced. This day, in fact his whole time in Chezgh'un, was an experience he would forever hold dear. As promised, lovely gifts awaited him on a table across the room: a batch of the treasured half-smoked sockeye, moose-meat jerky and a year's supply of tea made from locally harvested herbs, handmade beaded moccasins and a painted hand drum.

The following Friday, James packed up his Sidekick—six boxes, all his worldly possessions, other than a few things he'd left at Franyo's place. He loved the simplicity of his life. He didn't need anything more, best to keep life simple. It was early morning, but already people were outside of their houses to wave goodbye as he drove by.

Stands of lodgepole pines flew by—an illusion of rolling bilateral symmetry punctuated here and there by stands of trembling aspen. James stared straight ahead with his hands loosely at ten and two on the steering wheel. He was driving away from Chezgh'un for the last time and his thoughts were intense.

Art had been a brother to him; Sally, a sister. Bid'ah, a baby sibling. Henry—he'd admired and respected the man so much. Even though he was awkward in showing it, Leyo had cared for him deeply. He had taken a beaten for the sake of James' honour. Saying goodbye, Leyo gifted him the large, beaded pendant he'd always worn around his neck, saying he recalled how James had admired it. Angie and Loretta gave him more dried moose meat, wind-dried salmon and canned berries, all from the Tsilhqot'in.

The trees were now flying by faster than ever.

When he'd gone to say goodbye to Monique, he had intended only to say, "Goodbye—ekosi." Two simple words. But when Monique's gaze captured his, he was rendered speechless. His eyes flooded with tears as he handed her the leather pouch he'd stuffed with ceremonial tobacco, beautifully beaded with the four sacred colours: red, yellow, black and white. She, in turn, put a petite buckskin pouch into his hand and said, "Keep this with you, Princip'l, wherever you go. S'protecshun."

As James was leaving Monique's place, X.J. had caught up with him. He presented James with a rabbit's foot keychain. "I made it myself." The two exchanged an intense gaze. In a moment of weakness, James had put his arm on X.J.'s shoulder—shuddered as it touched down. Unsure what to say or do next, he turned and strode to his Sidekick.

James noticed he was biting his inner cheek, and his feet were damp in his leather booties.

He loved Chezgh'un—the people and the place, but spending another year there, running a school program in a condemned building—he'd decided he just couldn't do it. He told himself he couldn't face another year of watching the community struggle to survive while being discriminated against by their own tribe for being closer to the land and their culture—for speaking their language fluently—with pride. Even worse, the oppression by the white people around them—all the purulent rumours along with the refusal to serve them in restaurants and banks, being denied entry into stores—shooed away like pesky dogs. Fuck, he remembered his own experience at the local CIBC where he'd gone to open an account, and the clerk simply drew a big *X* across the employment section, assuming he didn't work.

Then there was the government—the *gor'ment*—its failure to fund any aspect of special education even though, if accurately assessed, initially half of the school would've qualified for some type of special education program—so many lagged far behind the appropriate grade level for their age. Over the past nine months the teachers had worked overtime with the kids—one on one—and nearly burned themselves out turning that statistic around. Where were the resources they would need to carry on, for counselling, special needs education, speech therapy and addictions support? And now with Felix gone as chief, there was little or no chance of the community being able to negotiate the level of funding they would need to address these and other challenges.

At times, he'd worried about not consulting anyone about big changes in his life. First there was the move from Vancouver to

Chezgh'un, and now from Chezgh'un to Salmon Arm, after just one year. Even though he respected her tremendously, he hadn't sought Catherine Bird's advice—it would've been unfair—even though she was an elder, she was also one of his staff. Besides, Catherine had enough on her mind. With Louise's encouragement, Catherine and her daughters had launched a legal claim to the lakeshore on which Louise's house was built.

As much and as often as he experienced bliss in Chezgh'un, life there was perilous. There'd been two threats on his life by people who had spent time in jail for violent crimes. There were the horrific deaths by fire that wintry day at Henry's house. Then there was the time when Leyo showed up at his place, his face bruised and swollen, fractured nose, missing teeth. All because of an unpaid debt and suspicion of a gay liaison with James.

And there were the whispers he heard as he was trying to sleep. Rachel, who had not turned up at school with the other teens. He could not forget her—*"No X.J. Not tonight. Pleasss..."*—or that he had been too paralyzed to help her.

Then there was Chief Felix and the intrigue that had unfolded shortly after Justa's death. The family weren't naive; they knew something strange had been going on between Felix and Justa and they'd called James to confirm their suspicions. James had been reluctant to disclose anything, but Justa's sister had trusted him profoundly, so he spoke up. Still, James was careful to not make any public statements—kept what he knew completely confidential—not wanting to create animosity with a powerful Dakelh man like the chief. Felix Joe had considered resigning as chief after the scandal broke, but Justa's family convinced him that hosting a feast—a shaming feast where he would confess what had happened with Justa and make amends with the family—was more appropriate. They didn't want to ruin him, they'd said—understanding the lengthy family feud that would result if they had.

Just a few weeks later there had been a new scandal involving Chief Felix. The accountant he had hired disappeared, taking with him the computers with all the financial records. Payroll cheques for the band were returned, NSF. Also, $500,000 had gone missing from the community's bank account, and rumour had it that half or more of that amount had ended up in Felix's personal bank account. The elders forced Felix to resign and leave the community, and in exchange for a promise to never run for elected chief again, they gave him the title of Grand Chief. Ali, with his background in economics, had been hired as the band administrator with the lofty new title of CEO. He'd promised to keep James posted on how things evolved between the people of Bilnk'ah and Chezgh'un, and he vowed to attempt to ensure all business dealings with Chezgh'un were open, transparent and fair. He'd promised to visit James in Salmon Arm a couple of weeks after settling into his new role.

What would life be like in Salmon Arm? Well, at least he'll be closer to Franyo—just a five-hour drive away. And Franyo promised to help him set up the cabin he'd rented at the lake for the summer. They would be friends for life, he was sure.

Maybe as executive director of an education resource centre that serves the whole province, he'll help more communities to advance their education programming, which in time will lead to a better life for all. He'll find ways to circumvent oppressive and limiting government policies that keep Indigenous people down, uneducated and poor—abysmal social indicators. The oppression and poverty had to end—things had to improve, everywhere—and quickly. In his darker moments, he'll find ways to exculpate himself for leaving Chezgh'un—his new Dakelh family—after only one year, to those who would ask, *why only a year?*

James's mental ruminations stop when he spots a dark spherical object in the middle of the road ahead. He pushes in the clutch, taps the brake then shifts down into fourth gear. He taps the brake once again. Third gear now. The books on the passenger seat fly forward onto the floor. As the vehicle approaches the object, he guesses it's a bear. This is a first—he's never seen a lone bear cub on the road before, where could its mother be?

The animal sits still—frozen. Is it dead? James clutches and downshifts again, flashes his headlights and honks the horn. It's not a bear... it's a beaver. After a moment it moves ahead slightly. Wait, it's hobbling—it must be injured.

James steers onto the shoulder and continues advancing slowly until he is close to the animal. He honks again, but the animal remains still. He sees its beady eyes peering at him. He's never been this close to a beaver before. How can he get it off the road and back to its lodge? Over to his right, beyond the ditch, he sees a pond. Maybe he could push the beaver in that direction—at least get it out of harm's way. He's heard that beavers can be dangerous—more so if they're rabid. He doesn't want to touch it, but he can't just leave it there. Surely, the animal will sense that he is trying to help it and will cooperate.

He stretches his arm back to locate a straw broom he has in the back of his vehicle—hopefully within reach. He opens the driver's door and hops out. The oneiric scene he steps into baffles him. He quickly realizes that now that he's stepped out of the realm of civilization—his Sidekick—like it or not, he is part of the wilderness. The vacuum created by the stillness and dark draws him in. The stage he is about to step onto is illuminated only by the twin spotlights of his Sidekick. He feels alone and vulnerable. There's just him and the beaver (and perhaps other sets of eyes he can't see watching him from the forest). What if something were to happen to him here? Are there cougars around? Had a bear been hunting this beaver—interrupted in taking her prey?

Slowly sweeping the broom out in front of him, as he's seen curlers do, James approaches the injured animal—its plush fur looks so familiar. He stands still like that for a moment, hoping the animal will flee.

He pictures the lovely beaver fur hat he has stashed in his vehicle—a spectacular fur stole along with it. Beaver fur is so warming against the frigid cold of northern winter—gifts he will treasure for years to come. It flashes through his mind how important the beaver was for his people. His grandfathers and uncles used to trap them to sell the pelts to feed the family—for generations, trapping beaver was their main livelihood.

Just as James is about to push the beaver's paws with the straw base of the broom, it leaps up and latches onto to his thigh with its formidable teeth. James gasps, hollers and stumbles backwards, grabbing his injured leg. Startled, the beaver lets go and waddles toward the ditch. James feels a dampness in his jeans and is hit by the unmistakable metallic odour of blood. He hobbles back to the car, climbs in and fumbles to find a plain white T-shirt in one of the boxes.

He unbuttons his jeans, opens his zipper and stuffs the rolled T-shirt tightly into the leg of his jeans, at the level of the wound. Thank God the beaver didn't get his penis—his *tuguy*—or his femoral artery. Once his pants are zipped and buttoned up there will be enough pressure to assuage the blood flow and he'll drive to the next town for help.

Bitten by Beaver—*amisk!*

Mah, sosquats!

Now this will be a story to tell.

Ahpo ekosi

Acknowledgements

I started this novel in 2018, while taking a course with the Sarah Selecky Writing School, with my amazing mentor/writing coach, Jennifer Manuel. On the basis of five story starters I wrote in that program, I was accepted into the Writers' Studio at the Banff Centre, where I had the pleasure of working with Caroline Adderson and Shyam Selvadurai, as mentors. Caroline and Shyam helped to shape and form the plot line and characters and provided tremendous guidance with respect to fiction writing in general. Kathy Page, another mentor of the program, also gave rich advice and powerful encouragement. My agent, Carolyn Forde, was supportive and patient as I navigated the sometimes churning waters of the world of fiction writing, as was my publisher. My editor, Barbara Berson, was a kind and astute collaborator. Getting to the present version of this novel was quite a process, not unlike getting to the refined final version of a wonderful sculpture.

I thank my circle of lovely friends and family for their encouragement. In particular, I thank Joanne Mitchell, Kim Echlin, and Ümit Kiziltan, who were my advance readers (and champions).

About the Author

Darrel J. McLeod is Nehiyaw (Cree) from Northern Canada, Treaty 8. His first memoir, *Mamaskatch: A Cree Coming of Age*, won the 2018 Governor General's award for non-fiction and was shortlisted for many other prestigious prizes, as was its sequel, *Peyakow: Reclaiming Cree Dignity*. McLeod has been a French immersion teacher, school principal, director of a provincial curriculum center, executive director of Education and International Affairs at the Assembly of First Nations, and chief negotiator for the government of Canada. Darrel is fluent is French, Spanish and English, and he is studying Cree. He lives near Sooke, BC and winters in Puerto Vallarta. He is also an accomplished jazz singer.